I0552556

The Path to Us

By

Christine James

Copyright © 2018 BGP Publishing

All rights reserved

No part of this book may be reproduced in any form
or by any electronic or mechanical means, including
information storage and retrieval systems, without
permission in writing from the publisher, except by a
reviewer who may quote brief passages in a review.

The characters and events portrayed in this book are
fictitious. Any similarity to real persons, living or dead
is coincidental and not intended by the author.

Cover: Kristy Charbonneau
Photo by: Alexy Ibly on Unsplash

ATTENTION: PLEASE READ

Dear Readers,

First, I want to say thank you for picking up this book. Whether it is because it was a gift or because it was purchased, please know that I appreciate it from the bottom of my heart.

PARENTS, I need to talk about a few things before you and your child reads this book.

This book was written with the thought of how today's society is. Our young adults and teens go through so much at such a young age. There are elements in the story that are uncomfortable and outright awful. While there are no explicit details, the implications of certain types of situations are there. So please be advised.

It seems that being a teen is 100xs worse than it was fifteen years ago. I say this because I have a young teen myself, and his friends have had to deal with some of the situations mentioned in this book.

So many teens are forced to carry around dark secrets that are scared to see the light of day. Perhaps they fear the consequences if they tell. Maybe they are afraid someone they love will be hurt if they speak up.

Our young people carry these burdens around like cancer inside them, eating away at their mind, spirit, and soul. It slowly eats away at them until it's too late. Some of these burdens are even carried into adulthood, affecting relationships and their view on life.

I'm hoping the words on these pages will help those—both young and old—see that they are not alone. There is hope even when the situation feels hopeless.

Be blessed.

Always,

Christine James

This book is dedicated to everyone that has ever felt alone. To the ones that live with demons haunting them every waking and sleeping hour of the day. To the ones that feel like there is no hope. To the ones screaming, but have no voice. You are beautiful just how you are. Don't change for anyone, and NEVER BE AFRAID of who you are! Be bold. Be beautiful. Be you!

Special Thanks

While I'm the author of this book, I wasn't the only one who had a hand in it. Hours of research went into this. I want to thank God for giving me the nudge to do it. He is the reason I'm able to do what I do.

I want to say a special thanks to Aaron Allen for his help and giving me some useful pointers. Then, to Catherine Black for her never-ending assistance as I navigated through some new areas in this journey. Girl, I'd have been lost without you.

Also, I want to say thanks to Mel for always giving me honest opinions! Thanks, lady!

As always, a HUGE shout out and thanks to Kristy Charbonneau with Cover Me Creative for the beautiful cover. You never cease to amaze me with your talent!

My best friend, Babs. I don't even know where to start, so I won't. I'll simply say that if it weren't for you, I'd never be able to do what I do. You give me the kick in the pants when I need it, which was often during this process. I'm so glad we met ten years ago because you have made me a better person, a better writer, a better mom, and just . . . better. Two halves of a whole! I'd be lost without out you. I love you!

My sister, best friend, and oldest friend . . . not old as in old but the friend I've had for the longest! You're a freaking inspiration. I don't know what I would have done these past 29 years without you! I love you more than I will ever be able to tell you.

Rhonda, for helping me keep up with my youngest. You, my dear friend, have a true gift from God. I don't know how you do it, but I'm here to say, I admire you so much!

To my parents, who, thankfully, took care of my children while I disappeared inside my writing cave for weekends at a time. Thank you for loving me, teaching me what it's like to be a good parent, wife, and person. I am who I am today because of both of you. You gave me strong examples of remodels, and you still do to this day. You taught me to be me while teaching me to respect others, love others, and cherish life. I've said thank you, but in truth, those two words will never be enough for what you've done for me.

To my amazing in-laws for helping with the kids, and the nights of playing cards so I could clear my mind and feel normal. A lot of people can't say they love their in-laws. I am not one of them because I can honestly say, I love and adore you! Thank you for loving me despite all my crazy.

My three brothers and sister-in-law. Life sometimes interferes and we don't talk for days at a time. However, I know that if I ever truly needed you, you'd be here. I love you guys!

NOW, to my amazing husband. You've had to put up with my late hours, my crazy rambling, my slacking in the housework department, my moods. You, my love, deserve some kind of reward for your patience and loving understanding of my need to get this book done. You've been my rock for 17 years now. You've cheered me on when I've succeeded and picked me up when I wanted to give up. You give me the dose of reality I need and the bitter truth when I need to hear it. You're my soulmate, my love, and my best friend. Thank you so much.

To my oldest son, Dillyn. I never told you this, but you are the reason I was inspired to write this book in the first place. You move me with the amount of compassion you have for your classmates. I see how much you want to help someone who is hurting. You inspire me to be a better person. I see the fantastic young man you are becoming, and it makes me excited to see what life is going to give you. I am so proud of you. You're my mini-me. You're going to go amazing places in life, son. This book wouldn't have been possible without the other people I've already mentioned. However, if it weren't for you, this book would never have been created. I love you, baby! I probably just embarrassed you, but that's okay, it's what I'm here for!

I saved the best for last. I want to say a *humongous* thank you to all my fans and readers. Some of you have been with me from the very beginning, and some of you are new. Thank you, from the very bottom of my heart. You are all the reason I do what I do.

To my sons
You are my heart, my soul,
and reason for breathing.
I love you

Whatever our souls are made of,
his and mine are the same.
— Emily Brontë

Prologue

The screaming was bad this time—really bad. Sitting in the corner of her dark bedroom, she covered her ears with her hands, but it didn't help. It never did. Through the thin walls of the trailer house, she could hear her step-dad screaming bad words at her mom. She didn't know what they were fighting about this time, but it was awful. She wondered if it had anything to do with him being caught in her bedroom the night before. She wondered if her mother had finally found out about all the other times he'd watched her.

The sound of breaking glass slamming against the wall caused her to jump. Heart racing through her chest, she pushed to her feet and ran to her window. Quickly and quietly, she pushed aside the cardboard box that was being held together with tape. The actual window had been gone for years, which made it awfully cold in the winter time.

Looking over her shoulder to make sure no one was coming through the door, she threw a leg over the window sill and slipped out into the night. The air was heavy, causing her to sweat as she ran between the rows of trailer houses that made up the trailer park.

Her heart beat quickly as she stayed in the shadows, making her way to the only safe place she knew. She pressed her back to the side of his trailer, giving her heart a minute to slow down. Then finally, taking a deep breath, she climbed on the overturned milk crates and lightly tapped on the window.

The sudden appearance of a face directly in front of her caused her to yelp. As she did, her feet slipped from the crate sending her flying backward and landing hard on her butt.

The window slipped up, and he leaned out, giving her a wide smile.

"What you doing here?" he asked in a hushed whisper.

1

She looked up at her best friend with tears in her eyes. He gave her a knowing nod. "Give me a second," he said as he disappeared inside.

Anxiously she looked around, scared that someone was going to see her. Being out at night in the trailer park wasn't a good idea, and it especially wasn't for little girls. She could see something moving in the shadows but wasn't sure if it was her imagination.

"Hurry," she whispered urgently, moving closer to the window.

"I'm comin'," he called back as he climbed from the window.

Once his feet were on the ground he turned and looked at her. He cupped her cheeks with his hands. "Did he touch you?"

She shook her head. "Not this time," she whispered.

"Have you told your mom about that one time he touched your butt?"

She nodded and frowned. "She said I shouldn't be makin' lies up like that. I got a whoopin. Is your mom home?" she asked as he took her by the hand and quickly began to lead them down the path that would cut through the woods and directly into the park.

"Yeah. She's work'n 'til tomorrow morning."

"She left you alone again?" She frowned. They were only eight years old, and yet they'd had to fend for themselves on more than one occasion.

He scratched at his arm and nodded. "Yeah."

"So why did you use the window?"

He shrugged. "Habit."

"I don't like the woods," she whispered as she clung tightly to his arm.

He moved away from her and then wrapped an arm around her shoulders. "I'll protect you," he whispered back. They never spoke about the things that sometimes happened in her house. He just knew that if she showed up at his window, things were bad, and he had to protect her. That's all that mattered.

"But who will protect you?" she asked in a small voice.

"I don't need protecting," he said as he led them down the path.

It didn't take long before they reached the other side. "What you wanna do first?" he asked as they walked to a picnic table.

She was about to say something when she noticed someone sitting on the swing set, all alone. The boy looked familiar, but from where she stood, she couldn't be sure.

"Hey, look," she said pointing at the boy. "Who is that?"

"Dunno. Let's find out."

They walked over to where the boy sat, and their eyes widened when they saw who it was.

"What are you doing out here by yourself, Richie?" he asked. The other boy wore a pair of pressed khaki slacks and an expensive looking polo shirt.

The boy from the swing looked up. "My dad's a dick, and my name's not Richie," he said as he scrubbed the tears away from his face.

She gave her friend a dirty look. Feeling bad for the boy, she moved away from his side and stopped in front of the other kid. "I'm Lilian, and this is Chase. You're Tyler Anderson, right?"

He nodded. "Yeah. How do you know?"

"Because we're in the same grade. You're in Ms. Jackson's class, and we're in Mr. McGee's. You moved here this year, right?"

He nodded again.

Lily took a seat beside him. "What'cha doing out here alone?"

He sniffled and wiped his nose on the back of his hand and just shrugged. He lifted his watery eyes and looked at them. "Why are you guys out here?"

"Because anywhere is better than where we live," Chase answered.

"Had a fight with my parents," he said regarding them with cautious eyes. "They left for a while."

"So, who is staying with you?" Lily asked.

"My aunt, but she's old and goes to bed at like seven thirty."

"Hey, where'd you get that?" she asked, pointing to the bruise peeking out from beneath the collar of his shirt. Tyler shifted uncomfortably and fixed his shirt. "Was playing rough with my dog. He bit me."

"Oh. What kind of dog you got?" Lilly asked.

Tyler frowned. "You ask a lotta questions."

Lily shrugged, bouncing her heels off the wall. "So?"

"It means you're a pain in the butt," Chase taunted.

"You take that back, Chase Michael!" she demanded.

"Make me!" he laughed, slapping at her ponytail.

Lily frowned and poked her tongue out at him.

Behind them, loud voices could be heard from the trailer park. Lily could hear her mom and step-dad fighting even from the playground. Her cheeks burned with embarrassment.

When she looked up, Tyler was watching her. "What's that all about?"

She stiffened against Chase's side, not wanting to say anything. Chase looked at Tyler and explained, "Her stepdad is a jerk, and her mom's a junkie. We usually come here until morning."

"Why not your house?" Tyler asked curiously.

"Because."

Lily knew that the state of Chase's house was something that always embarrassed him. While his mom worked hard, the place was a mess and kind of gross.

"It's just better out here," she said quickly.

Tyler's eyes widened. "You sleep out here?"

She shrugged. "Sometimes."

The three of them were silent for a long time. Chase kicked at the dirt with the toe of his second-hand converse sneakers.

"Why don't you come home with me?"

Chase and Lily exchanged looks as Tyler climbed to his feet.

"What if your aunt finds us?"

Tyler rolled his eyes and started walking. "She won't. Trust me."

Chase looked at her. "What do you think?"

Lily shrugged. "I don't wanna sleep in the tunnels tonight."

Chase nodded. "Then with Richie, it is."

"My name's not Richie," Tyler called over his shoulder as he walked down the sidewalk.

Chase and Lily followed Tyler for three blocks. When they rounded the corner, they came to an abrupt halt. 8163 Claymore Avenue, the richest neighborhood in Raven's Bend.

"*This* is your house?"

Tyler turned and gave them a sheepish look. "Yeah."

"Damn," Chase whistled as they gawked at the massive two-story structure with its pillared front porch and enormous security gate.

"Come on. We can get in this way," Tyler said as he lead them around to the corner. At the base, a couple sections of missing fence was covered by a few limbs. Pushing them aside, he nodded for Lily to go first and then Chase. Once the three of them were through the hole, they quickly made their way to the back door.

Little did they know, finding Tyler in the park that night would be the moment that forever changed their lives.

Part 1

Chapter 1

Our history is not our destiny.

~Alan Cohen

"I don't want to go back," Lily groaned to herself as she sat on the brick wall outside Tyler's house. The heels of her Goodwill Converse bounced off the brick as she swung her feet back and forth.

The August sun was already causing her blond hair to stick to her neck. A thick fog hovered over the land. When the sun shone over the tree line and onto the ground, made everything look like something from a fairytale.

In Raven's Bend Alabama, life was miserable in the summer, and even worse in August. It was too hot to play outside unless you were at the creek, and there was no way she wanted to be in her house.

Chase walked down the long concrete drive, stopping in front of her. He gave her a lopsided grin as he jumped up to sit beside her, nudging her in the arm with his shoulder. His shaggy blond hair was in severe need of a cut. It fell in curls around his forehead and into his eyes— one of which was black from the fight with his mother's latest boyfriend.

Chase picked at the hole in his jeans. They looked trendy, but she knew they were just worn out.

"How's the eye this morning?" she asked as she looked at him from beneath her lashes. Chase had changed a lot over the summer. At first, he'd been tall and lanky, all legs and arms, but working odd jobs at one of the local farms combined with football practice had changed that. As a result, his arms and chest had filled out. He was taller too. She had been close to his size at the beginning of summer, but now, he was a good four inches taller, putting the top of her head just beneath his chin.

7

That wasn't the only change he'd gone through. His voice seemed to be a little deeper. It had made her giggle at first because he would be talking normally without voice cracking. He didn't find it as funny as she did.

"It's fine. That man's a douche bag," he grunted as he shifted his backpack on his shoulder.

"Why is she dating him again?"

Chase rolled his eyes and shrugged. "Who the hell knows?" Their heels kicked back and forth against the brick.

Lily could feel his annoyance just in the way he was sitting. There was something about his mom's newest boyfriend that always had him in a bad mood. The black eye was just one of the reasons. "I just don't know why she keeps bringing home these losers. If they don't bolt after seeing me, then they bounce after they nail her a few times."

Lily winced at Chase's crass words. "Jeez, Chase. She's your mother. Don't talk about her that way."

Chase's head swirled around, his blue eyes meeting hers. He just arched his brow at her. "You're defending her?" he asked incredulously.

The last several years had drastically changed his mother. Things had always been hard on Chase and his mom, but they managed. Somewhere along the way, she'd just given up the fight. She no longer cared what happened to her or even her own son. She kept her job, but that was about it. Lily knew his mom wasn't making good enough money at the diner, and she had to rely on other sources of income. The thought of what the woman did for that income made Lily's skin crawl, but it wasn't much different from her own mother.

"Well," she said with a frown, "at least she's not a coke-whore that sells your stuff for her next fix." Her tone was bitter.

The subject of mothers was always a bit of a tense one between them. His mother—while being far from perfect—was still better than hers was. At least Diana Kramer was able to hold down a job as a waitress. They only things Vicki Lancaster could hold down were her booze and her panties.

Her statement made Chase flinch. He knew she was right, the entire time they'd been friends she'd been forced to hide more times than she could count because of the loud noises and strange sounds coming from her mother's bedroom.

When she was ten years old, Chase had to explain what those noises were. Once that cat was out of the bag, it made her sick to think about what was going on. Especially, when the men would walk through the house naked. Or, watch her with a weird look in her eyes. It made her skin twitch.

It was usually on those nights she snuck off to Chase or Tyler's—which had been often lately. However, there were those times when Chase's mother was also entertaining guests, and they were both forced to crash at Tyler's.

She looked up at the massive house Tyler lived in. "Where the heck is he?" Lily wondered out loud, not liking where the conversation was going. She was desperate to change the subject. She hated talking about her mother.

"I don't know. Have you talked to your dad?"

Lily's face turned into a deep frown. "The last time I talked to him, he said I couldn't call him anymore. Apparently, *Brenda* says they need to focus on *their* family," she said bitterly. Brenda, her dad's new wife, was the trophy wife from hell, which surprised Lily because her father was nothing but a lumber mill foreman. How he landed Brenda was still a mystery. She was a spoiled trust fund brat from Montgomery barely old enough to drink. Lily had met her once, and that was more than enough to suit her.

She'd discovered who her biological father was during one of her mother's coked-out rants. Chase and Tyler had helped track him down. She'd gotten her hopes up that he'd want her, maybe even whisk her away from the sick-os always at her house. No such luck.

"About freaking time," Chase grunted, ticking his head to the front door as it opened and successfully pulled Lily from her gloomy thoughts.

"How long you guys been out here?" Tyler asked as he walked down the fancy brick stairs of his dad's mansion.

Seeing him impeccably dressed in plaid shorts, flip-flops and a matching polo reminded her that he was from a different world entirely. Sure, his family was just as dysfunctional as hers and Chase's, but still, she was often reminded that he had more money than they could ever think about having. Sometimes it made her wonder why he bothered hanging out with them at all.

"Probably about fifteen minutes," Lily muttered, staring down at the frayed end of her shorts.

"You know you guys can come in, right?"

They shook their heads. "Your dad's here."

Tyler frowned. "So?"

"He don't like us, man. You know that," Chase said with a shoulder shrug.

"Who gives a rat's ass what he likes?" he grunted.

"Why's he home anyway? Thought he was in Milan or something like that," Lily said noting that Chase wasn't the only one that had changed.

Tyler stood almost the same height as Chase. His black hair was neatly trimmed. His shoulders were growing thicker and broader. When had he changed? He'd been gone for a week to visit his grandparents. When he came back, he looked different. How had he transformed so much in a week since she'd last seen him? Both boys were changing, and she felt like she was being left behind. She was still all knees and elbows and flat as a board, both in the front and back. Her legs were scratched and scraped from playing baseball with the boys. Sliding into home plate always did make her legs bleed, but she did it because it made her feel good to be noticed.

The sound of Tyler's slightly deeper voice pierced through her thoughts. "He was—" He paused and then restarted. "He had to come home to take care of some of his shares before he leaves again tonight."

"Whatever that means," Chase snorted.

Chase and Lily always nodded like they knew what Tyler was talking about. In truth, they didn't know much of anything about Elliot Anderson, aside from the fact that he didn't like the "little hoodlums" hanging around his house when he was gone, or even when he was there for that matter. Thankfully, he was rarely home.

Chase jumped to the ground, and Tyler moved to stand beside him. Both boys looked up at her expectantly, holding out their hands. Trustingly placing her hands in their palms, she allowed them to help her down.

Bending her knees slightly, she landed softly on the balls of her feet. When she straightened, they were looking at her with weird expressions hard for her to read.

She dusted her backside off and frowned, looking over her shoulder and at the back of her denim shorts. "What? Do I have something on my butt?"

Both sets of eyes quickly looked at her backside, but then darted away. Her frown deepened when she saw their cheeks turn pink, shifting awkwardly from one foot to the other. What the heck was that all about?

"Seriously, is there something wrong?" she asked, beginning to run her hands over the front of her tank top, making sure there was nothing out of place.

"Uh . . . no," Tyler croaked. Then, after clearing his voice, he started again. "No. I just . . . thought I saw a hole in your shorts."

Her eyes widened. "What?" She looked down in a panic.

Tyler then laughed, and when she looked up, both boys were looking at her with amused grins. Realizing that they'd been messing with her, she landed a hard punch on to each boy's arm. Tyler and Chase winced at the connection of her knuckles.

"Ow, Lils, that really freakin hurt," Tyler said rubbing the sore spot on his arm.

"No kidding," Chase grunted.

Lily rolled her eyes. "Come on, ya big babies. We best get going or we're gonna be late," she said as she pulled her backpack from the wall.

"Oh yeah, before I forget," Tyler said as he unzipped his bag and pulled out two brown paper bags. He handed one to each of them. Chase and Lily hesitated for a second before finally accepting them and putting them into their backpacks.

"Thanks," they mumbled in unison.

Tyler only smiled. Lily could feel tears of humiliation burning her eyes, but she refused to let them fall. She stopped crying in front of the boys a long time ago. They were strong and didn't cry, and their lives sucked as much as hers did. So, she refused to cry.

Tyler had been looking out for them for a few years now, even though they'd been the ones to find him alone in the park when they were eight. He'd made sure they were taken care of by giving them a place to stay when they needed one, as well as making sure they had food. In exchange, they provided him with the friendship that he truly craved. They'd become nearly inseparable, and while they had different circumstances and people looked at them oddly, they each needed one another for various reasons.

The nanny, Maria, was in charge when his father was gone. She understood very little English but seemed to understand their situation perfectly. Lily liked the woman, and it was sad that over the last six months, Tyler's nanny was more of a mother to the three of them than any of their own mothers.

When Lily had gotten her period, she'd been terrified and embarrassed. She'd locked herself in her bedroom. The boys didn't understand and wouldn't leave her alone until she finally broke down and told them what was happening. They'd been grossed out immediately. But, when they realized that she was upset, they went to the store and came back with tampons and pads. How they'd known what to get was still a huge mystery. Unfortunately, even though she had the supplies, she had no idea how to use them.

She'd walked to Tyler's house with wads of tissue stuffed in her panties. Thankfully, the boys were out running around somewhere. The older, Spanish woman, didn't look at her with pity, nor did she shoo her away. Instead, she'd guided her into the house and explained the best she could in her limited English about the products.

"Have you heard from your mother anymore?" Lily asked Tyler as they began to walk to toward the school.

He looked down at the ground and shook his head. He hefted his backpack and then kicked at a soda can that was on the sidewalk. It skittered and bounced onto the street where it was promptly smashed by a car. The horn blared, and the middle-aged man flipped them the bird as he sped by.

"Do you know when she's going to get out?"

Again, he shook his head. "No. According to my dad, if she's out by the time I'm forty, it'll be amazing," he muttered.

Tyler's mother had been caught trafficking anything. It was a massive scandal that made the national news. A few months after they met him, Tyler said the reason they'd moved was that she'd been arrested.

When she'd asked her mother what it meant, she'd just said that the woman should be put before a firing squad for her crimes.

Lily hadn't pushed any further because she didn't want to know anymore. The thought of something happening to Tyler because of his mother made her stomach upset. She remembered the police showing up at Tyler's house one night. Even month's after her arrest and moving to a new town, they were still conducting their investigation. They questioned Tyler and his father for hours.

She looked over at Chase and frowned. He was unusually quiet, and she couldn't figure out why. Talking about their crappy lives was seriously crushing their first day of school vibe. She decided to change the subject.

"So, how was football?"

Both boys seemed to liven up. "We're gonna be really good this year. Coach said Tyler is good enough to be starting quarterback for the junior varsity. I'm gonna be running back," Chase said proudly.

"What 'bout it, Lils? You gonna try out for cheer this year?"

A nervous feeling twitched in her stomach. She wanted to cheer but knew that she wasn't as pretty or as good as the other girls in her grade. At least that's her mother always told her when she talked about trying out in junior high.

"Honey, you're just not that pretty. Nobody wants to see an ugly cheerleader."

She shifted her bag awkwardly and shrugged. "I don't know. I mean, I've thought about it, but I don't know."

"I think you totally should," Tyler said hooking his arm around her shoulder. The smell of deodorant and cologne drifted to her. It wasn't an unpleasant smell. However, it did cause her to chuckle.

"Are you wearing cologne?" she asked with a giggle.

He frowned and dropped his arm down to his side. "Maybe."

"Why?" she asked.

"Because . . . well, because I want to smell nice."

"It's so Kiera will notice him," Chase snickered with a wide grin aimed at their friend.

"Dude, shut the hell up," Tyler said throwing a punch in Chase's direction.

Chase anticipated the swing and quickly dodged out of the way. He jogged ahead and turned around to where he was walking backward.

"Did you tell Lily how you French kissed her this summer behind the skating rink?" Chase teased.

Lily's eyes widened as she swung her gaze to Tyler. "You what?" She felt her cheeks turn pink. The thought of Tyler kissing *anyone* made her stomach feel weird, probably because she'd always had a secret crush on him.

He shrugged and looked away. "It wasn't big deal, okay?" He scowled at Chase.

Lily reached out and stopped him. "Why didn't you tell me?" She didn't want to be hurt, but they never kept secrets from each other.

"I'm sorry, Lils. It's just . . . I don't know, weird. You're a girl."

She scowled at him. "No kidding. What difference does that make? Kiera's a girl."

"But she's a girl I *want* to kiss. You're not."

Lily didn't know why, but his comment stung. Was there something wrong with her? Was she not kissable? "Am I'm not good enough to kiss?"

"What? No! I mean, yes! Wait?! What? I didn't mean it like that. I mean . . . ugh," he groaned, placing his palm on his forehead and squeezing his eyes closed.

Lily crossed her arms, interested to see how he was going to dig out of the Grand Canyon size hole he'd just put himself in.

He looked at Chase for help, who was standing there with his arms crossed over his chest and an amused smirk smeared across his face.

"Don't look at me," he chuckled. "You're the one that put those feet of yours in your mouth. I wanna see how you're gonna get'em out."

Tyler looked back at Lily and took a small step closer. "You're my best friend. I can't see kissing you because, well, that's what you are. That don't mean you're not kissable. I'm sure some guy would love to kiss your lips."

She blew out a small breath, unsure of why his words made her stomach feel weird. In fact, everything about him was making her feel weird. She slowly nodded and took a step back. "Yeah, okay. I doubt that."

As she turned to walk away, he gently grabbed her by the arm. "Hey, next time I promise to tell you." He held up his pinky, and she wrapped hers around his. It was something the three of them done when making promises to one another.

"I would never hurt you on purpose. You know that right?"

She nodded as they unlinked fingers. Chase rolled his eyes. "Come on. We'd better get going."

They rounded the corner, and the massive school building loomed in front of them. It was an imposing, two-story structure made of red brick and plain windows. The welcome sign beckoned them to enter, but it was the last thing any of them really wanted to do.

"Can you believe we're finally freshmen?" she asked.

"Three more years and we're done," Chase muttered.

Tyler took a deep breath and smiled, giving them strength like he always did. "Well, here goes nothing." The three of them crossed at the crosswalk and into the building that would essentially become their home during the week. She couldn't help but feel that as soon as they walked through those doors, everything was about to change.

She couldn't have been any closer to the truth if it had smacked her square in the face, and more than anything, she wished she'd been wrong.

Chapter 2

No one saves us but ourselves.
No one can and no one may.
We ourselves must walk the path.

~Gautama Buddha

"How bad does it suck that I don't have a single class with you guys," Lily complained as she placed the lunch Tyler had given her on the table across from Chase.

Chase stopped stuffing the sandwich into his mouth and looked up at her.

Lily twisted the top off her juice and took a sip. "Where's Ty?" she asked with a frown.

Chase lifted a shoulder and chomped down on his sandwich one more time, shoving the last half hungrily into his mouth. Lily winced, realizing that he probably hadn't eaten breakfast or even dinner the night before. The paper bag beside him was empty and crumbled into a ball. Her heart pinched a little.

She unfolded the top of the bag and pulled out the contents; a Ziploc baggie with pb&j, a bag of chips, a candy bar and an apple. They were her favorites, and Tyler knew it.

Chase was still scarfing down his apple when a group of girls walked by their table. Lily fought the urge to cringe under their pointed stares. Instead, she lifted her chin and squared her shoulders, preparing for the inevitable.

"What's wrong, Chase, your whore of a mother forget to feed you again?" Kiera Stockton said snidely. She flipped a strand of glossy black hair from her shoulder and looked down at Chase as if he were a bug she was ready to squash.

Anger simmered in the pit of Lily's stomach as Chase looked down and avoided eye contact. Kiera Stockton was the princess of Raven's Bend. At least that's what she wanted everyone to think. Daddy dearest was a hotshot plastic surgeon, and her mother was the Mayor. All in all, the girl *was* everything and *had* everything, and she didn't mind reminding everyone within earshot either. At any time, she had four or more girls flocking around her hanging on her every word.

Lily wasn't sure if it was the general dislike of Kiera that was bothering her, or that Tyler had confessed to kissing her behind the skating rink. The thought of the two of them being together made Lily's empty stomach turn sour.

Placing her sandwich back in the bag, Lily glared at the girl and her cronies. "Back off, Kiera," Lily snapped.

Kiera's frosty blue eyes swung in her direction, taking her attention off Chase. It had been Lily's primary goal, especially after seeing the shame that slipped over his face.

"What did you just say to me?" she asked, narrowing her eyes dangerously in Lily's direction.

Lily didn't flinch. She just met the girl's unwavering glare with one of her own. "I *said,* leave him alone."

Kiera was silent for a minute before throwing her head back and cackling. The sound was like nails on a chalkboard to Lily. Her little gaggle of friends did the same thing. When Kiera suddenly stopped, so did they.

"Saw your momma on the corner last night," she said coolly.

The corner of Lily's mouth ticked up in a slow smile. "Yeah? Was she working your daddy over?"

Chase sputtered in the milk he was taking a drink of, spewing it all over the table in front of them. Lily chuckled, and when she looked up at Kiera, her smile only grew wider. The other girl's eyes had become wide with shock. Lily didn't let it go there.

She lifted a shoulder flippantly and took another drink of her juice, never taking her eyes off the other girl. "It wouldn't surprise me. He's her best customer. I think it's up to three nights a week he comes for a visit."

Kiera's face turned blotchy with anger as she took a step closer. Lily pushed up to her feet, daring the girl to step closer, and get closer is exactly what she did. Lily was spoiling for a fight. Adrenaline was beginning to surge through her veins as her fists tightened at her side. It wasn't the first time she'd ever been in fight, and she was confident it wouldn't be the last.

"What's goin' on here?"

The sudden sound of Tyler's voice pierced through her anger induced haze. Kiera's entire expression changed, lighting up as if someone had rammed a flashlight up her nose and turned it on.

"Just girl talk," Kiera cooed, looping her arm through Tyler's. "Why don't you come eat with us, Tyler? Leave these losers to their table."

Tyler frowned and looked from Lily to Chase. "No, thanks. I'm good," he said as he tried to extricate her from his arm. She reminded Lily of an octopus, her tentacles suctioning onto Tyler whenever he got to close. Once free, he sat beside Chase.

Kiera glowered at him and then back to Lily. "We're not finished here," she seethed as she flipped her hair over her shoulder and strutted off, her hips twitching back and forth with entirely too much effort.

Lily sagged onto the bench beside Tyler who was already stuffing his face. She laughed, feeling better now that both of her friends were with her. However, when she looked up at Chase, his expression was tight. His lips were pressed together, and his eyebrows were pulled down into a frown.

"You shouldn't have done that," he snapped.

Lily blinked, taken back by the sharpness in his voice. "Done what?" she asked, thoroughly confused.

"I don't need you to stand up for me, Lily," he hissed as he grabbed his tray.

"I wasn't . . . she was. . . ."

"I have enough crap to deal with, and now, thanks to you, I'm going to have to deal with the fact that a girl has to fight my battles."

"What were you gonna do Chase? You know you ain't gonna hit her!" she fired back hotly.

"Mind your own damn business," he growled as he stormed off.

Several other students backed away as he stormed by them and through the double doors. The only thing Lily could do was stare after him.

She looked at Tyler. "What did I do?"

"You embarrassed him," he said simply as he took a bite of an apple.

Lily frowned. "How did I embarrass him? I was just—"

"Defending him like he couldn't do it himself," Tyler offered.

"What?! I did not!"

He arched a dark black brow at her and stared at her from impossibly thick lashes. A knowing smirk slid across his lips.

"I didn't!!" she protested a little louder.

"Really? Because, when I walked up, it looked like you were about to mop the floor with Kiera. You just shouldn't have done anything."

"And let her pick on Chase?"

"He can handle himself."

"She's a girl, and you *know* he ain't gonna do anything," she said again.

He shrugged. "Still don't change the fact that you embarrassed him."

Lily sat back down and stared at Chase's half eaten lunch. When she looked up at Tyler, he was looking at the table that was full of his teammates and the cheerleaders. There was a sort of sadness in his eyes that said he would much rather be sitting with them.

"Go sit with them," Lily said softly.

He jumped slightly and turned to face her. "I don't want to," he said as he unwrapped his sandwich.

"You're lying," she said evenly.

"So. Even if I did sit there, what would you guys do?"

"We don't have to spend every minute together, Ty. You can have other friends." Even as she said the words, they left a funny taste in her mouth. The thought of Tyler hanging out with any of those knuckle-dragging apes made her stomach ache.

He watched her for a long moment and then looked over to where Kiera was waving discreetly to him. Anger burned the inside of her chest, but she kept it tamped down.

Clearing her throat, she grabbed what was left of her lunch and Chase's and pushed to her feet. "I just remembered I need to go see Mr. Smith about our Algebra assignment."

Tyler frowned at her and looked down at her partially eaten lunch. "But you haven't eaten much."

She shrugged. "Not that hungry."

They both knew she was lying. Tyler's frown deepened as he stared at her. "Ugh, fine," she said pulling an apple from the bag and taking a big bite.

"See, all better," she said between chews.

Chapter 3

You yourself as much as anybody in the entire universe deserve your love and affection.

~ Mahatma Gandhi

The next several weeks seemed to drag by in a routine that made monotony look exciting. Everyone slid into their schedules with ease. Tyler and Chase were spending more and more time on the football field, and Lily saw less and less of them. It was during this period that she realized she lacked in the friend department.

Lily fumbled with the combination on her locker door, cursing under her breath as she jerked and tugged on the latch. "Damn it," she snapped as she slapped her palm angrily against the locker door. The metal rattled loudly, causing several other students to look at her curiously. Some of them gave her snide looks and whispered behind their hands as they walked away.

She frowned. "Take a freak'n picture," she snapped at the ones still lingering.

"Hey, Lils," Chase said cheerfully, appearing out of nowhere.

"Hey," she grumbled as she tried the stubborn lock once more. "Where's Ty?" she grunted as she tried to concentrate on spinning the dial. When it still didn't budge, she cursed longer and louder.

"Jeez," Chase said reaching around and spinning the dial with her combination. The lock clicked open, and she frowned.

"Thanks," she mumbled as she reached inside and removed her books and ratty backpack.

"He's already in the locker room getting ready for practice."

She slammed the door, spun the dial and looked up at him. "Why aren't you there?"

He lifted a shoulder. "Wanted to see what you were doing after school."

She shouldered her backpack, and they started walking down the hall. It was mostly deserted, with just a few students lingering about.

"Probably going to the park," she said. Since her stepfather moved out a few years prior, there was a never-ending stream of men coming to her house. There was no way in hell she was going to be staying the night in her house with her mom's flavor of the day. There was something seriously off about that man. It made her skin crawl. She didn't even know the man's name, nor did she care to.

"Perv still lurking about, huh?"

"Yeah," she grumbled as they turned down the hall that would lead to the locker room.

"I don't like you staying there when he's there."

"Where else am I gonna go? I can't always crash at Tyler's, and your mom's boyfriend is a dick."

"Why don't you come to practice?" he suggested.

Lily frowned, not sure if sitting alone in the bleachers was any more appealing than sitting alone at the park.

"I don't know," she said as they at the locker room door.

He lifted a shoulder. "I just don't like you being at that park by yourself. You know that."

It was the truth. While the park wasn't exactly an urban war zone, it did have some questionable characters that lingered around.

She looked up at him, and he looked away sheepishly. "What?" she asked.

He lifted his shoulders and tucked his hand into the front pockets of his jeans. Rocking back on his heels, he chewed on the inside of his lip. She frowned. "What's going on?"

"We just kinda miss you, that's all."

She chuckled. "I miss you guys too. Sucks that we don't have the same classes." She thought about it for a few moments. As she did, Chase's crystal blue eyes watched her. No, watched wasn't the word she was looking for. It was more like study. He was studying her.

Typically, she didn't mind watching them practice, but that was when it was pee-wee ball. Now, it was against other schools. They were spending less time together, and she couldn't help but feel like a void was growing between them. *They* were doing their thing and getting more popular by the day. She, on the other hand, was still the girl that lived in the trailer park with a whore mother.

"Fine," she relented. "Not like anyone other than you guys care where I'm at anyway."

Chase's face split into a broad smile as he backed away. "See ya later, Lils."

She rolled her eyes and laughed. "Later."

The shrill cry of Coach Oxland's whistle echoed through the air and mingled with the grunts of boys as they crashed into one another, helmets clacking loudly. She winced as Tyler took a sac and landed hard on the ground. Suddenly, he disappeared beneath a heap of boys.

Her eyes stay trained on the pile of boys until she saw Tyler finally emerge. Even through his helmet, and even though he got smashed, she could see the wide grin on his face. She let out a sigh of relief when his eyes met hers. He gave a slight nod—his way of letting her know he was safe.

She'd learned a long time ago, that Tyler and Chase's safety was important to her. When they hurt, she hurt. Over the last six years, they'd become such an integral part of each other's lives, it was rare to see one without the other two. That was another thing that was bothering her.

She'd noticed that while both boys were on the football team, their popularity was only growing. Tyler had always been popular because of his family and the situation revolving around his mother. However, she and

Chase were always known as kids from the wrong side of the proverbial tracks.

Everything was shifting because now, Chase was becoming more popular and not because Tyler was his best friend. Well, at least not all of it. He was genuinely good at football, and in their school, if you were a jock, you had it made.

And where did that leave her? "Sitting in the stands like a loser with no life," she muttered as she slammed the textbook resting on her lap closed. With an exasperated sigh, she tossed it aside. She knew she needed to be studying, but her focus was not cooperating. Her nearly perfect GPA wouldn't suffer if she didn't study for thirty minutes.

Pushing thoughts of school work to the side, she shifted her gaze to the cheerleaders prancing around in their short, shorts and their tank tops. Kiera had her sights set on co-captain, and knowing the tenacity of the girl, it was likely she would gain the crown before they were juniors.

She almost groaned as Kiera bounced up and down excitedly, wiggling her fingers in the most ridiculous version of spirit fingers Lily had ever seen. Cheer tryouts had come and gone, and Lily had chickened out. Not because she was worried that she couldn't do it, but because she had no way of getting all the things she would need. Her mother had zero money and what money she did have was spent on her next score.

Before her stepfather left, her mother hadn't been doing drugs, and she barely drank a sip of alcohol. That was just before Lily's tenth birthday. However, as soon as the man walked out the door, everything changed. It was like her mother had gotten a taste of freedom and was reliving her younger years. Half the time she wore clothes that high school girls were wearing. It wouldn't have been so bad if she wasn't in her forties and about fifty pounds lighter.

Lily was lost in thought when she felt the presence of someone else. Turning to see the newcomer, her breath hitched in her chest, and her eyes grew wide. It was the new kid everyone had been talking about.

"Hey," he said golden eyes fixing on her.

She looked around, wondering if he'd been talking to someone else that was nearby. When she realized there was no one around, she looked back at the kid.

"Uh, hey," she said awkwardly, tucking a strand of hair behind her ear. Mentally, she kicked herself for not applying a little makeup that morning. She'd been running late thanks to her mother's last conquest hogging the bathroom doing God knows what.

"I'm Lucas."

"I know," she blurted. Heat filled her cheeks. Did she really just say that? She wished the ground would swallow her whole.

Trying quickly to recover, she gave a laugh that she prayed didn't sound as nervous as it felt. "I mean you're the talk of the entire school. Hard not to know who you are." And it was the truth. The second Lucas Delray had stepped through the doors; the sophomore had been the topic of all the raging gossip. He was good-looking, in a bad boy kind of way.

The sides of his head were shaved, leaving thick black hair hanging over his forehead and into his eyes. He was wearing a pair of black jeans with a silver chain dangling from hip to back pocket. While he was wearing a leather jacket, she could see the faded logo of some band on the front. On his feet were black converse sneakers.

Realizing that she'd been staring, she jerked her attention back up. He arched a brow at her knowingly and gave her a lazy smile. Butterflies fluttered in her stomach. The palms of her hands grew sweaty. She rubbed them against the thighs of her worn jeans before shoving them inside the hooded sweatshirt Chase had given her to wear. The October evening air was already getting chilly, an odd occurrence for the south.

"I'm Lily."

It was his turn to smile, revealing two rows of absurdly perfect white teeth. "I know," he said with a wink.

Lily flushed and looked down at her worn sneakers.

"The *entire* school, hmm?"

She nodded and shrugged. "It's a small school in a small town. I'm pretty sure people knew who you were and your entire life story before lunch."

"I can imagine what they are saying," he grunted as he reached into his leather jacket and pulled out a pack of cigarettes. "You want one?" he offered when he saw her staring at the pack.

Her eyes widened as she looked around. "Are you crazy? You can't do that here," she said pushing his hand down and quickly making sure no teacher caught them.

"Scared of getting into trouble?" he asked softly. A sly smile tilted the corners of his mouth up.

"What? No!" she sputtered.

"Is that so?"

She turned and looked at him. There was a glitter of mischief in his eyes, and she could feel herself getting pulled in.

He licked his lips, and she watched his mouth. What would it be like to kiss him like Tyler had kissed Kiera? She could feel heat warming her cheeks once more as her eyes met his. She'd never kissed a boy before. She just added it to the ever-growing list of things that she was missing out on.

"Prove it," he challenged.

"What?"

He stretched his long legs and stood above her. He took a few steps down the bleachers before turning and looking at her. "You say you're not scared of getting into trouble. Prove it."

Without another word, he walked the rest of the way down the bleachers and disappeared around the side.

Lily stared at the spot where she'd last seen him and then looked back out to the field. Chase and Tyler were in the huddle, and the cheerleaders were working on a pitiful looking human pyramid.

What would it hurt? She needed to make new friends. Lucas seemed like a good option. With quick, jerky movements, she stuffed her books back into her bag and slung it over her shoulder. With hurried steps, she walked down the bleachers. Before disappearing through the breezeway, she cast a look over her shoulder to the field.

Tyler was watching her from the water cooler. He held up his hand, questioning where she was going. She just shrugged and gave a little wave before disappearing around the corner.

It didn't take her long to find Lucas. All she had to do was follow the smell of cigarette smoke. When she finally saw him, he was beneath the bleachers. It was all very cliché—smoking under the bleachers—but it gave her a little rush of excitement.

He was leaning against the wall with one foot propped behind him and his eyes closed. A stream of smoke billowed out of his nose. When he opened his eyes, they landed on her immediately.

"I was beginning to think you chickened out," he said with a smirk.

She bristled slightly. She hated being called a chicken. There wasn't a dare that she wouldn't do. She gave him a tight smile and dropped her bag at her feet.

He watched her with curiosity as he shook a cigarette from the crumpled pack and handed it to her. She held it in her hands for a few moments, studying it thoroughly. Every lecture and lesson she'd ever heard about cigarette smoking came to mind. Her mother smoked, and she hated the smell. Before today, she'd never thought about taking up the habit.

"That end goes in your mouth," Lucas said interrupting her thoughts.

"I know that," she snapped, narrowing her eyes at him.

He held up his hands in surrender. "Hey, I was just helping." He tugged a golden zippo from his front pocket and flipped it open.

Here goes nothing. She placed the orange filter between her lips as he held the flame to the tip. Unsure of what to do, she inhaled and immediately sputtered and coughed.

"Shit," she wheezed as tears filled her eyes. Her lungs burned and ached as she continued to hack.

Lucas threw his head back and laughed loudly. "Easy there. Not such a big drag on your first time."

He then held his own half-smoked cigarette up and gave her a demonstration. After watching him a few times, she decided to try again. The second time wasn't as bad, but she still coughed. However, by the third and fourth times, it wasn't so bad.

Nicotine flowed into her system, giving her a pleasant little head rush. She smiled and flicked her ashes, trying desperately to look cool.

"Well, look at you," he said with a wink.

She rolled her eyes and took another drag. "So, Lucas, where did you move from?"

He gave her a smug smile. "I thought everyone already knew my life story."

Lily just shrugged and dropped her cigarette to the ground before crunching it out with her toe. She exhaled the last plume of smoke and gave him a grin. She couldn't help it. The rush of doing something she wasn't supposed to combined with the fact that this incredibly hot, older guy was talking to her made her feel brave.

"I'm not like everyone."

He stared at her long and hard, his lips were still pulled back into a smile, but it was the look in his eyes that made her heart thump harder in her chest. "No, Lily, you most certainly are not."

The way her name rolled off his lips made her stomach flutter.

"You want to get out of here?"

"Uh . . . um, well. I'm kinda waiting for my friends."

"The two jock straps I've seen you with?"

She smiled. He'd been watching her?

"Yeah. They're my best friends."

Lucas shrugged and dropped his cigarette to the ground beside her smooshed one. "Suit yourself," he said as he began to walk off.

Lily frowned and looked through the cracks to where the team was still practicing. It would be at least another hour before they finished.

Acting on impulse, she called out, "Wait." She scooped her bag from the ground and trotted after him.

He stopped and smiled down at her. "Come on, let's go find some trouble to get into." He slung his arm over her shoulder, and that's when Lily knew that Lucas Delray had just become a part of her life.

Chapter 4

Not everything that is faced can be changed,
but nothing can be changed until it is faced.

~James Baldwin

"Where's Lily?" Chase asked as he left the locker room. Tyler was flirting with one of the cheerleaders.

"I don't know," he grunted as he leaned in and whispered something into the girl's ear. She giggled and blushed, playfully batting at his chest.

Chase frowned at the couple. "What do you mean you don't know?"

Tyler let out an annoyed huff and looked up. "I mean I don't know. She was in the bleachers studying or some crap; then she wasn't. I'm not her keeper."

"I saw her leave with that new guy," the blonde offered. He thought her name was Tiffany, but he wasn't overly sure. She'd just transferred from Atlanta.

"The sophomore?" he asked.

She nodded and tugged on her bottom lip. "Yeah. He got up and left. She followed him a couple minutes later. Not sure where they went after that."

Chase's scowl deepened. "Thanks," he muttered as he walked down the hall leaving Tyler to his flirting.

Where on earth could she have gone? Lily wasn't the overly adventurous type. In fact, she rarely deviated from her routine.

He rounded the corner and almost immediately ran into Kiera. Inwardly he groaned.

"Hey, Chase," she said in an overly chipper voice.

"Hey," he grunted as he started walking again. Since football season began, Kiera's tune toward him had changed.

The annoying squeak of her shoes quickly began to follow. "What'cha doing?"

"Going home."

"Wanna go to Frank's?"

Frank's Pizzeria was the only place for kids their age to hang out. There were pool tables and arcade games from the eighties, but they still worked great.

"No. Hey, have you seen Lily?"

Her smile fell, and her nose scrunched up in disgust. "Why do you want to know where that skank is?"

Anger caused the hair on the back of his neck to stand up. Kiera could be nice when she wanted too. However, it was a rare occurrence, especially where Lily was concerned. The girls had never gotten along, and now that they were in high school, it seemed to be worse.

"You know what, forget I asked. Later, Kiera."

He turned and walked away, even though she was still talking to him. He hated it when Kiera talked about Lily. There was nothing he could do about it. If she'd been a guy, he would have cuffed her a good one, but he'd been raised never to strike a woman. It was something he firmly believed in. He'd seen his mom get knocked around more times than he cared to count. He refused to be a man like that.

He walked through the front doors of the school and looked at the deserted parking lot. He couldn't wait until he turned sixteen and got his own car. He'd been saving his money, but he was still a long way from having enough money.

He dropped down onto the steps and waited. A few minutes later Tyler plopped down beside him with a wide smile smeared across his face.

"Dude, Tiffany is so freaking hot," he said as he leaned back on his hands. "And one hell of a kisser," he added.

Chase chuckled. The laugh died on his lips when he saw two people emerging from the shadows across the lot. Immediately he recognized Lily. He sighed a little when he saw that she was safe. The only time he didn't worry about her safety was when she was with them.

"There's Lily," he grunted to Tyler.

Tyler's attention snapped to the couple walking across the parking lot. Lily's hair was down around her shoulders. This caused both to frown. Lily almost never wore her hair down.

"Who's with her?" Tyler grunted, leaning forward and resting his arms on the tops of his legs.

"Must be the new guy."

They stiffened when the new guy's eyes met theirs. A smirk tilted one corner of his mouth up, and Chase felt his blood begin to simmer. As if to further make things worse, the guy draped his arm possessively over Lily's shoulders.

Lily's gaze met first Chase's and then Tyler's before quickly looking away. As they got closer, he could see the pink in her cheeks. She almost seemed to glow.

They finally reached the steps and stopped.

"There you are," Chase said pushing to his feet. Tyler followed suit and openly assessed the new guy. Immediately a bad feeling swelled in the pit of Chase's stomach. There was something about the guy that just didn't sit well with him, and judging from the way Tyler's jaw was clenching and unclenching, he felt the same thing.

"Sorry. I got bored. Guys, this is Lucas." She turned and looked up at Lucas, giving him a warm smile. Her eyes were glossy, and the smarmy grin on Lucas's face widened. "Lucas, these are my best friends. That one's Tyler and he's Chase."

Not even one of the boys offered a hand for a shake as they sized each other up. "Sup," Lucas said with a quick jerk of his head.

"Hey," Tyler and Chase muttered in unison.

"Where ya been, Lils?" Chase asked casually.

"I—" she started but was cut off by Lucas.

"Don't see how that's any of your business." Lucas's tone was clipped and edged with a warning.

The tension snapped between the four of them immediately as Chase tensed. Tyler knew if he didn't diffuse the situation, things were going to get out of hand quickly. Chase's temper was a powder keg with a short fuse. It took very little to set him off, and in that moment, he was already primed and ready to go. On top of that, the dick standing in front of him was holding the proverbial burning match.

Chase took another step forward, going toe to toe with the sophomore. Chase was big for his age, but Lucas was bigger. "What did you just say to me?"

Lucas's eyes narrowed. "You heard me."

Chase's nostrils flared angrily. Lily's eyes were wide with shock and confusion as she looked back and forth between the two.

Tyler put a hand between the two hot heads and gently pushed. "Okay, let's not do anything stupid."

"Oh, I think something stupid is exactly what I need to do to get that damn smug grin off his face."

"Welcome to try it, pretty boy," Lucas taunted.

Chase's fists flexed, and his shoulders tensed.

"Stop," Lily yelled, finally finding her voice

It was only after hearing her voice that Chase backed down. Before another word could be said, Maria honked the horn.

"Time to go, Lils, our ride's here," Chase said through clenched teeth.

"Okay," she said starting to move away from Lucas's arm. However, his arm tightened around her, and he pulled her to his side. She looked up at him just as his lips dropped to hers.

A flurry of emotions took off in Chase's stomach as he watched Lucas ram his tongue down Lily's throat. He looked at Chase over Lily's head. The look in his eyes challenged Chase to make a move.

When Lucas finally broke the kiss, he released Lily and pulled a cigarette from his jacket pocket. "I'll talk to you later," he said with a wink as he lit his smoke and walked away.

Lily watched him walk away and then turned to face them. Her dreamy smile faded when she saw their dark looks. Her brows pinched together.

"What?"

"You've known him for a couple hours, and you're already sucking face," Chase said vehemently.

Her frown deepened. "And your point is?"

"How much do you know about him?" Tyler questioned as the three of them walked to Maria's idling car.

"Enough. What's with you guys anyway?"

"I just don't like watching you make out with a guy. It's gross," Chase snapped as he opened the door and waited for her to climb in.

Lily just stared at them with fury burning in her green eyes. She crossed her arms over her chest, and both boys looked down. Tyler and Chase hadn't been the only ones to change over the summer. Lily had developed rather . . . well.

Their eyes jerked back up to her face.

"Are you kidding me right now?" she yelled.

"What?" they both said dumbly.

She snorted and rolled her eyes in a way that only Lily could. "I sit and listen to you two talk about boobs and butts all the time. You talk about sex and making out with girls constantly, but *me* kissing a guy in front of you is gross?"

"Pretty much," Chase said.

Tyler groaned inwardly. Chase was not helping the situation one bit. He never did when they fought. His brain to mouth filter rarely worked, and Lily's temper always seemed to clash.

Lily took a step closer and jabbed him in the chest with her finger. "You know what?! Screw you!" She then whirled and jabbed a finger into Tyler's chest. "I don't know what y'all's problem is, but you embarrassed me! I don't know what that little pissing contest was about, but y'all need to knock it the hell off~"

"We're just worried about you," Tyler defended.

"I don't need a damn babysitter so back the hell off."

Spinning on her heels, Lily angrily marched away.

"Lily. Wait," Tyler called.

Lily spun around and walked backward. As she did, she lifted both middle fingers at them before promptly turning and marching away.

Both Chase and Tyler just stared after her for a long moment before looking at each other.

"What the hell was that about?" Chase asked.

Tyler just shook his head and laughed. "One of these days, she's gonna punch you in that mouth of yours."

"Why?"

"Because you goad her."

"Do not!"

"Whatever, get in. You can eat at my place tonight."

"What about her?"

They slid into the backseat and closed the door. "She'll come around," Tyler said as he watched her walk away. "She always does."

Chapter 5

To exist is to change, to change is to mature,
to mature is to go on creating oneself endlessly

~Henri Bergson

Lily's old sneakers crunched over the gravel on the side of the road as she made her way home. The sun was just beginning to dip behind the trees. The air had grown cooler, and by the time she walked down the weed-choked driveway of the trailer park, she was shivering. Her thin jacket did very little to ward off the cold. Thanksgiving was just around the corner. She couldn't believe in a few short weeks it would be Christmas.

She was pissed at Chase and Tyler for the way they'd treated Lucas. How dare they treat him that way? They had no right. They didn't see her acting like a lunatic when they were flirting with girls. At the thought of Lucas, her thoughts softened. She'd known him for less than two hours, and he'd already been two of her firsts. She'd smoked a cigarette, which had made her feel rebellious. The exhilaration of getting caught was like adding a cherry on top.

Then, while she'd been leaning against the rough brick wall of the elementary school, he'd kissed her.

"I'm going to kiss you now," he'd said. The sound of his husky voice made her body tingle in funny places. She didn't altogether understand what the weird feelings were, but as soon as his lips touched hers, she'd forgotten all about them.

She wasn't sure how a first kiss was supposed to go, but it felt weird. His mouth was all over hers and then there was his tongue. She'd heard about French kissing but never thought much about it. His tongue had awkwardly pushed into her mouth, and she was unsure of what she was supposed to do after that.

So, doing what she thought she was supposed to do, she rolled hers against his. She must have done something right because he pressed his body tighter against hers. One of his hands rested on her hip while the other was on the wall beside her head.

She'd soon gotten into the rhythm he'd set when he moved the hand from her hip and cupped her bottom. Her eyes widened as he squeezed her. She could feel herself blushing. This was the first time she'd ever allowed anyone to touch her like that on purpose. She was feeling conflicted.

Reaching behind her, she moved his hand back to her hip. He didn't move it again. His mouth, however, did move. It moved from her lips down to her neck. Again, her body began to tingle, and she had another weird sensation *down there.* They'd learned about boy parts and girl parts, but she wasn't sure what was happening. She did realize, however, that she very much liked the feeling of his mouth on her neck.

After a while, he pulled away and gave her a sexy smile. Her heart was beating so fast she was sure it was going to explode from her chest. They'd started to walk back to the front of the school when he told her that she needed to pull her hair down around her neck. At first, she'd been confused, but they'd walked by a car, and she saw her reflection. He'd left two hickies the size of quarters on each side of her neck.

Lily knew what people said about girls getting hickies. They called them a tramp or easy. The good folks of Raven's Bend liked to call her mother a tramp and much worse.

She'd been embarrassed when Tyler and Chase had looked at her questioningly. They knew she never wore her hair down. Her best friends had shattered her good mood.

Lily walked up the drive of the pitiful looking trailer. Once upon a time, there had been flowers in the flower beds and brightly colored pots hanging on the porch. Her mom used to keep their place in good shape. That all changed when the step-father walked out.

Now, the flowerbeds were overflowing with weeds, and the yard was in no better shape. The dry, knee-deep weeds, crunched under the soles of her shoes as she cut across the yard. She climbed up the rickety steps, praying that she wouldn't fall through them and break her leg or get cut on a rusty nail.

Taking a deep breath, she hoped that no one was home. The lights weren't on, but that didn't mean anything. Well, it could have indicated that the power had been cut off, again. As quietly as possible, she stepped through the front door, and immediately she was greeted by the stench of mildew and unwashed laundry.

Though it was cool outside, the inside of the trailer was stifling. She opened the refrigerator and winced at the harsh light streaming from the inside. "Power's not out. There's that," she muttered as she scanned the contents for something to eat. The only thing on the inside was a three-week-old half gallon of milk and three bottles of beer. There was also a small chunk of cheese with green and white fuzz growing on the corner.

Her stomach cramped and rumbled hungrily. She'd hadn't eaten breakfast that morning because her mom either didn't bother coming home again or had left early. The lunch Tyler packed had faded hours ago.

She picked up the block of cheese and took it to the counter. After switching on the light over the sink, she inspected the cheese. There was only one corner with the mold. Maybe if she cut it away, the rest would be okay to eat.

Her stomach grumbled again.

Deciding to take the risk, she pulled a knife from the drawer and cut away the moldy spots of cheese. She then dropped the knife into the three-day-old slimy dishwater. Bugs and gnats flew into the air, hovering over the nastiness.

I hope she cuts her hand off, she thought as she grabbed her bag and made her way down the narrow hall. She passed her mother's room and heard a loud thump. It was followed by a giggle then muffled grunts and moans.

Lily's cheeks burned as she hurried to her room and quietly closed her door. She had no idea who was in her mother's room, but she did have an idea of what they were doing. The thought of it made her stomach queasy.

Dropping her bag on top of her ratty desk, she switched on her desk light. She plopped down into the chair and began pulling her books out. If she was ever going to get out of the hell hole that was her life, it was going to have to be by a scholarship.

She tried not to think about the cheese she was nibbling on as she went over her notes for her science class. After three hours, her mind was beginning to wander to Lucas. Knowing that she wouldn't get any more work finished, she closed her book and pressed the heels of her hands against her gritty eyes.

Lily switched off the lamp and fell against her bed. Shafts of moonlight filled the room in a bluish-gray haze. The poster above her bed was of her favorite actor. Many nights she'd stared up at the pirate, silently praying for him to take her away from her life. Life as a pirate had to be better than the life she was living.

Her stomach clenched again, reminding her that the small block of cheese was not enough to ease the hunger pain. She could go to Tyler's house, but she was still angry with them for the way they'd treated Lucas. She refused to go crawling to them when they had acted like complete dicks.

To keep her mind off her aching stomach, Lily thought more about Lucas. He hadn't told her much about himself. When she'd asked, he'd shrugged it off and changed the subject. She thought about the way his hands had touched her, wondering how she felt about it.

She then wondered what it would be like to have sex with him. Over the summer, she'd walked in on Chase and Tyler watching one of his mom's dirty movies. Like them, she'd been curious. By the end of the film, the only thing the three of them could do was sit there in silence. The whole thing was awkward and uncomfortable. Especially when they realized *how* people had sex and what happened. Up until that point, it was all they had known about sex without having really *known* about it. To say it was a shock would be an understatement.

After that day, the three of them no longer shared a bed when they spent the night together. It was after that day that things felt weird. Now, as she lay in the darkness, she was beginning to understand things.

While she loved Tyler and Chase, they were boys. They thought of things differently than she did. To them, she was their best friend and not a girl. It only confused her more when she thought back to how they'd reacted to Lucas. Chase hadn't acted like that when Tyler had told him about kissing Kiera. So, what was the difference?

Exhausted and starving, Lily's eyes slowly drifted closed.

She didn't know how long she'd been asleep, but the sound of her bedroom door creaking open woke her. She still had her shoes, clothes, and jacket on.

"Mom?" she asked sleepily rubbing her eyes.

There was no response, but she could see someone standing in the door. Her eyes widened when she realized it wasn't her mother but a very large man.

Lily's heart launched into her throat. "What are you doing in here? Get out!" she said raising her voice.

"Well, looky here. Aren't you a pretty little thing," he said as he stepped deeper into her room, closing the door behind him. The soft click of the door sounded like a shotgun going off in her head. Lily began to panic.

He stepped into the light the moon cast and her heart hammered harder. He was a middle-aged man with a rounded stomach, and the only thing he was wearing was a pair of white underwear.

"What are you doing in here? This is my room. Get out!" she shouted, backing herself into the corner of her bed. She knew immediately it was a mistake. As he got closer, he blocked her path for escape.

He ignored her and moved forward. "Young and pretty. What are you, fourteen?"

She didn't answer, and he shrugged.

"No matter. You're about the perfect age. A ripe piece of fruit just ready for the plucking," he leered. He licked his lips and made a wet smacking sound.

Lily's stomach rolled violently, the sound making her want to vomit.

She was cornered like a frightened rabbit with nowhere to go. Her entire body trembled with fright.

If she could just make it to the door, she would be free. She scrambled to try to get off the bed. As soon as her feet hit the floor, however, his hand flashed out with speed she hadn't expected. His hand fisted in her hair as he roughly jerked her backward on the bed. Her skull landed against the wall with a dull *thud* sending stars dancing across her vision. His hand tightened in her hair, causing her scalp to burn and her eyes to water.

His weight pushed her into the mattress as he savagely jerked her arms above her head. Her shoulder popped loudly, sending pain ricocheting through her body.

His breath was hot, and the rancid smell caused her to gag.

"I swear, I'll scream," she threatened weakly.

"Go ahead. I like it when they do."

And that's precisely what she did.

Chapter 6

Evil is unspectacular and always human
And shares our bed and eats at our own table.

~W.H. AUDEN, Herman Melville

Chase frowned as he walked through the darkness. Tyler said he could stay the night if he wanted to. He'd decided not to because Mr. Anderson had shown up. While the man hadn't been unkind, Chase could tell by the disgusted look on the man's face that he was not thrilled with Chase being there. It was as if Chase was a bug and Mr. Anderson would rather squish him under his expensive shoes.

Instead, Maria had given him a plate of food to take home in case he got hungry during the night. The older woman was always making sure that he had plenty to eat. She also knew that he wasn't going to take it home and eat it. The nanny knew the first place Chase would go would be to Lily's to give her the food.

He'd expected her to show up at Tyler's house. When she didn't, they began to worry. Tyler offered to walk with him, but his father had refused to allow it. Chase tried to keep the peace and said he'd go check on her. It had done little to ease Tyler's worry though.

As he walked up the gravel drive, he could feel the sharp rocks through the thin soles of his shoes. He desperately needed a new pair, but with his mom gone on another bender, he had no idea when he'd be able to afford it.

Chase bypassed his own trailer and made his way toward the one Lily lived in, four houses down. After he passed the third one, an eerie feeling began to creep up his spine. He jumped into the shadows when the figure of a large man exploded from the front door of Lily's house.

He was yelling something and behind him stood Lily's mother. She was crying and screaming. "I'm so sorry, baby. Please don't leave. She didn't know what she was doing."

Chase's blood turned cold in his veins as he watched the man jump into his car and slam the door. Red taillights lit up the shadows as the tires spit gravel wildly behind it. Chase looked back to the house, but he could no longer see Lily's mother.

His feet began to move on their own, but as he got closer, Viki stormed out of the house drunkenly slamming the door behind her. He pressed his back against the side of the porch, clinging to the shadows. He could smell the alcohol on her breath even from where he stood.

"You ruin everything, you stupid little bitch! You shoulda just agreed. If you had, it wouldn't have hurt so bad!" she screamed. Viki struggled to put on her shoes as she teetered dangerously on the top step. "I should have drowned you when I had the chance."

Chase's fists curled into his sides. All he would have to do was reach out and trip her. She'd break her neck and Lily would be safe. However, he knew that she truly wouldn't be. So, biting down hard on his lip until he tasted blood, he waited until the woman was in her car and speeding away before he took the steps two at a time.

The smell of the house was nearly overpowering as he dropped the covered dish of food to the roach-infested table.

"Lily!" he cried, searching frantically through each room. "Lily! Damn it, answer me."

His heart slammed against his ribs violently as he approached her bedroom door. With clammy hands, he reached for the knob. "Please let her be okay," he prayed as he pushed the thin door open.

It took a minute for his eyes to adjust to the dark room. "Lily? Lily, answer me, please," he begged.

He listened, but the only thing he could hear was his heart and the sound of his breathing in his ears. He was reaching for the lamp when he heard a whimper.

"Don't turn on the light." Her voice was so soft he barely heard it.

"Lily, where are you?"

"Just go away," she whimpered.

"Like hell. What happened? Why can't I turn on the light?"

There was no answer. Deciding that having her angry with him would be better than her being hurt, he walked over to her desk and switched on the lamp. He'd been in her room dozens of times and knew it like he knew the back of his hand.

He blinked, waiting for his eyes to adjust to the sudden light. Lily's room was tiny but immaculate. There wasn't an article of clothing out of place or a scrap of dirt anywhere. It also smelled like vanilla and wild berries.

He looked at the bed, but it was empty. The blankets were scattered everywhere. Then he saw a dark puddle of blood staining the light blue sheets. His blood turned to ice in his veins. Frantically, his eyes searched the room before finally settling on the small ball curled in the corner.

"Lily!" He rushed to her side and realized that her shirt was ripped to shreds, hanging off her shoulders and exposing parts of her breasts. Blood rolled down her shoulders from what looked like a savage looking bite mark. She clutched at the fabric, trying to hide her body but failed miserably.

The need to vomit rolled up his throat, but he pushed it aside. He reached out, but she flinched and tried to scoot tighter into the corner.

"Shhh, it's me," he said softly. Keeping his movements slow, he pushed some of her hair from her.

His eyes widened in horror as she stared back at him with a black eye that was already almost entirely swollen shut.

"I'll kill him," he seethed feeling a rage boil inside him hotter than fire.

She just sobbed, and Chase's heart broke. He didn't know what he should do. "Should I call the cops?"

Her eyes widened. "No! Please don't call the cops." She was nearing hysterics as she released the front of her shirt and urgently gripped his jacket. "You can't, Chase.

Don't call the cops. P-p-please!" Her sobs came harder and faster. Her entire body shook violently.

He nodded slowly, and she sagged back to the floor in a heap.

When she shifted, he saw that her legs were completely bare. The realization of what happened gutted him. Her tanned legs were marred with dark bruises that looked like fingerprints. There were also scratches on her hips and ribs.

"Did he—" he couldn't even bring himself to finish the words.

She looked away in shame. Chase's heart shattered into millions of pieces because he knew he would never be able to make her forget this night.

"Can you put pants on?"

She only shook her head and sobbed harder. Tears leaked from her red and swollen eyes.

He quickly shrugged out of his jacket and wrapped it around her. "Come here," he said. She climbed into his embrace like a frightened animal. Pushing to his feet, he shifted her so he could grab a clean blanket from her closet. She clung to him as if her life depended on it. Then with some maneuvering, he secured the blanket around her body.

"We're going to take care of you," he whispered against the top of her head as he carried her from the house and slipped into the woods that would take him back to Tyler's house. "No one will ever hurt you again. I'll kill anyone that tries."

"Here, take her for a minute," Chase said as he handed Lily over to Tyler.

She had cried herself to sleep against his chest, so when she was being passed into Tyler's arms, she didn't stir. "What the hell happened to her?" he asked as Chase pulled the blankets back.

"That asshole her mom has been seeing."

Tyler's eyes widened and then narrowed in rage. Chase knew the anger well because he was feeling it too. "Did he—" Tyler couldn't finish the question. Chase only gave him a dark look. It was all Tyler needed before he knew the truth.

"We have to call the cops," he hissed as he gently placed Lily in the center of the bed. Chase pulled the blankets over her.

"We can't. She freaked out earlier. I don't know what to do." Never in his life had he felt so powerless. He was thirteen years old, and there was nothing he could do.

"Should we clean her up or something?" Tyler asked.

"Probably."

Tyler walked into his attached bathroom. A few minutes later, he returned carrying a wet washcloth. Gently, he pulled the blankets back, exposing her bruised legs. Careful not to expose her further, he gently wiped away as much of the dried blood as possible. Lily barely stirred.

"We can't just leave her like this. She needs to get checked out. Those scratches look so bad. If we call the cops, they can catch him. He'll go to jail, and she can go to the hospital and get the help she needs," Tyler said as he dabbed antibiotic ointment on the cuts and scratches. Once he'd tended to as much as he could, he pulled the blanket back over her body.

"Maybe. Her mom might go too."

"And that's a bad thing? Obviously, she doesn't give a shit about her own daughter!" Tyler said his voice rising. Chase watched his friend. It was rare that Tyler got upset over anything. However, since it involved Lily, things were much different.

Chase shook his head. "You don't understand."

Tyler frowned. "I don't understand what?"

"What happens if her mom gets taken away?"

"She'll go live with her dad."

Again, Chase shook his head. "I don't think so. A couple years ago Lily told me that he signed a piece of paper. He was no longer her dad."

"What? How is that even possible?"

Chase shrugged. "I don't know, but if her mom gets put away, Lily will get taken away."

"Taken where?"

"She'll be put into foster care."

Chase had seen it happen several times in the trailer park. A white car and a police car had shown up to people's houses. There were usually two nicely dressed people and an officer. They always left with the kid or kids screaming and crying. He'd never seen those kids again.

He didn't know much about how foster care worked, but he couldn't see that happen to her. "We'll never get to see her again."

Tyler's face paled as he looked from Chase to Lily. She was tossing and turning in her sleep, sobbing lightly.

"She can stay here," Tyler said.

"But your old man?"

"He leaves in the morning and will be gone for three weeks this time. It'll work for now, but eventually, her mother is going to wonder where she is."

Chase ground his teeth together. "Let that bitch worry. You should have heard what she was saying. She was blaming Lily."

Tyler sighed. "You going to stay?"

Chase just gave him an incredulous look, and Tyler chuckled. He removed the sleeping bags he kept stored under the bed. When Chase and Lily stayed the night, Lily always got the bed while they slept on the floor.

"I'll take left," Tyler said as he rolled the sleeping bag out on the floor.

"I'm not sleeping right now. I want to keep an eye on her."

Tyler nodded. "I'll sleep for a few hours and then you can while I stay up with her."

Chase sat at the foot of the bed. Resting his back against the rail, he drew his knees up to his chest.

Tyler turned out the lights and stretched out on the sleeping bag. Thoughts circled their friend as she lay whimpering in bed. Chase wanted to reach out to her. He wanted to hold her and keep her safe. This was his fault.

If he hadn't pushed her so hard and made her so angry, she would have come with them instead of going off on her own.

Hours later, Tyler lay snoring on the floor, and even after he tried to take over watching over her, Chase refused him. This was his responsibility.

"I'm so sorry," he whispered as tears streaked down his cheeks.

The days following Lily's attack were a complete nightmare. When asked what happened to cause all the bruises, she claimed it had been an accident. The school counselor reported it, but when the department of child services showed up at their house, everything appeared perfectly normal. Her mom had cleaned the house close to spotless and refrained from drinking and the drugs.

They had questioned her relentlessly, and when asked about the bruises and cuts, the response had been a car accident. The case was dismissed and the file closed. It didn't take long for Lily's mom to return to her old self. However, the man that had tormented Lily never showed up again.

As a result, Lily's mom had taken her anger out on her daughter. This time, the bruises weren't visible, but the mental scars would leave a lasting impression.

Lily turned in on herself. She became distant to everyone—except for Lucas. He understood her better than anyone. While he never promised to be there any time she needed him—like Chase and Tyler did frequently—she knew he would. She *hoped* he would.

The days turned into weeks, and the weeks turned to months. Christmas and New Year came and went. They never talked about that night again. Tyler had tried to get her to get help, but she adamantly refused. It was because of his insistence to keep talking about it that she began to pull away from them. She didn't want to, but when she looked at them, she was reminded of that night. It hurt. It hurt like hell. Lucas became the person she clung to. They snuck out all the time. She began drinking more frequently, showing up to school either hungover or still drunk.

Logically, she knew she couldn't blame Tyler and Chase for her behavior, but like Lucas told her, they would never truly understand how she felt. They would only pity her. She'd adamantly defended them, believing they would never pity her. Then she'd seen it for herself one day after lunch.

Kiera walked by, intentionally knocking Lily's books from her hands, scattering papers all over the hall.

"Watch where you're going, skank," the girl had sneered. She tossed her glossy black hair over her shoulder and cackled loudly. The girls always following her like helpless twits mimicked her laugh. It was like something out of a terrible teen movie.

Humiliation and anger boiled inside Lily's chest. "Don't you have a manicure or something to get too?" Lily grumbled as she knelt on the floor to gather her books.

"Excuse me? What did you just say?" Kiera asked, looking down her nose.

She should have kept her mouth shut, but she'd never really had the ability to do that when Kiera was concerned. "Nothing," she muttered lowering her gaze, trying to focus on gathering her things and getting the hell outta dodge. But it was too late, she'd already been put on Kiera's radar.

"Oh look," Kiera said loudly. Against her better judgment, Lily looked up at the other girl, mentally bracing herself for what was going to come next.

"Maybe you are just like your mother." Her voice dripped with venom. The girl's eyes pinned Lily to the floor with an arctic gaze. "Since you're already on your knees, do you just want all the guys to line up here or would you prefer to go to the boy's locker room and taking them all on at the same time?"

Lily's eyes had widened. She wasn't sure why, but it never failed to surprise her at the pure hatred that Kiera seemed to spew.

Lily's cheeks burned brightly as several of the guys in the hall made lewd comments and groped themselves.

Suddenly there was a scuffling sound followed by someone being shoved into a locker. Lily didn't look up. She didn't dare.

"Do that to her again, and I swear you won't have any balls to grab next time!" Chase's voice was low and menacing.

"Back off, Kramer. It was just harmless fun."

Chase's grip tightened on the guy's shirt, and he slammed his back into the locker again, jarring the guy's teeth. "Does it look like she's having fun, Ellison? Huh?"

A group of guys had gathered around them. Tyler stood with his back against Chase's, making sure none of the other guys jumped him. When one of them took a step forward, Tyler leveled a cold glare in the guy's direction. "I wouldn't do that if I were you." His voice was dangerously low. People knew Chase and Tyler well enough to know that if push came to shove, they would not hesitate to throw down. They'd done it on more than one occasion.

Chase was a ruthless fighter. Growing up being beat on by men his entire life, he'd learned early on how to fight. Tyler, was thinner than Chase but could fight just as hard and just as well.

"I asked you a question, asshole. Does it look like she's having fun?" Chase barked, slamming the guy against the locker once more.

"N-no," he stuttered.

Chase released him and backed away. Slowly, he turned. "If we see *any* of you dickheads so much as look at her wrong again, you won't be able to see out of your eyes for a month."

The crowd that had gathered around her scattered. Lily could hear the anger in Chase's voice. He was struggling to maintain his control. Tears had filled her eyes. Her hair fell around her face, acting as a curtain to shield her from the lewd stares and catcalls. She didn't have the strength for a fight. She was in the process of picking up her books when Chase and Tyler came to the rescue.

"Let us help," Tyler had whispered.

"I don't think she has the right to talk about easy mothers. Her mom's legs fly open the second she's on her back." Chase grumbled as he had stacked Lily's books in a pile. Lily was prepared to laugh with them because, in all honesty, she'd missed them. However, it was when her eyes met each of theirs that she saw what Lucas had been talking about. Pity. It was as plain as the nose on her face. They weren't nice to her because they were her friends. They were nice to her because they pitied her.

From that moment on, Lily completely withdrew. She and Lucas spent almost every waking moment together. When summer rolled around, she couldn't have been more excited to get out of the hell they called school. She was tired of the never-ending drama. Kiera had continued her torment, but Lily was growing harder and harder.

The slights and jabs lost their effect, and she began to blow Chase and Tyler off. They just reminded her of too much. When she was with Lucas, things were easier— simpler. He made her forget. One of his methods of forgetting was introducing her to weed.

The first time she'd smoked it with him, she'd vowed to never do it again. However, after a couple more run-ins with her mom, she quickly realized the best way to get away was to get as messed up as possible. It worked. Unfortunately, the fix was always temporary. As soon as she sobered up, the problems returned, and on the nights that she smoked and drank, they brought a wicked hangover with them.

That created a vicious circle. She would drink whiskey and smoke pot to forget her crappy life. Then, when she sobered up, she started all over again to kill the hangover. That summer was one she would never remember!

Lucas became what Chase and Tyler would never be—someone who didn't care too much what happened to her.

Chapter 7

The past is never where you think you left it.

~Katherine Anne Porter

Sophomore Year

"Shhhh, someone is going to see us," she giggled as they staggered to the front of the truck. Her head was swimming. She wasn't sure if it was because of the weed or the cheap vodka Lucas had swiped from his old man. Either way, she felt great—for the most part.

"Come on baby. No one is going to see us," Lucas slurred, his mouth pressing sloppy kisses to her mouth and cheek. She was pretty sure that he was smearing her new lipstick all over her face. It had been a present to herself, swiped from the Gas-N-Sip for Christmas. Her mother hadn't bothered.

No one had given a damn about her for Christmas. She'd worked at the Chicken Barn and spent the holiday completely alone. Chase and Tyler had gone skiing with their girlfriends over the break—courtesy of Tyler's douche-canoe father. They'd invited her, but her invite came with rules, one rule to be specific. No Lucas. They didn't like him and didn't bother hiding it. It pissed her off and only further served to push a wedge between them. She didn't like their girlfriends, and yet, she wasn't treating them like dog crap scraped off the bottom of her shoe.

Things were different with Lucas. He was there and didn't look at her like she was going to snap. She liked the feeling he gave her. He helped her forget about her craptastic life. Eventually, Chase and Tyler got the hint and stopped hovering. They settled for disapproving glances from across the room.

Time slipped away, and so did their friendship. When she was alone, she thought about all the summers they spent together. The memories of the Fourth of July always made her smile. When she was alone was when she missed them the most. She thought about going to hang out with them, but Lucas always seemed to show up right when she made up her mind.

A year had come and gone, and she'd spoken maybe a handful of sentences to both of her old friends. They'd become stars of the junior varsity football team, catapulting them further into the popularity stratosphere. She'd been left behind while they were living their lives.

Squeezing her eyes tightly closed, she tried to pull her focus back to the present before the darkness of the past threatened to pull her under.

Lucas had been trying to get her to give *it* up for months now, but she adamantly refused. Each time they got close, flashbacks would slam over her like a tidal wave. The evening always ended with an angry Lucas and a remorseful Lily.

"Why can't we, Lily? You know I'm the only one that will want you after what he did to you. No one wants to be with a woman that's been damaged like that." His words cut deep and at first, she didn't believe him, but the longer they were together, the more she began to see it was true. The other boys would look at her differently at school. Even though they didn't know what happened, they knew something was wrong with her.

These fights were always the worst because when she inevitably turned him down, he would swear at her and call her a stupid tease. Then, without fail, he would leave her at whatever party they'd been at in search of someone else's pants to get into. A couple of times, she'd spent the night in the parking lot in another town because he'd left her. Each time she swore it would be the last time. However, the next day he would always beg her forgiveness, and she would take him back.

Maybe tonight she would give in and finally give it up for him. Start the new year off with a bang. At least it would keep him from getting angry again.

All around them the sounds of the New Year's party roared. The bonfire crackled and popped as people danced to the country music blaring from someone's pickup. It was always the same thing at the same place. There was a party almost every weekend on the back fifty acres of Old man Jordan's farm.

"I think I need another hit," Lily said as she tried to wiggle away from Lucas's probing tongue and roaming hands.

He huffed out an annoyed breath and produced a half smoked joint. She took it from his hands and placed it between her lips. Lucas held out a lighter and lit the tip.

The smoke burned her lungs on the first drag. She exhaled coughing and sputtering before handing it back to Lucas. Her eyes watered as she felt the fog begin to roll back in.

He took a drag, held it in and then pulled her in for a kiss, exhaling into her mouth. As her mind became hazy again, she pulled away and smiled up at him. He took it as an invitation and pushed her against the side of someone's new truck.

A small whimper escaped her lips as his cold hands found their way up her shirt.

A flash of hands not belonging to Lucas rushed through her mind. She squeezed her eyes tighter and forced the image away. Lucas took it as another invitation and roughly groped her breast.

"Oh look, it's a skanky trailer trash makeout, shesh," came the high pitch voice of a very drunk Kiera Stockton. The three girls at her side cackled loudly. It was like nails on a chalkboard against Lily's nerves.

Lily had never been more thankful for the head cheerleader's interruption. "Beat it," Lucas growled as his mouth fastened to Lily's neck—leaving another hickey no doubt.

Kiera snorted. "Looks like you found your calling, Lily. Taking after your whore mother after all."

Anger simmered through Lily's veins as she placed the palms of her hands on Lucas's chest and pushed him away. "What did you just say to me?" she hissed.

Kiera raked her gaze over Lily, making a sucking sound with her teeth before looking at her flawless manicure. "You heard me loud and clear, trailer-tramp."

"You should really work on new material, Kiera. Or is it you can't, because your tiny little brain can barely come up with anything other than *Rah-Rah-Rah.* Oh, and don't forget the spirit fingers!" Lily did her best impression of a Valley-girl bimbo as she wiggled her fingers, ending with a double bird.

"Get those hands out of my face. No telling what skeezy dick they've been on."

Fury burned through Lily with the force of a wildfire as she glared daggers at her. Kiera was dressed in tight skinny jeans and a hooded sweatshirt. Her black hair was pulled back into a slick ponytail, and even though she was very obviously drunk, she looked flawless.

Lily took a step closer to the group of girls. "You know what, Kiera," Lily started, her fist curling in at her sides. Each year, Kiera had become a bigger bitch. She took jabs at Lily daily, and in most cases Lily would walk away, seething with rage and humiliation. However, at that moment in time, she was feeling just the right amount of courage.

"Ooo, Lily has grown a pair of lady balls, girls," Kiera taunted as she took a sip from the red plastic cup in her hand. Her eyes never left Lily's face.

Lily chose that opportunity to smack the bottom of the cup, spilling the red liquid all over Kiera's face and down the front of her very expensive hoodic.

Everything around them became dangerously quiet. Kiera gasped and sputtered, her eyes growing wide. The red punch dripped off her chin, causing Lily to laugh. Lily's amusement only added fuel to Kiera's fire.

"You stupid bitch," Kiera seethed.

Lily smirked again. Adrenaline was pumping through her veins like gasoline as Kiera took a step closer. "You know, Kiera, you always call my mom a whore, but do you know where *your* mother's been three nights this week?"

Kiera blanched, and Lily continued. Lily looked at the crowd gathering around them. "She's been balling the quarterback from Mason County."

A hush of whispers and murmurs began to filter through the crowd. When Kiera didn't respond, Lily pressed on. "That must have really sucked, huh. To have your mother—our beloved mayor—steal your boyfriend. Bet you never thought you'd have to take your own mother's sloppy seconds."

Her taunts had the desired effect. Kiera launched herself at Lily, claws out and lips twisted into a very unflattering snarl. Her hand landed soundly against Lily's cheek with surprising strength. Kiera had lit the fuse, and now, Lily was going to explode.

Lily wasted no time striking back. She curled her fist and struck Lily against the side of the head. All hell broke loose as both girls screamed and clawed at each other—both aiming to do as much damage as possible to the other.

Kiera's hand fisted through Lily's blonde hair as she jerked her to the hard ground. A rock pressed into her ribs as Kiera landed on top of Lily. They rolled over the frozen, dirt-packed ground, coming to a stop with Kiera sitting on top of Lily.

"If you wanted to go for a ride, all you had to do was ask, sweetheart. Although, you're really not my type."

Her taunts only made Kiera angrier. "You're nothing but a worthless waste of space."

"Bet that's what your boyfriend said about you while he bent your mother over her desk at town hall," she said as she dodged a punch.

Kiera screamed and struck again, this time her fist landed against Lily's face. The metallic taste of blood bloomed inside her mouth. She was done playing. Lily bucked her hips and threw Kiera to the ground. Once free from the added weight, Lily slowly climbed to her feet, spitting a mouth full of blood to the ground beside Kiera's expensive sneakers.

She dropped down over Kiera, pinning the girl's arms to the ground with her knees. With a balled fist, she struck out against Kiera's perfect face. The world around her ceased to exist as she focused all her rage on the girl beneath her. Growing up in a trailer park had conditioned her for fighting. If she didn't want to be picked on, she'd learned at an early age how to fight.

Lily lost track of how many times she struck the girl before she was hauled backward by a strong arm around her middle. "Let me go!" Lily screamed wildly, kicking out with her feet. Her hair flew wildly around her face. She could feel the blood from her split lip dribbling down her chin. The thick arm circling her middle only tightened as she was being carried away from the scene in front of her.

"Lils, stop," said a deep masculine voice in her ear. Just like that, all the fight left her, and she sagged. Reality began to slip back through her tunnel vision. Faces full of pity and fear gawked at her as Kiera's friends helped their friend to her feet. Everyone looked at Lily like she was a monster.

"What the hell are y'all looking at?" she screeched wildly.

Blood poured from the other girl's face. "We need to get her to the hospital," Molly Trent said. She was one of the girls always at Kiera's beck and call.

"You're a psycho," Kiera said through her split lip and a broken nose.

Lily began to struggle once more. "Come ov'rhere and shay that, you shkeezy tramp!" she screamed, her words beginning to slurring together. She swung out madly, cuffing someone in the jaw. Suddenly, Chase loomed in front of her, a dark scowl marring his handsome features as he rubbed his jaw. This guy was drop dead freaking gorgeous. She wondered why she'd never seen him around school.

Suddenly, her alcohol-induced fog shifted, and her eyes widened. "Chase?" His name came off her lips in a surprised whimper.

"Quite a right hook you got there, slugger," he said. His voice was low with a southern drawl.

"Lily!" another voice whispered in her ear. She was being pulled toward the front of the truck, away from the crowd. Someone turned the music back up, and the party resumed. Once she was placed on her feet, she slowly turned.

"Tyler?" Her voice was small as she stared at the handsome features of her friend. His face was an unreadable mask as he watched her.

She grinned up at him. "When'd y'all get back from s-sk-skiing?" she slurred. Suddenly, everything around her seemed like it was suspended in molasses. Her vision began to warp, and the ground vaulted dangerously beneath her feet. Lily's head began to swim, forcing her to sway dangerously on her feet.

"Whoa there, I got you," Chase said reaching out to steady her.

"I don't feel so—" She didn't get a chance to finish her sentence as everything in her stomach surged forward and all over Tyler's chest.

She tried to apologize, but couldn't through all the vodka reappearing. She doubled over and clutched her stomach. Over and over she wretched. One of the boys moved behind her, gathering her hair behind her head, while the other gently rubbed her back.

Tears burned her eyes as she continued to turn herself inside out. When she thought she was done, she doubled over again only to dry heave for fifteen more minutes.

When the spasms finally stopped, she tried to stand up, but her legs refused to work. She felt herself falling forward. In a matter of a second, she was going to be lying in a puddle of her vomit. However, the second never came. She was being hoisted up into a strong pair of arms. She shivered against the sudden chill.

She was vaguely aware of an engine starting and then movement. Heat blasted from heaters, and there were voices, but she couldn't make out what they were saying.

When she opened one eye, she saw Chase behind the steering wheel; his profile lit up by the dash lights of the truck. His head was turned to the side as he talked to someone standing outside the truck.

"Is she going to be okay?" a soft, feminine voice asked. Lily struggled to place a name with the face, but she couldn't get her mind to focus.

"I think so. We just need to get'er home," Chase answered.

"Well, call us if you need anything," another girl said.

"Thanks," Chase said. The next thing she heard was the unmistakable sound of kissing. Lily's stomach lurched again, but not because of the alcohol.

She watched as he rolled the window up and wiped the back of his hand across his lips. Lily wanted to laugh, but her face felt numb. She also wanted to reach out to him and say thank you, but her throat felt like it was on fire.

Instead, she looked up at Tyler. He must have sensed her looking at him because he pulled his gaze from the windshield and looked down at her. Gently, he pushed a strand of hair away from her face.

"Sorry for upchucking all over you," she rasped. It felt like she'd swallowed razor blades and then drank a gallon of lighter fluid.

A half-smile lifted the corner of his cheek.

Has he always had that dimple in his cheek when he smiles? Her drunken mind wondered.

He shrugged. "It was Chase's."

"Hey, asshat. I loved that shirt," Chase grunted from the driver's side.

She chuckled, and silence filled the cab once more.

"Wanna tell us what all that was about?" Tyler asked, smoothing more hair away from her face.

Lily looked up at him as he studied her face. Tears burned her eyes while humiliation burned her insides. "Why are y'all always around when the bad shit happens?" she whimpered, avoiding the question.

Once again, Chase and Tyler were seeing her at the lowest point in her life, and once again, they were there to rescue her.

"It's what we do," Chase said softly. He took his eyes from the road and stared at her. She could see worry in his beautiful blue eyes, and it hurt her heart knowing that she was the one that had put that look there. The last thing she wanted was for them to feel sorry for her. She didn't need their help. She needed Lucas. He could make it all go away.

"Where's Lucas?"

Chase snorted. "That douche nozzle split the second you started heaving."

"Don't call him that."

"Why are you with him, Lily? He treats you like shit." His voice was tight.

"Because I care for him. A lot." Even as she said the words, they tasted bitter. She knew Lucas didn't care for her, but he was what she deserved. He was the only one that would ever care for her after what she'd been through. Nobody would want her.

Tears rolled down her cheeks.

"Let it go, man," she heard Tyler say. He draped a clean sweatshirt over her curled up body, and she welcomed the scent of his cologne.

"I'm glad your back," she mumbled. Even though they hadn't been close lately, they were her home. No matter what happened, she knew she would always be safe with them. Finally, she succumbed to the darkness because, it was there and only there, she could truly find the peace she desperately needed.

Chapter 8

You cannot control the results, only your actions.

~Allan Lokos

Warm light slanted over her face, and with a groan, she tossed her arm over her eyes. As she did, a dull pain throbbed to life just above her eyes. "Ugh."

Slowly, she pushed herself into a sitting position. Her tongue felt swollen and glued to the roof of her mouth. The walls of the room warped. She squeezed her eyes closed and pressed the tips of her fingers against her temples, trying to massage away the ache. She could feel her pulse pounding in her head like a bass drum, probably thanks to the vodka/pot combination. She knew better than to do both.

Pulling her knees to her chest, she rested her forehead against the tops. "Deep breaths. Deep breaths," she muttered.

When the room stopped spinning, and the roar between her ears lessened, she lifted her head and studied her surroundings. The room looked vaguely familiar, but she couldn't be sure. The walls were painted deep navy blue with the curtains a lighter shade of blue.

A desk sat against the far wall with a laptop sitting neatly on top. Posters of cars and sports players hung on the walls. The hardwood floors were spotless, except for a thick rug in the middle. Beside the bed was a rolled up sleeping back. She leaned to the other side of the bed and found another neatly rolled sleeping bag.

Emotions welled in her chest as tears filled her eyes. The last time she'd been in this room had been after a miserable night she'd never forgotten. Now, she was in the same room, sitting in the middle of the same bed struggling to remember the night before. She groaned. What in the hell had happened?

A picture on the bedside table drew her attention. She lifted the frame and studied the three smiling faces staring back at her. A smile tugged her lips as she remembered the summer the photograph had been taken. It was at the lake two weeks before they started junior high. It was the last time Lily remembered genuinely being happy.

Slowly, she drew the tips of her fingers over their faces. However, the sight of her bruised and bloodied knuckles caught her attention.

"What the hell?" she muttered as she crossed her legs and placed the picture in her lap. She squinted and studied her hand, gingerly pressing the tips of her fingers against the bruises. She winced at the ache.

"You should see the other girl," came a deep voice from the other side of the room.

Lily jumped, the photograph that lay forgotten in her lap crashed to the floor. Shards of glass exploded from the frame and covered the floor.

Without thinking, Lily jumped from the bed.

"Shit," Chase muttered pushing away from the door frame. "Don't move or you'll get cut."

Lily stopped in her tracks as Chase knelt in front of her. She watched as he carefully picked the glass up from the floor and tossed it into the trashcan beside the bed. He was still kneeling in front of her when he dumped the last of the glass.

His eyes were trained on her legs. She frowned and then looked down, realizing that she was wearing nothing but a pair of black boy shorts and someone's t-shirt. She could feel Chase's eyes on her legs. When he looked up, his beautiful blue eyes meeting hers, she noticed his pupils were dilated, and his jaw was clamped together tightly.

She noticed the flecks of darker blue in his irises and found herself wondering if they'd always been there. There was a slight fluttery feeling in the pit of her stomach. His eyes roamed over her legs, stopping at the white scars crisscrossing over the tops of her thighs.

Then it felt as if a bucket of cold water had been dumped over her head. Why hadn't she realized that she didn't have pants on earlier?

Before she knew what was happening, he reached out and gently cupped her thigh, just above her knee. Tenderly, he drew his thumb over the scars, some of them not yet completely healed. His eyes met hers once more, pleading for answers. She looked away, humiliation forcing her to take a step back. She gripped the hem of her shirt and tugged it down over her scars.

"Lily?" he said hoarsely. She could hear the sorrow in his words.

"Don't," she said taking another step back and holding up her hand. She could feel emotions bubbling to the surface. No! She couldn't let them out. The pain. Too. Much. Pain. She couldn't stand seeing the horror in Chase's eyes as he realized what the scars meant.

"Lily! What the—"

"Don't, Chase," she said again. She meant for it to come out strong and forceful, but instead, it only came out a weak plea. Tears filled her eyes, but she refused to allow them to fall.

Chase pushed to his feet and took a step closer. He gently took her by the wrists and turned them in his hands. He wasn't satisfied when he didn't see any scars. The sleeves of the t-shirt hung to her elbows. With tender fingers, he pushed the fabric up, revealing more of her dark secrets on the underside of her arms.

"How long?" he asked.

She lifted a shoulder. What was she supposed to say?

"Lily!" The firm tone of his voice caused her to wince. "How long have you been doing this?" he asked, this time his voice calmer.

Lily pulled her arm away and pushed her sleeve back down her arm. "It doesn't matter, Chase. Leave it alone."

"The hell I will," he said roughly cupping both of her arms and holding her tightly. Anger burned brightly in his eyes.

Panic sucked the air out of her chest. Terror stole through her like thick black tar creeping through her veins. She began to struggle. Chase's face was beginning to fade, and another took its place.

"Get off me!" she screamed thrashing and struggling against him.

Chase released her suddenly, causing her to fall back on the bed. She scuttled back, tugging the blanket to her chest as reality began to wash away the terror.

Logically, she knew Chase wasn't going to hurt her, but there was a part of her mind that refused to acknowledge that he was no threat.

Chase held up his hands. "Shhhh. Lily. It's me," he said calmly. His eyes were wide with worry and regret. "I'm so sorry. I shouldn't have grabbed you like that. I wasn't thinking."

She nodded, but her body still trembled violently. Suddenly, her stomach began to roll, and the need to vomit became almost overwhelming. Rolling off the bed and to her feet, Lily sprinted across the room and into the bathroom, slamming the door behind her.

She managed to get the lid on the toilet lifted just in time to spew yellow bile into the water. Her throat burned, and her body shook as it continued to revolt against her. Tears burned her eyes as they dripped down her face.

The pain was too much. She felt like she was about to explode. They had seen her scars. The look of horror on Chase's face was burned into her mind.

With shaking hands, she flushed the toilet and walked over to the sink. She stared at her reflection in the mirror and winced. Her hair was caked with mud and twigs. There was a bruise under her right eye, and the bottom of her lip was split. Bits and pieces of the fight with Kiera emerged from the haze of her mind.

She'd gotten into a fight with Kiera, but what had it been over? Lily searched her mind trying to find the reason she'd gotten into the fight but came up blank. Then another thought reached her. Where was Lukas? Where had he gone? She vaguely remembered being towed off Kiera, but it hadn't been by him. It had been by Tyler and Chase. They'd been the ones to pull her off the other girl.

Lily studied her reflection longer. There were dark rings of mascara mingling with the dark circles of a restless night. All in all, she looked like something that had crawled out of a horror movie. With a heavy feeling of despair and humility swelling in her chest, she slid to the floor beside the tub. She pulled her knees up to her chest and rested her forehead against their tops.

Everything was spinning out of control, and she was trapped in the vortex threatening to suck her under. For the first time in weeks, she was sober, and she hated every minute of it.

Chase just stared at the closed bathroom door. The girl on the other side was not the girl from his childhood. He'd noticed over the last several months that Lily's look was changing. At some point during the past summer, she'd colored her hair from its beautiful blond locks to jet-black. She'd gone from wearing little to no makeup to wearing entirely too much.

There were always dark shadows beneath her eyes as if she hadn't slept in months. The black clothing coupled with the piercings made her look like a completely different person. He hadn't even realized how skinny she'd gotten until last night.

"What happened in here?" Tyler asked, walking into the room with a bottle of pain reliever and glass of water.

Chase turned and looked at his friend. "Did you see the scars on her legs?" he asked in a hushed whisper. The shower was turned on in the bathroom.

Tyler placed the glass and the medication on the bedside table. He nodded as he sat on the edge of the bed. Picking up the picture, he stared at their three smiling faces. "I noticed them last night when I was pulling her dirty clothes off."

"And you didn't tell me?"

"It was kind of hectic," he said never taking his eyes off the photo.

Chase sat on the bed beside his best friend. "She's been cutting, and judging from some of those scars, it looks like it's been going on for a while now."

"It would seem so."

Chase raked his hands back through his blond hair. "We've been shit for friends. You know that right?"

Tyler looked up at him; his eyes were saying precisely what Chase was feeling. "It's not like she wanted us around."

"We should have pushed harder. If for nothing else, than to keep her away from that butt plug Lucas."

"And do what, Chase? What could we have possibly done to make things better for her? You know once she gets her mind set on things, there's no changing it."

Chase angrily shot to his feet, frustration gnawing a hole through his chest. "I don't know, man. Something."

Tyler opened his mouth to respond, but his phone buzzed. He pulled it out of his pocket and looked down at the screen. "The girls are on their way over," he said.

"Do you think that's a good idea?" Chase asked.

"Why wouldn't it be?"

Chase looked at him and then pointed to the bathroom door. "She really needs our help."

"But what can we do?" Tyler asked, his voice beginning to rise with frustration.

"I don't know, but I do know we can't just say sorry you're having a shitty time, see ya later."

Both boys felt helpless. Their friend was suffering, and neither one of them had any idea how to fix it. Chase opened his mouth to say something, but the sound of the bathroom door opening stopped him.

Lily stepped out; her face scrubbed clean of any makeup and blood. Her hair fell in damp ringlets around her shoulders. She was wearing nothing but a towel.

Tyler and Chase both looked at her with wide eyes. The girl standing in front of them was no longer the gangly girl they'd grown up with. Somewhere over the last couple of months, she'd grown up. She was stunning.

Her shoulders were dotted with freckles, still showing slight signs of a summer tan. The bite marks on her shoulder reminded them what happened to her.

"Um, I hope you don't mind. I took a quick shower," she said keeping her eyes cast down. She nervously chewed on her bottom lip.

Tyler shook his head. "Not at all."

"Can I borrow some clothes?"

Chase snapped his mouth shut.

"Uh, yeah. I have some sweats and a shirt you can wear. They might be too big, but they're clean," Tyler said.

Leaving Chase gawking like a fool, Tyler walked over to the dresser and began to rummage through the drawers. As he was pulling a pair of black sweatpants and a t-shirt free, an audible gasp sounded from his bedroom door.

Chase, Lily, and Tyler whirled around to find Amanda and Kimber staring at them. Their eyes were wide with shock, and their mouths were pressed together into thin angry lines.

"Ah hell," Chase grumbled.

"What's going on here?" Amanda asked as she walked over and stood in front of Chase. Her green eyes blazed fire up at him.

Kimber looked at Tyler. She didn't have to say a word for him to know that she was asking the same thing.

"It's not what it looks like," Chase said trying to keep his voice calm.

Amanda nodded, never taking her eyes off him. Chase held her gaze evenly. He'd seen her put many boys in their place with that frigid glare. He cared about her, but wondered exactly why they were together. She didn't seem to care that much about him. At least not as much as she did his football jersey.

She snorted and rolled her eyes. Spinning on her heels, she looked at Tyler who still held clothes in his hands while Lily was shifting anxiously from one foot to the other.

Tyler ignored Kimber's scathing glare and handed Lily the clothes.

"Thanks," she muttered as she walked into the bathroom and closed the door behind her.

Kimber whirled on Tyler. "We thought you were going to take her home last night. Didn't know you were going to shack up with her here," she accused, crossing her arms over her chest.

Tyler rolled his eyes. "Take the jealousy down a notch, Kim."

Kimber gave an unladylike snort and rolled her eyes. "Seriously? You think I'd be jealous of her? Puh-lease. Pretty sure she's banged every guy except for you two in this town. Unless—"

"Now wait just a minute," Chase cut in taking a step forward, his voice rising in anger.

"Don't you dare yell at her," Amanda snapped, stepping in front of him. "How dare you bring that trash here? We trusted you. We thought you were doing what was right. Not bringing her here to bang,"

Chase narrowed his eyes and clamped his jaws so tightly together he was sure his teeth were going to crack. Anger filled him.

"First of all," he said between his gritted teeth and taking a step closer to her. "Don't you dare call her trash again. Secondly, nothing happened. She crashed on the bed, and we slept on the floor."

"Besides, we don't have to justify shit to you two," Tyler chimed in.

Amanda and Kimber both snorted in derision. "Well, then I guess you can," Kimber motioned to her entire body before continuing, "kiss all of this goodbye."

Tyler looked at Chase as he glared at Amanda. Then, walking to the door, he turned. "Then don't let the door hit your flat ass on your way out."

Both girl stared at them in disbelief.

Chase grinned. "You heard the man. Get to stepping."

"You'll be sorry," Amanda said as she linked her arm through Kimber's.

"Keep telling yourself that, princess."

Once they were outside the door, Tyler slammed it shut in their faces. A slew of curses flew at them from the other side. They grew fainter as the girls walked down the stairs. It was only after the front door slammed closed that Tyler walked over to the bathroom door. He gently rapped his knuckles against it.

"They're gone. You can come out."

The knob twisted, and Lily emerged. "I'm sorry I caused so much trouble."

Chase shrugged and flounced down on the bed, crossing his ankles and folding his arms behind his head. He gave her a smile that he hoped would make her laugh. "Nah, they were too high maintenance," he said wagging his brows at her.

She chuckled, and it gave Chase a warm feeling in his stomach. "Good to hear that again, Lils," he said softly.

She only shrugged, and both boys could see the sadness in her eyes. Was their friend broken beyond repair? Had they pushed her too far away?

"Why don't you hang out with us today? We can grab some pizzas, watch some movies or whatever you want," Tyler said wrapping his arm around her shoulders and guiding her to his desk chair.

"I don't know," she said softly.

"Come on. Our day has suddenly become wide open. Why not spend it like we used too?" he said. He looked at Chase over the top of her head, and their eyes locked. They both knew that they needed to keep an eye on Lily, and if that meant spending every second of time they had with her, then it was going to happen.

"I guess that would be okay," she said tucking a strand of hair behind her ear.

"Awesome. Come on, slip some socks on and your sneakers and we'll go get a pizza." Chase bounced from the bed and stood in front of them.

Her eyes widened. "I can't go out like this."

"Why not?" Tyler asked.

She stood and pointed to her baggy attire. "I look awful."

"No, you don't. You look pretty damn hot dressed like that," Chase said. Tyler nodded his head in agreement, and the blush in Lily's cheeks deepened.

She thought they were joking.

They weren't.

Chapter 9

Nothing is ever lost to us
as long as we remember it.

~L.M. Montgomery

On the way into town, Lily sat between Chase and Tyler in Tyler's pickup. "Hey, stop by my house really quick. I need to change clothes," Chase said.

Tyler nodded. A few minutes later, they pulled down the drive that lead into the trailer park. Lily winced. The place was really in bad shape and looked far worse in the harsh light of the frigid January day. A lot of the homes had been abandoned, and over the Christmas holiday, some had been raided in a massive drug bust. There were only a handful of families still living there. Unfortunately, her mother was still one of them.

"I'll be right back," Chase said hopping out of the truck.

"Do you want to go get some clothes from your house while we're here? I can go in with you if you want."

She shook her head. "No. I'm fine wearing this, as long as you don't care."

He shrugged. "Looks better on you anyway," he said with a wink.

His thigh brushed against hers again. She could feel the heat of his body seeping into hers, and there was something about it that gave her peace.

He turned the engine off and shifted in his seat. She could feel his brown eyes watching her. Looking up, she met his gaze. She was stunned to realize that up close, he looked much different than he did from across the hall.

The roundness of his childhood was gone. His jaw was square and firm and dusted slightly with dark shadow. His lips seemed to be fuller than she remembered. There was a small silvery scar just beneath his left eye.

"Do you remember when you got this?" she asked, lightly brushing the tip of her finger over the imperfection.

His eyes drifted closed, and for a moment, it seemed like he shivered under her touch. When he opened his eyes, she concluded that she must have imagined it.

A slow smile tugged the corners of his mouth up. "Because you were being a pain in the ass."

A bubble of laughter exploded from her lips, and it startled her. She couldn't remember the last time she'd actually laughed.

"Me? You were the one that told me to do it."

He gave her a playful frown. "I didn't think you would do it though."

She shrugged. "You dared me to punch you. You know I don't back down from dares."

"You could've at least taken that ring off," he said tipping his head toward the small mood ring she wore on her middle finger.

Immediately, she touched the ring and began to twirl it around her finger. They laughed, but soon silence settled in the truck. It was a heavy silence, and it made her feel uncomfortable. Things never used to be so hard.

Tyler picked up her hand and threaded his fingers through hers. The pad of his thumb brushed against the back of hers. It was a familiar act that they'd done since they were young. When one would get too lost in thought, they would grab the other's hand and pull them back from the darkness. One would act as the anchor so the other wouldn't get lost. It was something that only the two of them shared.

"Um, how did you guys undress me?" Lily asked. Heat warmed her cheeks as she looked down at their hands in an attempt to avoid eye contact.

He laughed. "It wasn't easy, that's for sure. Man, you were out last night. I kept a sheet pulled up over your bottom half. The top, well, sorry but you were covered in puke. I just took it off."

She shrugged. "I don't really care. It's more than what my swimsuits cover, and besides, they are just underwear. We all wear them."

"Not Chase."

She snorted and laughed. "I don't want to know *how* you know that."

"Trust me, I wish I didn't."

"How long?" he asked suddenly when their laughter died down.

She tensed. Tyler and Chase were alike in almost every way. However, Tyler was the calmer of the pair. Chase wore his feelings out in the open for everyone to see. Tyler, on the other hand, did not. While he opened up to Chase and Lily, he was pretty closed off to just about everyone else. She could see the sadness in his deep brown eyes and often wondered what it was that had put such a look there. Then, there were some days that he seemed miles and miles away.

When they were younger, Tyler had severe nightmares. They often resulted in bed wetting; something that hadn't stopped until they were nearly eleven years old. Still, when she asked about the nightmares, he never seemed to remember them. There was more to Tyler than he let on. If he didn't want to share, then, she would never force him.

As far as temperaments went, his was consistent. He was calm and rational about everything. Chase, on the other hand, had a nasty habit of exploding first and asking questions later. They balanced each other out very well.

She stared down at their linked hands, feeling the tears sting her eyes. Could she tell him? Would he look at her like she was damaged? Everyone always looked at her like she was damaged. Would one of her oldest friends do the same?

"The first time I did it, it was an accident."

Tyler didn't say anything. He just held her hand and gave her the strength that he somehow knew she needed. "Mom and I had a nasty fight. She hit me, and I hit her back. It was the first time that I'd ever fought back. She beat me good that time. I remember taking a shower and watching the blood wash down the drain. She'd stabbed me in the arm with a fork. I just remember staring at the blood as it swirled down the drain, wondering what it would be like if my pain would just wash away so easily."

She took a deep breath. She'd never told anyone about the cutting, and until that moment, she'd never wanted to tell anyone.

"I was shaving my legs when the razor slipped on my thigh. It hurt, but at the same time, it eased the ache in my chest. I watched the blood swirl and realized that I felt better. I didn't do it again for a long time. Then the first time Lucas and I got into a fight, I did it again. It became a habit. It was the only way to get the pain out. It was the only way to make it hurt less."

He lifted their hands and brushed his lips against her knuckles. It was something new. Out of all the times they'd held hands, he'd never kissed them before. Her skin warmed under his lips, and butterflies took flight in the put of her stomach. "Then when Lucas and I got into fights. . . ." she hesitated for a moment.

"What?" Tyler hedged.

"Sometimes they were really bad."

She watched as his Adam's apple bobbed. He was clenching he teeth so tightly together she could see the muscle in his jaw twitching.

"Did he hit you?"

Lily looked down, ashamed to admit how bad things sometimes got with Lucas.

"Lily. Did. He. Hit. You?" he asked through clenched teeth.

Unable to form words, she only nodded. When she looked up and met Tyler's eyes, she could see every thought passing through his mind. "It was only a couple of times. He was sorry after it happened."

"Why didn't you come to us?" he asked. She could hear the raw pain and anger in his voice.

"Because. It was my mess. He didn't mean to."

"Stop defending him. You should know better than anyone, that's not true."

"Still. . . ." She couldn't argue with him because he was right. Lily knew that the situation was bad. She'd seen other women in the same circumstances. She remembered her step-dad beating her mother and swearing she'd never be with a man that did that to her.

"Besides. . . ."

"Besides what?"

"He had what I needed to make the pain go away. I felt so alone, Tyler," she said tears rolling down her cheeks.

"You're never alone! You've never *been* alone," he whispered as he pulled her in close for a hug. She took a deep breath, breathing in the scent of his soap and cologne. When she pulled away, their faces were only inches apart. Electricity crackled between them. She licked her lips, and his eyes darted to her mouth.

Before she knew what was happening, Tyler leaned in and brushed his lips softly against hers. Her eyes widened before drifting closed. She leaned into the kiss and waited for the fireworks to go off. Tyler deepened the kiss, but it felt weird, awkward somehow. It was a nice kiss, but it wasn't at all like she'd figured it would be.

When he pulled away, he chuckled and shook his head. "Was that. . . ."

"Awkward?" she supplied.

He seemed to sigh in relief. "Okay, I'm glad I'm not the only one that felt that."

She laughed nervously. "Right? I mean don't get me wrong. It was a good kiss. You're an excellent kisser, but it just wasn't there."

Tyler's cheeks turned pink, and he looked away. "In all the years we've been friends, have you ever thought about doing that before?"

Lily shifted in her seat, unsure of where this conversation was going. "I'd be lying if I said no. You?"

He chuckled. "For the longest time, all I could think about was kissing you. Watching you with Lucas used to drive me insane."

She turned wide eyes to him. "Did you *like* me? Like, like me like me?"

He nodded bashfully. "I think I've always had a bit of a crush on you," he admitted.

"Well, now I don't feel so bad for having a crush on you!" she said with a small bubble of laughter.

"I guess that kiss settled something."

"Oh yeah, what's that?" she asked.

"That there's nothing between us more than friendship."

She fidgeted in her seat. "Does that bother you?"

He lifted a shoulder. "Yes and no."

She arched a blond brow at him. "Care to explain?"

"It's a no because I wouldn't want something like that to mess us up. We almost lost you once. If I were to lose you because of a relationship, I'm not sure what I'd do. Yes, because I know what an amazing woman you are, and you're going to make some man so happy one day. I kind of wanted it to be me."

A feeling of sadness began to overwhelm her. "No one's going to want me," she whispered. "I'm too broken."

Tyler frowned and lifted her chin with his finger. Her watery gaze met his stern one. "You're not broken. You might be a little bruised, scrapped or even scratched, but never broken."

"I feel broken. I don't think I'll ever be normal again."

Tyler scoffed. "Normal is overrated. Besides, what is normal really?"

"I just don't want to feel like this anymore." She sniffled.

"Maybe you should talk to someone, get some help."

A feeling of panic bubbled in her chest. Her eyes widened as she gripped his arm. "NO! Tyler, please. I can't talk to anyone about this. Please!"

"Shhh!" he said pulling her into his arms once more. He kissed the top of her head. "Then don't, but you can't be doing that shit anymore. You're going to get into serious trouble. What's going to happen if you cut and go to deep? OR, if you take something and it causes you to die? Did you ever stop to think about what that would do to me, to Chase?"

Lily nodded, knowing that he had a valid point. She dashed the tears away and sniffed. Then, she smiled wide and gave another nod. "Okay. I promise. I'll do better."

"And if you feel the need, you will. . . ." he hedged.

"I'll call."

"Good!" He flicked the end of her nose. "You always were such a pain in the ass."

Lily chuckled. "Only because I have to keep up with you two."

They listened to the radio as they waited on Chase. After a song finished, Lilly broke the silence. "Hey, Tyler, about all that stuff with Lucas. . . ."

He smiled and looked at her. "I won't say anything to Chase," he promised.

Lily let out a sigh of relief. If Chase found out that Lucas had hit her more than once, there's no telling what he'd do. His temper was volatile where Lucas was concerned. A few minutes later he was jogging across the yard. Lily wiped her eyes as he jerked the truck door open and jumped in.

"What'd I miss—hey why are you crying?"

She just smiled at him and patted his thigh. "No reason." She looked up and saw a woman standing on the front porch. She was wearing a fur-lined jacket and waving at them.

"Is that your mom?" she asked.

Chase nodded. "Yeah."

"She looks. . . ."

"Better?"

"Well, yeah."

"She's been doing really good. She was in rehab for a while, and when she got out, she lived in a halfway house for a couple months."

Lily's eyes widened. "What? What happened?"

"It's a long story, but the short of it is, she got busted for narcotics, but since they technically weren't hers, she was sentenced to mandatory rehab. My aunt Jenny moved in and took care of me while mom was in rehab."

Lily shook her head incredulously. She'd missed so much of their lives. It was almost to the point she felt like a complete stranger. She lived a few houses down and never once realized anything was going on. Mentally, she kicked herself for being such a rotten friend. Then again, they didn't know much about her either.

"But she's doing good?"

He nodded. "Yeah. It's crazy. I spent so long not having a mom, and now she's suddenly there. It's weird."

She bumped him with her shoulder. "At least you have a mom now. It seems like she really cares. I mean look at her, she's still waving."

The three of them looked up, and sure enough, Chase's mom still stood on the front porch grinning from ear to ear while waving. "She looks better than I've seen her in a long time," she mused.

Chase gave a little wave to his mom and nodded. However, Diana remained waving with exuberance.

"Yeah. She's finally starting to put some weight back on, and her color is getting back to normal."

"I swear if she waves any harder she's going to fly away," Tyler chuckled as he started the engine.

"Shut up and get out of here," Chase snickered, slapping Tyler playfully on the back of the head. He left his arm on the back of the seat, playing with Lily's hair as he'd done for years.

She let out a sigh and scooted down in her seat. For the first time in a year, everything felt like it was going to be okay.

"I'm sorry," she finally muttered as they drove down the two-lane highway that would lead them into town.

Both boys gave her a questioning look.

She shrugged and chewed on the loose skin around her fingernail. "For not being around."

Chase casually dropped his arm over her shoulder and pulled her into his side. He smelled like chocolate and mint. She snuggled closer into his warmth as his hand squeezed her shoulder.

Lily looked up at him. She realized that Chase had changed more than she'd thought. His lips were fuller, and light blond peach fuzz dusted his chin and cheeks.

Have his lips always looked so soft?

Chase was watching her. Something flickered and swirled in his eyes. It looked like a fog being cleared away. He gave a slight frown, cleared his throat and shifted in his seat, putting a little distance between them.

She looked at her folded hands, needing to focus on anything but the two boys—men—in the truck with her. She hadn't lied when she said she'd thought about kissing Tyler. She'd had a crush on Tyler for the longest time, and when she turned thirteen, the crush became a little more substantial. She had often found herself daydreaming about them getting married and living in a mansion in Oklahoma.

However, her crush had died out when he'd continued to look past her and to every other girl. It was like he could never quite see her—like she was just on the outside of his periphery. She used to think that if he would just notice her, it would be like all those cheesy romance movies. Guy realizes his girl best friend is the woman of his dreams. The girl has been waiting for the guy to only notice her.

Eventually, it had faded completely, and she hadn't thought about her crush on him for years. Then there was Chase. She'd never once had those kinds of feelings for him. He was just like her. He came from the same type of life she did. He had been like an older brother protecting her. That was how it always had been, but, suddenly, it felt like something had shifted between them. It made her stomach queasy because she wasn't sure she would ever see Chase as anything more than a brother.

"We feel the same way," Tyler's voice said, penetrating her thoughts.

Lily's head whipped around, causing her to curse the abrupt movement. It felt like her brain was sloshing against her skull, but that took a back burner to what Tyler had just said.

"W-what?" she rasped. Why did her throat suddenly feel so dry? Why did her tongue suddenly feel coated with sand?

Tyler chuckled and fidgeted with the knobs on the radio. He finally settled on a local country station playing only Johnny Cash songs. He dropped his hand back to the gearshift and downshifted, causing his hand to brush the inside of her thigh, just above her knee.

"I said we feel the same way."

"The same way about what?" she asked dumbly.

"About not being around much," he said. His lips pressed into a thin like as he stared out the windshield. The muscle in his jaw ticked slightly with annoyance.

"We should have been there for you more," Chase said filling in the silence. She looked at Chase and saw the same expression on his face as Tyler's.

Lily's heart swelled in her chest. These amazing people still cared for her after everything they'd been through; even after they'd been estranged.

She reached for Chase's hand and then for Tyler's. She then lanced her fingers through theirs. "I'm alive because of you two. No matter what happens or where we go, we can always find each other. Always!"

For the first time in months, Lily felt peace cover her like a warm blanket, and she knew that the only reason she felt like that was because of Chase and Tyler.

Unfortunately, not everything is that simple.

Chapter 10

Out of all the things I have lost,
I miss my mind the most.

~Mark Twain

For three days, things began to feel normal—well as normal as they could. Lily found herself laughing more than she had in months as they fell into a routine she'd thought lost forever. Things with Chase and Tyler were back to normal, mostly. The only difference was the small things—the brush of a hand against the small of her back from Tyler or the way Chase moved a strand of hair away from her face. These things felt different somehow, and before she couldn't think about them for too long, she brushed them off as her overly active imagination.

Since the day after the party, they'd spent all their time together. Tyler insisted that she stay with him for a while. She tried to refuse, but while they were away from the house, he'd instructed Maria to set a spare room up for her. At first, Lily refused, knowing that Lucas wouldn't like the idea of her staying the night with another guy. However, after spending one night alone with her mother, she quickly made her mind up.

Part of her decision had been—in large part—thanks to Lucas. He'd pretty much been MIA since the night of the fight. When she tried calling him, it would ring twice and then go to voicemail. All her messages and texts went unanswered. Anxiety began to creep into the edges of her happiness, but she refused to allow it to steal the peace she'd made up her mind about.

She'd made a promise to herself to start working harder on her grades. If she was going to get out of town as soon as she graduated, she needed to get her act together and focus.

School would be starting in less than twenty-four hours, and Lily felt like she was starting junior high all over again.

She stood staring at her reflection in the mirror of the bathroom Tyler had appointed her, Lily cringed. She'd lined her eyes with heavy black liner, and saw now, just how awful it looked. An angry bruise colored her jaw, and her bottom lip was split and tinted with purple. However, that's not what disgusted her. As an act of rebellion, she'd gotten her eyebrow, nose, and lip pierced. Thankfully, the fight hadn't pull any of the rings or studs out. "You don't fool around do you?" she asked her reflection. Reaching up, she removed the hoop from her eyebrow. She then took the ring out of her lip. She was in the process of removing the tiny stud in the side of her nose when she stopped.

Slowly, she turned her head from one side to the other. The fake diamond winked under the bathroom lights. She decided that the nose stud could stay.

Then the faded pink and black stripes in her hair caught her attention. She'd full-on rebelled against everything and everyone. She'd tried to hide behind piercings, heavy makeup, and poor hair color choices. The person staring back at her was not a person she recognized.

"I want me back," she whispered as she turned on the water and washed away the heavy black eye makeup. It took several tries, but she finally managed to scrape away all the makeup. As she stared at her freshly washed face, she wondered if she could get herself back. Did she even want to go back to the person she was before?

You can never go back. You're dirty. Tainted. No one will ever want you.

Lily's heart began to beat rapidly against her ribs as her mind whispered to her. Leaning forward, she clutched the edge of the sink until her knuckles were white and ached. She took deep, cleansing breaths, trying to will away all the negativity.

You can't hide. They will see the real you and then they will leave you too. Just like your dad and just like

Lucas. They will look at you with disgust like your mother does.

"No," she whispered as tears leaked from her eyes. "No. No. No." Over and over she chanted the words. "I won't let you win. You can't win," she told nagging doubts in her mind.

Pressure began to build up in her chest, threatening to choke her. Her breaths were coming out in short bursts. Her grip on the sink loosened, and her hands began to tremble.

You're going to drown. Let it out. Let the pain out, and it will all go away.

Tears rolled down her cheeks as the heavy feeling in the pit of her stomach began to solidify. Too much. It was all too much.

Taking a deep breath, she opened the medicine cabinet in search of what she needed. The tips of her fingers brushed against the cool metal handle, and she knew relief was only seconds away. She twisted the lock on the bathroom door and closed the lid on the toilet. Since she'd been lazing around the house with Tyler and Chase, she wore a pair of Tyler's gym shorts.

With shaking fingers, she pulled the leg of the shorts up to expose her inner thigh. Dozens of ghost white scars crisscrossed across the soft skin. She traced a few of them with her fingers, finding comfort in the release she was about to find.

Lily took a deep breath. The pain was intense, causing tears to burn her eyes and cloud her vision.

You must let the pain out. This is the only way.

Her head began to swim as she grew lightheaded, and soon, the pain vanished, and she was left with the blessed comfort of emptiness.

"What you want to do today?" Chase asked Tyler from across the room.

"I'm going to finish this project," Tyler grunted as the pencil in his hand scribbled furiously over the notes he was taking.

"Man, seriously? This is the last day of our winter break, and you're spending it doing homework?"

Tyler still didn't look up. "It's extra credit, and I need it if I'm going to get into the summer program at USC."

Chase frowned. "You're going to spend all summer in California and not have time to do anything. Don't see how that is going to be fun."

"Because it will help me get into school. Besides, I'm not the beach boy type."

Chase snorted and leaned back on the couch, tossing the football above his head. "And you know Coach isn't going to like you missing camps."

"I've already talked to Coach. He thinks it's a good idea. The camps out there will really help me."

"Uh-huh. Whatever, Richie," Chase grunted as he continued to toss the ball.

"Don't call me Richie," Tyler said without looking up.

"What about Lily?" Chase asked.

This gained his friend's full attention. "What about her?" Tyler asked.

"Well, it feels like we're just getting her back and you're taking off."

Tyler rolled his eyes. "A bit dramatic? One, she's not *ours* in the first place, and two, she's a big girl. If she stays here and away from that twat monkey Lucas, she'll be fine. Besides, I'll only be gone six weeks. I'll be back by the end of July, and we will still have four weeks of summer."

"Where are you going?"

Tyler and Chase's eyes snapped to the bottom of the stairs where Lily stood. *Thunk.* "Ow, damn," he growled when the ball he'd been tossing landed between his eyes.

Lily giggled, but her smile fell when Chase's eyes grew wide, and a smile twitched at the corners of his mouth.

"What are you laughing at?" she asked as she shoved her feet into her boots.

Chase shrugged. "I just forgot what color your eyes were. You know, since you wore all that batshit around them all the time. I thought you were some vampire or something."

Lily rolled her eyes. "It was just eyeliner."

"That looked like it was rolled on with a paintbrush."

Tyler chuckled and moved from the table. Chase shot him an annoyed glance. He couldn't be bothered to look up from his work to have a conversation, but the second Lily walked into the room, he had the time.

"You took your piercings out too," he noted, his blue eyes roaming over her face.

She nodded. "I kept the nose ring. I kind of like it."

"I do too. Now, if we just do something with this hair," he said picking up a couple strands with the tip of his index finger and thumb while scrunching his nose in mock disgust, "we will have our beautiful Lily back and not Elvira mistress of the damned."

She batted at his chest playfully. Even through the material of his shirt, he could feel how cool her touch was. Acting on instinct, he covered her hand with his, pinning it against his chest. His heart beat a rapid tattoo against his ribs.

Lily lifted her bright green eyes to meet his gaze, and his breathing stopped altogether. Tyler cleared his throat, and everything suddenly snapped back into focus.

Chase released her hand and took a slow step back. He needed to put a little distance between them before he made a rash decision—a decision that would screw everything up.

"Where you headed?" Tyler asked.

Chase looked at his friend, and if Tyler noticed his odd behavior, he didn't show signs of it. Relief flooded through Chase. The last thing he needed was to not only screw things up with Lily but mess his friendship up with Tyler. They were pretty much all he had.

"Well, I was going to see if you wouldn't care to take me down to Alice's shop today."

"Feel the need to throw some electric purple in with the pink and black?" Chase teased.

Lily rolled her eyes and smacked him in the chest. "No. I'm not really sure I know what I want. I just want something . . . different."

"Sure. I can run you down there," Chase said. "Tyler is working on his extra credit report, so he can go to California this summer."

Lily's eyes went wide as she swung her gaze to Tyler. "You're going to California?"

Chase could hear the hint of disappointment in her voice, and it bothered him. He wasn't sure if it bothered him that she was bothered, or if it bothered him because she seemed genuinely upset that Tyler wouldn't be around.

He nodded. "Yeah, just for couple months. I should be back by July."

"But you'll miss everything," she protested and took a step closer.

Pain pinched Chase's chest as he realized what was happening. He was jealous. It wasn't an unusual feeling where Tyler was concerned, but this was something different, something much deeper.

"I can run you down to Alice's," Tyler volunteered.

"I thought you had to study?" Chase said with a frown.

Tyler lifted a shoulder. "Maybe a break is what I need after all."

"Well, why don't all three of us just go," Chase suggested.

Lily looked up at them puzzled. "You want to sit in a salon for two hours while I get my hair done?"

Both boys shrugged. "Why not?" Tyler said.

"Because you have a paper," Chase blurted.

Tyler frowned. "You were just telling me I needed to take a break."

Chase huffed and looked at Lily who was looking back and before between him and Tyler.

"I don't really care who goes. I just know I need to go before I change my mind."

"Then I guess it's settled. We'll go to the salon with you. Y'all wanna grab a pizza after?" Tyler asked as he tugged his boots on.

"Sure," Chase and Lily answered at the same time.

The three of them stepped out of Tyler's house and into the frigid January air.

"Damn, it's cold out here," Chase grunted.

"Well, it is January," Lily teased, nudging him with her shoulder. The contact made heat rush through his veins and warmed his cold body.

"I know. I just meant it's cold for Alabama," he grumbled as he opened the truck door for her.

He watched as Lily climbed into the truck. For the first time, he noticed the curve and shape of her backside. His heart thumped a little bit harder, and blood began to rush faster through his body. Unfortunately, it wasn't to his brain that blood was rushing to.

Tyler jumped in and started the engine, and Chase climbed in beside Lily, slamming the door closed with a little more force than was necessary. Cold air blasted from the vents and Chase had to clamp down on his cheek to keep his teeth from chattering together.

"It's s-s-so c-c-cold," Lily stuttered through her clacking teeth.

Chase slung his arm over her shoulder and pulled her into her side. It was a move he did purely on instinct and one he'd done a million times since they'd known each other. However, this time, it felt different.

"It'll be warm soon," Tyler said reaching down and patting her thigh.

Lily sucked in a short, hissing breath and lowered her gaze. Tyler shot Chase a look over her head.

"What's wrong?"

"Nothing. I must have a bruise or something from the fight," she muttered.

Chase knew better, and judging from the look Tyler gave him, he was thinking the same thing. There hadn't been a bruise on her leg from the fight. They'd seen her wearing shorts since the fight and nothing had been there.

Lily clasped her hands together tightly in her lap.

Chapter 11

You are what you think.
Pain will follow bad thoughts
as certain as happiness will follow good ones.

~Buddha

Lily sat on the edge of the bed staring down at her worn sneakers. The clock on the nightstand said seven-thirty. School started in thirty minutes. Her heart began to beat faster.

"You've got this," she whispered.

She'd spent a lot of her savings at the salon to get her hair colored back to blond. Afterward, she'd spent what she had left on a few new clothing items. She tried not to be angry at her mother, but she was. It was a parent's job to provide clothes for their children. It wasn't supposed to be the other way around.

When she mentioned going to the second-hand store in town, Tyler decided to ignore her request. Instead, they'd driven two towns over to the mall. There, she'd spent the remainder of her savings on three new pairs of jeans, five shirts, and new undergarments. To her surprise, Tyler and Chase had both been patient with her while shopping. In fact, they'd chipped in and helped her buy a few more shirts and a couple more pairs of jeans.

She was humiliated, but at the same time, grateful that her friends cared so deeply for her. Still, even though she wore new clothes and showered several times, she still felt like she was dirty. There was an emptiness and ache in her chest that just refused to go away.

Tears blurred her eyes and spilled out onto her legs. She wondered what Lucas was doing. There was a part of her that missed him, but there was also an equal part that knew he was bad news. Still, she felt like she needed him, especially when the emotions became too overwhelming. Her hands began to tremble as the pain started to build up once more.

She cast a glance at the bathroom door, wondering if she had enough time to ease the ache before school. Then, as if to answer her question, a heavy knock sounded on her door.

"Lils?" Chase asked from the other side.

With her question answered, she quickly dashed away the tears and plastered a fake smile on her face.

"Yeah?" she called with more cheer than she felt.

"You ready? It's time to—" Chase's words died on his lips as his gaze bore into her. He crossed the room in two long strides, kneeling in front of her so he was at eye level.

"What's wrong?"

She rolled her eyes, trying to shrug everything off playfully. "Allergies."

Chase's blond eyebrows drew together in a severe frown. "Bull. Truth, Lily. Now."

She just huffed. "I'm just a little nervous," she admitted. It wasn't a complete lie. She was nervous because she knew the minute she stepped through the doors of the school, she would be the center of attention.

Chase gathered her hands in his. "Listen, you have nothing to be worried about. You're a complete knock-out." He flashed her a cheeky grin, wagging his brows.

Unable to help herself, she snorted and chuckled. "Oh yeah. So hot." She gestured to her new jeans and the long sleeve, plain black V-neck sweater she wore.

"You don't see it, do you?" he asked suddenly. All humor was gone from his voice as he deep brown gaze bore into hers. Thick lashes framed his eyes, and she was slightly jealous of their fullness. Why couldn't she have lashes that looked that good?

"See what?"

Lily lifted her gaze to his and gasped. She saw something there. She couldn't put a finger on what she was looking at, but it was different than all the other times he looked at her. It seemed softer, more tender, even . . . affectionate.

Chase swallowed, and her eyes followed the way the muscles in his throat worked. It seemed like such an odd thing to notice. Slowly, she drew her eyes back up to his full lips. Her mouth went dry. She could feel her heartbeat pulsing in her ears.

Chase's calloused thumbs slowly moved over her hands. "How beautiful you *really* are," he said huskily. The room grew warmer around them as electricity sizzled in the air. She could feel the heat rising into her cheeks.

She didn't get a chance to respond because Tyler walked through the door. "We need to get going," he said looking down at something in his hands.

Lily jerked her hands out of Chase's and bolted to her feet, knocking Chase onto his backside. He landed with a soft *ooff* that drew Tyler's attention.

"What's going on?"

Chase pushed himself to his feet and smiled. "Our friend here is nervous."

Tyler smiled widely. "Is that so?"

She shrugged. "Maybe just a little bit."

"Is that it?" Chase asked ticking his chin toward the white, rectangular package Tyler held in his hand.

Tyler's face lit up with a brilliant smile as he smiled.

"Is what what?" she asked.

"You know if you ever need us you can just call, right?" Tyler said as he took a step closer. The three of them made a triangle with Lily at the top.

"Er, well, yeah I know that, but I don't have a phone so. . . ." she trailed off.

Tyler thrust the box toward her, and she reluctantly accepted it. "What is it?" she asked cautiously.

"It's a gift. Can't you tell by the bow?" Chase teased.

"I know it's a gift, doofus. I just don't know why."

"Because," Tyler said with a shrug.

"Because is not an answer. You do realize that, don't you?"

"I do."

Chase shoved his hands into the pockets of his jeans and bounced excitedly on the balls of his feet. She was suddenly acutely aware of everything about Chase. He wore a stocking cap pulled down over his head, blond curls peeking out from beneath the front. His cheeks seemed to be more angular than they had been when they were little. She noticed how his *American Eagle* thermal shirt hugged his shoulders and arms.

Holy muscles Batman. Where did those come from?

There was no mistake. Chase was no longer a boy. Somewhere along the way, like Tyler, Chase had turned into a man. Her eyes flickered to his lips, and she wondered what they would taste like. Would they be soft? Would they be dry?

You seriously cannot be thinking about kissing Chase. You were just thinking about kissing Tyler the other day. Do you want to be a whore like your mother?

And just like that, it felt like a bucket of cold water was thrown in her face. Feeling her cheeks burn with embarrassment, she cleared her throat.

"Why?"

Tyler shrugged and looked down at his hands. He shuffled nervously from one foot to the other before looking back up at her. "We feel like part of everything that has happened to you has been our fault."

Lily did a double take. "What? No!!" She opened her mouth to protest, but Tyler held up his hand.

"Just open it, and we'll explain."

She untied the silvery ribbon and lifted the lid. Inside the box was a brand new, cell phone already powered on. Her eyes widened.

"A phone?" she gasped and looked up at both.

They nodded, and Tyler stepped closer. The smell of his cologne reached her. "We haven't been there over the last little bit. It started off as us giving you space after—" his voice trailed off, but they all knew what he was referring too. He cleared his throat and tried again. "It started with us giving you space, and then things just kind of, I don't know, came up. We had football practices, games, camps, and then all our school work."

Chase stepped forward and stood beside Tyler. "We're not using those as excuses because honestly, there shouldn't be any excuses. We were shitty friends that let you slip through the cracks. If we'd have been there, then *none* of this crap would be happening."

Lily stared incredulously at both of them. *She'd* been the one that pushed them away. *She'd* been the one to make stupid and careless decisions. Yet, here they were, saying they were the ones at fault. Her heart thumped wildly in her chest. What did she do to deserve friends like them?

Tears rolled down her cheeks, but she was unable to say a word. What could she say?

"Thank you," she whispered.

Tyler smiled wide and moved to stand beside her. He slung his arm around her shoulder and kissed the side of her head. The tantalizing scent of his cologne wrapped around her. Her gaze found Chase's. There was a dark look in his eyes as he looked at her and then glared at Tyler. What was happening?

What would have happened if Tyler hadn't walked into the room? Would Chase have kissed her?

It was in that moment that she felt the shift between the three of them. It wasn't a huge difference, but it was there. There was an awkward tension that hadn't been there before, and as the three of them silently piled into Tyler's truck, she couldn't help but wonder if she'd just jumped out of the frying pan and into the fire.

Trying to ease the tension, she held up her phone. "Come on guys. Squeeze in! I want a picture of this. It's a new day!" Chase and Tyler both scooted closer, and she snapped the picture. Three friends captured forever.

Chapter 12

It's so much darker when a light is lost
than it would have been if it had never shone.

~John Steinbeck

"I can't do this," Lily said as she stopped at the base of the cement steps that lead into the high school. People walked around them, whispering behind their hands and casting sidelong glances at her. Her heart thundered in her chest like a jackhammer. "People are gonna talk about me."

"Yeah! They are," Chase said. Tyler gave him a disapproving look before slugging him in the arm. Chase frowned and rubbed his shoulder. "Let me finish asshat," he grumbled.

Lily wanted to laugh, but her terror was threatening to choke her.

"I was saying, yes, they are going to stare and whisper and talk, but we're gonna be right here with you."

"You can't. I don't have a single class with either of you."

"You're going to be fine," Tyler said assuring, giving her a warm smile and causing butterflies fluttered in her stomach. She quickly looked to her feet. When did things get so complicated?

Chase nudged her with his shoulder. "Don't worry. You look like your old self again."

"That's what I'm worried about," she grumbled as she shifted the weight of her backpack and shuffled from one foot to the other.

Her mind was running rampant with thoughts. What if she had another run-in with Kiera? The longer she thought about the incident at the party, the worse she felt. She'd been so drunk and stoned; things had just become too much. Even after the vicious things the other girl had said, Lily had no right to say the harsh things she had. She knew what she had to do but wasn't sure how much good it would do. However, if she was going to make things better in her life, she needed to apologize. Still, the thought of apologizing to Kiera left a bitter taste in her mouth.

Deciding that she'd had enough self-pity and doubt, she took a deep breath and squared her shoulders. The old Lily wasn't scared of anything.

That was before he touched you. That was before he made you his.

No! She wasn't going to allow thoughts of that night to plague her existence any longer. She'd had enough of misery. It was time for a change. She wasn't going to deal with what happened.

Mentally, she pushed all the anguish, terror, humiliation, and disgusting feelings into a box and locked it tight. This was a new year, and she was going to spend the rest of the school year trying to get back to where she wanted to be.

With a nod, she started up the steps. She stopped and turned, giving both Tyler and Chase wide smiles. "Well, what are you waiting for? We've got classes to get to."

Both boys chuckled and jogged up the steps. This was going to be a good day. No matter what happened, she was going to be okay.

The three of them walked through the double doors and were greeted by several stares. Lily just smiled and walked by all the spectators. Even some of the teachers gave her a second look. "I've got to go see Ms. Lanahan before I go to my locker. I'm not sure how long I'll be," she said as she stopped in front of the guidance counselor's door.

"Okay, we'll see you after first period, okay?" Tyler said meeting her gaze intently.

She nodded and smiled. "See y'all then."

"Later, Lils," Chase said as they turned and walked away. She watched them go for a few moments, noting how each one walked differently. Tyler walked with ease, his steps confident and sure. Chase walked with a bit of a swagger that made her giggle. Not only was she noticing how they walked for the first time, but she was seeing how each one filled out their jeans.

Chase's jeans were tattered and worn. The outline of his wallet worn into the denim of his back pocket. So many of the boys in their school had the worn circles of chewing tobacco in their pockets. She was thankful Chase was one that didn't. When did Chase's backside begin to look so sexy?

Before her thoughts could get carried away with her, she shook her head slightly. Lifting her hand, she knocked on the door, and to her surprise, it swung open immediately.

Her breath hitched in her throat, and her palms became clammy. Lucas stopped suddenly in front of her after closing the door behind him. At first, he appeared not to recognize her; then clarity seemed to shift through his bloodshot eyes. He toyed with the ring in his lip, and she couldn't help but follow the movement.

Lucas made her insides tremble, but she knew it wasn't because he was a good guy. It wasn't because he cared for her. It most certainly wasn't because he was the right one for her. It was because he was the exact opposite of all of those reasons. When push came to shove, the truth behind it all was that Lucas was bad for her. He was the bad boy that always made the girls feel naughty for caring about them.

"Well, look who's decided to surface," he said bitterly. He raked his gaze over her disapprovingly.

"Lucas, I—" She cleared the gravel from her voice and tried again. "I've been trying to call you. Why haven't you answered your phone?"

He shrugged and looked at his short fingernails in disinterest. "Had shit to do. Looks like you been busy too," he said ticking his head down the hall to where Chase and Tyler stood glaring at him.

Feeling defensive, Lily scowled at him. "I haven't done anything. I've been trying to get a hold of you so we can talk. Where the hell have you been?"

Lucas's face darkened, and Lily took a small step back. She recognized the look all too well.

"I-I'm sorry. I just missed you." It wasn't a complete lie, but it also wasn't the truth. Lucas was getting mad. He didn't like it when she talked back to him.

He took a step closer to her. From the corner of her eyes, she could see Chase and Tyler move in their direction. Both of them dropped their bags to the floor, not wanting anything to slow them down in case of a fight.

"Better call your guard dogs off," Lucas said slowly. The icy edge in his voice made her realize how truly dangerous he was. "I'd hate for something unfortunate to happen to them," he added.

Scared for her friend's safety, she looked at them and gave a slight shake of her head. They stopped but leaned against the wall, indicating that they wouldn't get involved, but at the same time, they weren't letting her out of their sight.

Lily turned her attention back to Lucas. Her mind whirled with different ways this scene was going to play out. If she provoked him further, he could—and likely would—get violent. That would result in Chase and Tyler getting involved and possibly hurt. She couldn't let that happen.

Reaching out, she placed a hand on Lucas's arm. "I'm sorry, baby. I was just worried. You left me at the party the other night."

He glared down at her hand and then up to her face. She'd hoped to see his anger subside, but it didn't. He took a step closer, putting a scant inch between their bodies.

"I know where you've been. I've seen you with them," he spat. His face was growing red with anger. If she didn't defuse the situation quickly, someone was going to get hurt.

She closed the distance between them. "I'm sorry, baby. I don't remember anything. They took me home and looked after me. I wished it would have been you," she said as she reached up and cupped his face. She could smell tobacco and cologne masking the hint of the marijuana he'd obviously just smoked. His hand rested on her hip as he subtly pulled her against his body.

His hand snaked up and cupped the back of her neck tightly. The sharp pain from his fingers caused her to wince, but she couldn't show the pain. She kept her face stoic as she stared up at him.

He lowered his lips to her ear. "I know what you've been doing with those two. You're trying to leave me behind. You're trying to go back to the way things were. Do you think they will ever look at you without thinking about what *he* did to you? Do you know what they say when you're not around? They call you pathetic. They say you deserved it. They call you a slut." He drew the backs of his knuckles over her cheek. It was a tender motion and had it not been for the biting grip he had on her neck, she'd think he cared. "I'm trying to protect you." His voice was husky against her ear. Once upon a time, the feeling of his breath on her neck and ear would have turned her on. Now, it only made her ill.

"They know what happened. They would never do that to me," she argued.

"Why do you think they've been ignoring you all this time? Why do you think they haven't talked to you in close to a year and a half? Do you think it's because they were *giving you space?*" he said with air quotes.

Lily didn't want to believe him, but Tyler did say that they'd been giving her space. Was it because they were disgusted with her? She wanted to believe her childhood friends, but Lucas quoted them almost word for word.

"I've just been hanging out with them, baby. Nothing's changed," she said linking her fingers with his. She felt the tension leave his arms and the tautness of his face lightened.

"Give me just a minute," she said.

Turning, she hurried over to where Chase and Tyler waited for her. "What's going on?" Chase said through clenched teeth. His gaze was focused over her shoulder at Lucas.

"Nothing. I just need to talk to him. That's all."

Tyler shook his head and moved closer to her. "I don't like that idea at all, Lily," he said in a low voice.

She smiled and placed a hand on his arm. "Listen, if I'm gonna get my life and stuff back on track and finally put demons to rest, he's where I have to start."

Even though she knew the words coming out of her mouth were true, she wasn't sure she'd be able to follow through with them. The thought of being without Lucas made her antsy.

"It's not a good idea," Chase replied, finally settling his blue gaze on hers.

"This is my mess. I've got to clean it up."

Both of guys huffed and looked at Lucas, who stood behind her. Their eyes narrowed. The only outward show of emotion Tyler revealed was the slight flaring of his nostrils. However, the evidence of Chase's anger was written plainly on his face. His teeth were clenched so tightly that the muscle in his jaw ticked rapidly. His fists were curled in at his sides, and the veins in his forearms bulged.

Hauling hay last summer really beefed him up, her mind noted. Mentally she rolled her eyes.

She grabbed Chase's wrist and tugged slightly. "I'll be fine. I know how to take care of myself now."

He sighed heavily. "Fine, but I swear, if he so much as leaves a mark on you, I'll kill him."

Lily searched his face for any sign of playfulness. She then realized that he was completely serious.

She gave him another squeeze and then shot Tyler a look she prayed conveyed that she wasn't afraid.

"See you at lunch. Okay?" Tyler said pointedly.

She nodded once. "I'll be there."

She watched as they hesitantly turned and walked away. Guilt plagued her because she knew that she wouldn't be seeing them for lunch. If she was going to deal with Lucas, it couldn't be at school. It needed to be somewhere that they could talk openly without people hearing or listening.

Turning, she walked back over to where Lucas was leaning against the wall. One of his scuffed boots was propped on the wall behind him. He lifted his gaze from his phone.

"I need to talk to Lanahan and go to my first classes, but do you want to get outta here at lunch?" She moved closer, twisting her fingers through his.

"I dunno," he shrugged.

"Please? I thought we could . . . talk."

Hunger clouded Lucas's eyes as he rolled his tongue over his bottom lip. "Talk, eh?"

She nodded. "Yes, just talk. There are some things we need to discuss."

"I can't leave campus today, or Lanahan is going to nail my ass to the wall. Meet me in the locker room at lunch, and we can *talk* in there."

She swallowed the lump in her throat and bobbed her head. Lucas smiled and dropped his mouth to hers. His tongue slowly rolled over her lips and into her mouth, and despite herself, she sighed and felt herself press against him.

Around them, there were loud whistles and a few lewd comments. The door beside them opened, and Ms. Lanahan stepped out. Her eyes narrowed. "Ms. Lancaster, you're late," she said tightly.

Lily took a quick step back from Lucas. "Sorry," she mumbled.

"Get inside and have a seat. "Mr. Delray, I suggest you get yourself to class," she said firmly. Lucas's golden eyes flashed challengingly, however, to Lily's surprise, he nodded. "Yes ma'am," he said in a clipped, sarcastic tone.

Lily scuttled through the open door and took a seat in the plush chair in front of the counselor's desk. Patricia Lanahan was not a woman to be messed with. She was supermodel gorgeous with long chestnut hair, hourglass figure, dark brown eyes, and thick black lashes. Her skin was smooth and flawless, making Lily want to ask her what kind of skin cream the woman used.

Nevertheless, beauty aside, the woman was formidable. She was firm and did not play favorites. She'd never believed the story that Lily fed her after the incident with her mom's boyfriend. It was a huge reason child services had gotten involved. Lily didn't begrudge the woman, though. She knew it was her job.

"You said that you wanted to see me when school started again. What about?" Lily asked as the other woman closed the door and sat behind her desk. The hardness of her features seemed to soften as she turned her deep brown gaze to Lily.

For a few moments, she openly assessed her. Lily shifted nervously in her seat as the woman's eyes tried to peel away layer after layer of Lily's protective barrier. Soon, a soft smile curved her red colored lips.

"What brought on the change of your appearance?" she asked.

Lily lifted a shoulder. "Don't know."

Ms. Lanahan nodded once. "Well, personally, I think this look is more fitting. You're looking well, except for that bruise I see. Care to tell me what happened?"

Lily shrugged.

The woman tapped her pencil between her fingers on the desk. "Wouldn't have anything to do with the black eye and busted nose I saw a certain head cheerleader with, would it?"

There was no hiding the smug smile that spread across Lily's face. However, when she looked up, she was shocked to find the counselor smiling in return.

"About time someone put her in her place."

Lily's eyes widened in shock. This caused Lanahan to laugh.

"Listen, I know you've had a rough year and a half, but it's time that we focus on a few things. Seeing you looking like you once did makes me feel better, but there are a few things that have me very concerned."

Lily squirmed in her seat. "O-okay?"

"Your grades for one. Lily, you're in genuine danger of failing not just one, but all your classes. As it stands right now, you're most likely going to have to take summer school."

Lily's heart sank. She'd known her grades had taken a hit, but she hadn't realized it was that bad.

She licked her lips. "Okay. But is there a chance I can get them up so I won't have to repeat the grade?"

Lanahan opened a file on her desk and skimmed the contents. "It's not going to be easy, but I think it's doable. But, Lily, you're going to have to put the effort in. You're going to have to get your act together and focus."

"I can. I will. Most of the stuff I know already."

"I don't doubt that. Lily, you were at the top of your class when you started your freshman year. Then, suddenly, everything just dropped. What happened?"

Lily's heart began to race. Her palms grew sweaty, and she rubbed them against the thighs of her jeans. "Nothing. Fighting with my mom. We don't get along that well."

Lanahan's eyes were pinned to Lily's face, and there was no denying the fact that the older woman just did not believe her.

Lanahan closed the file and leaned forward, crossing her arms over the folder. "Lily, you do know that you can talk to me. Right?"

Lily nodded.

"Not just about school, but other things."

The way she said *other* made the bubble of apprehension that was growing in Lily's stomach expand up through her chest and into her throat. Did she know what happened?

"Everything is fine," Lily managed to get choked out.

"Being in unstable relationships can sometimes make you feel very alone. I've noticed the way you act when you're with Mr. Delray." Lanahan was very careful to keep her voice even, but Lily could see the distaste in her eyes.

"What does he have to do with anything?"

She just lifted a shoulder. "I noticed things with you started to decline about the same time you began to keep his company."

Lily frowned. "That's not true."

"It's not?"

Lily's mouth fell open, trying to find the words to defend Lucas. "He's like me," she finally said.

"How so?"

"He just is. He knows what it's like to have parents that don't seem to care."

"Is that how you feel? Like your mother doesn't care."

If she had cared, she wouldn't have let that monster into our home.

Lily lowered her gaze to her folded hands. "She's just busy." It was a lie, but it was the best she could come up with.

She could feel the counselor's eyes watching her like a hawk. When she looked up, the woman nodded. "Okay, so, here is what we're going to do to get you back on track. Every day during your homeroom, I want you in here. We're going to have a session for thirty minutes, and then afterward, we will work on your studies."

"Um, session?"

Lanahan nodded. "Yes. We are going to be doing sessions. You're going to talk, and I'm going to listen."

Lily gulped in panic. "You mean like a shrink?"

Lanahan chuckled. "We're just going to chat. Talk about anything you want; how you're feeling; what's going on in your life; whatever you need to talk about."

"What makes you think I need to talk about anything?"

"I've been doing this job for a few years now. I can tell when something's going on."

"And if I refuse?"

"I'm afraid that's not the option. I'm required by the state to evaluate any student that I feel might be in trouble."

"I'm not in trouble. Lucas would never hurt me."

Lanahan arched a dark brow. "I was referring to your studies. However, I am curious as to why you automatically jump to defend Mr. Delray."

Lily didn't get a chance to respond before the woman pushed away from her desk. As she did, the first bell of the day rang. "Time for you to get to class. We will continue this afternoon."

A wide smile spread across Lanahan's face, and Lily frowned. The last thing she wanted to do was go emotional dumpster diving with someone that could potentially get her thrown into a foster home or worse, a group home.

Feeling more dejected than ever, Lily left the counselor's office and made her way to her locker. With each step she took, her mind whispered.

You're going to break. You're not strong enough. The pain will get through. She will see everything that has happened, and you'll be put away.

She'd hoped that talking to the other woman would help. Unfortunately, the only thing it had done was make her feel worse.

Chapter 13

*It's so much darker when a light is lost
than it would have been if it had never shone.*

~John Steinbeck

Lily made it through the first hour with relative ease. She found herself aptly listening to her literature teacher discuss Frankenstein and its juxtaposition to real life. She also realized that it was going to take a small miracle to get caught up after coasting by. Her current grade was bordering on failing and could tip at any time.

After the class, she'd talked to her teacher and he'd gladly given Lily extra credit work to help her get caught up. He'd also stated that he was glad to have her back as if she'd been gone for months. In a way, she figured she had been absent.

Lily walked back to her locker, anxiety creeping into her as she hugged her books tightly to her chest. People whispered while she walked by, but she ignored them. She kept her eyes trained on the ground, loathing the cowardly person she'd become. She just wanted to try and fix everything that was broken.

She reached her locker and twisted the dial. The lock gave with a soft *click,* and she tugged the door open.

"There she is," Chase crowed as he strolled up to her and slung his arm over her shoulder.

"Did you make it through Thompson's class?"

She nodded. "Yeah, he's letting me make up a lot of the work."

Chase's eyes nearly bugged out of his head.

"You're telling me that that hard ass is letting you do makeup work?"

She shrugged. "I guess so."

"Well hell."

"Well hell, what?" Tyler asked coming up on her other side.

"Thompson is letting her do makeup work."

"Huh," Tyler said. "That's a first."

"So, how'd the meeting with Lanahan go?" Chase asked as he turned and leaned his back against the lockers beside hers. He kicked his foot up behind him as he tucked his hands into the hip pockets of his work jeans.

"I have to see her every day during my free period. She wants to talk," she said as she removed the books for her next class.

Silence passed between the three of them as Tyler and Chase shared a look.

"What?" she said looking back and forth between them.

"Maybe talking to someone isn't such a bad idea," Tyler offered.

"Not going to happen," Lily said slamming her locker door closed with more force than she could muster.

"He's right, Lils. Maybe telling someone other than us, like an adult, can help you get through this and move on with your life."

"I *am* getting on with my life," she said. The three of them moved away from the lockers and walked together down the hall.

"You know what we mean," Tyler said. "It's just that she can probably help you deal."

Lily blew out an exasperated sigh. "I'm fine, guys. I promise. Right now, I just need to focus on getting my grades back on track. It's the only way I'm going to get out of this hell hole."

"And Lucas?" Chase hedged.

She huffed out and stopped in the middle of the hall. A few students grumbled and cursed as they were forced to go around.

"Listen, I appreciate everything you're trying to do, but listen, there are some things I have to handle in a certain way. Lucas is one of those things. I need you both to just back off and let me take care of him."

"We don't trust him, Lily," Tyler said as they stopped outside Lily's class.

"I know. You've made that more than a little clear, but this is something I've got to do. I need you to trust me."

"Fine," they both lamented.

"Good, now go on. You're going to be late."

Tyler tapped the end of her nose, and Chase flicked her ponytail as they walked by. She just chuckled and rolled her eyes.

The instant she walked through the door, she could feel all eyes on her. Tension crackled in the air like electricity. Her eyes scanned the room and instantly settled on the source of her unease. Kiera glared at her with the force of a thousand deaths. Both of her eyes were black, though heavily covered with makeup to conceal the worst part of it. The white of her left eye was bloodshot from burst blood vessels. There was a white strip of tape across the bridge of her nose.

She did look worse for the wear. She'd thought that seeing the sad shape the other girl was in would make her feel better. However, it had the direct opposite effect. People stared at Lily as if she were a monster, most of them already knew what had happened at the party. They had either heard about what happened or were there to witness it. Either way, it wasn't Lily's proudest moment.

Kiera broke eye contact first, as she shifted from her chair and walked to the back of the room. Lily dropped her bag on her desk and took a deep breath. If she was going to make things better in her own life, then she needed to try to mend some broken fences.

She cautiously approached Kiera, who was flipping through pages of a book in her hand.

"Can I talk to you for a second?" Lily asked quietly.

Kiera spun around and narrowed her bloodshot eyes. Lily winced, the other girl honestly did look awful.

"What do you want?" she hissed.

Lily cleared her throat. "To apologize."

Kiera laughed, it was loud and brittle sounding. "Oh, that's rich coming from you. What on earth makes you think that I would want anything to do with your skanky ass?" Kiera asked a little louder than necessary.

"Things got out of hand Friday night, and I didn't handle things the way I should have. I'm sorry." Lily could tell by the incredulous look on Kiera's face that any attempt at an apology was going to be futile.

Kiera snorted and then flinched. Lily bit back a smile because as badly as she felt for doing what she'd done, she still found it mildly satisfying that the queen had been taken down a peg or two.

"You're nothing," Kiera hissed, taking a step closer. She was an inch from Lily's face. "You're a tragic waste of space. No one would miss you if you would just up and die." She laughed. "You know what, that would solve everyone's problem. It sure as hell would solve your problem."

"What problem?" Lily whispered.

"The problem that you're a mistake. You should really think about ending it all. You know, kill yourself and just make the pain and rage go away. We all know that your momma beats on you. We don't know much about your daddy, but we know what he did to you. The way he touched you and told you not to tell."

Bile began to climb up the back of Lily's throat. Images began to flash through her mind.

Hands touching. Pain. So much pain.

"Just do it," Kiera whispered. "Kill yourself and be done with it."

Tears burned Lily's vision as a sly smirk twisted Kiera's split lip. With a flip of her hair, she walked around Lily and took her seat.

The floor wobbled beneath Lily's feet as she struggled for air. Lily walked through the door just as the bell rang.

That's it. That's the answer. Kill yourself. Just kill yourself and get it over with. The voice inside her head sounded like Kiera's, and it made her feel even more hopeless.

As she walked down the hall, the walls seem to press in on her. Her breathing became ragged as her steps grew quicker.

With shaky hands, she pulled her phone out of her back pocket and ducked into the girl's locker room. Tears rolled down her eyes as her fingers trembled over the screen.

Me: *Meet me under the bleachers in 5.*

She then quickly added, *this is lily,* remembering that she had a new phone and number.

Minutes ticked by. She chewed on her bottom lip as she waited for a response she knew would never come. Her hands trembled as Kiera's words ricochet through her head. Tears burned her eyes, begging to be released. The urge to release the pain any way possible was growing stronger. Her eyes darted around the locker room looking for something to help her ease the ache. There was nothing.

She waited until the second bell rang and then waited three more minutes before she slipped from the locker room and hurried down the back staircase that would lead her outside. She pushed the door open, and the frigid January air slapped her in the face, forcing her to take in a sharp breath.

With each step she took, she cursed herself. She should have taken the time to go get her jacket. The cold air bit into her bare arms. Her feet crunched over the gravel as she hurried across the lot and through the gate. The pressure was building behind her eyes, and her heart was racing through her chest.

After ducking through the barriers, she made her way to where she prayed Lucas was waiting. Relief came when she smelled the strong scent of cigarette smoke before she saw him. As she rounded the corner, she saw him leaning against the wall, cigarette dangling from his lips as he stared in concentration at something in his hands.

Her feet carried her closer, and she realized what he was doing, and she sighed. He was rolling a joint. He looked up and gave her a sloppy grin. "I knew you couldn't stay away," he said slowly. His eyes were glassy and bloodshot.

Lily stopped in front of him, tears finally rolling down her cheeks. "Make them stop," she said softly.

His smile widened. "What's it worth to you?" he asked. There was a hungry look in his eyes. She knew exactly what he was implying.

She took a step back. "Seriously?"

He lifted a shoulder and dropped the cigarette to the ground, crushing it beneath his boot heel. He then placed the newly rolled joint between his lips and lit the tip. After inhaling, he then blew the smoke into her face, dangling the freedom from the dangerous thoughts running through her head. The acrid smoke made her cough, but at the same time, it beckoned her.

She licked her lips and looked up at him, weighing her options. Was it worth it? Maybe she should just find Tyler and Chase. They could help her through it. She could lean on them, and it would be much better than what Lucas was offering her.

Lucas took a step forward and pulled her body against his. Her heart raced faster as the smell of smoke drifted around her more. What did it matter? It's not like she didn't know what would happen. Maybe if she did, things would be better with him. If she finally got over her hesitations, being with Lucas could be a good thing.

She lifted herself up on her tiptoes and brushed her lips against his. "Okay, but not for the smoke. I'm doing it because I'm ready."

Keep telling yourself that, her mind screamed.

Taking him by the hand, she led him to the concession stand door. At least it would be warm inside. The school usually kept a space heater on the inside to keep the pipes from freezing. She stood waiting, shivering against the cold—or possibly her nerves—while Lucas used his pocketknife to jimmy the door open.

The lock finally gave with a pop, and the door swung wide. Lucas took her by the hand and pulled her into the darkened interior of the room, closing the door behind them. The only light on inside was coming from the small heater in the corner. The room was slightly warmer, but not by much.

Lucas found some clothes and spread them out on the floor. There were no tender kisses or caresses. It was only a fumble of hands on buttons, clasps, and zippers.

As he lowered her to the floor, Lily closed her eyes and ignored the horror that was trying to come back to her with each of his wet and sloppy kisses. She kept reminding herself that it was Lucas and not *him.* It was the only way she was going to get through it.

It was the only way she *did* make it through.

Lily stood in the corner of the room, watching as Lucas shrugged his jacket on over his shoulders. Her skin felt like it was about to climb off her body, and while she'd prayed that finally giving in to Lucas would make her feel better, she realized, she'd been dead wrong. More thoughts swirled inside her head, causing it to buzz like an angry hornet's nest. Self-doubt plagued her, making her second guess everything she'd done.

She just wanted a few minutes of peace. The only thing she wanted was to be completely numb and forget about everything that was going on, and all the nasty stuff Kiera had said to her. Lucas reached into the breast pocket of his jacket and removed a small plastic bag. Finally, some peace, but when she stepped closer, she realized that what he was holding wasn't what she was wanting.

Lily frowned and glared up at him. "What the hell, Lucas?"

He chuckled and held up his hands. "Chill. This is better than a little weed."

She watched as he opened the baggie and withdrew a small white pill. He took her by the wrist and deposited it into her palm. For a moment, she just stared at the tablet. When she looked up at him, he gave her a broad smile.

"Take this. Trust me. It's a rush!"

Lily hesitated for a moment before tossing it into her mouth and swallowing it dry. Lucas then hooked his fingers through the belt loops on her jeans and pulled her into his body. He lowered his mouth to her neck and suddenly it was like every nerve ending in her body was on fire. His teeth sank into her neck before he kissed her and took a step back.

Reaching up, he brushed a strand of blond hair away from her face. He pressed his thumb against her bottom lip. "If you want more, just say the word. I'm sure we can work out a payment arrangement," he chuckled.

Lily couldn't react. Her head was swimming through molasses. Her body was warm, and the best thing of all, the nasal tone of Kiera's voice was finally quiet. She giggled as she left the concession stand and leaned against the outside wall. The cold air didn't faze her. Everything around her became sharper, and she just tilted her head back and embraced the feeling of floating. Lucas had disappeared, but she didn't care. She didn't have to care because everything was okay!

At least, that's what she thought.

Suddenly, the ground tilted, and her stomach revolted. Her eyes snapped open, and it was like she was staring at her surroundings through a funhouse mirror. Everything bowed and warped in front of her. She heard someone walking behind her as she walked to the side of the concession stand. If it were a teacher, she would be busted for sure. The air was cold, but the warming effect of the drugs made her hot. Sweat covered her forehead with a thin sheen.

"Slut!"

Lily whipped around looking for the sound of the voice. Someone was leaning against the side of the concession stand, watching her. The figure blurred and warped. Lily squinted, trying to bring the person into focus.

"Who's there?" she called out. Her voice echoed, sounding as if her head was inside an empty barrel.

"You're such a whore," the voice rasped as it stepped from the shadows. Lily's eyes widened as she watched Kiera walk closer.

"Hell you doing?" Lily asked, bracing her hand on the rough cement wall, trying to keep herself upright. Her words weren't coming out right.

"I know what you just did. You sold your body for a fix. You're just like your mother."

"You don't know shit, you dumb cow," Lily hissed.

She watched as Kiera moved closer, however, as the other girl got closer, she faded and was replaced by her mother. Lily frowned and scrubbed the heels of her hands against her eyes.

Her mother's makeup was smeared, and her clothes barely covered her body. "Always thought you were better than me. Always looking down your nose." Her mother got closer, and Lily could smell the cheap whiskey on her breath. "We're not so different now, are we? How does it make you feel to know that you're a whore like me?"

"No," Lily whimpered, tears filling her eyes. "I'm nothing like you."

Her mother threw her head back and cackled loudly. "Oh yes, daughter. You're a dirty, filthy whore, just like me." Her laughter echoed off the walls. Lily turned and tried to run, but her feet felt heavy.

Her heart began to race as the pain from earlier crept back in. "No, no, no, no," she whimpered, clutching the sides of her head. "You're not real!" she screamed, pulling at her hair.

Her mother transformed into Tyler, and Lily felt her heart crack as he looked at her in disgust. "I knew better than to help you. You're such a waste of space. You're always going to be trailer trash."

With her back pressed against the wall, she slid down to the cold concrete floor. Tyler knelt in front of her, his face inches from hers. "Go ahead and do it. No one will miss you. You know there's only one way to get rid of the pain."

Tears blurred her vision.

"Do it," he whispered. "Let all the pain out."

Tyler slowly backed away, and the source of all her nightmares surfaced. Her body grew cold as he moved closer to you. "My, but aren't you the pretty thing." His breath was rancid as he drew his knuckles over her cheek.

"Don't touch me," she sobbed.

"Go ahead and scream. I like it when they scream."

"No," she gasped.

Her mother was back, and so was Kiera. Tyler stood behind the group, arms crossed as he watched her with a leer.

"You can make it all go away," he said. He stepped through the others and knelt in front of her once more. "Don't you want the pain to just go away?"

Sobs wracked her body as she nodded.

"Then do it. Release the pain."

Lily's hands brushed against something on the ground beside her. With trembling hands, she picked it up. A knife. Who would just leave a knife lying around?

Her head was spinning, and her heart was racing. Everything around her was a mixture of bright colors and muffled sounds. Slowly, her fingers closed over the handle of the knife.

"R-r-release the pain," she chattered. Her teeth clacked together loudly, partially because of the drugs and partly because of the cold.

Her head was growing heavy as her grip slipped on the knife. She'd done it hundreds of times. She knew the easiest way to get rid of the pain was to cut it out.

She struggled to pull the sleeves of her shirt up. Then, pressing the sharp tip of the blade against the skin just beneath the bend in her arm, she drew it across. The pain was instant, but so was the relief.

Minutes, maybe hours, later, Chase's face appeared in front of hers. "Not you too," she whimpered. Seeing his face was too much. Hearing how disgusted he was, was too much. Darkness crept around the edges of her vision as the pain leaked down both of her arms and dripped onto the cold concrete. Then . . . it was just . . . gone.

Chapter 14

Not until we are lost do we begin to find ourselves.

~Henry David Thoreau

Chase leaned against his locker staring at his phone. He'd sent half a dozen messages to Lily without any response.

"What's with the frown?" Tyler asked as he opened his locker and removed his books.

"Lily left class," he replied.

"I'm sure she's just talking to Lucas or Lanahan."

"I haven't seen her since the bell rang."

"I don't know," Tyler said closing his locker a little harder than was necessary.

"I haven't seen Lucas either."

Tyler's face turned dark. "Do you think she's with him?"

A cold feeling settled in the pit of Chase's stomach. He honestly hoped that she was, but after what had happened with Kiera, he wouldn't be surprised. He'd heard about what Kiera had said to Lily. The whole school had, and yet, Kiera was still in the limelight, genuinely believing she'd done nothing wrong.

Feeling restless, he shoved away from the locker and turned to put his books back inside.

"What are you doing?" Tyler asked when Chase slammed the door closed.

"I'm ditching and going to find her. You coming?"

Tyler shook his head. "Man, I can't. I have a test and if I skip, Rogers will flip his shit."

Chase nodded. Tyler's grades were important to him, and he respected that. Chase, on the other hand, couldn't care less about his grades. He wasn't going to be going anywhere after graduation other than the local feed store or lumber mill.

"Okay, I got this." Chase zipped his jacket and began to walk away. Tyler's hand grabbed his bicep.

"Don't get into it with Lucas."

Chase gave him a cocky grin. "You know me."

Tyler's scowl deepened. "I do know you. That's the problem."

"Relax. I'm looking for her, not trouble."

Tyler snorted. "You're always looking for trouble."

Chase walked down the hall and turned around, walking backward. "Hey, I can't help it. Trouble finds me."

"Well, you focus on finding Lily."

He gave him a nod and turned. Finding Lily was precisely what he planned on doing. When the second bell rang, Chase hurried out the back doors and around the side of the building. He tried to think of where Lily would be.

Chase checked several different places, and each time he came up empty. He looked at the student parking lot and scanned the cars. Lucas's piece of shit rusted Camry was nowhere to be found. A heavy feeling landed in the pit of his stomach. Worry began to creep into his veins as the cold January air turned his skin to ice.

The sky overhead was saturated with thick gray clouds. There was a heaviness in the air that promised a winter storm just around the corner. Maybe she'd gone to the football field. The soles of his shoes crunched over the gravel. He was rounding the corner when he heard screaming.

Without thinking, Chase bolted through the gates. To get to where the sound was coming from, he had to cross the field and go through the stands. As he feet pounded against the AstroTurf, the football field never felt so wide.

He was just climbing up the stairs and heading behind the bleachers when he heard a voice. "Lily," he called. His eyes frantically scanned the surroundings but found nothing.

He listened, a difficult task considering his heart was thundering behind his ribs and his breathing was erratic.

Then he heard it again; soft whimpering.

Chase bolted across the breezeway and rounded the corner. There was nothing in the world that could have prepared him for what he came across. Terror ripped through him like a lightning bolt. Lily sat crumpled against the outer wall of the concession stand. Her head was lolled over her shoulder, and both arms were listless by her sides. In her open, blood-filled palm was a long-jagged piece of metal. It looked like she'd ripped through her skin with the tip.

Her arms were streaked with blood and long jagged cuts while her hands rested in pools of blood. The color leaked from his face as he closed the distance and knelt in front of her.

"Lily!" he said frantically. Her lips were turning a pale shade of blue, and her face had lost all color.

He pressed his fingers to the side of her neck. "Please. Please. Please," he begged as he searched for her pulse. He sighed when it beat weakly beneath his fingers.

Her eyes fluttered open, and tears filled them. "Not you too," she whimpered.

"Hang in there, Lils, okay? Please just hang in there."

Working as quickly as he could, he pulled his phone out of his pocket and dialed 9-1-1. Then tapping the speaker button, he placed the phone on the ground and removed his jacket. As the operator came on the other end, he quickly explained the situation. She promised help was already on the way.

He removed his long sleeve shirt and began to wrap it around one of her bleeding arms, applying as much pressure as possible. The blood soaked through immediately. He then removed his t-shirt and wrapped it around the other.

The frigid winter air bit into his skin, but he didn't pay attention. Nothing mattered to him except making sure she lived.

"Chase?" she said weakly.

"Shhh, I'm right here, Lily." He cupped her cheeks noting how cold her skin was against his palms. "Stay with me, okay. Help is on the way." Once her arms were covered the best he could, he draped his jacket over her trembling body. Her skin was turning ashy.

"I'm sleepy," she whispered.

"No. Damn it. Don't you dare go to sleep."

"I just. . . ." her voice was growing fainter, and terror began to seep into every fiber of his being.

"You remember the first time we met," he sniffed, tears filling his eyes.

When she didn't respond, he gave her a little shake. "Lily, remember the first time we met!" he repeated.

A faint smile touched her lips. "Johnson's Mill Creek," she whispered.

He sniffed. "That's right. I fell and twisted my ankle, and you helped me get home. Said you'd take care of me."

"Chase . . . I can't . . . drugs. . . ."

He froze. "What? Did you take something?"

"Lucas said it would make it go away."

Chase was about to respond when the booming voice echoed through the breezeway.

"What's going on here!"

"Coach!" Chase called. "Coach! Please, help!" This time tears were falling. He felt helpless as his coach hurried over to his side.

"Sweet Jesus," the man said as he knelt.

"I-I found her. Blood. There's so much blood."

Coach nodded calmly. "Go inside the concession stand and get the first aid kit." When Chase didn't move immediately, Coach gripped him by the arm. "Hurry, son."

Something snapped to life inside him, vaulting him to his feet. He hurried through the door and flipped the switch on. He raced across the room and retrieved the first aid kit from beneath the counter. As he was making his way out, something caught his attention on the floor.

There was an opened square foil packet on the floor. Beside it was a discarded condom. His stomach threatened to revolt as pieces of what happened began to fall into place. Anger burned through him brighter than anything he'd ever felt before.

Coach's bellowing voice pulled him out of his haze, propelling him forward.

By the time Coach got Lily's arm wrapped in bandages, the ambulance had arrived. Everything happened in a flurry of activity as the paramedics pushed him aside and did their tasks.

"Is she going to be okay? Hey, I'm talking to you."

"Step back, kid. Let us do our job," the paramedic said firmly, though not unkindly, as she pressed her stethoscope to Lily's chest.

"Is she going to be okay?"

"We're going to do everything we can." The woman then looked at her partner. "BP is dropping. Let's get fluids started."

Seconds later a massive fire truck pulled to a stop beside the ambulance. More people rushed to Lily's aid. There was a flurry of activity as Chase was scooted out of the circle. When he moved to get closer, Coach grabbed his arm. "Let them do their job, son."

It seemed to take them hours to care for her, but, it was probably less than two minutes before they had her on a stretcher and rolling her to the back of the ambulance.

He stopped and watched as they loaded her into the ambulance. The woman from earlier looked at him. "Are you coming?"

Chase cast a look at Coach. "You need to stay here," he said. A crowd was beginning to gather. They were pointing and whispering as Lily was being loaded. He wanted to scream at them all but didn't.

"Listen, we've got to go. In or out!"

He looked to his coach. "I'm all she has."

Coach removed his windbreaker and handed it to him. "I'll take care of the rest of your classes," he finally said.

"Thank you," he replied. He climbed into the back of the ambulance, and the paramedics slammed the doors. In seconds they were tearing out of the parking lot, sirens screeching. He gripped Lily's cold hand and brought it to his lips.

"Don't you dare leave me. Do you hear me? Don't you dare," he whispered. Tears dripped from his lashes and splashed onto their hands. Her hand faintly squeezed his.

The heart monitor beeped rapidly, and then, suddenly, the continual beeps turned into one long beep. "We're losing her," the paramedic said shoving Chase out of the way.

Everything around Chase moved in slow motion as he watched her begin CPR. There was no response, and it was that moment, that his entire world crashed down around him.

Chapter 15

*It's so much darker when a light is lost
than it would have been if it had never shone.*

~John Steinbeck

Chase sat in the waiting room of the hospital for hours. Leaning forward, elbows rested on knees, he cradled his face in his hands. No matter how hard he tried, he couldn't get the doctors or nurses to tell him anything. There was an overwhelming sense of helplessness that washed over him each time a nurse or doctor would walk by.

One of the nurses took pity on him and gave him a cup of coffee. "Here you go, young man," the older woman said.

"When can I see her?" he asked for what felt like the hundredth time.

She let out a slow sigh. "I know how frustrating this must be for you, but until we get a family member in here, we aren't allowed to discuss anything.

Chase felt his anger simmering just beneath the surface. However, he knew that there was nothing he would be able to do about it. Instead, he just nodded and accepted the coffee. The woman gave him a sad look and walked away, her orthopedic shoes squeaking softly against the tiles.

He took a sip of the tepid coffee and winced. It tasted like he imagined liquid tar would taste. He checked his phone when it dinged in.

Ty: *School's out. On my way. Any news?*

Me: *No. Won't tell me anything without a family member.*

He didn't have to wait long a response.

Ty: *I'll take care of that. Don't worry. We'll be able to see her soon.*

Chase just frowned at his phone. He wasn't sure what Tyler was going to do, but whatever it was, he hoped he hurried. The smell of disinfectant mingling with the strong scent of citrus was making his already queasy stomach churn. Whoever it oversaw the cleaning needed to lay off the cleaners just a little bit.

With an exasperated sigh, Chase leaned back, resting his head against the wall. He closed his eyes and tried to push out all the sounds of the hospital; people talking in hushed voices; the droning of different machines beeping, clicking or otherwise making noise; the squeaky wheel of an IV cart as it was being pushed.

He opened one eye and looked to where the sound was coming from and immediately groaned. An elderly man pushing the cart by him was wearing a hospital gown with the back completely hanging open. With another groan, he squeezed his eyes together again and tried to breathe. Hospitals were not places he enjoyed visiting.

Feeling restless, he shoved to his feet and began to pace the halls. He walked to the double doors marked *Authorized Personal* and stared through the round windows. He prayed for Lily to walk down the hall at any moment. However, the heavy feeling in his chest and the uneasiness he felt in the pit of his stomach told him that this time was going to be different. They wouldn't be able to protect her now.

Not this time.

Chase looked down at his hands. He'd been in such a rush to follow the gurney through the hospital. Tears burned his eyes as he began to scrub his hands vigorously against his jeans. His vision blurred as they dripped. His heart thumped wildly in his chest. If he'd only gotten to her a few minutes sooner. If he hadn't stopped and talked to Tyler.

The what if's tumbled through his head. The faster and harder he scrubbed his hands the more his thoughts began to consume him.

Sobs racked his body as he began to cry in earnest. He was so lost in his own head, it wasn't until he felt a soft hand on his back that he jerked his head up.

"Here, son," the nurse from earlier said as she handed him a wet towel.

Chase sniffed and took the towel from her.

"I know it's hard," she said leaving her hand in the middle of his back, gently rubbing soothing circles.

"I should have known this would happen. It was too soon."

"Honey, there's nothing you could have done. People like her. . . ."

Chase's head whipped around. "People like her?"

"That's not what I meant," she said firmly. "What I should have said is that people in her situation are hard to predict. They might seem okay one day, and then the next they're being pulled under by a darkness that no one understands. Not even their closest friends know the depth of their pain."

Chase listened. "What are we supposed to do?"

The nurse just gave him a sad look. "Pray. You pray and do the best you can. Then, the following day, you do it again, and again and again and again. When she tries to lash out, you stand strong. Now, I don't know what that baby has been through, but I know it's gotta be something bad to bring her to this."

The woman placed her hand on his shoulder and gave it a squeeze. "I can see you care for her. I can't tell you the details, but I will tell you this," she said lowering her voice. "Your friend was in bad shape. Whatever she took slowed her heart way down. The only good thing about it was it slowed her heart down enough to slow down the blood loss. She's critical, but as of right now, she is stable. I can't tell you any more than that without a family member present."

Chase sniffed, wiping his nose on the sleeve of Coach's jacket. "Thank you." His voice was thick from crying.

She gave him a sad smile and returned to the nurse's station. Once again, Chase looked down at his hands.

Most of the blood had come off, but there were traces still there. Turning, he made his way down the hall and into the bathroom. After pushing in the lock, he leaned his back against the cold wood and slid to the floor.

There were very few times in his life he'd felt as helpless as he had when he found Lily bleeding out on the concrete. Leaning forward, he crossed his arms behind his head and rested his forehead on his knees. He'd almost lost her. If he'd been just a minute later, it would have been too late.

Chase lost track of how long he'd been sitting on the floor. It could have been minutes or hours. It didn't matter. It felt like he was in a dream. With an exasperated sigh, he pushed from the floor and walked to the sink.

He filled both palms with soap and scrubbed Lily's blood from his hands. Red swirled with the suds before slipping down the drain. Once the soap and blood were off his hands, he leaned over and splashed cold water on his face.

His hands gripped the side of the sink as he stared at his reflection. He really did need a haircut. Water dripped off his nose as he stared into the eyes of his reflection. His irises were surrounded by red lines left behind by tears and worry.

Suddenly, the feeling of helplessness and despair disappeared. It was replaced by a rage so hot and intense he was sure he would be consumed. His hands trembled as he imagined Lily laying on her back on the cold cement floor with Lucas over her.

He'd given her the drugs.

He was the reason she was in that room.

A burst of anger rushed through Chase so strong and fierce his entire body began to tremble. His head spinning, he whirled around and stormed from the bathroom. He turned and started marching down the hall. He angrily pressed the button on the elevator and tapped his feet anxiously as he waited for the doors to slide open.

As they did, he stepped forward just as Tyler stepped out. His black hair was mussed from running his hands through it repeatedly—a nervous habit Tyler had. His eyes were wide with worry.

"Have you heard anything?"

Chase shook his head. "They won't say anything because of the whole family bullshit. One of the nurses said she was critical but stable."

"Come on," Tyler said stepping around him. It was in that moment that Chase realized that Tyler's father was in tow.

Chase fell into step with Tyler. "What the hell man? Your dad? He hates us. I thought he was out of town?"

"He owes me, and he came back for a meeting. I just happen to catch him," Tyler muttered under his breath.

Chase wasn't going to argue. He and Tyler just stood back and watched as the imposing man towered over the nurse at the nurse's station. To the woman's credit, she wasn't intimidated.

"Until a member of Lillian's family can be reached, I am acting as her attorney. I need you to allow us in to see her." Chase could not stand Elliot Anderson, but he had to give the man credit; he was imposing and slightly terrifying. He towered over nearly everyone at six-foot-eight. His shoulders seemed to be as wide as he was tall. He was imposing with steely gray eyes that seemed to cut everyone down. What Chase just couldn't understand was why he was helping them.

The nurse nodded, and Elliot turned and looked at the boys. He straightened his tie and glared down at Chase before sliding his cold look to his son. "I expect you to stay out of trouble. Whatever that girl has gotten herself into is not good. You'd do well to stay away from her and keep your damn nose clean." He looked down his nose at Chase once more causing the anger that had been cooling in his belly to rise again. "I told you that hanging out with trailer scum like them would lead you to no good. She's just like her mother."

"You arrogant sonofa—" Chase took a challenging step forward. While he was tall for his age, Elliot still had at least four inches on him. Tyler's firm hand on Chase's arm pulled him back.

"Not here. Not now," Tyler said, though Chase wasn't sure if he was addressing his father or him.

"Thanks," Tyler muttered.

Elliot nodded once and marched back down the hall to the elevator.

The nurse cleared her throat. "He's charming," she said drily, her shrewd eyes following Elliot down the hallway.

Chase snorted. "That's one way of putting it. If you find gonorrhea or the plague charming."

This caused the nurse to smile. "Well, he's not the first one to try to pull a power trip on me. I know damn good and well he is not that girl's guardian. However, I know that she means the world to you, but I'm going to tell you now, things are already in motion."

Panic seized Chase's chest as he looked at Tyler and then back to the woman. "Things? What kind of things?"

She just shook her head sadly. "Because she attempted to take her life, she will be evaluated. From there, the police may or may not get involved. If she's deemed a danger to herself, she will be placed in a facility until she can make a recovery.

Tyler and Chase both listened. "She's going to be locked up?"

The nurse nodded sadly. "Maybe it's for the best, son. At least this way, she might be able to get the help she needs. It's obvious that that poor baby doesn't have anyone to care for her other than the two a'you."

The only thing they could do was stare at her. What was there to say? What could she say? "She's in room 1503. If anyone asks, you're her brother. That shit stunt that your dad pulled is crap, and I'm supposed to report it. I won't. Just keep everything quiet and don't cause problems. Okay?"

"Thank you," Chase said touched by the woman's kindness.

She nodded and walked away. Turning, he looked at Tyler. His friend's face was blank. Worry lines creased his forehead, and his mouth was tugged down into a frown, but aside from that, it was hard to see what was going on in his mind.

"Let's go," Chase said as he pushed through the double doors.

Chapter 16

Don't believe everything you think.
Thoughts are just that, thoughts.

~Allan Lokos

Chase felt like his heart was going to explode from his chest. At his sides, his hands trembled. He stuffed them in his pockets and fidgeted with his keys. Then something Tyler said earlier struck a note in his mind.

Reaching out, Chase grabbed Tyler's arm and pulled him to a stop. "Hey."

Tyler looked at him puzzled. "What was that back there?"

His brows turned down in confusion. "What are you talking about?"

"I'm talking about with your old man. What was all of that? You said he owes you?"

Tyler shrugged, but there was an odd look in his eyes that Tyler had never seen before. "It's nothing man."

Chase frowned. "Ty, what's going on?"

Tyler shifted from one foot to the other, looking anxiously. Finally, he huffed a sigh. "I found out some shit on my dad. I used it against him as leverage to get us back here."

Chase's eyes widened. "What kind of *shit?*"

"Just leave it alone, man." He didn't give Chase a chance to argue because he brushed by him and walked the rest of the way to Lily's room. Chase noted the way Tyler's shoulders were slumped. He understood his friend's pain. He was worried about Lily too.

He stopped beside Tyler in front of her door. What were they going to find on the other side? His stomach rolled violently.

"Here goes nothing," Tyler said as he reached forward and pushed the heavy door open.

The interior of the room was dimly lit. The only light on was glowing softly behind the hospital bed. Chase stopped in his tracks at the sight of Lily. Her blond hair had been cleaned and was fanned out against the white pillow. The back of the bed was lifted slightly to keep her from lying completely on her back.

She was so still that if it weren't for the steady beep of the heart monitor, he would have questioned if she were alive. A clear oxygen tube was secured beneath her nose.

Beep. Beep. Beep. Beep.

The heart monitor was steady, and yet, it looked like she was dead. Her skin was pale, almost waxen, fighting with the contrast of the bed linens. His eyes continued to study as he slowly walked to her bedside. They wandered down her arms, seeing the pale scars from past cutting experiences.

When his gaze finally landed on the white gauze encasing both of her forearms, just below her elbows, his heart stuttered. Splotches of red were already beginning to bleed through the bandaging. Then, he noticed the leather cuffs around her wrists, securing her to the bed. His eyes widened.

"Ty," he whispered.

Tyler seemed lost in his own little world as he stared down at Lily. "Tyler!" he whispered again, this time a little louder.

Tyler's head snapped up. He blinked his eyes several times and focused on Chase. "They have her strapped to the bed!" Chase hissed.

His friend nodded and opened his mouth to say something, however, before he got the chance, nurse breezed into the room. She was a younger woman with a round face and kind smile.

"Are those necessary?" Chase asked, jabbing his finger in the direction of the restraints.

She gave him a sad look and nodded. "I'm sorry, but yes. It's hospital policy that all suicide attempts are to be kept in restraints until they are ruled to no longer be a threat to themselves."

"That's ridiculous. She's going to freak when she wakes up and finds those on her. She hates being held down," Chase said looking at Tyler for help. When his friend didn't say anything, he frowned and turned back to the woman. She seemed unfazed by his annoyance as she went about checking Lily's vital signs.

"I'm sorry. I wish there was something else I can do," she said apologetically. He could see the sincerity in her eyes.

"But she's not a threat to herself."

She sadly shook her head. "I wish I knew what to tell you, but I can honestly tell you this. Your friend is in good hands. She will get all the help she needs, and the best care."

Chase's chest fell in defeat. He should have been the one to give her the care she needed. Seeing her lying in bed so still and unmoving stirred things in the pit of his stomach that he never knew existed. A gamut of emotions surged through him like the ebbing and flowing of the tides.

"What happens next?" he finally asked. He looked at Tyler, confused as to why he wasn't saying anything. His eyes were still trained on Lily's face as he stood with his arms crossed tightly over his chest. His face was a blank mask, making it impossible to see what was going on. It was weird to see him so stoic.

"Well, she will be evaluated by a psychologist when she wakes up. Right now, she's on a seventy-two-hour hold."

"Meaning?"

"Meaning that she will be here for a minimum of seventy-two hours because of the risk she poses to herself. After that, the doctors will make their decisions about the next step."

"The next step? What does that mean?"

The nurse fixed the blanket around Lily's still form and gently tucked a strand of hair behind her ear. It was undeniable the woman cared for her patients.

"It can be a few different things, so it's tough to say."

"Pick an option."

She sighed. "Legally, I can't tell you what they are going to do because we don't know yet. However, I can tell you that a few different choices are mandatory rehab and counseling. Another would be to place her in a facility to help her overcome whatever demons she's fighting," she said casting a look at Lily. Chase followed her gaze. "Mental illness isn't something that is taken lightly around here."

Both Tyler and Chase's attention snapped to the nurse. "She's not mentally ill," Tyler said defensively.

"She's just been hanging out with this guy. He's a bad influence. Got her into some stuff," Chase said.

She nodded. "That would account for the toxins found in her body."

"Toxins?"

Again, she nodded. "There were some powerful chemicals in her blood that are never supposed to interact. We've been seeing several cases like this a week. They are getting more and more frequent. They cause the neurotransmitters in the brain to misfire, causing hallucinations as well as slowing the heart rate. While the situation here is bad, your friend is lucky."

Chase frowned. "She's strapped to the hospital bed, in a medically induced coma. How is she lucky?"

"First, she will be pulled from the coma in a few hours. It was just a precaution while the surgery was done and to help get the drugs out of her system." She jotted a few notes on her clipboard.

"And the second reason?" Tyler asked.

The nurse looked up from her notes. "The second reason she's lucky is because she's not dead. The dose in her system could have killed her. It *should* have killed her." The woman lovingly patted the top of Lily's hand. "Your girl here, she's a fighter."

"You have no idea," Chase said softly.

"There's only fifteen minutes left of visiting hours. Then I'm going to have to ask you boys to leave. You can come back tomorrow."

"That's not happening," both boys said in unison.

She huffed. "Please don't make me call security."

"Please, don't make us leave," Tyler pleaded.

Chase turned imploring eyes to the nurse. He knew she was only doing her job, but it sucked. They couldn't leave her alone. They couldn't let her be alone when she woke up. They'd left her alone for far too long. It couldn't happen again.

"We're all she has," he said casting a look at Lily and feeling an unfamiliar tug in his chest.

The nurse looked back and forth between them and then to Lily. "Fine. Leave when hours are over, and then come back in a couple hours. I'll be able to allow you in, but *do not* cause trouble and don't make me regret this. It's my ass on the line, not yours."

Chase's eyes widened. Suddenly, the sweet little nurse turned scary and intimidating. "Yes ma'am," Chase and Tyler said in unison.

She gave them one last warning look before leaving the room.

"Well, didn't see that one coming," Chase said as he pulled a chair to the bedside. Tyler did the same on the other side. Then, the only thing they could do was sit. So, that's what they did. They sat and waited.

Chapter 17

Whoever can see through all fear will always be safe.

~Lao Tzu

Lily could hear voices, but she was having a hard time struggling through the fog to figure out what was being said. Everything around her was cold and dark. When she tried to call out, there was no sound. She could hear the hum and beeping sound of monitors and other devices, but she didn't know where the sounds were coming from.

It felt like she was trapped in a dark, cold room with no light. She lifted her hands to feel in front of her but felt nothing but an empty void. She tried to walk in the direction of the voices, but as soon as she took a step, they moved. She spun around, trying to figure out where they were coming from.

How long do you think she'll be out?

Wait a minute. The voice was familiar. Chase?

"Chase? I'm here," she tried to call, but when she opened her mouth, nothing came out. Panic wanted to claim her. Why couldn't she talk? Why couldn't she make a sound? Where was she?

I don't know man. She heard Tyler say.

What was wrong with her? Why couldn't she wake up?

I'm going to get some coffee. It's going to be a long night. She strained to listen as Tyler spoke, but his words began to blend. He sounded so sad.

She listened for a little longer. The only thing she could hear was the sound of her heart thumping and the obnoxious beeping sound.

"What the hell is that beeping?" she muttered.

Desperately, she wanted to wake up, but no matter how hard she tried, she just couldn't get her body to follow her mind's instructions. She could hear and feel everything going on around her. She just could not wake up.

She felt her hand being lifted and held gently. There was the brushing of something soft on the back. It was so faint and light, it felt like butterfly wings. The grip tightened as her hand was lowered back to the bed.

"You've got to come back to us. Do you hear me? Damn it, Lilian. You can't check out on us—me. I can't do this without you."

Suddenly, in the distance, Lily saw the faintest flicker of light.

"I'm so sorry. I'm so, so sorry." The sadness in Chase's voice stole her breath. He sounded so broken. Her heart clenched, and the small light she saw through the darkness grew a bit brighter.

"Keep talking, Chase," she said softly.

"We just got you back. You can't do this to us. Please, Lily. Wake up."

The light continued to grow brighter. With each step she took, and with each word he said, the darkness began to fade to gray.

"As much as I want you back, you need to know I'm pissed. I'm so pissed at you right now!"

She heard him sniffle and continued to walk toward the growing light.

"You're so much better than this. Why can't you see it? Why didn't you go to Tyler? Why didn't you come to me?" She could hear the hurt and anger in his voice, and it made her heart ache. She'd done this to them.

"Me and you, we've been friends since we were two years old. Why didn't you trust me?"

"I didn't want you disappointed in me," she whispered, knowing that he couldn't hear her. She was closer to the light now. Just a few more steps and she'd be free.

"We're going to get through this." She heard him sniffle.

Two steps. One step. All she had to do was step into the warmth that she knew was right in front of her. She cast a look over her shoulder. The darkness behind her seemed to pulse, begging her to stay. The thought was tempting. In the dark, she could remain hidden from everything that had happened to her. No one would see what she'd done just to get a fix to make the pain go away. She wouldn't be judged.

"Please, Lils." Chase's voice was soft as he pleaded one final time.

Lily turned around and stepped forward.

Chase's head rested on the side of the bed. He clutched Lily's hand in his own. Though she was restrained, there was a little room for him to maneuver the back of his hand to his lips. "Please, Lils," he whispered into the mattress.

Her hand twitched in his, and his head bolted up. He stared at her face, watching for signs that she could be waking up. The nurse chose that moment to come into the room.

"She's waking up," he said hopefully.

The nurse frowned and looked at Lily's form. "She's not supposed to wake up until we bring her out of it. Why do you say that?"

"Her hand moved. I was talking to her, and it twitched in my palm."

She gave a knowing nod and a kind smile. "That is common with comatose patients. Their subconscious is still working. It's like the bridge between her brain and parts of her body is broken. The brain can't figure out how to cross the gap until her body repairs the bridge. Feeling the muscle twitches and spasms is just her body repairing the roads in her mind."

"Can she hear me?" Chase asked looking at Lily. The vibrant creature she'd once been seemed so far gone. This girl seemed like a ghost.

"Some think so. It's tough to say."

"When will the doctors be waking her up?"

"They decided to wait until tomorrow morning," she said as she moved around the room checking Lily's vital signs and fluids.

"Is that safe?"

"Is what safe?" Tyler asked from the door. He walked in carrying two cups of coffee. After handing one to Chase, he looked at the nurse. "Is what safe?"

"We were just discussing Lily's coma. It's medically induced. It means when the doctor is ready to wake her up, he can."

"Why isn't he?"

"Because, as I stated earlier, it's to make sure all of the drugs are out of her system and she has calmed down. She's very fortunate to be alive at all." She walked to the foot of the bed and jotted down a few more notes before replacing the clipboard back in its holder. "Your friend seems very strong. Her vital signs are getting much better. It's just an added precaution. Now, as for you two. You need to get out of here for a while. I'll let you back in a little bit later."

When neither one of them moved from Lily's bedside, the nurse crossed her arms and stared them down. "I said, scram. She needs to be bathed anyway. Go out, grab some food, change clothes, shower or whatever else you need to do. By the time you get back, you'll be set to stay with her tonight."

Chase and Tyler hesitated for just a moment before shuffling to the door. Tyler walked out, but Chase stopped at the doorway. He cast a look back to Lily. As he watched her, something snapped inside him. All the anger he'd felt from earlier began to surface.

He would make this right. It didn't matter what happened to him. With a new-found determination, he marched down the hall. Tyler's long strides soon fell into step. "What's going on?"

"I think it's time we handle business once and for all."

Tyler didn't have to ask what he meant because he already knew. "Let's go!"

It didn't take them long after leaving the hospital to find Lucas. He was lounging in his living room at the trailer park. Chase kicked the flimsy door in, causing it to fly from the hinges.

Lucas sat up, his eyes glassy and confused. "What the hell man," he slurred.

The second Chase set eyes on the low life, he stormed across the small living room and jerked him up by the shirt. "You worthless piece of crap. Do you know where your girlfriend is right now?"

Lucas snickered. "Probably boning somebody to get another fix."

"Sonofabitch!" Chase roared. He released the other guy and then swung his fist as hard and fast as he could, catching Lucas square in the nose. He felt bones and cartilage snap under his fist, and it was satisfying, but he was far from finished. He pulled back and landed another blow to Lucas's ribs. The bones cracked.

"She's in the hospital," Chase roared as he punched Lucas in the stomach. Lucas recovered and spat blood onto the floor, hugging one arm around his middle. He stretched to his full height and turned narrowed eyes on Chase.

He spit again and then took a step closer. "That little whore didn't take too well to the drugs, did she? Didn't figure she would. They have a nasty habit of making people see things."

"You knew she would react that way?" Tyler asked.

Lucas shrugged and wiped the blood away from his nose with the back of his hand. "I wasn't sure, but man, she was quite the lay. I've been working for months to tap that piece. I knew she would give it up for the right offer."

"You raped her!" Chase accused.

"You can't rape the willing," Lucas smirked. His teeth were covered with blood. "And I promise you, she was willing. She had it coming to her anyway. She was such a cock tease, making me think she was going to give it up and then change her mind. I got tired of her endless whining."

Chase was preparing to charge, but a loud, angry roar from behind him caused him to hesitate. Tyler rushed by him and grabbed Lucas by the shirt. Whirling him around by the fabric of his stained shirt, Tyler slammed Lucas against the wall. The entire house shook as pictures fell to the floor, shattering. "She's in a coma because whatever it was you gave her made her slit her wrists," Tyler yelled, slamming Lucas on the wall repeatedly. "She almost died."

"She should have finished the job," Lucas growled pushing back against Tyler. However, it didn't work. Tyler was much stronger and quicker. Lucas swung, and Tyler easily sidestepped. As he recovered, he threw a punch into Lucas's head.

Then, all hell broke loose. Tyler and Lucas began exchanging punch after punch. They crashed into furniture and broke lamps. Even though Lucas was under the influence of whatever his drug of choice was, he was surprisingly strong.

When Lucas grabbed an empty whiskey bottle and lifted it above his head, Chase decided it was time to step in. Chase lowered his shoulder and rammed it into his gut, pushing him through the front door and landing them both on the rickety deck.

They rolled through the cheap lattice covering the side and hit the ground with a hard *thud.* The air rushed from Chase's lungs as Lucas landed on top of him. Lucas landed blow after blow to Chase's face. Stars exploded through his vision as blood filled his mouth. He tried to pull his arms up to keep the punches from reaching his face, but Lucas's knees were pinning his arms to the ground. The weight of Lucas sitting on his chest was making it impossible to breathe.

Suddenly, Lucas's weight was pulled from his body. He gulped air into his lungs as he staggered to his feet. As he did, he found Tyler sitting on top of Lucas. He was landing fist after fist against the guy's face. Lucas was nothing but a bloody mess.

"Ty, man, that's enough," Chase said clutching his aching ribs. Tyler didn't respond.

"You sorry piece of shit," Tyler said punctuating each word with a blow to the face.

Chase could feel the urgency in the air. Tyler was getting close to going too far. He watched for a few seconds longer. This was not normal for Tyler. Sure, they'd gotten into fights together, but he'd never thrown more than one, maybe two, punches. Chase was the fighter.

"You hit her. You made her do things she didn't want to do. You forced her to have sex with you!" Tyler yelled.

Chase's eyes widened. "He what?"

Tyler stopped his attack, resting his bruised and blooding fists on his thighs as he breathed heavily. "She told me he used to hit her."

A new anger lit in Chases' belly, but he put it out. He looked at Lucas's, barely conscious body on the ground. Before he could say anything, Tyler slammed his fist into the guy's face again.

Chase wrapped his arms around Tyler and hauled him backward. They both tumbled to the ground, and Tyler jumped to his feet. "You're just going to let him get away with this?!" he bellowed, turning his rage on Chase and shoving him.

"Look at him, Tyler!" he roared back. "He can barely move."

"It's not even close to what he deserves," Tyler raged. His chest heaved up and down as he breathed heavily. "He beat her. He tore her down. He *poisoned* her and today he almost killed her."

Chase watched his friend crumble. It was something so out of character that it took him a minute to process what was happening. Tears mixed with blood and dirt on Tyler's face. Stepping forward, he pulled Tyler into a hug.

"We almost lost her today!" Tyler sobbed into his shoulder. "We still might lose her."

Chase returned the hug, despite the ache in his ribs. They took a step apart, and he looked Tyler over. The anger and hurt were gone, and his calm, controlled friend was back in place.

"Let's just get the hell out of here," Chase said.

"I couldn't agree more."

He began to walk to the truck, but when he didn't hear Tyler's following, he stopped and turned. Tyler was squatting down beside Lucas.

"Can you hear me?" he growled.

Lucas's head moved slightly.

"Good. You listen and listen well. If you ever come near Lily again, I *will* kill you. Do you understand?"

Lucas nodded. A chill raced up Chase's spine. In all the years he'd known Tyler, he'd never seen him so dark.

He watched Tyler finally push to his feet and march silently to his truck. The only thing Chase could do was follow.

Something had snapped inside Tyler, and for the first time in six years, Chase was worried about someone other than Lily.

Chapter 18

*No great mind has ever existed
without a touch of madness.*

~Aristotle

Lily's tongue was glued to the roof of her mouth, and her head throbbed painfully. Everything in her head was a jumbled mess tangled in fog. She had no idea where she was or how she'd gotten there. Slowly, she pried her eyes opened. They felt like they were dried out and covered in layers of grit.

Her surroundings were fuzzy at first, but then, they slowly came into view. She turned her head and reclining on the couch with his chin slouched on his chest was Tyler. He was snoring softly. She noted the bruises and swollen eyes. This caused her to frown.

Turning her head slowly, she looked for Chase. She found him resting his head on the bed beside her, his hand protectively over hers. She tried to move, but it was at that moment she realized that her arms were restrained.

Panic filled her chest. Why was she being held down? Why was she tied up? The heart monitor beside her head began to beep faster as her panic climbed.

She began to struggle, trying to kick the blankets away, but she was also strapped by the ankles. Terror pure and unfiltered filled her veins with ice.

"Chase?!" she croaked, trying to struggle.

Chase shot upright, looking around anxiously. "Lily, calm down," he said once the fog of sleep lifted.

"Chase, why am I strapped down? Let me go," she said feeling the terror creep into her throat. "Please, let me go. Don't hold me down."

"Lily, we're not holding you down," Tyler said standing on the other side of the bed.

She couldn't hear what they were saying. The only thing she could understand was the roaring of blood as it pulsed through her head.

She could hear both boys calling her name, but couldn't respond. Chase yelled for Tyler to get help. The next thing she knew, she felt Chase's warm palms against her cheeks.

"Lily! Lily, listen to me. Hear me!"

His voice punctured through the cloud of terror surrounding her.

"That's right. There you go. You hear me now?" he asked.

She nodded slightly.

"That's my good girl. Listen to me. Okay, it's okay. You're not in danger. They are for your safety. I'm going to take them off, but you have to promise you'll be calm."

His voice became clearer. "Focus on me and take a deep breath."

When she didn't do it immediately, his hands tightened on her cheeks ever so slightly. Lilian! Focus on me. Breath with me."

He took several deep breaths, and she did the same. Within moments she began to calm. As she did, nursing staff raced into the room. The whole thing lasted less than a minute, but it felt like so much longer.

When she was finally calm, Chase released her face but didn't move from the bed.

"Sir, I need you to step back," the male nurse said.

"Just give me a second, man. Okay? She's got to calm down." He didn't let the man reply as he turned and faced Lily once more. Tyler was awake and on his feet on the other side of the bed.

"You good?" Chase asked.

Lily knew she was far from good, but she nodded anyway.

"I'm going to let these people do their job, okay? We're right here," he assured her.

She frowned. "I'm not a baby, Chase," she grunted, perturbed that she was being talked to like one.

Chase chuckled and patted her hand before moving away. Lily watched with wary eyes as the doctor, a middle-aged woman with shock white hair and a kind smile, drew closer.

"Hey, sweetheart, I'm Doctor Asher. Do you know where you are?" she asked as she clicked on a penlight and flashed it into Lily's eyes. Lily winced as the light stabbed into her brain.

"I'm guessing the hospital since you're a doctor," she replied dryly.

Chase and Tyler chuckled, and Dr. Asher just smiled. "That's right. Do you remember why you're here?"

Lily wracked her brain as she tried to remember what events had led her to be in the hospital. The last thing she remembered was leaving the school and heading to the football field. Suddenly, a sharp pain bolted through each of her arms. She flinched and looked down. Blood began to soak through the bandages on her arms.

"We need to get these dressed and check to see if she's reopened the stitches," the doctor told the nurse.

"Yes, doctor," the man said.

"This is Andre."

"As in *the giant?*" Lily supplied while watching the massive man move around the room. He stood well over six foot tall and was bald. He had a black goatee and a slight, sliver scar in his dark eyebrow. He looked better suited to be a wrestler than a nurse.

"I've been called worse," Andre said as he gathered the items he needed and placed them on the tray.

Dr. Asher laughed. "I'll be back when he's finished, and we'll chat, okay?"

Lily only nodded and watched as the doctor left the room. Tyler whispered something to Chase and then followed her. Lily frowned but then turned her attention back to the man that was wielding a particularly sharp pair of scissors in her direction.

She had to admit, Andre, was rather attractive. His eyes were a rich, chocolate color, and his smile was warm and inviting.

However, her good nurse was forgotten as he pulled back the bandages and revealed angry looking cuts.

"Well, you didn't pull any of the stitches, but we need to clean this up. Okay?"

She nodded, unable to take her eyes off her arms. What had she done? She'd never cut so deep before. There was a total of four jagged cuts in all different angles on her forearms. They were dangerously close to her wrist.

Pain burned through her arms as Andrew cleaned and rebandaged each arm. Once he was done, Andre patted her arm and offered her a warm smile.

"Can we take these off?" she asked indicating the restraints.

He studied her for several long minutes.

"Please," she begged. "I don't know why I'm tied down, but please, I won't do anything. I just can't handle it. Please?"

Andrea studied her for a long moment and finally nodded. He unfastened the Velcro and looked at her. "Don't make me regret this," he said firmly.

"You scare the hell out of me. I don't think I'm gonna try anything." She'd meant it as a joke, but it was the truth.

"I'll be back in just a bit to check on you. Dr. Asher will be back to talk about the next steps. Okay?"

Lily nodded. Terror stole through her. Next steps? What did that mean? When Andre left, he pulled the door closed behind him. She looked at Chase and frowned.

"Next steps? What's he talking about? And why do you look like you've been hit by a truck? Tyler too?" She'd noticed the bruises and cuts on Tyler's face, but she was just now seeing the ones on Chase's. They weren't nearly as bad as Tyler's though. There was a cut and some bruising on his bottom lip and a small cut under his right eye that had been covered with a white butterfly bandage. Angry purple and black bruises colored his jaw.

Chase didn't smile. He just sat on the bed and looked at her.

"What?" Anxiousness began to creep through her body.

"You seriously don't remember what happened?"

She looked down at her hands. Her eyes skimmed the stitched cuts crisscrossing and marking up her arms. As she stared at her injuries, bits and pieces began to creep through the fog. She remembered sending a text to Lucas. Then meeting him at the concession stand.

Her eyes widened as she met Chase's intense stare. Her stomach rolled violently when she remembered what happened; what she'd done.

"I'm gonna be sick," she gasped covering her mouth.

Chase reacted quickly, grabbing the basin beside the bed just in time for her to spill the meager contents of her stomach. Over and over she wretched until there was nothing but dry heaves and gagging.

When she finished, she collapsed back on the bed while Chase took the basin into the bathroom. A few seconds later she heard the toilet being flushed. Tears streamed down her cheeks, dripping off her chin as humiliation and disgust burned through her.

Chase returned to her bedside. The edge of the thin mattress dipped under his weight. Reaching up, he drew the cloth over her forehead, but she turned her head away. She couldn't stand to see the look of disappointment in his eyes. She'd done the very thing that her mother did for a living. Everything rushed back to her; sex with Lucas on the cold concession stand floor; the drugs; the voices and hallucinations; the cutting. Every detail came back with a clarity that she wished never existed. She wished it would have stayed forgotten. It was in that moment that she realized, she was at her rock bottom.

She sobbed softly as he gently gripped her by the chin and turned her to face him. Using his thumb, he brushed a tear away. It wasn't the first time he'd comforted her. Over the lifetime they'd known each other, he'd comforted her more times than she could count. He'd helped bandage scrapes and bumps when they were little. Chase was as tough as they came. In his mind, showing emotion was a weakness, but he never made her feel that way. He never judged her for falling or crying. He just dusted her off and wiped her tears. This time it felt different, though.

"Look at me," he urged. There was a tenderness in his voice that she was sure that no one had ever heard, not even Tyler.

Still, she couldn't look at him.

"Lilian, look at me," he demanded firmly. He only used her full name when he was upset with her.

"I can't," she whispered.

"You owe me that much," he snapped softly.

Lily's eyes widened, and she forced herself to turn around. When she did, she gasped. Chase was staring at her with watery eyes. It caused her heart to break.

"I—we nearly lost you yesterday," he said. "If I'd been a second later, you would have bled out."

"I'm so sorry," she cried softly. Sobs overtook her body.

"You need help, Lily. You can't keep going on like this. I—we can't lose you."

"I saw things—people," she whispered. "They said some horrible things; my mom; Kiera; *him*," she said with a shudder as she remembered the face of the man that haunted every moment of her life surged forward. Her heart jumped, causing Chase to look at the monitor.

He grabbed her hand and squeezed it. "Hey. Look at me. They aren't real. They weren't there."

"It felt like they were. Some of the stuff they said was what Kiera had said to me at school."

His eyes narrowed. "What? When did you talk to Kiera?"

"Before fourth period. I went to apologize for the fight. I felt bad and wanted to, I don't, know fix things."

"With Kiera?"

She lifted a shoulder. "Some of the stuff she said just got to me."

Chase stiffened, and he clenched his jaw together tightly. "What did she say?" he asked through gritted teeth.

"That I was a waste of space and needed to just end everyone's misery and kill myself." She could still hear

Kiera's voice ringing in her head—both the hallucination and the real one.

"And you believed her?"

She shrugged.

"Listen, you know how toxic she is. You also know that she has no soul. She will do or say anything to make you miserable."

She knew what he was saying was true. She'd tried to do it on her own. She'd even relied on Chase and Tyler to help her. She knew she was in too deep. It wasn't fair to keep putting them through all her drama and emotional baggage. They had to live their lives and stop worrying about her.

"I don't know what to do," she said softly.

"Then we will all figure it out like we have our entire lives. We will help you through this. It might take a while, but we will do this. We're going to get you healthy again."

"They aren't the only ones I saw," she admitted.

Before Chase could ask her what she meant, the door opened, and Tyler stepped through. Lily stiffened and dropped her gaze. She felt Chase's reaction react to her odd behavior toward their friend. When she looked back up, Chase was watching her. Then it was like a switch flipped, and he knew what she'd been talking about. He knew who the other person was she'd seen.

"Hey, you," Tyler said softly as he sat on the other side of the bed. She knew he was trying to keep calm and act like everything was okay. However, she knew him better. His emotions played across his face like a flashing billboard.

He reached for her hand, but she pulled it away. He looked at her questioningly. She flinched at the hurt she saw in his brown eyes and looked away.

"What happened to you two anyway?" she asked, avoiding eye contact with Tyler.

Both guys shifted uncomfortably. Tyler climbed to his feet and walked over to the window, keeping his back to them. She frowned.

"What's going on?"

"We had a little . . . chat. With Lucas," Chase finally admitted.

"You did what?! Why would you do that?" she asked.

Tyler spun around and pinned her with a glare. It was cold and dark. "Are you seriously asking us that question right now?"

"Yes, I'm asking that question. Why wouldn't you do such a thing? He's not worth the trouble, certainly not all the damage it looks like you two got."

"He's not worth it," Chase said looking from Tyler to Lily. "But *you* are. Lily, he all but forced you to sleep with him."

"That was my decision. I *chose* to do that."

"Why? He had something you wanted, and the only way you were going to get it was to sleep with him. You were upset after your run-in with Kiera."

Tyler's scowl deepened. "What run-in? What's he talking about, Lily?"

Knowing that he was going to find out from Chase anyway, she retold the story and about how she tried to apologize. Tyler's face paled and then turned red with anger.

"Still doesn't change the fact that you went to him. And, to get what you wanted, you had to have sex with him," he spat out.

Lily's shoulders sagged with humiliation. Tyler didn't stop there.

"Then, after the fact, you go and try to commit suicide! How could you?!" He was breathing heavily. "Do you not know how much you mean to us? How important you are to our lives?"

"Ty, man, chill," Chase said moving around the bed and stepping between them.

Lily watched as Tyler turned angry eyes from her to Chase.

"She's been through enough," Chase said firmly. She could tell he was trying to keep a tight rein on his patience. "She doesn't need it from you too."

"You know what, maybe she does, Chase. Maybe she needs a bit of tough love to see how stupid she's being.

That she can't do stupid shit like that and think it wouldn't affect anyone but her."

She listened as he ranted. Chase had said his peace and even though what Tyler was saying was the same thing, it still stung. Emotions welled in her chest, and once again tears filled her eyes. "Why would you do that?" he yelled.

"*Because you told me to!*" she screamed.

Tyler took a startled step back. Chase's gaze swung in his direction.

Tyler looked horrified. "What?"

"You were there!" she yelled. "I saw you there! I heard you tell me to end the pain! You told me I could make it all go away!"

She hadn't meant ever to tell him that he was one of the people she saw. The pain in his eyes spoke volumes. His face paled, and his mouth dropped in horror.

Chase spun around to face her. "He wasn't there, Lily. You have to know that."

She just stared at Tyler for several long moments. Finally, she let out a long breath. "I know he wasn't there."

"Why would you see me there?" Tyler asked. His hurt evident in his hoarse voice. "I would never . . . Lily, you guys, are my world. You and Chase are all I have. I would . . . to think that you think. . . ."

"Tyler, I don't think that. I don't even know why I saw you. You two are the best parts of my life. I don't understand anything. The only thing I know is that I'm broken, and I don't know how to fix it."

The three of them stared at each in silence. What was there to say? She'd made a mess of things. She'd been weak and unable to say no. She opened her mouth to say something, but the doctor walked in.

"Lily, I think it's time we talked."

Once again, Lily knew her life was about to change. She didn't realize it then, but things were about to get a lot harder before they got easier.

Part 2

Chapter 19

Look deeply into the nature of suffering
to see the causes of suffering and the way out

~Buddha

Chase,

I feel like I'm going crazier than what I was when I got here. It's been five months, and the only thing I can do is stare at these walls. My therapist says I am making progress, but I'm a long way from where I need to be. I don't feel like I'm getting anywhere. The nights are the hardest. When I'm all alone, and it's quiet, I can hear people down the halls crying and screaming. For a moment I think that I'm dreaming. Then I realize that I'm not. I know that I'm stuck in this place for another seven months, and that's only if I show progress. I don't know if I can do this.

Tell me something about home. What's new? I missed you this month. I know you had to work. Has Tyler left for California yet? I haven't heard from him. We kinda left on bad terms. All I can think about is trying to make things right with him. Have you talked to my mom? I don't guess I should be surprised that she hasn't tried to contact me. How's your mom? You said that she got the job as the overnight manager at the hotel in Warren. How's she liking it?

What about you? Are you working at Armstrong's ranch again this summer? I hope he's paying you good. Has football camp started yet?

"Time for session, Lily," Jasper, the sweet-natured nurse said as he approached her table.

Lily tucked a strand of hair behind her ear and smiled up at him. "Give me a few more minutes?"

He smiled. "Just a few. You want me to mail that to Chase for you?"

153

"If you wouldn't mind."

He flashed a wide smile. "No problem at all." Jasper turned and walked over to Mr. Wellington, an elderly gentleman that sat in his wheelchair and stared out the window day in and day out.

Lily looked down at the letter in front of her. She pressed the tip of the pencil to the paper and continued.

Jasper just told me I've got to go to session soon. I like him. He's nicer than most of the people that work here. His wife just had a new baby—a little boy. They named him Link. He's cute too. Chubby little cheeks and all drool.

Tell Tyler thank you for setting me up in this place. I've tried to reach out to him, but he's not answering my calls or my letters. I know his dad helped, but can you please tell them that as soon as I get out of here, I'm going to repay every penny. I can't believe I'm saying this, but I'm ready to be home. I know I need to get better first, and I'm working really hard at that. I promise.

Well, I need to go. Hope to see you soon. Hopefully, if things continue to go well, my doctor said I might be able to have visitors once a week instead of once a month. I hope so. They moved me to another wing. Doctor Harrington felt that I was doing well enough that I didn't have to be under 24/7 surveillance. I guess that's something.

I miss you.
All my love,
Lily
P.S. Please tell Tyler hi for me.

Lily folded the piece of paper and tucked it in the envelope. She didn't bother sealing it because she knew Jasper or one of the staff had to read it before it was mailed.

With a sigh, she moved from the table in the common room and walked over to Jasper. "Here ya go! I appreciate you doing this for me. I'll pay you back."

He winked at her. "I think I can handle a few cents, Lily."

She nodded.

"Ready to go?"

"As I'll ever be," she said with fake enthusiasm.

Together they walked down the long hall. This side of the hospital, unlike the one she'd previously been in, was different. The hallways were decorated with calming abstract art. Plants stood on pedestals. As if trying to give the place a little more of a homey feel would make it feel less like and institution.

As they rounded the corner, she saw Hercules. A wide smile crossed her face as she knelt in front of the massive chocolate. He went to her immediately and ran his tongue up the side of her face.

"Eww, gross," she giggled as she scratched behind his ears. His back leg tapped the floor excitedly as he plopped down and presented her with his belly.

"Aw, now you're just being greedy," she cooed, scratching his belly anyway. Hercules's owner talked to Jasper while Lily continued to talk and pet the dog. Finally, she pushed to her feet and wiped her slim covered hands on her pale blue scrub bottoms.

"He's always so happy to see you," Ronnie said patting the dog's massive head.

Lily smiled. "Well, that makes two of us. I love when he comes to visit."

Ronnie's smile faded a bit. "He might not be back for a while, though."

"Oh no. Why?"

"He's got to go get a tumor removed. It's pressing against his spinal cord."

She gasped. "Is he going to be okay?"

"The vet said there shouldn't be a problem. The tumor is self-contained. It should be an easy operation. Recovery will be a few months though."

Her heart sank a little. Several therapy animals made the rounds. There were a number of dogs, cats, birds, and even pigs that made weekly visits to the patients.

"Well, at least he'll be okay," Lily said.

"We need to get going," Jasper said kindly.

"Oh, right! Well, I'll see you guys soon." Lily scratched the dog's head. "You get better and come back to see me. Understand?"

He licked her hand and then trotted off down the hall, his nails clicking against the white tiles. She and Jasper continued down the hall until they stopped in front of a frosted glass door with the name Anastasia Harrington embossed on the door.

She hesitated.

"You've got this," Jasper said kindly.

She took a deep breath and slowly released it. Therapy was the hardest, most draining part of her day. When it was over, she typically had dinner and then went to bed.

Reaching out, Lily grasped the cold doorknob and twisted it. She looked over her shoulder at Jasper. He was still waiting patiently with an encouraging smile.

Lily pushed the door open and was instantly cocooned in the smell of pineapple and vanilla. Anastasia loved fruity scents. Her office wasn't cold and formal. Instead, it was calming and put Lily at ease.

She stepped through and closed the door behind her. "Ahh, Lily, right on time," she said by way of greeting. Anastasia moved from her desk and to the mini fridge in the corner of the room. She removed a can of Pepsi and bottle of water. She handed Lily the soda and then with her notebook in hand, moved to the wicker beach chair she always sat in.

Her entire office was decorated in the beach motif with the walls painted a calming blue. Various pictures and sea-themed articles hung on the walls. In front of the windows, colorful globes refracted the evening light, casting a myriad of colors around the room. In front of her chair was a table full of sand. It was used to aid in her sessions. It gave the patient something to focus on while using the small rake to rake different designs as they talked about their most painful memories.

"You're looking well," she said with a warm smile. Anastasia Harrington was a woman in her late twenties. She'd been working at the Asher House for three years and was still young enough to actually care about the patients in her care. Some of the other patients weren't so lucky. They had some of the other doctors, some of the ones that had been jaded by working entirely to many years.

Her features were exotic, with hazel, almond-shaped eyes fringed in heavy black lashes. Her lips were full and almost always smiling. The fact that she wore virtually no makeup only enhanced her natural beauty. Today she wore a light-yellow sundress under her white lab coat.

Lily took her usual seat, a giant overstuffed chair. As she sat, she removed her shoes and pulled her feet beneath her.

"How are you feeling?" she asked.

Lily lifted a shoulder. "Better today, I guess. I didn't have any dreams last night."

Her eyes brightened. "Oh Lily, that's such a good sign."

"I guess," she said with a shrug.

"It is. Don't you see it? We've lowered your dose of anxiety meds. Your body is handling it remarkably. I'm thrilled with this news."

Lily felt her spirits lift a little. "Yeah?"

She nodded. "Yes." She jotted something down, and then looked up. "I've also got some news. I wanted to run things by you."

"Okay?"

"Since you're sixteen and you'll be seventeen by the end of the school year, you have an option to become emancipated."

Lily frowned. "I didn't think I could do that until I was eighteen."

"Technically, no. Since the legal age limit of an adult is nineteen in Alabama, it would have to be extenuating circumstances."

"Are these extenuating circumstances?"

She nodded. "It would seem that your mother has gotten into some trouble."

Lily snorted. "There's a big shock. What happened?"

"That's not important."

She wasn't surprised at all that her mother had finally gotten picked up. She was surprised that it had taken so long. What hadn't surprised her was that Viki Lancaster had all but jumped at the chance to send Lily away.

The day her mother finally visited her in the hospital was still burned into her mind.

"Oh, my sweet baby!" Viki rushed across the hospital room and showered Lily with affection. Lily just stared at the woman. Chase and Tyler exchanged glances. "What have you done to yourself?" she crooned, laying on the motherly affection thick.

Viki's hair was washed and styled, and Lily wondered where she'd gotten the money for the new cut and color. Then she realized, she didn't want to know. Her mother was also wearing a new skirt and blouse, and for a minute, she almost looked like someone that gave a damn about her daughter.

The older woman sat on the edge of the bed and smoothed Lily's hair away from her face while saying how much she loved her and how sorry she was that this had happened. If only she'd seen the signs. For a moment, Lily wanted to pretend that her mother cared. She knew better.

That evidence came as she signed the papers to take Lily away. "It's for the best, baby girl. I just want you to be happy and healthy again." Boy, she was laying it on thick for Andre.

Andre's eyes slid to Lily, and she could see the sympathy there. He wasn't buying her mother's act either.

After all the staff left the room, Viki turned her eyes to her daughter. The warm smile turned frigid as she leered at her from the foot of the bed. "You know, I think it is for the best that you're locked up for the next year.

Maybe it will teach you to run around making false accusations about innocent men."

Lily never got a chance to respond because Chase and Tyler jumped from their spots on the couch. Tyler stood protectively at Lily's side while Chase got in Viki's face.

"You need to leave now!" he said. His voice was so cold and calm; it made Lily shiver.

Viki turned her gaze to Chase. "You know she'll never pick you, right. She's a little whore just like me. I should have known she'd tried to steal my boyfriend."

"Steal. Your. Boyfriend?" Chase said through gritted teeth.

"Chase, don't," Lily whispered. She clung to Tyler's hand as the storm between her mother and Chase exploded.

"She did not steal your boyfriend you crazy old hag. That man brutalized her so badly that she's going to be physically scared for the rest of her life. HE'S the reason she's in here. You're the reason she's in here because you let him have her."

Viki's eyes widened, and she took a step back.

Chase nodded. "That's right. I was there after he left. I heard what you told her. I watched you chase after the man that tortured your daughter. I'm the one that carried her away and we," he pointed to Tyler, "are the ones that picked up the pieces. As far as I'm concerned, you're the one that should be strapped to that bed. You crazy, psychotic bitch!"

Viki leered at him and then looked at Lily. "Good riddance. You were a mistake."

"Lily?"

Lily blinked away the memory and looked at Anastasia. "I'm sorry. What?"

"Where did you go just now?"

"Nowhere I needed to be," Lily said.

Anastasia pulled tissues from the box and walked around her desk. She handed them to Lily, and it was only then that Lily realized that she'd been crying.

"Sorry," she mumbled.

"Don't be sorry. You were back in the hospital room that last day with your mom, weren't you?"

Lily nodded and looked at the tissue in her hands. "How'd you know?"

"I mentioned your mother. It's to be expected, and it's something I promise we're going to work through. Okay?"

Lily sniffed and swiped the tears away. "Okay. What were you saying?"

Anastasia smiled. "Since you're going to be seventeen when you leave, I believe that I can pull some strings and get you the right paperwork to become emancipated."

Hope soared through Lily. "Really?"

She nodded but then her smile slipped a little. This caused Lily's smile to fall. "What's the catch?"

"You're going to have to continue to do well and prove that you can be stable. Mr. Anderson agreed to help you in all legal and financial ways while you're in here."

Lily's eyes widened. This was news to her. Tyler's father was not the most pleasant man on the face of the planet.

"This seems to shock you."

"What? The fact that a man, like Elliot Anderson, is helping a mental case like me?"

"Lily!" Anastasia gently scolded.

"What? It's the truth. He's a narcissistic jackass that doesn't give two wet farts about his own son. So yes, I do have a hard time believing that he's doing this out of the goodness of his heart."

In fact, she was sure of it. Elliot did not do charity if it wasn't going to benefit him in some way. It bugged her to know that she was going to be indebted to him.

"Be that as it may, he's taking care of things. I suggest you use it to its fullest extent. The plan is for you to take classes here with a few other of the patients so you won't fall behind in your studies. Starting tomorrow, you'll be getting caught up on all the work you've missed from your sophomore year. Then you'll immediately begin your junior year. If you keep your head down, focus and work hard, there's a good chance you can finish your junior year by the time you get out of here."

"How is that possible?"

"Well, I've been going over your previous transcripts. Lily, you're a brilliant young woman. You were top in your class. I believe that if you set your mind to it, you can do twice the work."

Lily shrugged. "Sure, why not! What else am I going to do all day?"

Anastasia laughed. "That's one way to look at it. If—when—you accomplish this, it will give you a fresh start for your senior year."

"Really?" Lily asked. She had mixed emotions about the whole situation. Getting out in time to finish high school was great, in theory. It also meant that she would have to go back and face all the stares, the whispers, and rumors. Was that something she could do?

Anastasia nodded. "We will start tomorrow so we can get you caught up to speed with all the classes you've missed since you've been in here. I can't make you any promises, but it's not outside the realm of possibility. You've done very well so far, but I'm not going to lie, Lily, you still have a long way to go. It's going to be hard, and there might be setbacks, but our ultimate goal is to get you healthy. The rest will fall into place with time."

Lily nodded. "I can do this."

Anastasia's smile widened. "I absolutely believe that, but it's time for us to dive in and get to the source of everything so we can truly begin the healing process."

Lily shifted uncomfortably in her seat and chewed on the skin around her fingernail. It hurt, but it was distracting.

"Isn't that what we've been doing?"

She nodded. "Yeah, in some ways. But, what I like to do in cases like yours is start out slow, as I'm sure you have noticed. In the beginning, it was about establishing trust between us. It was about getting to know one another, and now that we've reached that stage. It's time to set our sights forward and go for it."

Lily was silent for a long while. The clock on the wall count the seconds. Her eyes watched the seconds as the mermaid's tail on the clock moved back and forth—acting as a pendulum—ticking away the minutes of her session.

"Today we're going to start where all of this started. We're going to go back to the day that is the catalyst for everything."

And just like that, Lily's good mood plummeted. Since being committed and starting therapy, they've been slowly going through her childhood. They started as far back as she could remember, and now, they were getting to the source of her pain. They'd tried to address it in the beginning, but Lily had a breakdown and was forced to be restrained because the flashbacks had gotten so bad. Initially, she was only supposed to stay six months. However, after a more in-depth evaluation, they'd decided that she would be better suited to take a full year for recovery.

Since beginning sessions, they only brushed against the *incident*, but it was just for about five minutes and at the end of each session. Anastasia was changing the pattern, and it made her uncomfortable.

She squirmed in her seat and frowned. Anxiety began to twist her stomach in knots and work its way into her chest. What if therapy wasn't going to work? What if she stayed locked away forever?

"Lily."

Her breathing was becoming harder. "Lily, I need you to look at me," Anastasia said calmly.

Before the darkness could ultimately take over, Lily lifted her gaze to meet Anastasia's. "There you are."

"What if I can't do this?"

Anastasia gave her a warm smile. "I don't think that's an option for you. Not because you don't have a choice, but because you're one of the hardest fighters I have ever seen. Some people bounce back from the stuff you've gone through. Others don't."

"You don't think I'm dramatic?"

"Do you?"

Lily frowned. She hated it when she did that reverse question thing. It was annoying. "Sometimes, yes. I don't like being the victim."

"Then don't be."

She could feel the pain welling up in her chest. The only thing she could do is nod.

Anastasia pursed her lips. "Do you know what the mandala is?"

Lily frowned. "Yeah. It's that flower-thingy. Doesn't it have something to do with Buddha or someone like that?"

She chuckled. "Flower-thingy, yes. It is also used in the Buddhist faith. It means different things to different people. Some believe it can represent a person's journey through life. They can sometimes be linked to where one has been and the path they are meant to take in life. For some, it's thought to be a great symbol of inner peace."

Lily watched as she moved across the room and removed a book from one of the shelves. She returned to her chair and flipped through the pages until she stopped. Turning the book, she tapped the picture of a black and white, intricately designed mandala. It was beautiful in its complexity. The lines all intersecting and crossing to form a beautiful image. Behind the mandala were leaves and flowers, drawn with the same intricate swirls and patterns.

Lily looked up at her. "How's this have anything to do with me?"

"You see, when the mandala was created, it was so beautifully made that it was believed when an individual's mind absorbed the patterns, it blocked out any negativity. When this happens, it allows the individual to feel calm and centered, giving the mind a rest from the rat-race of life. If you focus on the mandala, it almost works like hypnotism."

Lily stared at the picture for a moment longer. "I can see how that can happen."

"I want you to think about this mandala as we start our therapy. When you begin to feel all the bad begin to come at you, focus your attention on this. Find your center."

Lily arched a brow at her and chuckled. "I didn't take you for the hippy-dippy sort, doc?"

Anastasia chuckled and placed the book on Lily's lap, still opened on the page with the mandala. Lily looked at the picture for a moment and then took a deep breath. "Okay. Where do we start?"

"How about we talk about *that* day. How did it start?"

When she didn't answer right away, Anastasia added, "Take your time."

It was now or never. There was no way of going around this roadblock. She was going to have to plow through, hoping and praying that when she came out on the other side, she wouldn't be broken beyond repair.

Reaching forward, Lily took her Pepsi from the table and swallowed a long drink. The carbonation burned, but she didn't notice.

When she set it back on the table, she took a deep breath. "The day started out just like every other. Chase, Tyler, and me met at Tyler's house and walked to school together. . . ."

Chapter 20

Not until we are lost do we begin to find ourselves.

~Henry David Thoreau

Lily,

Sorry, it's taken me so long to write back. I've been working almost non-stop. It's nearly two in the morning, and I have to get up at four to go to work. It's good to hear from you. I can't imagine what it's like in there. Hey, do you remember when we used to sleep in the tunnels at the playground? Remember when we used to lay on the tops and stare at the stars? I do. I think about it sometimes. The stars were our happy place.

I still look at those stars, and think of you. Sometimes, clouds are covering the stars, and I can't see them, but I know they are still there. I know what you're dealing with can't be easy. I can't imagine what you're going through. As for the broken part . . . we're all broken in some way. If you're still broken when you get out, I will help you put the pieces back. I will use duct tape, crazy glue, or whatever it takes. You're going to get through this. We're here for you.

So, now that I've gotten all the sappy business out of the way, you wanna know something about home. Hmmm, let me see. Well, you're not the talk of the town anymore! I know, that probably upsets you, but you've been dethroned in the gossip department. As it happens, Kiera is pregnant. I know, it shocks me too. (okay, not really) But still. It's actually kind of sad, and while she is still a royal bitch, she was played. Dude knocked'er up, and when he found out, he bolted.

Not sure if you've heard bout your mom or not, but she got picked up for solicitation and busted for narcs. Apparently, she was dealing meth and coke and tried to do so to an undercover DEA agent. She's going to be away for a while.

Aside from that. Ain't much to report. Mom is doing well. We actually moved into the old Whittaker house at the end of Orchid Street. My mom met a guy and, dare I say it, he's not a complete douchecanoe. I met him a couple weeks after you left. Mom said she wanted to make sure he's the real deal before she introduced us. Guess they been dating for about three months already. He's been working with me on some of my football moves. We all sit down to dinner every night. It's still weird, but nice. I guess. He's firm and grounded me because I was late for curfew. CURFEW. When in the hell have I ever had a curfew? As weird as this is, I was okay with that.

OH!!! AND!!!!! She's going to have a baby. Can you believe it? I'm going to be a big brother. It seems weird, but I'm kind of excited about it. I guess it was an accident, but they seem happy! I haven't seen mom smile like this in . . . well ever. I don't think I've ever seen her smile like this.

Yes, I'm working at Armstrong's. He's paying decent. It's hot as balls hauling hay, but it pays. He said he wants to keep me on to help with the ranch year-round. Says he needs a foreman that he can trust. Can you believe it? The town hoodlum, a person someone else can trust. Yeah, me either.

Football camp starts next week. I'm excited cause Coach said that I have a real shot at going to college on a scholarship for football. Can you imagine? Getting the hell outta this place and going to college. Who would'a thunk it?

I'll give Tyler your message when I hear from him. He left for California three weeks ago, and I haven't heard from him yet. He's in a weird place right now. That stuff you told him at the hospital before you left really hurt him. I know—and he knows—that you don't believe he was there, but it still cut him. I get it. Just give him time. That's all he needs.

Okay, I'm super proud of the progress you're making. As soon as you get out, we're going to spend days doing nothing but eating pizza and watching movies. So, get your ass better so I can have my best friend back.

Remember, when you're feeling lost just look up and find the path to us. It will help you. I know it has helped me.

I miss you more!
I'll see you soon.
Always,
Chase

Chase folded the letter and slid it into the envelope. After addressing it and placing it on top of his desk, he leaned back in his chair and scrubbed the heels of his hands over his eyes. Exhaustion begged him to go to bed, but his mind refused to shut up long enough to allow it. He was torn between his friends.

Tyler was in California at a football training camp at USC and Lily was in a sanitarium. It wasn't until they were both gone that he realized how dependent on them he'd become. Watching Lily being hauled away was almost more than he could handle. She'd had to be sedated when they told her she would be spending six months in a mental institution, and it hadn't gotten any better once she got inside. The day he found out she would be gone for an entire year, broke his heart.

Everything was changing. The dynamic between the three of them seemed to be upset. Tyler was withdrawing and keeping to himself; Lily was trying to get healthy, both mentally and physically. That left him alone. Which, was both good and bad. Good because it gave him a chance to figure out who he was without Tyler and Lily around; bad because he missed them something fierce and was having a hard time finding out who he was.

"When did I become the sane one?" he muttered.

Chase pulled his boots off and got dressed for bed. He was just about to turn his desk light off when there was a soft knock on the door.

"Yeah?"

His mom pushed to door open and walked into the room, her swollen belly leading the way. Her hair was wadded into a knot on top of her head. She wore a long t-shirt, a thin robe and a pair of giant wool socks. In her hands was a pint of ice cream.

He snickered, and she just spooned ice cream into her mouth and shrugged. "Don't judge!"

This time he laughed and held up his hands. "Hey, no judgment here."

"What you doing up so late? Don't you have to work in a couple hours?"

He nodded. "Yeah, just had some things to take care of." She looked over his shoulder at the desk.

"Is that from Lily?"

"Yeah."

"How's she doing?" she asked as she shoved another spoonful of chocolate ice cream into her mouth.

Chase shrugged. "Hard to tell. Seems like she's doing okay. Her letter seems a bit brighter than the last one. I don't know." He sighed and sagged heavily onto the bed. "I just keep replaying everything in my head, trying to find where I messed up. I shoulda done this or that. If I woulda been there more and not—"

"You stop right there, young man," she said firmly. She placed the ice cream on the dresser, sat in his desk chair, and rolled it to where she was sitting in front of him. "You listen to me and listen to me well."

He looked into his mom's blue eyes.

"You didn't have no control over what happened. That child lived through the most horrific thing a person could ever go through. Her innocence was ripped from her. You helped her the best you knew how. Did you do it the right way? Probably not. You shoulda went to someone. Then again, you weren't exactly in a position of trusting any adults. Lord knows I wasn't no help. So, that's on me. The important thing is, you're there for her now. You continue to be there for her. You be there for Ty, 'cause he needs it too."

Chase nodded. "Yeah, he does.

"But don't forget that you need care too. Take care of yourself. Don't carry all the burden alone. You've had to do that for far too long. You don't have to no more. I wasn't there for a lot of years, but I'm here now. Let me carry some of this stuff. Okay?"

The only thing he could do was stare at the woman in front of him. She'd changed into a completely different person. The dark circles were gone from beneath her eyes. She'd gained weight but in a good way. All in all, she was the mother he'd always dreamed of having.

"Thanks, Mom."

She gripped his chin and tilted his face up. "I can't believe you're not a little boy anymore. You've turned into an amazing young man. I'm just sorry I missed so much of it." Tears filled her eyes and slipped down her cheeks.

"The past is the past, mom. You're here now. That's all that matters."

"I'm gonna do right by both of you," she said resting her hand on her swollen midsection.

He nodded. "I know."

She pushed herself to her feet, groaning the whole way. After patting him on the shoulder, she grabbed her ice cream and closed the door softly.

He picked his phone up from the dresser and tapped out a message.

Me: *How was practice?*

He didn't have to wait long before the response came in.

Ty: *Not terrible. The quarterback is a prick, but other than that. It was okay.*
Me: *That's good.*

Before he could send his message, another popped in.

Ty: *how's your mom doing? The baby? sorry hvn't msged back. been hectic.*

Chase's fingers hovered over the screen of his phone for a moment before responding.

Me: *she's doing good. It's still weird seeing her happy.*

He pressed send and then quickly tapped another message.

Me: *got a letter from Lily today. She's doing good. Asking bout you. You need to tlk to her.*

Chase stared at the screen for a long time. His eyes grew heavy as he waited. Five minutes passed and then ten. He must have dozed off because his phone dinged fifteen minutes later, and it caused him to jerk awake. He was amazed that he'd fallen asleep sitting up and without face-planting into the floor.

He woke up his screen and read the message.

Ty: *I know. I will. Not ready.*
Me: *soon?*
Ty: *Yes.*
Me: *promise?*

A media message appeared, and it was a picture of Tyler's pinky, causing Chase to chuckle. The pinky promise was something that each of them did with Lily. This was the first time it was done between them. He chuckled and plugged his phone into the charger and groaned when he saw 3:09 on the clock. Work was going to be miserable.

With a weary sigh, he crossed the room and switched off his lamp. He grabbed Lily's letter and fell into bed. His mind was racing a million miles a second. The light of the full moon streamed through the window. He read the letter a dozen times. His eyes kept reading *I miss you.* They were the last thing he saw as he closed his eyes.

"I miss you too, Lils."

Lily stared at the ceiling. It had been three days since *the* session with Anastasia. She called it *the* session because it was the one she finally opened up about being molested—holding nothing back. There had been a lot of tears shed, sobs and rage released on that day; not to mention the contents of her stomach two different times as she relived the horror of that night.

She'd left the session wiped out and so drained that she went straight to her room and slept from six in the evening to nine the following morning. Lily had found out that Anastasia had ordered her to not be disturbed. For that, she was grateful.

Closing her eyes, she turned her face into the rays of sun streaming through the glass. It warmed her skin, and for a moment she was transported back to a time when she, Chase, and Tyler were happy. They were playing in Wilson's creek. They were just barely twelve years old, and that's when she thought she had a crush on Tyler.

When she opened her eyes, she realized that she was smiling. She felt lighter. She'd faced the demon. While she still needed to address it and begin to heal, she knew she was on her way. For the first time in her life, she felt hope. Like the sun warming her skin, the feeling of hope warmed her.

She was just climbing to her feet when a knock sounded on the door. "Yeah?!" she called, clearing her throat. She reached for the water glass beside her bed and washed away the grit as her door opened.

Anastasia walked in, carrying the sweet smell of Jasmine with her. "You look really good this morning, Lily," she said.

Lily nodded. "I feel good. I mean I still feel anxious and nervous about our next session because I know we're going to have to do that again, but, as a whole, I feel better."

"That's wonderful. Well, I came to give you some news."

"Okay?"

"Well, I've gone over my notes and your progress. I've decided that you can have open visitation."

Lily's eyes widened. "Really?"

"Mmhmm!"

Lily gave a little squeal and launched herself to her feet. She wrapped her arms around Anastasia's neck without thinking. She then immediately took a step back. "I-I'm sorry. I know that probably wasn't appropriate."

Anastasia shrugged and laughed. "You initiated it. I did not. No harm."

"Okay, so what exactly does this mean?"

"It means you can have a visitor up to two times a week. I've also pushed through to get you some phone privileges. I'm happy with your progress, *but*," she began, making sure she had Lily's full attention, "I'm doing this in good faith, okay. If I see for a minute that you're slipping or going backward, we'll go back on limitation. I'm going to leave you on your antidepressants for a while longer, but we're going to start weaning you off the anti-psychotics."

"You don't think I'm schizophrenic?"

"No. After reviewing your case and your sessions, you don't have the symptoms."

Lily frowned. "Then what about the voices?"

"They were manifestations of your subconscious. In short, they were your brain's way of working through the trauma you went through. Now that we've had this break-through, we are going to focus on getting you better. I have high hopes for you, Lily. Just in these last five months, you've changed. I've seen the way you work and the way you struggle. You broke, and you broke hard. I don't believe you were suicidal. The accident at the school was just that, an accident."

"What's next then?"

"We're going to open up every single facet of your life. Every day. Every minute. We're going to explore your relationships and your life. Then, once that is done, we are going to work on coping mechanisms. You were a cutter. We're going to find a way for you to channel your issues into something constructive instead of destructive. It's important for you to understand and realize that while you're having good days now, there will be things that might trigger you in the future. You're going to have days that are high and some that are low. I want to approach these days without medication at first. I don't like to medicate people unless absolutely necessary."

"Is it like PTSD, the good days and bad?"

"It's exactly that. We're going to also work with methods for that, explore different avenues that will help you overcome any situation you might find yourself in. I'm thrilled, Lily. You're the reason I do my job. You're the reason I love my job."

Heat filled Lily's neck. She wasn't used to getting compliments. If felt odd to have an adult give her praises.

"Thank you."

"You're very welcome. I'll see you this afternoon," she said turning to leave. She was out the door when she abruptly turned back around. "Oh, I almost forgot. You got two letters today."

Excitement bounded through her as she grabbed the letters and walked back over to her bed. She recognized Chase's handwriting immediately. The second letter was from Tyler. She wasn't ready to read that one yet.

Hooking her finger beneath the tab, she popped the tape that one of the staff members was kind enough to place on the opened envelope. Then feeling giddy, she leaned her back against the wall and with the sun streaming through the window, she read Chase's letter.

She smiled fondly as she read it once, twice, and a third time before folding it and tucking it in her nightstand. Then, with a deep breath, she lifted the letter from Tyler.

She noticed that the return address was from California. "Well, at least he's not hiding from me," she muttered as she removed the letter from the envelope. Her heart thrummed in her chest. What did he have to say? Was he still upset with her? Would he forgive her?

Her hands shook with anticipation as she unfolded the paper.

However, her heart plummeted as she read the short note written in Tyler's beautiful handwriting.

Lily,

I need time to sort through things. I don't know how much or how long. You focus on working on you. I've got to do the same for me. I don't need distractions right now.

Be well.
Tyler

And just like that, Lily understood what Anastasia meant when she said some days would be better than others because she felt like she'd just been punched in the gut.

Two steps forward and five steps back.

Chapter 21

Release the past, the present and the future.
Give your mind the freedom it needs
to take you beyond suffering.

~Buddha

The days faded into weeks, and pretty soon the weeks faded into months. Lily established a routine and began to find herself. As Anastasia has said, there were setbacks, but when they happened, Lily just pushed herself harder.

She began to take advantage of the physical therapy facilities when she wasn't studying. She quickly discovered that running was the way she coped. When she was on the treadmill, especially after a hard session, everything seemed to melt away.

It had taken months, but she was finally able to move past the rape. She could talk openly about it without feeling violently ill. She didn't like talking about it, but she could do it if need be. After dealing with that, and the abandonment of her mother, Lily focused on her abusive relationship with Lucas. It was after she'd dealt with the first two issues that she realized the problem Tyler and Chase had with him.

Chase visited regularly. However, she hadn't heard from Tyler since his first and only letter. This was a major sore point for her, and after feeling sorry for herself, she'd gotten pissed. She was still working through the anger issue with him. She understood that he was hurt, but it hadn't been her fault. Chase had informed her that instead of returning home for their junior year, Tyler was going to stay in California. He claimed that the athletics department at the local school was second to none. However, Lily suspected that he didn't want to be around her. It hurt, but she tried not to let it discourage her too much.

"You look beautiful," Anastasia said as she knocked on Lily's room door.

Lily brushed her hands down the front of her jeans. She wore a simple, scoop neck t-shirt that hugged her. Since working out daily, her body was toned and defined. She had curves in places she had no idea existed. She looked like herself and yet, at the same time, she didn't.

Her hair fell in glossy blond waves down her back. Anastasia had given her lip gloss and mascara, which was all she said Lilly needed. The girl that she was staring at was no longer the little girl. This was the first time the reality of everything was sinking in.

"What if I'm not ready? What if I have a breakdown and flip? Are you sure about this because I'm not sure? What if I can't find a job? What will I do?" The questions and panic tumbled from her.

Anastasia crossed the room and placed her hands-on Lily's shoulders. "Look at me," she said firmly. Lily sucked in a deep breath and held it in her lungs for the count of five before releasing it. "You've got this. We will still have our sessions once a week. You have my cell and home number. You're ready for this. Don't think for a minute that I would be releasing you if I thought you weren't."

Lily nodded, and Anastasia continued. "I'm so incredibly proud of you. There are not a lot of people that can't say what you can. The truth is, more people remain victims of their mind. You fought, and you won. Yes, some days will be better than others, but you've got this."

Lily felt her confidence swell and realized her beloved doctor was right. She had this.

"Oh, and one more thing. Chase is here."

Excitement bubbled in the pit of Lily's stomach. Chase had been to see her almost every week since she could have more frequent visits. There only a few times he hadn't been able to make it. In fact, because his work schedule had become intense over the holiday break, especially with the cold weather, he'd been working long days and nights at the ranch. The last time she'd seen him had been three weeks ago at Christmas. They'd talked every day on the phone for thirty minutes. He told her about his day, and she'd told him about hers. Sometimes, they just sat in silence. Their bond was growing stronger, yet, at the same time, she still had a bit of a hole in her heart where Tyler was supposed to be.

"I'm ready," she said shaking away the sad thoughts she was having about Tyler and checking her reflection one last time. She grabbed her backpack and slung it over her shoulder. Then, without looking back, she walked out of her room.

Together they walked to the end of the hall and through the security double doors. In the main lobby, standing in front of the fireplace, Chase stood staring into the fire. Lily's heart stuttered in her chest. She took a quick moment to study his profile while he wasn't looking.

He wore a long-sleeve gray, thermal shirt that was pulled tight around his broad shoulders and hugged his midsection. Low-rise jeans fell perfectly on his hips, the cuffs at the bottom cut an inch up the sides so they would fit over his dusty work boots. He was much bigger than she remembered. His shoulders were broad and muscled, tapering down into a narrow waist. The person standing in front of her was no longer Chase the tough little boy. No, the person standing in front of her was all man. When had that happened? It had only been three weeks.

His hands were stuffed into his pockets as he watched the fire. He wore a hat she'd seen him wear hundreds of times. It was a hat she'd gotten him years ago for his birthday. The trucker style hat had a green front with the bill fraying along the sides. It had been worn so much, the white was dingy and stained, but it gave it character. Everything about it screamed farm boy, which is why she'd bought it for him in the first place.

When they'd been kids, he'd dreamed about owning his own spread. Around the front of the hat was green with the words *Farm Boy* stitched on it. Blond hair curled around the nape of his neck, in desperate need of a cut. The dancing firelight flickered, highlighting a strong, square jaw dusted with light blond stubble. Her heart did a little leap, and butterflies fluttered in her stomach. This was Chase. He was her best friend.

He must have sensed her watching him because he turned. When his eyes met hers, a bright smile tilted the corners of his mouth, revealing white, slightly crooked, teeth. Lily didn't think twice as she propelled herself across the short distance between them and catapulted herself into his arms. His arms circled her waist as he lifted her feet from the floor and held her tightly. This had been the first time they hugged since the day she left the hospital.

She squeezed him as if her life depended on it, and he returned the hug. The comfort of his arms had always been a place she felt safe. It was no different now, a year later. It felt good to have his arms hold her again. She took a deep breath. This was it. *This* was how she knew she was going to be okay because when he hugged her, she was home.

The moment seemed to last forever as he just held her. She breathed in deep, the scent of fabric softener and cologne filling her senses. Tears burned her eyes, but they were happy tears.

Finally, he placed her back on her feet and held her out at arm's length. "Look at you," he said his blue eyes roaming over her. She could feel flush rising into her cheeks as she tucked a strand of hair behind her ear.

"I have to say, Lils. You look amazing." The low, husky tone of his voice made goosebumps scatter across her arms.

"Don't look so bad yourself," she replied. Reaching out she gripped his bicep. "Wow, looks like working on the ranch agrees with you."

Chase chuckled, pulling his hat off and raking his hand through his blond curls. "And you need a haircut," she said ruffling his downy soft hair.

"Ain't really had a whole lot of time."

Anastasia walked up to them, and Chase turned. "Doc, good to see you again."

"You as well, Chase. Take care of our girl here, okay?"

Chase draped his arm over Lily's shoulder and tugged her into his side. "You got it."

"I have no doubt." There was a glimmer in Anastasia's eyes as she looked at Lily and then back to Chase. She chuckled to herself as if thinking of something funny.

Before Lily could question her, Anastasia lifted the backpack Lily had dropped. "Our appointment is next Friday. You have the address?"

Lily nodded.

"I'll get'er there Doc."

"I know you will." She then turned and looked at Lily. "I think you're in good hands. Be well, sweetheart. Call me if you *ever* need anything."

Lily stepped forward and embraced the woman. She could feel emotion bubbling in her chest. "Thank you for not giving up on me," she whispered.

Anastasia's embraced tightened briefly before she stepped away. Lily noticed that the woman's eyes were misty.

"Well, what are you waiting for? Get her outta here. Frankly, I'm getting tired of her," she teased.

Chase and Lily walked through the front door and down the steps. Parked out front was a bright red pick-up. It was an eighties model Chevrolet, but it looked brand new. The Cherry red paint glistened in the afternoon sunlight.

Lily's eyes widened. "Is that yours?"

Chase nodded proudly. "Trevor helped me buy it with the money I make at the ranch and the other odd jobs I take around town I'm just about to get it paid off. We actually rebuilt her from the ground up."

"We?" she asked as he opened the passenger door for her. She climbed in and settled into the warm seat. She shivered slightly as Chase climbed in.

"Here, wear this," he said reaching behind the seat and pulling out a hoodie.

"Thanks. I didn't think about having you bring me a coat. It's not like I really had a use for one in there."

"It's all good." Chase turned the key, and the engine roared to life. The low rumble vibrated through the cab.

"She sounds like a beast," she chuckled as he put it into gear and sped from the parking lot.

"Oh, she is."

"So, who is this we?"

"What?"

"We? You said *we* built her from the ground up."

"Oh, right. Trevor. He owns a chain of body shops. He'd just put one in town when he and my mom met. He let me work at the shop to pay for the parts and paint job."

"Wow. He sounds like a nice guy."

Chase nodded. "He is. I keep waiting for the other foot to drop, but it's been a little over a year, and he's still cool. He also volunteers with the fire department."

"And you have a sister! How is Coraline?"

"She's spoiled," he chuckled as he reached into his back pocket and removed his wallet. He flipped it open while holding onto the steering wheel with one hand and handed her the wallet with the other.

There were four pictures inside. The first one was of a toothless, chubby-cheek little girl with dark brown eyes and a riot of blond curls. "She looks like you," she noted.

"I get that a lot."

She flipped to the next picture. It was of the two of them when they were seven or eight years old before they met Tyler. They were sitting together in a mud hole covered head to toe in thick brown goop. Chase had his arm slung around her as they both grinned back at the camera—each missing their front teeth.

"I remember when we took this," she said showing him the picture.

"I know. I was so mad that you lost your tooth before I did."

Lily laughed. "You stayed up all night wiggling and pulling on yours until it finally came out."

"Hurt like hell too," he mused.

She turned to the next picture, and her heart tightened. It was a picture of the three of them. Tyler was sitting on the park bench with Lily in the middle and Chase on her other side. They both had their arms behind her as the three of them ate ice cream. She remembered Chase begging his mother to take the picture. It was taken the summer after they met Tyler.

She flipped to the last picture, and the air left her lungs. Tears burned her eyes as she stared at their three smiling faces. The two boys she recognized, but the girl was someone she didn't. Her face was sunken in with dark circles under her eyes. Her freshly colored hair looked lackluster and dull.

"Wow," she muttered.

Chase looked at her and then the picture. He shifted in his seat. "Yeah, I got it off your phone. It was the most recent one I had of the three of us."

"I don't even recognize myself," she whispered, tracing her thumb over the ghost of a girl she'd once been.

"Because that's not you."

She didn't know what it was, but the tone of his voice caused her to look up. There was something different about the way he was looking at her, and it made her uncomfortable, but not in a bad way. His eyes were on hers, and the inside of the truck seemed to grow warmer. They were stopped at the intersection that would take them back into Raven's Bend.

The blaring of a horn behind them caused both to startle. Chase cleared his throat and pointed his truck toward home. As they drove through the city limits of their tiny town, she noted all the things that had changed.

"There's a McDonalds now?"

He laughed. "Yeah, it's where all the cool kids hang out."

"Sign me up," she joked.

They drove down Maine Street, and everything seemed so different and yet, the same. "Do you care to take me to my house," she asked.

He slowed the truck and turned down the street that would take them to the trailer park they once lived in. "Are you sure?"

"I need to," she said.

"There's nothing there anymore. Your place caught fire after it was raided. Your mom was cooking meth, and it exploded. Nearly killed the Thompson's and the Smiths."

"Oh."

Chase turned into the driveway, and Lily realized the place looked much different. The yards were neatly kept, and some even sported decorations.

"It's different."

"Back in July, some guy from Montgomery bought the whole park. Cleaned it up and repaired all the trailers. He's turned it into a pretty decent place. It took him a while to get all the trash out, but now, some good people live here.

Trepidation crept up her spine as the tires crunched over the gravel. They pulled to a stop in the very last lot. As he'd said, there was no longer a house there, but a brightly painted playground. Despite the chilly thirty-nine-degree weather, children were laughing and playing. They slid down the slides, pumped their legs on the swings to make them go higher, and climbed fearlessly all over the equipment.

Chase put the truck in park, and they just sat there watching. There was a little girl, not more than seven or eight, running away from a little boy who was carrying what looked to be a frog. Nostalgia washed over her.

"It seems fitting," she said thoughtfully.

"What's that?"

"That something so simple, pure and perfect has taken root where something evil happened. It's replacing years of pain and sorrow. It gets to hear the laughter of children where it was once nothing but tears. There's happiness instead of terror."

"I never really thought of it like that."

Lily laughed softly. "I've had nothing but time to think."

He took a deep breath and pushed it out. "Well, you ready to go home?"

She chewed anxiously on her bottom lip. "Are you sure your mom doesn't mind me crashing for a while?"

Chase snorted. "Are you kidding me? She's talked about nothing but you coming home for days. Honestly, she's about to drive us crazy. I might just be sick of you already."

Lily laughed as they left her childhood torment behind her once and for all.

"Seriously though. The house is huge. You even get your own bedroom."

Lily's eyes widened. "The couch would have been fine."

He rolled his eyes. "Yeah, okay. You tell my mother that."

"It's so weird."

"What's that?"

"Seeing you happy."

"I know right?"

He pulled his truck under a carport beside a small SUV. He opened the door but when Lily didn't turn do the same he stopped.

"Lils? You okay?"

"Yes. No." She laughed anxiously. "Just being back is a bit overwhelming. I don't know what I'm going to do when school starts."

He grabbed her hand and squeezed it. The rough calluses scraping against her skin gave her the assurance she needed. "It's a good thing we've got seven and a half months to get adjusted, huh?"

He let go of her and rounded the front of the truck. He pulled the door open, and she slid out into the chilly air.

"Welcome home," he said holding his arms out proudly.

The two-story house was painted a cheery yellow with light blue shutters. The wrap around porch boasted wicker furniture and a porch swing. It looked like something out of a magazine. "It's so nice," she said as they walked up the sidewalk.

"Yeah. Mom and Trev have been working a lot on remodeling. There are still a few things that need to be fixed, but for the most part, it's been almost completely rebuilt."

Both stopped in their tracks when they spotted someone sitting on the top steps.

Her heart jumped into her throat as she watched him climb to his feet. He gave her a warm smile as he walked down the stairs and stopped in front of her. Tears spilled over her lashes as she felt the hole in her heart began to heal.

"Tyler," she whispered.

"Welcome home, Lils."

Chapter 22

What seems to us as bitter trials
are often blessings in disguise.

~Oscar Wilde

The only thing Lily and Chase could do was stare. The first thing that Lily noticed that the Tyler she'd last seen was not the same one standing in front of her now. Like Chase, he'd changed. He was now taller and leaner. He wore a dark red thermal shirt, much like the one Chase was wearing. The material stretched to fit his broad shoulders and muscled arms. The front was tucked back behind the simple belt he wore. His hands were thrust into the pockets of his jeans.

His clothing, however, wasn't what she noticed. The roundness of childhood was no longer on his face. Now, his face was lean and angular with prominent cheekbones lightly dusted with dark shadow. A gray beanie covered his black hair. Beneath his dark brown eyes were dark shadows making it seem like he hadn't slept in days.

She couldn't say anything. The only thing she could do was stare, unsure of what there was to say. The last thing he'd told her was that he needed time. That was almost a year ago. A million questions raced through her head, but not even one of them made it through her lips.

Chase must have sensed her unease because he was the first to move; to speak. "Ty, man, it's good to see you," he said taking a step forward and pulling Tyler in for a manly hug. It was only then that Tyler broke his gaze from hers as he embraced Chase.

Chase took a step back, smiling from ear to ear. "It's good to see you, Richie. I thought you weren't going to be home until August."

Tyler shrugged. "Don't' call me Richie and I know. I wanted to come home. I missed—" He shifted his gaze to Lily, but only briefly. "I missed you guys."

185

He walked down the last step and came to a stop in front Lily. She held her breath unsure of what she could say. There was so much that needed to be said. She needed to explain everything, and more than anything, she needed to apologize. But, how was she supposed to do that? She'd hurt him, and even though it hadn't been intentional, the pain had still cut deep.

She was aware of Chase watching them as they stood awkwardly in front of one another. She opened her mouth to say something, but Tyler beat her to it. "You look amazing," he said softly.

She flushed. "Thanks. Spending a year in the looney bin'll do that to a person," she joked. It had the desired effect because he smiled.

Without a word, he pulled her into his arms, holding her tightly. She sighed and wrapped her arms around him, clinging to him as if her life depended on it. Taking a deep breath, she breathed in the scent that she knew belonged to only him. It was of cologne and fabric softener. She felt the tension leave his body as he held her tightly.

"I'm so sorry," he whispered against her hair. "I'm so, so sorry."

Tears burned her eyes and spilled from her lashes, soaking the front of his shirt. She sobbed softly into his shirt front. It finally felt as if her world was whole again. All the pieces of the puzzle of her life were finally back in place.

When they finally pulled away from each other, Tyler's eyes were wet with tears. He sniffed and smiled. "Look at you," he said holding her out at arm's length to inspect her.

Lily flushed under his gaze.

"You truly do look incredible, Lils. You look happy."

She chuckled. "I'm getting there. A step closer now," she said as she looked back and forth between Chase and Tyler.

"Oh, you *are* here!"

They turned and saw Chase's mom standing in the doorway. She looked over her shoulder. "Trevor, they are here. I told you," she called before turning and running down the steps.

"Tyler!!!" she exclaimed excitedly. "Honey, it's so good to see you home again," she said pulling him into a giant hug. It was funny considering Diana was almost a foot shorter than Tyler. When she withdrew, she turned her attention to Lily.

"Oh Lilian, look at you. Damn if you're not as pretty as a magnolia blossom." She didn't give Lily a chance to say a word as she wrapped in a hug.

Chase laughed. "Jeez, mom. Let them breathe already."

Diana took a step back, her smile wide and eyes watery. Her blond hair was pulled into a ponytail. She wore a ruffled apron over a dress. It reminded Lily a lot of Donna Reed. A few moments later, a tall man wearing a simple pair of jeans and a blue t-shirt stepped onto the porch. In his arms was a wiggling girl whose face was wet with slobber.

"Bub, bub, bub," she babbled when she saw Chase.

Immediately, Chase jogged up the steps and took the giggling little girl from Trevor and tossed her into the air.

"CHASE MICHAEL!" his mother screeched, pressing her hands over her heart. "Don't do that! You scare me to death."

"Relax, mom. She loves it. Don't ya, squirt?" he cooed into the neck of the girl. The only response he got was giggles and babble.

Trevor walked down the steps, and as he got closer, Lily could easily see what Diana saw in the man. He was thickly built, but not in an imposing manner. His black hair was dusted at the temples with silver. On his face was a neatly trimmed beard. Bright green eyes looked to Diana with nothing but love and adoration.

"And you must be Lily," he said extending his hand.

"Yes, that's me, Mr. Sanderson. It's nice to meet you," she said taking his hand. It swallowed hers and was rough with callouses but otherwise gentle.

"Please, call me Trevor. After all, you're going to be living here."

She flushed and shifted from one foot to the other. Chase had given the squirming toddler back to his mother and now stood just behind Lily. Trevor turned and looked at Tyler.

"And you're Tyler."

"Yes, sir," Tyler nodded, accepting Trevor's hand.

"Well, come on. Dinner is nearly ready. Tyler, honey, will you be staying?"

"I don't think so. I need to get home and unpack. My father's going to be home this evening."

The way he regarded his father was cold and distant. It made Lily believe that things were still no better between them. Chase had told her in one of his letters that Elliot and Tyler had some sort of falling out. That was part of the reason he'd chosen to stay in California.

"Are you sure? There's plenty of food. Diana cooked enough to feed a blessed army."

Tyler chuckled. "Thanks, but I'm going to have to rain check."

"Okay then."

Trevor and Diana walked back into the house. Lily, Chase, and Tyler stood in awkward silence for several long moments. It felt right that the three of them were together again, and at the same time, something just felt off between them. It felt as if something has shifted. It made Lily anxious.

"So, why'd you decide to come home?" Chase asked as he leaned against the stair rail.

Tyler shrugged and shoved his hands into his pockets. A soft breeze blew around them. Though it was January, it was unseasonably warm, but it was still a bit chilly. "I don't know really. I guess I got a little homesick."

"I understand that," Lily said.

Tyler looked at her. "So, how are you doing? You're smiling. I've not seen you smile in a long time."

She nodded. "I haven't smiled in a long time. I'm doing good, though. The time away did me some good. I worked through most of my issues. I still have to do therapy once a week, but for the first time, I feel like I'm truly going to be okay."

He seemed to sigh in relief. "That's good to hear."

The silence stretched out between them. Finally, Lily couldn't handle it anymore. "Chase, can you give me a few minutes with Tyler."

Knowing that she needed to make peace with their friend, he nodded and hurried up the steps. Once the door was closed, Lily sat on the steps, and Tyler sat beside her. She looked down at her folded hands, mentally going over everything she needed to say to him. In the last year, she'd rehearsed hundreds of times. Now that she had the chance, she couldn't think of a word to say.

Tyler reached over and laced his fingers with hers. Immediately, she was granted the courage and strength she needed.

He gave her hand a gentle squeeze, letting her know that he was right there and waiting. She squeezed back.

"The last year has been absolute hell," she started. "The first few months I was in that place, I didn't think I was ever going to make it out. I felt crazy—I mean truly, certifiably insane. The nights were the hardest though because I couldn't turn my mind off. It was at night that I went through every single conversation I'd had with every single person in my life. I told them what I needed to say. I yelled at them, and I punched them. It was also the time that I went over everything I'd done wrong and all the people I'd hurt."

Lily turned and looked at him. "I hurt you. I wished like hell I hadn't done that. I thought of a million different ways I was going to make it up to you. None of them ever seemed good enough. I tried to rationalize why I would have seen you that day, but I never got an answer. I still don't know why your face was mixed up with the ones that I saw. I may never know. But, I need you to know this. The entire time I was in there I never felt whole. I had Chase, but that wasn't enough. Knowing that you were out here hurting because of something I said was keeping me from getting better. Tyler, you and Chase are all I have. One-third of my heart was missing knowing that I'd hurt you. The thought of you never speaking to me again was devastating. I'm sorry. I wish there were some elaborate gesture I could do to prove it to you, but there's not. I'm just sorry. I know you would never tell me to hurt myself. You've protected me and taken care of me since we were eight years old.

"When I didn't have a place to go, you let me stay with you. When I was molested, you kept my secret. I never once thought about what that would do to you. I never considered how holding onto that kind of secret would affect you. I'm sorry you had to carry my burden."

She took a deep, shuddering breath. "Can you please forgive me?"

"Yes!" he said almost before she could finish her sentence.

"Really?"

He held up his pinky. She curled hers around his. "Really," he said with a nod.

"Lily, I wasn't mad at you. I was hurt, but never mad. You had a lot on your plate, and seeing you so helpless made me feel like I'd let you down. I put the distance between us because I needed you to focus on you. The best thing I could do for you was give that to you. That day Chase told me you were in the hospital was a day I'll never forget. I thought we'd lost you. I'd thought I was about to lose my sister, and I was so pissed at myself because instead of going with Chase that day to look for you, I went to class. I should have gone with him."

"You couldn't have known. And Sister?"

He nodded. "Yes. You're like my sister, Lily. I will do whatever it takes to protect you. Even if that means hurting myself in the process. I had some things I needed to work through in California as well. I had some issues with my dad, and I needed the distance to clear my head."

"Did it work?"

He shook his head sadly. "No. My dad is my dad. He's never going to change."

"What now?"

"I'm going to go home and unpack and get ready for school. I'm going to focus on school and get a scholarship. Then, I'm going to get the hell out of here, just like I know you are going to do. Just like I know Chase is going to do."

She lifted her shoulder. "I don't know about me. I think I'm going to be stuck in this town forever."

He chuckled flicking a piece of lint from his jeans. "I think you're going to surprise us all, Lily Lancaster."

"We'll see."

"You watch. You're going to do great things."

She giggled and leaned her head on his shoulder. "I'm glad you're home," she said as she looped her arm through his.

He kissed the top of her head and patted her hand. "I'm glad *you're* home."

They sat there for a few moments more in nothing but comforting silence. When the sky began to darken, Tyler pushed to his feet. "I need to get home. See you tomorrow after school?"

She nodded. "Sure will. Do you want a ride?"

He shook his head. "Nah. It's not that far, and the walking helps me think."

"Okay. See you later."

"Later, Lils."

She stood on the porch, watching as Tyler walked down the street and disappeared around the corner. She turned and looked at the house; this was her new home, at least for a little while. She was both happy and anxious at the same time. When she walked through the front door she was greeted by the smell of fresh garlic bread and the tantalizing scent of pasta.

"Oh yeah, I've got this."

Chase and Lily washed the dinner dishes while Trevor and Diana put the baby to bed. "That was amazing," Lily groaned as she scrubbed the red sauce off the plate with a sponge. Her stomach was full, and her heart was light.

"I never knew how good of a cook my mother was until Trevor came around. When I was little, it was usually just eating leftovers she brought home from the diner or a TV dinner."

"I don't remember my mother cooking anything."

"Oh no, we know she's good at cooking some stuff."

Lily frowned. "I don't think so."

"She's good at cooking meth."

Lily's eyes widened, and she exploded into laughter. "You're horrible."

"Too soon?" Chase asked.

She giggled again shook her head.

"Come on, I'll show you the house," Chase said once they finished cleaning the kitchen.

She followed him out of the kitchen and to the stairs. "This is mom and Trevor's room," he said pointing to the first door on the right. "Cora's room is right next to theirs. There's the bathroom," he said pointing to the first door on the left. Then he pointed to the door beside the bathroom. "This is my room, and yours is right there beside it. There is a bathroom joining the two rooms."

"Well, that's cool," she said as they opened her room door and stepped inside.

Chase switched on the light and Lily gasped. The entire room was painted a soft yellow. A full-size bed was pushed up against the wall with a white dresser beside it. A desk with a computer sat against the wall opposite the bed. What drew her attention the most was the giant bay window that overlooked a peach orchard. Bright blue, green and purple pillows decorated a plush window seat that just begged her to curl up with a book.

"It's amazing," she gushed.

"My mom wanted you to have a place to call your own."

"It's my favorite color," she said placing her hand on the wall.

Chase scratched the back of his neck and shifted his weight from one foot to the other. "I know," he said sheepishly.

"I would have been content with a closet, you know. You guys didn't have to go to so much trouble."

"It wasn't trouble, Lils. She knows how much you mean to m—us. She wanted you to be in a place you felt safe."

Horror suddenly filled her. "Does she know what happened to me?"

Chase shook his head. "I had to tell her, Lily. She didn't know what was going on and when I told her you were in the hospital, I just kind of lost it. I tried to keep it quiet, but I just couldn't." His brown eyes bore into hers. "I'm sorry."

She shook her head. "It's me that should say sorry. It wasn't fair of me to ask you to keep that kind of a secret. It wasn't right. I didn't know that then, but I know it now."

He took a step closer. "There isn't anything I wouldn't have done for you." The temperature in the room seemed to climb as they stared at each other. She felt like she was getting lost in his eyes. Warmth crept into her cheeks as she blinked and turned, pretending to see something interesting.

"There are some clothes for you in the dresser. If you need more, then we'll go get some. She didn't know what to get you to sleep in, so there are a couple of my t-shirts and gym shorts in there until we can get you something better."

"They will work just fine."

"Okay, well, I've got to get up early and go to the ranch before school."

"Right. School."

Chase walked into the bathroom connecting their rooms. "There are towels and shampoo and all that girly stuff in the cabinet. If you need anything just let me know."

She smiled. "Thanks."

Chase nodded and began to walk off before stopping and turning. "I'm glad you're home, Lily. This is where you belong."

Chapter 23

Do not indulge in charitable acts for your own benefit.
Love them for the happiness they bring to others.

~Buddha

"I can't believe you don't have to go to school," Chase grumbled over his bowl of cereal. Lily chuckled as she sipped her coffee. He'd already gone to check on things at the ranch before the sun was even up. Though his job required him to be up at ungodly hours, Chase was the furthest thing from a morning person.

"Don't laugh," he grunted as he shoveled a spoonful of soggy frosted flakes into his mouth. Lily fought the urge to gag. For as long as she could remember, Chase had always preferred his cereal to be soggy.

"Don't be jealous!" she teased throwing a dishtowel at him. She handed him her coffee.

"Thanks," he grunted taking a sip. "Why you up so early anyway?"

"Getting an early start on job hunting. I need to get money saved up to pay rent and get me some new clothes. Hopefully, eventually, a place of my own."

He frowned. "You don't have to pay rent, you know."

"I know. I just don't feel right freeloading. I want to contribute."

"Then you can do my chores! That's contribution," he said with a cheeky grin.

Lily rolled her eyes. "Yeah, I have enough on my plate. I'm not doing your chores too. Hey, can you give me a lift to town on your way to school?"

Chase drank the rest of the coffee and poured the soggy remains of his cereal into the sink. "Yeah. I need to be leaving in about twenty minutes. I'm going to swing by and grab Ty. So, go do whatever it is you chicks do to get ready."

194

She socked him in the arm and rolled her eyes. Ten minutes later she hurried downstairs. Chase was pushing his feet into his boots at the base of the stairs when she came down. Thankfully, Diana had thought to get her a few nice things. Lily made a mental note to start a list of everything she owed Trevor and Diana. She knew she'd never be able to pay them off completely, but she was going to try her hardest.

Chase looked up at Lily as she came down the stairs and felt as if the wind had been knocked from his lungs. She wore a pair of fitted jeans that accented the shape of her long legs. The deep crimson sweater that she wore hugged her curves perfectly and Chase found himself wondering where exactly the girl Lily had gone because the person in front of him was no longer all skinned knees and elbows. The girl in front of him had transformed into a stunning woman.

Her hair was piled on top of her head that looked both messy and perfectly styled at the same time. Her bright green eyes were fringed with dark eyelashes. Chase felt his heart speed up as she walked down the steps.

"You ready?" he asked, clearing his throat and grabbing his bag from the floor.

She nodded and grabbed the jacket Diana had bought her. "Yeah."

Together, they walked out of the house and down the steps. At some point, Chase had started the truck. It grumbled as it idled in the driveway, the exhaust creating white plumes in the frigid air. Lily climbed into the truck and was greeted by heat and the smell of Chase. She took a deep breath and smiled. It was so good to be home.

Chase tossed his bag in the back of the truck and tugged the driver's door open. They pulled out of the drive and drove toward Tyler's house.

"So, what's on your agenda today?" Chase asked.

"You do realize that's the second time you've asked me that, right?"

Chase frowned. "What?"

"You asked me earlier what I was doing today. Then again, just now."

"Oh, right!" he said absently.

Lily frowned. "Are you okay? You seem a little off."

"What? No, I'm fine. I still can't believe you're already done with our junior year."

She laughed. "There wasn't much of anything to do, so I focused on school and stuff."

"Guess that makes sense."

"Have you decided what you're going to do after school?"

He nodded. "I think so."

"Really?"

"Yeah, I want to buy my own ranch and breed horses. I've been saving just about everything I've made since I've started working. I'm still a long way off, but maybe one of these days."

"Do you have your eyes set on a particular place?"

"I'd love to buy the old Triple J."

Lily tried to remember what place he was talking about. "Is that the one out by Cooper's Ridge?"

He nodded. "Yeah, it sits in the valley. Not far from Wheeler Lake." When they were in the sixth grade, their class had taken a day trip to the lake. It was a good four-hour drive away.

"That's a good distance away. Almost to Decatur," she mumbled.

"That means you'd have to leave Raven's Bend." A heavy feeling began to form in the pit of her stomach. If Chase left Raven's Bend and Tyler went to college at USC, she'd be alone.

He nodded. "Yeah, but I think a change is something I need."

"But what about your mom and Trevor or Coraline? Won't they need you?" She was trying desperately not to sound panicked. She'd lost a lot of time with both he and Tyler since beginning high school. The thought of everyone scattering after graduation made her anxiety creep a bit higher. She was going to be alone.

"Mom's got Trevor now. I just think a clean start is what I need." He paused and looked at her from the corner of his eye. "What about you? What do you plan on doing?"

She shrugged. "Probably end up a cashier at the Sip-N-Save," she said glumly.

"Somehow I doubt that."

Before she could question what he meant, they pulled in front of Tyler's massive, colonial-style mansion. Chase laid on the horn.

"You know if his dad's home he's gonna crap a brick wall."

Chase smiled and repeatedly beat on the horn. Even after Tyler walked down the steps. He tossed his bag in the back with Chase's. Lily scooted over in the seat straddling the gearshift. She tried to ignore the sudden fluttering in the pit of her stomach as her leg brushed against Chase's.

Tyler hopped in and glowered at Chase.

"What the hell, dude?" Tyler grumbled.

"Just wanted to make sure you were ready to go."

Tyler's frowned deepened. "Douche," he grunted and turned his attention to Lily, who was snickering between them. "Hey, Lils. Decide to join us at school after all?"

"Ha," she scoffed. "Not a chance in hell. I'm not going back to that place a day sooner than I need to. I'm going to try to find a job."

"Hey, that reminds me, I had to drive Maria to the vet clinic last week—her Rottweiler was sick. I saw they had an opening for a secretary or office manager or something like that."

Lily perked up. "Really?"

"Yeah. The vet is cool. Just tell her I sent you by. She's an old friend of the family."

Lily nodded. "I'll do that. Thanks."

The three of them drove into town, chatting about everything and nothing at the same time. It was the first time in almost two and a half years that things felt somewhat normal.

Chase pulled to a stop in front of the vet clinic. "You sure you don't want to use my truck today? You can just drop us off and then grab us after school."

"Yeah, I'm sure."

Chase slid out from behind the wheel and Lily followed. She looked back at Tyler. "Have a good day."

He flashed her his million-dollar smile. "Go get 'em, tiger," he said holding two thumbs up. Lily just giggled and stepped onto the sidewalk.

"I have to go to work after school. Can you find a way home?"

She nodded. "It's not that far of a walk. I'll be fine."

Chase looked at her, his brows knitting together with worry. She sighed. "Seriously, Chase, I'm fine. I'm not a fragile little girl anymore. I won't break if something goes wrong."

He began to climb into the truck and stopped. "Oh, I almost forgot." He reached into his jacket and pulled out her phone. "In case you need us."

"You kept it?"

He nodded. "Yeah, we suspended your line. I reactivated it and changed it over to my name when I heard you were getting out."

She reached out and took the phone but almost dropped it when their fingers brushed together. An electrical current seemed to snap between them. When she looked up, Chase was just watching her.

"Thank you," she said touched that he'd kept her phone for over a year.

He shrugged. "I cleared and deleted everything on it. I thought since you were starting out fresh, your contacts needed to be clean too."

She didn't have to be a genius to figure out he was talking about Lucas. She just nodded and tucked it into her back pocket.

"Okay, well, wish me luck," she said hugging the jacket Diana had loaned her tighter around her body.

He flashed her a broad smile. "You don't need luck, but hey, if the vet doesn't pan out, then there's always McDonald's!"

She rolled her eyes. "Har, har. Get out of here. Y'all are gonna be late."

Chase jumped back inside the truck and pulled away from the curb. Lily watched until the rounded the corner. It felt like something different was going on with Chase, but she really couldn't put the finger on what. She couldn't deny the spark of attraction she felt when he was around, but she just figured it was because she hadn't been around any attractive guys in the past year. Besides, Chase wouldn't feel that way toward her anyway. He could have his pick from any girl in town. He sure as hell wasn't going to choose a nut job.

Taking a deep breath, she began walking up the sidewalk. Three doors from where Chase had dropped her off was the vet clinic. When so got to the door, she frowned. The sign told her they didn't open until nine.

"Ugh." It wasn't even eight. Looking around, she decided to go to the coffee shop and wait. Thankfully she had a little money left in her checking account that her mother hadn't raided for drugs. A giant caramel mocha was precisely what she needed.

Walking across the street, she walked into the tiny shop. It was an eclectic little place with mismatched couches, ottomans, and chairs scattered around the room. There was a small stage by the windows where they hosted an open mic night every Friday night. Various posters were adorning the walls. Some were of old classic cars while others were of famous bands, basketball players, musicians, and just about every other kind of poster one could imagine. When mixed with the tantalizing aroma of coffee and fresh pastries, it made here remember when the three of them would come and study. It was a favorite place for the kids to hang out on the weekends.

As she walked further into the coffee shop, however, her sense of nostalgia vanished. An overwhelming sense of dread filled the pit of her stomach when she recognized a group of girls standing at the counter. She may have been gone for a year, but there were some people she would always remember.

For a moment, she thought about bolting before anyone saw her, but she decided against it. They lived in a small town. If word about her release wasn't out yet, then it would be soon enough. She might as well get it over with.

Taking a deep breath and squaring her shoulders, she walked by the table of girls drinking their lattes and stood in line. The chatter almost instantly stopped. It was then followed by whispers that were as subtle as a hurricane.

"*. . . she's out?*"

"*I wonder if she's still crazy.*"

"*Look at her hair.*"

"*I wonder if she's tried killing herself again.*"

"*Wonder if she wore a straightjacket.*"

Tolerating about as much as she could handle, Lily turned and fixed the girls with a cold glare but a sweet smile. "You know, I did have a straightjacket. It was purple with rhinestones. How are you girls doing? It's so good to see that some things never change." She placed her hand to her chest. "I mean, here I was thinking that surely people wouldn't be so childish, but thank you Amanda, Kimber for keeping that bar set so low. I'm glad I can count on you to never disappoint. Bless your hearts."

Both girls opened their mouth to reply, but Lily held up her hand, stopping them. "You know what, on second thought," she shrugged and continued, "I really couldn't care less. Now, you better run along to school before you're late. I know you're dying to get back and tell everyone that the town psycho is back!"

Amanda and Kimber's mouths fell open. Pink colored their cheeks as they scuttled from their seats. "Crazy bitch," Kimber muttered as they hurried by her.

Lily threw her head back and laughed. "Oh, you have no idea," she called after them.

Other people in the coffee shop stared at the exchange, but when Lily looked at them, they quickly averted their gazes or pretended to be interested in their own mundane lives. She couldn't help the smile that crossed her face as she stepped up to the counter.

She ordered a mocha and muffin and settled in at the table in the far back of the room. It was better to stay out of the line of fire if possible. However, the looks on Chase's and Tyler's ex-girlfriends were priceless. She didn't doubt that they were already burning rubber to get to the school to spread the latest news. Then something dawned on her, for the first time in her life, she didn't care.

Chapter 24

When we have found peace within ourselves,
peace and love follow us everywhere we go.

~Eknathe Easwaran

An hour later Lily stood staring at the clinic door. They'd opened five minutes ago, and Lily was sure that she was going to vomit all over the sidewalk. She didn't know the first thing about being a secretary or even working in a vet clinic. However, after spending time with Hercules and the other therapy animals, she discovered that spending time with animals was something that brought her peace. It helped her stay focused, and there was a sense of calm that came to her when she was with animals.

As she stood staring at the door, she felt her phone buzz in her pocket. She removed it and tapped the screen awake. The envelope message told her there was a waiting message.

She touched the icon, and the message popped up.

Chase: *how'd it go?*
Me: *hasn't yet. Too scared. What if I don't get the job? What if they know?*

She didn't have to wait long for a response. Apparently, he was waiting for her.

Chase: Well, how will you know if you don't go inside?

Lily frowned and looked up. At the end of the sidewalk, both Chase and Tyler stood, smiling at her. Her heart jumped in her chest as her eyes locked with Chase's as they walked forward. When they stopped in front of her, she shook her head.

"What are you guys doing here?"

Tyler shrugged and dropped his arm over her shoulders. "Do you think we're going to spend the first full day you're back in school?"

She laughed. "I don't think school is optional."

Chase shrugged, giving her that devil-may-care grin she loved. "Not much going on anyway."

"He called and had his mom check us out," Tyler snickered.

Chase frowned. "Dude? It sounded much cooler that we were ditching."

Lily couldn't help the deep belly laughter that exploded. "Aww, did he ruin your street cred."

"Douche," Chase grumbled half-heartedly.

"So, what gives, Lils?" Tyler asked hugging her tightly.

She just shrugged. "I don't know. Maybe I'm not ready for this."

"How do you know if you're not ready for something if you don't at least try?" he questioned.

Turning her head, she looked up at him. He smiled down at her, but there was something about his smile that didn't quite reach his eyes. "When did you become all wise and logical?"

He lifted his shoulders. "I've seen the world," he said dramatically as he pressed a kiss to her temple and stepped away. "Seriously, though. You've got this. You're not the same girl you were when you left last year."

"You say *left* like it was my choice."

"Whatever the reason, you're not her. I could tell the minute I saw you again. I barely recognized you, Lily. This . . . this right here," he said gesturing up and down the length of her body, "is the woman you're supposed to be. That little girl that was here a year ago, that's not you. This is you. Right here. Right now. And you have to believe us. We've seen you at your lowest. Now, let us watch you get to your highest."

Lily's eyes misted as and launched herself into Tyler's unsuspecting arms. "Thank you," she whispered. He held her tightly.

"You've got this," he whispered back.

"Hey, what about me? I said you could do it too!" Chase whined playfully.

She rolled her eyes. "You're like a jealous little boy." Nevertheless, she moved into his embrace. However, it was much different than Tyler's had been. With Tyler, it had felt platonic, much like a big brother hugging a little sister. That wasn't the case with Chase.

The second Chase's arms slipped around her ribs, she became hyperaware of him. She could feel the way his body molded against hers. She felt the warmth of his breath on the sensitive skin of her neck, causing goosebumps to climb over her arms.

Then there was the heady scent of his cologne wreaking havoc on her senses. It was different than the brand he'd used when they were younger. This kind, somehow, made him smell . . . enticing. It was giving her a light buzz and causing her head to swim, and suddenly she was lost. She could feel his heart against her cheek as it sped up. Then the most bizarre thing happened. Her heart sped up to keep pace until they were beating as one.

Tyler cleared his throat, startling the pair apart. Heat flared into her cheeks when she took a step back. She anxiously tucked a strand of blond hair behind her ear. Chase cleared his throat and jammed his hands into his jeans as he took a step back.

"Go on, Lils. You got this," he said hoarsely.

Nodding her head, she took a deep breath and put her hand on the door. She gave them a look before giving it a pull. Both guys flashed her dorky grins, giving her the thumbs up. Feeling confident, she pulled the door open and stepped inside. She was praying with each step she took that this would be the first step in her new life.

Chase watched as Lily walked through the door. When they first saw her standing in front of the clinic, she looked so small and frightened. She looked like she was about to bolt in the opposite direction at any moment. In fact, he was sure that's what she was about to do.

As soon as Lily disappeared into the clinic, his brows knitted together in a frown. What in the hell just happened? Better yet, what was *happening*? When he turned and looked at Tyler, his frowned deepened.

"What?" Chase asked stuffing his hands into the pockets of his jean jacket.

Tyler just chuckled and shook his head. "Let's go get some coffee," he said already walking across the street.

"Whatever," Chase grumbled, following Tyler across the street to the coffee shop. They walked inside and placed their orders. Then, after grabbing a couple of muffins each, they settled into a table in front of the large windows.

"Why are you back?" Chase asked after taking a huge bite of his muffin.

Tyler shrugged. "I was homesick and just missed you guys."

Chase studied Tyler's face as he stared out the window. He felt like there was something he was missing like he was only getting part of the story.

"I call bullshit," Chase said matter-of-factly.

"Nothing. Just drop it, man."

Chase shook his head. "The hell I will. I dropped the ball with Lily. I'll be damned if I do the same thing with you. What gives? The last time I talked to you, everything was going great. You even had a girlfriend. What was her name? Trixie, Bambi, Candi. . . ." Chase snapped his fingers while he pretended to search for the girl's name.

"Barbie, and don't be a douche. You know what her name was."

Chase threw back his head and laughed. "Well, it was some sort of stripper name."

Tyler didn't laugh.

"Chill, dude. I'm just playing," Chase said sobering. "Seriously, though, what's going on with you?"

"Nothing, man. Leave it alone."

"Try again. That's not happening." Chase frowned, all his humor vanishing. Something was eating away at his friend. Tyler was the glue that typically held their little triad together. He was the level-headed one. Chase was the hot head and Lily . . . well, Lily was Lily. Seeing

Tyler bothered by something didn't sit well with Chase at all.

"Tyler? What's going on? Why did you come home?"

Tyler took a deep breath and looked up at Chase. "I wanted to spend my last year here with you guys. You're the only family I know. After we graduate, who knows when or if we'll see each other again?"

"Don't be ridiculous," Chase scoffed. "Once you hit it big in the pros, you can fly us out to see you!" When he didn't laugh, Chase's smile fell.

Tyler just stared out the window. "I found out my mother might get out of jail on a loophole."

This got Chase's attention. "You've got to be shitting me."

Tyler just shook his head and absently picked at the cardboard holder around his coffee cup. "I overheard my dad talking on the phone the other night. I guess there was some paperwork screwed up while she was processed. If it makes it to appeals, then she could be out of prison as early as May of next year."

Chase felt his stomach churn with disgust. While he and Lily had been from the opposite side of the tracks as Tyler, the scandal that followed him around was much worse. It would only get worse if his mother was allowed to go free on a technically.

"Well, look at it this way, you'll be gone and won't have to deal with her shit."

He shrugged. "Yeah, I will be."

"Okay, I say we talk about something different."

"Like what?"

"Who you taking to prom this year?" Chase asked as he took a sip of coffee.

"How in the hell would I know that? I just got back." Then a sly smile curved his lips. "I might just ask Lily."

Chase sputtered in his coffee, causing it to splash on his hand and the table.

"Are you okay there, buddy?"

Chase gasped and wheezed, trying to catch his breath. "Yeah. Just went down the wrong pipe." He grabbed a napkin and wiped away the coffee. "You're going to ask Lily?" he asked.

"I might."

"I mean, is that such a good idea? Do you think she'd be ready for something like that?"

"It's not really my say. I just can't get over how beautiful she's gotten. I'm really seeing her in a new light."

Chase scrunched up his nose. "Seeing her in a new light? Is that the kind of crap they're spouting in California?"

"What? You haven't noticed it?"

Chase shifted in his seat. "Sure, I mean I guess. She's not hard on the eyes. She never has been though."

"She's all I've been thinking about since I got back. I think I might ask her to go out on a date with me."

"Sure, I mean if that's what makes you happy, then go for it. I mean I'd love to see my best friends together. I'm thinking about asking Lexa out anyway." Lexa was a sophomore he'd taken out on a couple of times. She was sweet enough, but something just didn't feel right.

Tyler's face split into a smile, and everything in his demeanor seemed to change. "Dude, relax. I'm just playing. I'm not going to prom. I'm going back out to California that weekend to register for camps this summer."

The tension that had suddenly come over Chase seemed to vanish almost as quickly as it had appeared. "I'm not going either. We're going to have another shipment of cattle coming in that weekend, and another heard of horses going out.

They'd been talking for an hour when Lily emerged from the clinic. Chase sent a text telling her where they were. They watched as she hurried across the street and through the front doors. Her smile was full, and her face was beaming.

"You got it!" Chase exclaimed.

She nodded excitedly.

Chase let out a loud whoop of excitement and lifted her in a huge hug, spinning her around in small circles.

When he put her down, her cheeks were flush, and her beautiful green eyes sparkled.

Have her eyes always been this beautiful?

He placed her back on the floor and took a step back. Tyler then darted between them and wrapped her in a hug that lasted a bit longer than Chase's had.

"We're so happy for you," Tyler said clutching her hands and lacing his fingers through hers. Chase felt a prickle of jealousy creep up his spine.

"I didn't just get a secretary job. They are giving me a position as a veterinarian's assistant. I'll have to take a couple classes a few hours a week after work, but I could be certified by the end of summer. And once school starts they are more than willing to work around my schedule."

"Wow, Lils. That's amazing," Tyler said hugging her again.

Chase took a step closer. "That is amazing. Why don't we celebrate?"

She released Tyler's hands and looked up at Chase. Her face was positively radiant. "And do what?"

"Anything you want!"

"Let's go to Jasper and go ice skating. I've not been on the ice in forever."

Chase nodded. "Then Jasper it is." He looked at Tyler who was watching them smugly. Why did it suddenly feel like the dynamic between the three of them had just changed?

Chapter 25

We are not built like a ship to be tossed,
but like a house to stand.

~Ralph Waldo Emerson

Seven months later

Lily stuffed a hand full of popcorn in her mouth as Tyler put the DVD into the player. "Tell me why we're watching this crap again?" he complained.

"Because we haven't had a chance to hang out in months. Me and Chase have worked almost all summer while you've been off gallivanting around California again."

Since beginning work at the clinic, she'd been spending almost all her time there learning as much as possible. She usually got home around eight in the evening, and after eating what dinner Diana had saved, she collapsed into bed exhausted.

She rarely saw Chase, and there were times when they went two or three days without seeing each other at all. He was gone to the ranch before five in the morning and usually in bed before she got home. On the weekends, they both worked nonstop. Diana even scolded them both for working too much. She accused them of being more "adulty" than the adults living in the house.

"Hey! I wasn't *gallivanting.* I was working too," he defended with feigned indignity.

"Yeah, some work, chasing all those beach bunnies in bikinis," Chase called from the kitchen.

"Hey, don't hate the player."

"Oh, hey, the nineties called. They want their catchphrase back," she laughed.

"Says the one who just quoted a catchphrase from the nineties."

Lily poked her tongue out at him. "Besides, since we're all lacking in the relationship department, a little

209

sappy romance won't kill you," she said tossing a few kernels of popcorn at his head.

"We're not *all* lacking," he snickered as Chase walked into the room carrying sodas and chips.

Lily frowned when Tyler directed his comment toward Chase. "What's that supposed to mean?" she asked.

"Nothing."

Chase placed the sodas on the coffee table and shot Tyler a scowl as he sat on the other side of Lily. "So, how's work been? Did you get your certification?" Tyler asked, changing the subject.

She didn't miss the subject change, but she let it go. "I did, and it's been amazing. More than amazing. Dr. Chaffey is freaking amazing; she's like the animal whisperer. I've gotten to go with her all week on house calls. I helped deliver a litter of puppies, two calves, a foal, and a sheep. It's crazy! I never thought that helping animals would be so . . . fulfilling! Her son has been helping out tremendously," she gushed excitely.

"The boss's son, eh?" Tyler teased, wagging his brows up and down suggestively.

Lily rolled her eyes, but it didn't stop the color from staining her cheeks. "Yes, the boss's son, and don't say it like that. You makes it sound dirty."

"So *that's* why you've been staying late after work," Tyler continued to tease, nudging her with his shoulder.

"Would you stop? You've been home for less than twelve hours, and you're already stirring shit. Besides, he's like five years older than I am."

"And didn't you say he'd asked you out?"

Chase's head jerked up. "He what?"

Lily frowned and then shrugged. "Yeah."

"Did you go out with him?"

"Not yet. Why?"

He just lifted a shoulder. "Because. Wouldn't that be a touch unprofessional? I mean dating your boss's son? I think it would make you look easy."

Lily's eyes widened. "Are you kidding me right now? Did you just call me a slut?"

"Those words did not come out of my mouth."

Anger burned in the pit of her stomach. "They might as well have."

"Don't put words in my mouth," he snapped at her.

She snorted. "How can I? You're so busy putting your feet in there, there ain't any room," she returned hotly.

"Whoa! I think we all need just need a timeout," Tyler said holding up his hand in the form of a T.

Lily ignored him and turned to fully face Chase. "What the hell is your problem, Chase?"

He narrowed his eyes at her. "Do you *not* remember the last older guy you dated?"

Lily gasped, stunned by the words that had just come out of him. "That's not fair!"

"Hey," Tyler barked. "Dude, that's a low blow." All the humor had left his face, and tension between the three of them suddenly began to fill the room.

"Let's just watch the movie," Tyler suggested in an attempt to defuse the situation.

"Fine," both Lily and Chase muttered at the same time. Lily crossed her arms tightly over her chest and sank down on the sofa. How in the world could Chase say something like that? She watched him from the corner of her eyes as he stared at the television. The muscle in his jaw ticked angrily, indicating that he wasn't watching the movie at all.

With an annoyed huff, Lily turned back to the movie. She was finally beginning to relax when Chase's phone buzzed.

"Hey, no phones on movie night!" she whined.

He ignored her and pulled it out of his pocket. A small smirk tilted the corner of his lips as he read a text message. He quickly tapped a response and then put the phone on his leg. It wasn't two seconds later before it buzzed again.

"Seriously?" Lily snapped.

Chase looked at her with narrowed eyes. "What are you, the phone monitor?"

"No, but I'd like to watch the movie and not have to worry about whatever flavor of the week you're talking to interrupting," she snapped.

"Well, I guess I'll just leave," he said shoving to his feet.

Lily watched, mouth hanging open as Chase tugged on his boots and left the house, slamming the door soundly behind him. A few moments later the engine of his truck fired up. Lily couldn't pull her eyes away from the door, even as the grumbling engine faded. She didn't know why, but his leaving in the middle of the movie bothered her.

"What the hell is that all about? Where's he going?" she asked, whirling on Tyler. He was just watching her with an odd look in his eyes.

"Don't know," he said flippantly as he shoveled more popcorn into his mouth. She narrowed her eyes at him. He was avoiding eye contact. Tyler only avoided eye contact when he was hiding something.

"Tyler Cooper Anderson, what aren't you telling me? Who was on the phone? Where's he going?"

Tyler swallowed and looked over at her. Everything on his expression said *busted.* He exhaled loudly. "He's probably going over to Molly's house."

Lily frowned. "Molly? Molly who?"

He swallowed, his Adam's apple bobbing nervously. "Molly Trent."

Lily's eyes nearly exploded from her head. "Molly Trent? Why would he be going over there?"

He looked down at something that was suddenly very interested in the bowl of half-empty popcorn. Finally, when she didn't stop glaring at him, he pushed out a heavy sigh. "He's been seeing Molly for a few months now. They aren't serious, yet."

She wasn't sure why, but the word *yet* left an acidic taste in her mouth. "He's been seeing Kiera Stockton's best friend and he, what, just forgot to mention it?"

"It's not like that, Lils. He just didn't want you to get upset. He knows your history with Kiera and didn't want to cause problems."

"So, he hid it from me?" Then something struck her. "All these late nights at the farm weren't late nights, were they?"

Tyler shook his head. "He didn't want to upset you."

"Little freakin' late for that."

The amount of hurt swirling around inside Lily's chest was too much to handle. She shoved to her feet. "I'm going to bed, you can let yourself out," she said as she rushed up the stairs, slamming the door behind her. She winced, praying that it didn't wake the baby or Diana up. When she didn't hear either, she let out a pent-up breath.

"Of all the freaking nerve," she hissed, kicking a pillow that had fallen from the bed across the room. He had got all bent out of shape when she'd even mentioned going out with doctor Chaffey's son. What gave him the right to read her the riot act when he was going out with one of the girls who had tormented her for years? She felt hurt, betrayed, and if she had to be honest with herself, a tad jealous.

"What right does he have saying I can't date someone? Not a single damn one," she muttered as she removed her phone from her back pocket. She sent a text to Dexter, asking if he still wanted to grab dinner one night. She wasn't surprised when he answered with a *yes* almost immediately. She'd thought that it would make her feel better. Anastasia had told her one day over coffee that it would be okay for her to slowly start dating again. At first, she'd adamantly refused, afraid that she would find someone like Lucas again.

Exhausted from work and the argument she had with Chase, she walked to their joined bathroom. She washed her face and brushed her teeth. She quickly unbraided her long hair and ran her fingers through it, sighing in relief as the mass tumbled over her shoulders and down her back. Once back in her room, she changed into one of Chase's t-shirts and a pair of track shorts that fell just below her butt cheeks. The shirt was three sizes too big for her, but it was the first thing she'd worn when she slept in her own bed. The neck was stretched out, so it fell off her shoulder. It really needed to be thrown in the trash, but she just couldn't bear to part with it.

School would be starting in two days. A whole new case of nerves attacked her as she sat at her desk and turned on her lamp. She lifted a schedule of all her classes. They were all advanced classes with a few easy classes tossed in the mix. She'd tried out for track over the summer and had made the team. Their first meet would be three weeks after school started. Anastasia had said joining a team sport would be good for her, not just physically but mentally as well.

It wasn't the classes or the team she was worried about. What did bother her was stepping foot back in a place that held so many ghosts. She'd learned a few weeks after she'd gotten back that Lucas had been arrested for a plethora of drug charges as well as felony theft. He was sentenced to twenty-five years in prison. She wished she could say she felt sorry for him, but she couldn't.

Another person she was not looking forward to seeing was the one and only Kiera Stockton. She'd heard that Kiera had a baby. Chase had informed her that Kiera had taken summer courses and gotten caught up and would be returning to finish out her senior year. Every cell in Lily's body dreaded coming face to face with the girl. But, part of her therapy was to face demons head on and make peace.

However, she remembered the last time she'd tried to make peace with Kiera. It had resulted in the lowest moment of Lily's life.

"I don't know if I can do this," she whispered as she looked at a picture of Chase and Tyler she kept on her desk. She'd taken it on the last day of school at the lake where they spent the entire day swimming, laughing, and celebrating life. Her gaze shifted to the notebook with a brightly colored mandala on the front. She traced the lines as a soft smile crossed her face.

When Anastasia had first talked about the symbol, Lily had thought the doc had cracked. There was no way on earth something as simple as drawing full of intricate lines, swirls, bright colors, and patterns would help erase all the bad things in her life. However, as their sessions had progressed, Lily had quickly discovered that what Anastasia had told her about the symbol had helped. Did she believe she was going to achieve some enlightenment or the supernatural ability of self-awareness? No. But, she did find comfort in the design. It did help her focus and find calm when her mind was raging like a violent storm. Since that session, Lily used it to help calm her frayed nerves.

It worked, for the most part. However, at that precise moment in time, she couldn't focus long enough on the mandala to focus on finding peace.

Deciding that she wasn't going to get anywhere by worrying about things in the past, she turned off the lamp and crawled into bed. "I'm not a ship tossed in the waves. I'm a house built on a solid foundation," she chanted. It was something Anastasia had taught her during of her hundreds of sessions. When she didn't drift to sleep, she started counting—another little trick she'd picked up.

Unfortunately, after three hours later, she lost track of what number she'd gotten too and was still wide awake. The only thing she could think about was Chase and Molly and all the stuff they were probably doing.

"Well, this just sucks," she grumbled, flouncing over onto her stomach and punching the pillow to fluff it. No matter how hard she tried, though. It didn't help.

"It's going to be a long night."

Chapter 26

*People take different roads seeking
fulfillment and happiness.
Just because they're not on your road
doesn't mean they've gotten lost.*

~Dalai Lama XIV

With a sigh of frustration, she kicked the blankets from her legs and climbed from the bed. Maybe a late-night spoonful of ice cream would make her feel better. She looked through the bathroom and into Chase's room to see if he was home. Seeing his empty bed made her heart sink. She hated fighting with him. It made her stomach ache and her anxiety climb. It was half-past three in the morning, and he was still out with Molly. She cringed. Would he bring her to the house? She didn't personally have an issue with Molly other than she was Kiera's best friend.

In fact, Molly hadn't been one to torment Lily. She'd always remained quiet, but still, guilty by association. Right? While she'd never tortured her, Molly had watched and at times, laughed at Lily's misery. If the girl had felt sorry about what Kiera and the others did, she never bothered to show it.

She became annoyed all over again with Chase as she quietly slipped from her room and tiptoed down the hall. Aside from the fact that Molly was Molly, Lily didn't know exactly why she was so against Chase dating her. He'd dated plenty of other girls. They never stuck around. While Chase was sweet and funny, he was still a sexy football god that could have any girl he wanted. Add in the fact that he was a ripped farm boy with a body that was every girl's dream, he was almost perfect.

Carefully walking by Diana and Trevor's room, she made her way down the stairs. She was careful to avoid the ones that squeaked. Without turning on any lights,

216

she made her way down the hall and into the kitchen. Soft light from the full moon filtered through the lace covering the rows of windows. Except for the bay window in her room, the kitchen was her favorite room in the house. Not just because it was always filled with food—something that she still wasn't entirely used too—it was also warm; not the heat kind of warm, but the Better Homes and Gardens type warm.

It was cheerily decorated in soft hues of blue and white, with mason jars and old tin buckets as decorations. They always seemed to be filled with flowers. While she'd come to love Diana dearly, Lily never quite gave out hope that one day she would have that kind of a relationship with her own mother. However, she wasn't naive enough to believe in fairytales, and if it got right down to it, she thought she would see talking mice making a ball gown before such a notion would come true.

As she entered the kitchen fully, she saw the light spilling from the refrigerator. Chase was bent over rummaging through the contents. With a smile, she snuck closer.

"*What* are you doing?" she said suddenly.

There was a loud *thud* followed by the rattling of jars and a string of curses a mile long. Lily doubled over in a fit of giggles as Chase emerged rubbing his head.

"Owe, damn it, Lily. Are you trying to give me a heart attack?" he whispered harshly as he removed several covered containers and kicked the door shut.

She walked around the counter and leaned against it, facing him. "Nah, I was going for a concussion because maybe *that* would explain why the hell you're shacking up with Molly Trent." Her good humor faded as she jumped right into the argument feet first. She'd never really had the ability for subtly.

"I'm gonna kill that big mouth," he muttered as he removed the lid from the container. He turned to the freezer and removed the pint of ice cream he already knew Lily was after. She tried to ignore the fluttering of butterflies in the pit of her stomach. Of course, he would know she was after ice cream. He knew her well enough to know that if she couldn't sleep, that was her go-to snack.

He opened the silverware drawer and removed two spoons. Then, after popping the lid off the pint of mint chip, he poked the spoon in and slid it to her. She accepted it but didn't take a bite. Instead, she looked at him.

"Why didn't you tell me?" she asked. She hadn't meant to sound so hurt.

He looked at her, and even in the darkness, she could see the remorse in his eyes. Silence hung heavily between them as he stared at her. Finally, he sighed.

"I don't know. It's nothing serious, really. We're just hanging out."

She rolled her eyes. "I'm not stupid, Chase. I know you don't just *hang out* with girls."

He frowned as he twirled his fork in the cold spaghetti. Chase never reheated food. He always preferred leftovers cold. When she'd asked him about it once, he said that it was all he was used too. "What's that supposed to mean?" he asked around a bite he shoveled into his mouth.

"You know what it means," she said feeling heat climbing into her cheeks.

He turned and faced her, leaning a hip against the counter. He was standing so close, she could smell faint hints of cologne mingling with sweat. To some, it might not seem appealing, however, for some reason, Lily had grown to like the smell.

"No, Lily. Why don't you tell me what it means?" His eyes bore down into hers, and she was thankful for the darkness because her cheeks were growing warmer by the second.

She broke the contact and stared down at the ice cream. Suddenly, a midnight snack didn't seem like such a good idea. "I'm not doing this. I'm going back to bed. Goodnight, Chase."

Lily turned to leave, but Chase's hand closed around her arm, pulling her back. Her feet became tangled, causing her to trip into his broad chest. His hand curved around her waist and rested on the small of her back. She could feel the heat of his palm warming her skin through her thin shirt.

She swallowed the lump in her throat as she looked up at him, unable to move. She wasn't sure if she couldn't move because he was holding her in place or because, at that moment, she didn't want to.

"Tell me," he said huskily.

Lily lifted her chin defiantly. "It means that you don't just *date* girls, Chase. I've heard about your conquests since we were in the eighth grade. I'm not stupid."

A slow smile curved his mouth, and he licked his bottom lip. Try as she might, she just couldn't keep her eyes from watching his mouth.

"Do you think I'm having sex, Lily?"

Again, she swallowed, but this time it was infinitely harder. His breath was warm as it brushed against the top of her head.

"It's none of my business if you were," she whispered. She flattened her hands on his chest, preparing to push away, but his grip tightened on her back, holding her against him. She could feel the steady *thump, thump, th-thump* of his heart beneath her palms.

"Would it bother you if I was?" he asked.

Yes. "No."

Again, he smiled. Chase leaned down, and for a moment, she thought he was going to kiss her. This was Chase—her best friend and other half. Why was she thinking about him kissing her? Her heart throbbed against her ribs.

"You're a rotten liar," he whispered. His warm breath brushed against her neck like a caress, forcing goosebumps to scatter along her arms and legs.

When he pulled back, his face was less than an inch from hers. Suddenly, she found herself wondering what it would be like to kiss him. It wasn't the first time she'd ever thought about it. However, it *was* the first time she'd seriously contemplated acting on it.

Just one kiss. She *had* heard about what an excellent kisser Chase Kramer was. What would it hurt to find out for herself?

She took a deep breath and felt herself leaning in. Chase also seemed to be moving closer. Just before their lips touched, however, he stopped and backed away, releasing her so quickly that she nearly fell forward.

Quickly righting herself, she looked up at him.

"I think you're right."

"A-about what?"

"You need to go back to bed."

There was no argument. She turned and hurried out of the kitchen and up the stairs. After closing her bedroom door, she sagged against the door. Had all of that really happened? Had she just about kissed Chase?

Then another thought struck her. For the first time since she'd been attacked, she wasn't scared to be touched. Being in Chase's arms didn't bring a torrential storm of memories or flashbacks. The only thing she'd felt was peace and calm.

Feeling more confused than ever, Lily walked across her room and collapsed into the bed. This time, sleep overtook her almost immediately, and for the first time in ages, she dreamed. The dreams weren't the kind that left her feeling vulnerable or waking up drenched in sweat. They were of the past and then of the future—a future with Chase.

Chase watched as Lily rushed from the kitchen. He hadn't realized he was holding his breath until he heard her bedroom door close and his lungs began to ache. What in the hell had just happened? He hadn't meant for things to go that far. Hell, until he turned and saw her standing in the kitchen, the pale moonlight streaming over her, he'd still been pissed at her.

The silver light streaming through the curtains covered her body, giving her an ethereal glow. Her blond hair fell in tangled waves around her face. The collar of her—his—shirt fell away, revealing the tanned and silky-smooth skin of her shoulder. She looked like a temptress and at the same time an innocent girl.

The way she'd asked him about Molly had struck a chord within his chest. He made a mental note to beat the thunder out of Tyler for opening his yap. However, seeing the shimmer of hurt in Lily's eyes tugged at something inside him. Guilt washed over him. He knew he should have mentioned Molly to her, but he hadn't exactly known how. At any rate, he hadn't even gone to see Molly.

He'd been so angry after leaving the house. The only thing he could do was drive around before finding himself at the lake sitting on the end of the dock. For hours he'd stared at the three carved names that had faded with time but were still plainly visible. The three of them had carved them when they were twelve and about to start junior high. It was that same day they promised to be part of each other's lives for eternity.

Looking back, it was a childish notion. He'd sat and stared out over the still waters reflecting the moon and thought about everything they'd gone through. There was Tyler with his mom who was messed up with trafficking and his asshat of a father. He admired Tyler more than he would ever admit. He was someone he looked up to because no matter what life handed him, he'd taken it and turned it around. Initially, he'd thought they'd been the ones to take him in the night he and Lily found him crying in the park. The truth of the matter was, he'd been the one to take *them* in. He'd made sure they had a place to crash and plenty of food to eat. Tyler was the backbone of their little triad. If it hadn't been for him, there was no telling what would have happened to them. The path they had taken through the woods that night to the playground was one they'd taken hundreds of times. Only, that night, it had taken them to Tyler.

Tyler would be going to college at one of the best schools on the west coast. He had a promising career in front of him with football. He hadn't let his absentee father or, the stain that was his mother, hinder his dreams and goals. Still, the thought of one of his best friend's on the other side of the country left him feeling empty. It left him wondering what he was going to do with his life. It was something he'd thought about often—every back-breaking, sun-scorched day he'd spent on the ranch he currently worked at. Sure, he'd been saving money for as long as he'd been working. He had a decent amount put back, but nothing compared to what it would take to reach his goals of owning his own place one day.

He thought about his own life and how it had changed over the last year. He'd gone from practically raising himself and relying on Tyler's maid to make sure he was fed, to having the family he'd always dreamed of. His mother was present in his life, and he'd discovered that she was pretty cool. He had a stepdad that was more like a father to him than whatever loser it was that had donated half of his DNA. He had a baby sister he adored more than anything in the world. He was content and for the first time in his life, happy.

Then his thoughts had gone to Lily. She was the strongest one out of everyone he knew. The things she'd gone through in her life were things that no one, young or old, should ever have to experience. It was those things that would have broken most people. It almost did. There wasn't a day that went by when he didn't think about the day he'd found her bleeding out against the concession stand wall. The beatings he'd taken from the men in his mother's life, the nights he'd gone without food, and the times the profoundly dark thoughts of taking his own life paled in comparison to the feeling he had when he saw her that close to death.

The day she got sent to the facility had been the worst/best day of his life. The worst, because he'd been without her for an entire year. Since growing up, there hadn't been a day they'd gone without seeing each other. But, he knew it was for the best. If Lily was going to have any kind of life, going away was her best shot.

The day he'd picked her up and brought her home was the day something had begun to change inside him.

He couldn't put a finger on what it was, but something had definitely changed.

As he sat for hours on the end of the dock, the one thing he continued to think about was the thought of her dating someone. It never really occurred to him that she would see anyone. Then again, why wouldn't she? She was a pretty—beautiful young woman. Any man would be lucky to have her. So why had it bothered him so bad that a man such as doctor Chaffey's son would be interested? He'd known of Dexter. After all, they lived in a tiny town. Dexter was several years ahead of them in school, but he'd been well known and well liked. As far as prospects went, Lily could have done worse. She *had* done worse. Lucas Delray was about as worse as one could get in that department.

By the time he'd left the dock and returned home, his head was throbbing from all the analyzing and obsessing.

Which brought him back to the present. He realized he was still standing in the spot he'd been in when he almost kissed her. At first, he'd only been taunting her. Then something changed. He'd thought about kissing her; his best friend. He'd been so close he could taste the mint from her toothpaste as her breaths escaped her parted lips.

The thought of her lips made him groan out loud. What in the hell was going on with him? This was Lily. She was his best friend and nothing more. There couldn't be more there—*ever.*

With his mind made up that it was nothing more than a heat-of-the-moment thing, Chase put the forgotten pint of ice cream back in the refrigerator. Just before closing the door, he thought about how he knew that's exactly what she'd been in the kitchen for at nearly four in the morning.

Because you know her better than you know yourself, his mind whispered.

Feeling exhausted, he slowly made his way up to his room. He quietly slipped into the bathroom and peeked inside Lily's room. She was sound asleep, the sheet covering all of her but one shapely leg. He'd seen her legs more than just this once, and over the summer he'd noticed that they were no longer lanky and knobby. They were the tone legs of an athlete and the most beautiful legs he'd ever seen in his life.

He gently pulled the bathroom door closed. He pressed his forehead against the door and squeezed his eyes tightly together. When had he begun to notice Lily as more than just his scuffed shoes, skinned knees best friend? When did he start noticing her as a woman?

Chapter 27

People cry, not because they are weak.
It's because they've been strong for too long.

~Johnny Depp

"I'm so glad you agreed to come out with me tonight," Dexter said as they walked together down the sidewalk.

Lily licked the side of her ice cream cone and smiled at him. "I am too." It wasn't a complete lie. After her little run-in with Chase in the kitchen the night before, she was more than eager to push it out of her mind.

"I was a little shocked that you wanted to do it so soon considering you're starting school tomorrow," he said as he licked his own ice cream.

"Well, I fully plan on jumping in head first. If I stand a chance at going to veterinary school, I'm gonna have to buckle down and work for a scholarship. I've got to keep my head down and focus. That's the only way I'm getting out of this town," she said thoughtfully.

"I can understand that, but don't forget to look up every once in a while," he said as they sat on a park bench that overlooked a small lake. Ducks and geese paddled around the surface.

She sat beside him and stared at the serenity in front of her. Couples were walking along the paths hand in hand. The sun was just beginning to dip behind the tree line. "Thanks for dinner," she said suddenly uncomfortable with the silence that had fallen between the two of them.

"It was my pleasure. You know," he began, turning a little to the side, so he was facing her a bit more. He pushed his frameless glasses up his nose. "My mother has talked about you for months now. She truly believes you have a gift."

Lily felt her chest swell with pride. "Yep, a gift for shoveling sh— poop and taking fecal samples. I'm a real

225

winner," she joked lightly. She was uncomfortable with compliments. This was something Anastasia assured her was common in cases like hers.

He gave her a warm smile. "I'm serious, Lily. I've seen your care with the animals. It doesn't matter if it's a turtle or a horse. You have a way about you."

She didn't know how to react. Her cheeks were warm with embarrassment. "Thank you," she said as she tucked a strand of hair behind her ear.

He leaned back against the bench and crossed his ankle over his knee. His khakis were neatly pressed with a sharp crease down the front. He wore a deep red button-down shirt with the sleeves pushed up at the elbows. Since Dexter had started working at the clinic, she'd never once seen him in anything other than slacks and a collared shirt. She searched through her memory trying to recall if she'd ever seen Chase in anything but sleeveless shirts or plain ole t-shirts.

Dexter was handsome, in a nerdy kind of way. His eyes were dark blue—the opposite of Chase's. His smile was warm. He didn't have the dimples like Chase did, but it was still charming.

Why are you comparing Dexter to Chase?

Suddenly, the thought of being out with Dexter didn't seem like such a great idea. He was a good guy, but she felt no chemistry whatsoever. There had been no sparks when his hand accidentally touched hers, or when he'd casually placed his hand on the small of her back to assist her into her seat at the restaurant.

In fact, it had taken every ounce of self-control she had to keep from flinching at his touch. When that happened, another wave of guilt attacked her. She thought that after last night's incident in the kitchen, she would be okay with someone touching her. Disappointment bloomed in her chest. Maybe she hadn't made as much progress as she initially thought.

Lily shifted in her seat. She could feel herself growing anxious as the sky began to darken. There were still plenty of people around. It wasn't that she didn't trust Dexter, she just wasn't sure how she felt.

Unable to stand the silence anymore, she climbed to her feet. "Well, I probably should get home." Another wave of guilt struck when she saw the flash of disappointment in Dexter's eyes.

"Oh. Okay," he said with a polite but forced smile. He climbed to his feet, and they turned and began to walk back to where they'd parked.

They'd agreed to meet in front of the clinic in case something came up, and one of them had to leave. He walked her back to her car in silence.

Before climbing into the car, she turned. "I had a really nice time tonight. Thank you." It was sincere and honest. She did have a good time. It was good to get out and be normal for a while.

Dexter's face seemed to light up. "I did too." Leaning in, he brushed a kiss against her cheek, causing her to flinch.

When he pulled away, there was no mistaking the hurt in his eyes. "Dexter," she started.

He gave her a sad little chuckle. "It's okay. I understand," he said as he put his hands in his pockets and stepped back onto the curb.

"It's not like that. I just . . . I've had a difficult past, and because of that, I just get a bit antsy when people get to close. Please, don't take it personally."

He nodded. "It's okay, Lily. Truly. There are no hard feelings."

She chewed on her bottom lip. "Promise."

This time he gave her a broad, genuine smile. "I promise. There are no hard feelings whatsoever. I'll see you at work on Tuesday?"

"Absolutely," she said with a little too much enthusiasm."

She opened the door and climbed into the car she was borrowing from Trevor. Dexter waved as she pulled away from the curb and made her way down Main Street. It was only once she was sitting in front of the house everything began to surge forward.

"It was just a kiss on the cheek. It was completely innocent. You were never in any danger," she tried to tell herself. "You were never in danger. You were never in danger. You were never in danger." Over and over she repeated the mantra, but it didn't seem to ease the pressure building in her chest.

Tears spilled down her lashes as she gripped the steering wheel so tightly her hands began to ache. She could feel the flashbacks trying to creep through the barriers of her mind. Her heart started to speed through her chest as the panic attack gained momentum. Her lungs began to constrict feeling as if hot needles were slowly being inserted into them. She couldn't breathe. Sweat began to cover her forehead, and her hands grew clammy. Her pulse throbbed like a bass drum in her ears.

Panic crept into every fiber of her being. She gasped as she doubled over and pressed her head against the steering wheel. Heavy breaths slipped through her lips as she panted hard and heavy. She was spinning, and she couldn't gain control. The fact that she was losing her grip only made things worse.

Tears burned her eyes, and her body shook violently. She'd been a fool. Against Anastasia's insistence and because she hadn't had a single attack since being out of the institution, Lily stopped taking her anxiety medication. She didn't like the way they made her feel and felt like she didn't need them. Then the night before with Chase in the kitchen, she'd thought that she'd made the right decision about going out with Dexter. She realized now how stupid of a decision it had been.

Now, she was having a full-scale panic attack with no one or nothing to bring her down. She was going to have to ride it out. Something that she wasn't familiar with considering when she was inside, she always had help coming down.

Every inch of Chase's body ached. He'd helped haul the last load of hay of the season, something that he couldn't be happier about ending. Every muscle screamed at each little movement. It even felt like blinking was going to throw his back out. He was gritty from the dust and sweat combination. It hasn't helped matters that it was ninety-seven degrees with a heat index of over a hundred and ten, but he pushed himself.

He turned onto his street and saw the car Trevor loaned Lily sitting in the driveway. Trevor and Diana had decided to take a quick, last-minute mini-trip into the mountains. They'd left shortly before he had left for work. Coraline was staying with Trevor's parents.

Chase frowned. Why was Lily home? She usually worked on Wednesday evenings. He pulled his truck into the drive beside hers. He turned, and in the darkness of the evening, he could see someone hunched forward. Had she fallen asleep?

He climbed out of his truck and made his way to her door. Before he even made it all the way over, he could hear the sobs and cries coming from inside. Panic clutched his chest as something inside him pushed him into gear.

Reaching out, he jerked the door open. "Lily!?" he reached for her arm, but she shied away. "Lily! What's going on? What happened? Are you okay?"

There was no answer as she cried and struggled to catch her breath. Again, he reached for her, but this time she shoved at him.

"G-g-g-get aw-aw-away!"

He reached for her again, and she began to thrash and kick. Her hand flashed out and caught him in the mouth. Blood bloomed in his mouth. "No!" she screamed. "D-d-don't touch me."

Keeping his hands down, he moved a bit closer. "It's me. It's Chase." No matter how hard he tried, he couldn't get her to see him. The last time he'd seen her this bad was when she was restrained in the hospital. Everything clicked into place. She was having a panic attack.

"Lily. Lily. Damn it, look at me," he said raising his voice. Slowly she lifted her bloodshot gaze to his. She was looking right at him but was like she couldn't see him. "Lily, I need you to listen to me. Okay? Do you hear me? You've got this. Listen to me. Come on. You can do this."

He took several deep breaths and exhaled them. "Breath with me, baby. Come on. Breathe." In and out. In and out.

At that moment, headlights washed over them as Tyler's pickup pulled into the drive. Only a split second passed before Tyler was standing at their sides.

"What the hell? What happened?"

"Lily, breathe with me. Please, sweetheart. Breathe." He continued to breathe, praying that he could get through to her. "Came home and found her in the car like this," he said between breaths.

"You don't know what happened?"

"Dude! I just got here like three minutes ago," he said impatiently, not once taking his eyes off Lily.

"What can I do?"

"Go in the house and get a bottle of water and a cold rag." Tyler crossed the yard and bounded up the front steps like the hounds of hell were on his heels.

"Come on, Lils. That's a girl. Come back to me. There you go," he said with more calm than he felt. Inside he was one big ball of raw nerves.

Finally, after what felt like hours, Lily's breathing began to slow. The dazed look faded from her eyes, and he knew she was on her way back. She still trembled. Reaching forward, he gently cupped her cheeks and turned her face gently toward his. His thumbs brushed away the tears that still rolled from her lashes.

He gave her the best smile he could muster. "Are you with me now?"

She nodded weakly as Tyler appeared beside them carrying a washcloth and bottle of water. He twisted the top off and handed it to her. With shaky hands, she took a small sip and Tyler put the cloth on the back of her neck.

"Thank you," she finally rasped.

"What happened?" Tyler asked.

She was quiet for a moment and looked down at her lap. "Lily? What happened? Did someone hurt you?" Chase asked, automatically assuming the worse.

"No. It was nothing like that. I-I went out with Dexter—" she began.

Chase dropped his hands and crossed his arms over his chest.

"Did he do something to you?" Tyler asked gently.

Her gaze shifted to Chase. "N-no. It was nothing like that. He kissed me on the cheek. I came home and then . . . everything happened so fast."

"He kissed you without permission?" Chase asked through gritted teeth.

"Chase," Tyler warned.

"No, it wasn't like that at all. It was like when you kiss me on the cheek or the forehead," she said to Tyler. "It was nothing more, nothing less."

"But you don't react like this with us," he stated.

She shrugged. "I don't understand it. It's different with the two of you. After last night. . . ."

"Last night?" Tyler questioned looking first at her and then to Chase.

"After being around you two, I thought I could handle it. I haven't been on my meds for months now. When I didn't have an attack after Chase picked me up from the institute and you guys both hugged me, I thought I would be okay without the medication. I thought—"

"*You haven't been taking your medication?!*" Chase roared taking a step forward.

Lily flinched and shied away. Her reaction was like a punch in the gut. "I-I'm sorry," he said taking a step back. "I just . . . Anastasia said you have to stay on your meds. It's important to your full recovery."

"I know," she agreed sheepishly. "I was so stupid." Her eyes misted over, and tears began to fall once again.

"Shhhh, hey, come on. Don't cry. It's okay," Chase said taking a cautious step toward her. When she didn't flinch this time, he moved a little closer. Gently, he cupped her chin and tilted her face up. "I'm sorry I yelled. You just scared the shit out of me, and when I thought he might have done something. . . ." He let the sentence trail off.

"It was my fault," she whispered. "I'm sorry I scared you."

He scoffed playfully and winked. "Oh, you know. I'm getting used to this whole saving you bit. I kinda like being the hero."

This made her laugh, and the tension seemed to ease up.

"Why don't we go inside? I'll make some tea," Tyler said taking her hand and squeezing it.

She nodded and slid from the car, but when her feet hit the ground, her knees buckled. "Whoa, easy there. I got you," Chase said acting on instinct and wrapping his arm around her waist.

For a moment, everyone tensed, unsure of how she was going to react. Even Lily seemed to hold her breath. When no one moved for several long moments, Chase ducked his head until he could see into her eyes. "We okay? You okay?"

She gave him a soft smile and slight nod. His heart tightened. She tried to walk but only made it a few steps before she wobbled again.

"Okay, hold on. Here we go," he said as he bent and scooped her into a cradled position against his chest. She sighed and rested her head against his shoulder. He grimaced, knowing that he probably smelled like a barnyard. She didn't seem to mind because by the time they made it to the front door, her body had relaxed, and she was breathing evenly.

"She's asleep," Tyler whispered as he opened the front door for them.

"I'm going to take her up to her room. Go ahead and make the tea. It's in the cabinet above the stove."

Tyler nodded and walked off toward the kitchen while Chase carried Lily up the stairs. It took a little maneuvering, but he managed to get the door to her room open. Without turning on the light, he carried her to the bed and gently placed her on top of the blanket.

Reaching over, he clicked on the lamp on the bedside table. His eyes scanned over her to make sure she wasn't physically injured. Her skirt had risen slightly just above her knees. The silvery scars marring her beautiful skin glared up at him, a harsh reminder of all the torment she'd been through.

Careful not to disturb her, he smoothed the skirt down over her legs and unfastened her sandals. After tossing them to the floor, he pulled a quilt from the foot of the bed over her body. She sighed and mumbled his name as she shifted in her sleep.

Chase sat on the edge of the bed and cradled his face in his hands. Then he did something he hadn't done in a year and a half.

He cried.

Chapter 28

The most effective way to do it, is to do it.

~Amelia Earhart

The sound of snoring brought Lily from her dreamless sleep. Warm air puffed out against her neck. A heavy arm was draped over her side, pinning her to the mattress. She stiffened as a wave of panic tried to claim her. Her eyes snapped open, and immediately her nerves were calm. She realized she was sleeping on her side, Tyler snoring lightly in front of her. A trail of drool dribbled from the corner of his mouth. His large hand was wrapped protectively around hers, and it made her heart squeeze, reminding her of how much he meant to her.

That meant that the warm body molded against her back, holding on to her protectively was Chase. At least she hoped it was.

"Shhh, you're okay," he whispered against her ear.

Chase moved away from her, instantly causing to miss the warmth his body had created. Gently, she eased her hand away from Tyler's and rolled onto her back. Chase sat on the edge of the bed, leaning forward while resting his arms on the tops of his legs.

Lily pushed herself into a sitting position and scooted to the edge of the bed beside him.

"How are you feeling?"

"A little drained but better. What time is it?"

He looked down at his watch. "Quarter til midnight."

She watched as he scrubbed his hands over his face and then exhaled. He climbed to his feet and stretched his arms high above his head. "Did you sleep any?" she asked as she slid from the bed.

"No."

"Have you eaten?"

He shook his head.

"Come on. I'll make us something to eat," she said. She walked from the room looking at Tyler. "Should we wake him?"

"Nah. He was sleeping so I could later," he said as he stepped out into the hall with her.

She frowned. "You take turns sleeping so you can watch over me?"

He nodded and yawned. He lifted his arms high above his head, stretching. She didn't miss the small stretch of skin that peeked from beneath his shirt as he moved.

"Why?" she asked as they walked down the stairs together.

"I don't know. It's just something we've always done."

She stopped on the bottom step. Reaching for his arm, she stopped him. "What do you mean it's something you've always done?"

"That night I brought you to Tyler's after. . . . We were afraid to both go to sleep. Each night we took turns. Once you were out, one of us would sleep while the other kept an eye on you."

Emotions swelled in her chest and lodged in her throat. "You did this every time?"

"Yeah." Sheepishly, he looked down at his feet. "You had really bad dreams for a long time. We didn't want you to wake up and be scared. At first, it was just going to be once in a while, but when we used to all sleep over at Tyler's, you would wake up screaming."

Lily frowned, trying to recall what he was talking about, but couldn't come up with anything. She remembered having bad dreams but nothing about waking up.

"I don't remember," she whispered.

"I didn't figure you would. You would just get this far off look in your eyes. The best we figured was that you were still asleep. So, we were there to help you go back to sleep, or whatever."

She didn't know what to say. Tyler and Chase had been such an integral part of her life for so long, she never thought about the lengths they went through to protect her. She didn't realize that they literally lost sleep because of her.

Tears welled up in her eyes, and she dashed them away. "I'm getting really sick of crying," she grumbled.

Reaching up, he cupped her cheek and thumbed away a tear. She couldn't help but lean into his touch. Her eyes fluttered closed.

"I'm sorry," she finally said when he cleared his throat and moved away.

"It's what we do. We look out for one another."

"But this . . . this is different."

Together they walked into the kitchen. She set out the ingredients for grilled cheese sandwiches. After making them each two, she retrieved her medication from the cabinet and shook a pill into the palm of her hand. For a moment, she just stared at it. She was disappointed that she'd been unable to go without her medication. It made her realize how truly broken she was. She'd been naive to think that she could go on with her life as nothing happened, and that made her feel so weak.

She ran water from the tap and tossed the pill to the back of her throat, swallowing it with a huge gulp of water.

"You're not being weak for taking it," Chase said softly.

She laughed softly. "How do you know I thought I was weak?"

He looked down at his sandwich and smiled. "How did you know to cut the crust off my sandwich?"

"Because."

"I know you," they said at the same time.

Lily felt peace wash over her as she climbed onto the barstool beside him. For a while, they ate in silence. "You know, I thought I could be normal."

"Pffft, normal is overrated," he scoffed.

She laughed. "I'm serious."

He looked at her with twinkling blue eyes. They were eyes she'd seen millions of times and yet, as she sat there with him, she felt like she was seeing them for the first time.

"Yeah, so am I."

"I thought that since I could handle you hugging me and Tyler holding my hand, along with your mother, I was okay. I thought that I was—"

"Miraculously cured?"

"Well, yeah."

He shook his head and took a drink of her water. "It doesn't work like that."

She arched a brow at him. "Oh? And just when did you become an expert on my issues?"

He flushed. "When you first went in, I began doing research. I checked out every book I could on sexual abuse victims, PTSD, and everything in between. Once my mom became more present in my life, I talked to her." He swallowed and shifted nervously in his seat. "I didn't know that she'd been raped. In fact, it was my father who raped her."

Lily's eyes nearly exploded from her head. "Seriously?"

He nodded. "Believe me when I say I was just as shocked. I thought he was just some random dude she'd met and shacked up with. Every case with every victim is different. Some lash out. Some self-harm."

She shifted nervously, but he continued.

"Some turn to drugs while others move on to become abusers themselves, and believe it or not, some of them turn to sex. My point is, every circumstance, every result is different. Some handle it betters than others. You didn't handle it well at first. You didn't cope, and you hid it. I take partial responsibility for that."

Lily gasped and covered his hand with hers.

"We both do," Tyler said from behind them. He shuffled into the kitchen and swiped the other sandwich from Chase's plate.

Horror filled her at hearing what they were saying. "No! None of this was your fault!"

Chase nodded. "But what you don't see is, that by us not doing anything, we were enabling you. You tried to bury it and keep it out of sight. It ate you up from the inside. When it started to surface, you started drinking.

When the booze didn't help, you looked for something else. You turned to Lucas."

"But I met Lucas before it happened."

"You met him the day it happened," Tyler reminded her.

Chase continued. "He was already lost, and after everything happened, he wasn't alone anymore. He preyed on you. When the pot and the booze didn't help, you started cutting."

She could feel emotions welling in her throat. "I don't need a trip down memory lane," she said, though not unkindly.

"I'm not saying this to make you feel bad. I'm saying had we spoken up and told someone like we should've, then this whole mess could have been avoided. You would've gotten the help you needed long before it got to where it ended up."

"You were only doing what I asked you to."

Chase rolled his eyes and snorted. "Yeah, remind me never to do that again."

The three of them laughed. "Anyway," he continued, "all people deal with it differently. After you came home, I talked to Anastasia. I needed to know what to expect. Damn it Lily, that day I found you. . . . I still relive that. Not as bad now that you're here, but I still have the nightmares. I never want you to get there again.

"Anastasia told me to take it easy around you, but when you didn't show signs of PTSD around me, I was hopeful. Then tonight, while you were sleeping, I realized that you're not likely to get triggered with us. That's not to say it won't happen, but from what I can gather, you haven't because you're comfortable with us. You feel safe and know that we would never let anything happen to you like that again."

Tyler nodded. "If you think about it, aside from us, Trevor and Diana, and the people you work with, you don't have contact with anyone. Not in a social manner. You're always here or at work."

"So?"

"*So*, that's going to change tomorrow," he continued. "We can't be with you every second. You have to help us. You have to keep to your meds until your *doctor* takes you off them."

She hadn't thought about it, but what they were saying was true. She would be in school, and people were going to talk and stare. She would bump into someone in the hall. Would she freak out and have an episode as she had earlier? "Is this an intervention?" she meant it to sound like a joke, but it fell kind of flat.

"If that's what it takes. Then yes, consider it an intervention," Chase said squeezing her hand.

Everything they were saying was true. She had been foolish in thinking that she could do everything on her own. Isn't that how she got into the mess in the first place?

"Okay. I promise to take better care of myself. I promise to try not to scare y'all again."

Both guys sighed dramatically. "Thank God. I'm getting really tired of always playing your knight in shining armor," Chase said with a wink.

Tyler wrapped his arm around her shoulder and pulled her into his side. He kissed the top of her head. "You mean the world to us, Lils. We just want you happy."

"Aww, this is a real Dawson's Creek moment," Chase snickered as he wrapped his arms around both of them.

"Just shut up."

Lily closed her eyes and soaked up the love and comfort from the two most important people in her life. With the strength they gave her, she knew that she would be able to handle anything.

Chapter 29

When our mindfulness touches those we love,
they will bloom like flowers.

~Thich Khat Hanh

"I don't want to go back," Lily groaned to herself as she sat on the wall outside Tyler's house. The heels of her new Converse sneakers bouncing off the brick.

The early morning heat was already sweltering. She'd wound her hair into a stylish, slightly messy, knot on top of her head. The tiny hairs were still clinging to her neck. A thick fog hovered over the land. When the sun shone over the tree line and onto the ground, it connected with the drops of dew on the grass, making them sparkle like diamonds.

She yawned. By the time Tyler left it was after two in the morning. She'd collapsed into the bed after insisting that Chase should sleep in his room. He needed rest because he had football practice. In truth, she needed time to go over things in her head and prepare for school. She'd finally fallen asleep an hour before she was supposed to get up. However, when she woke up, she felt strangely alert.

She'd dressed in a pair of new denim shorts, and a simple tank top. She'd even applied a little makeup and lip gloss. It wasn't much, but it made her feel more confident.

Anastasia had called her first thing, letting her know that she would need to meet in the guidance counselor's office when she got to school. Lily tried not to think about the last time she'd gone to the office.

Chase was leaning against his truck, watching her.

"Why are you staring at me?"

He laughed and just shook his head. "I don't know. You just look . . . different."

She scowled at him. "I do not."

He pursed his lips and nodded. "Yeah, Lils, you do." He walked over and jumped up onto the wall and sat beside her.

She wasn't going to argue with him—not when there was a kaleidoscope of butterflies flapping around in her stomach. Reaching over she touched the bruise and slight cut at the corner of his bottom lip. "How's the lip?" When he winced, she moved her hand.

He shrugged casually. "S'not s'bad. Good thing you hit like a girl."

"Say that again, and I'll smack you so hard Google won't be able to find you."

They both laughed, but it was cut short when the sound of yelling pulled their attention to the house. They turned to see where the source of the sound was coming from.

"Don't you walk out, you arrogant little shit! I'm not done talking to you!" Elliot Anderson boomed as Tyler slung his backpack over his shoulder and stormed down the stairs.

"Tyler! Tyler Cooper Elliot, get your ass back here right now!"

Tyler spun around when he got to where Chase and Lily sat. A cocky grin was plastered across his face as he lifted both hands and flipped the bird at his father. Their eyes widened when Elliot's face exploded in shades of red they'd never seen before.

When Tyler turned around, he was grinning ear to ear, something they weren't expecting. "Let's go," he said as he walked over to the truck and opened the door for Lily to climb in. As soon as they did, the three looked up to find a very pissed off Elliot standing in front of the truck.

"Go!" Tyler yelled.

Chase thrust the truck into reverse and sped down the drive. When they hit the street, he whipped the pickup around and jammed it into gear. Once their tires hit the pavement, smoke billowed out behind them as they sped away.

Excitement filled the cab as the three of them yelled. She wasn't sure why but, it amped them up. Once the surge of adrenaline settled and their laughter was under control, Lily looked at Tyler. "What was that back there?"

"Just stupid shit," he grunted as he opened his bag and rummaged through the contents. He was evading the question, something he frequently did when it came issues with his father. She'd learned early on not to push Tyler when it came to his father. There was no love there, and it was not going to be a surprise when Tyler moved out as soon as he turned eighteen. It didn't matter if he was in school or not. When his grandparents passed away, they'd left all their money--enough money to last three lifetimes—to Tyler.

The only person that would have access to that money would be Tyler; he'd have the access the day he turned eighteen. Lily figured this was one point of contention between Tyler and his father. It hurt Elliot's ginormous ego that his own parents hadn't left him a dime and their only grandson everything. Then there was his mother and the prospect of her getting out by the time they graduated high school.

When one got right down to it, Tyler's life was more messed up than any of theirs. How he held it together and dealt with it was incredible. He'd managed to make a considerable name for himself without his father's help.

He removed two brown paper bags and set them in her lap with a wide smile.

She laughed. "What's this for?"

"Tradition. Can't start our last first day of school without your lunches."

Touched by his sentiment, she opened her bag. Inside rested all her favorite, a Ziploc baggie with pb&j, a bag of chips, a candy bar and an apple. She could feel her eyes welling, but she shoved the urge to weep down inside and locked it tight.

"Aww, ya big ol' softy," Chase chuckled.

Tyler reached across the back of the pickup and smacked the back of Chase's head. The three of them laughed.

"What's with getting around so early?" Chase asked as they turned down a gravel road leading away from town.

"I wanted us to do something before we go to school," she said.

"And this would be?" Tyler asked.

"A new beginning! A new day! A new look on life!"

"Well, aren't you just miss cryptic this morning," Tyler laughed. "Hey, how you feeling anyway?"

"I'm fine. A little tired, but otherwise, I feel good."

"And your medication?"

"She took it," Chase chimed in. "I was standing right there when she did."

Lily crossed her arms over her chest. "You two do realize that I'm not a child."

"And *you* do realize that because of all that shit yesterday, one of us will be checking with you daily to make sure you take your meds."

She scrunched up her nose. "Fine. But I'm going to protest the whole time."

"We wouldn't expect anything less."

Reaching forward, Lily turned the dial on the radio. A country song about gravel roads, bonfires, and beer blasted through the speakers. They rolled the windows down. As the warm morning air filled the cab, carrying with it the scent of dust, hay fields, and freshness. The three of them sang at the top of their lungs, and Lily realized it was the lightest she'd felt in a long time.

Whatever awkwardness that had been going on with Chase was pushed away. Tyler's fight with his dad was forgotten. Chase's regret over not taking good enough care of her vanished. They were just three best friends, on a joy ride before going to school. For the moment, there were no significant problems, no anxiety over seeing the very people that tormented her for years of her life. Today was a new day, and Lily was going to live it to the absolute fullest.

They pulled to a stop at the lake they'd spent virtually every day of every summer at until things had gone wonky. This was the one place that Lily loved the most. It was the place that they were all free of all the crap that had gone on in their lives.

"C'mon," she said bouncing up and down in her seat while barely able to contain her excitement.

When they both just stared at her like she'd flipped her wig, she began pushing on Chase's arm. "Come on. If we don't hurry, we're going to be late for school. Now, scooch."

"Jeesh, woman," he grunted as she pushed harder. He opened the door and nearly fell out on his head. She giggled as she climbed from the truck and sprinted down the path. She turned and jogged backward. "Come. On. Already!"

She heard them muttering something about too early to run and about maybe she should be re-evaluated as they began to jog behind her.

By the time the caught up with her, she was already standing at the end of the dock. Her arms were spread out wide at her sides. She tilted her head back and closed her eyes, relishing in the warm kiss of the sun as it climbed into the sky. The air was hot and heavy, causing sweat to bead on her forehead, but she didn't care. Not a single thing was going to ruin this moment for her.

"Lily, what on earth has—"

"Shh. Just feel this moment. Just for a second, okay?" she said as she dropped her arms down, placing them behind each of the guys. She held onto them as they each put an arm around her while clasping each other's forearm. They were united. The three of them—heart, mind, and soul.

For several long moments, they just stood, welcoming the morning. Finally, Lily released them and took a step back. She knelt in front of their names. The ones they'd carved it seemed like a lifetime ago. She pulled out a pocket knife and began to carve. Chase and Tyler watched with curiosity as she worked. When she was finished, she blew the shavings away and climbed back to her feet.

"There. Your turn," she said giving the knife to Chase.

He knelt and carved something and then added his initial. When he was done, he passed the knife to Tyler.

Tyler stared at the knife in his hand for a moment, as if contemplating what to say. Then, slowly, he knelt and began to carve. When he was finished. The three of them stared down at their work. Lily took out her phone and snapped a picture of the carving and then turned, putting her back toward the lake.

"Come on. We're taking a picture!"

The three of them squeezed together, and she took a few pictures.

She stuffed her phone into her back pocket and looked at them. "I love you guys."

"We love you too," they said in unison.

"Now, let's go rule the school."

Thirty minutes later they were standing in front of the school. Lily wanted to ignore the pressure of nerves pressing against her chest, but she couldn't. Her backpack seemed to weigh a ton as she sifted it around on her shoulder.

"I'm scared," she admitted as they walked up the steps slowly.

"You're going to be perfectly fine," Tyler assured draping his arm playfully over her shoulder.

"Besides, we're the lucky ones. You're smoking hot, Lils. People are going to be staring because they're jealous."

She felt flush climb into her cheeks. "Shut up, Chase."

"He's right, Lily. You don't look at all like the girl that left here."

As they reached the top step, she could already see people openly staring at her. She tried not to let it bother her. She kept her chin high and continued to walk through the doors with her best friends.

I can do this. She repeated it constantly. Most of the younger classmen didn't know who she was, so that was a big bonus. However, there were still members of her class that she'd known her entire life. Some weren't so bad, but she had never taken the time to get to know them. It was more of a defense mechanism than anything. If she didn't put herself out there, she wouldn't be hurt.

The senior corridor was down the hall and to the left, but she still had to go to the guidance office. "Okay, this is where I get off," she said stopping in front of the school counselor's office.

"Want us to wait?"

"No. I'm fine. I promise." She wasn't sure who she was trying to convince more, herself or them. When they didn't move, she rolled her eyes and shoved at Chase's shoulder. "Go on, get out of here. I'll be fine."

"See you in a bit," Tyler said giving Chase a push when he refused to budge. After they disappeared into the crowd of kids milling about the hall, she turned and faced the door. She took several deep breaths as she put her hand on the cold knob.

"I've got this," she whispered.

Chapter 30

When we stop judging others and ourselves,
our heart begins to open.

~Swami Dhyan Giten

As she stepped into the office, she was greeted with the fragrant scent of lemon and vanilla. She took a deep breath and smiled. Lemon had always been one of her favorite aromas.

"Ah, there she is," Anastasia said rising from her chair and greeting Lily with a hug. "Me and you are going to talk about last night," she whispered.

Lily stiffened in her arms. "Chase gave me a rather alarming phone call last night, but we *will* discuss that later."

She could hear the disapproval in the woman's voice, but when the embrace ended, Anastasia was nothing but warm smiles.

Ava Lanahan stood from behind her massive oak desk. "Lily. It is so good to see you. You're looking very well."

Lily offered the woman a kind smile. "Thank you. I feel better than I ever have."

"That is what I love to hear. Please, have a seat so we can get started. We won't be long."

Lily nodded and sat in the chair beside Anastasia.

"Now, I've been brought up to speed on everything," she began, "and I just want to make sure that we're on the same page. *Really* on the same page, not like last time."

The heat of humiliation burned Lily's cheeks. "Yes, ma'am."

"I'm going to be honest, after finding out the severity of everything going on with you at our last visit, I must apologize. I feel like I was remiss in my job."

Lily's eyes widened. She was caught off guard by the apology, but she shook her head. "No, you weren't. I was a scared child. I was afraid of being taken away from my friends—Tyler and Chase to be specific. I take full responsibility for my actions. I handled everything very poorly. I accept that now, and I'm working on making things better."

Her statement seemed to please the woman because she smiled. "I'm so glad to hear that. I've been talking with your doctor, and we've both agreed that it is in your best interest to stop in and see me once a week. Doesn't have to be any set time. I just want to be sure to touch base and make sure everything is okay. I've been going over your schedule and transcripts from last year, and I must admit, I'm pleasantly surprised."

"Why?"

"Because Lily, I truly had no idea how exceptionally bright you were. You were such a chameleon for so long that I never once picked up your aptitude. I mean, I knew you were bright just from your junior high transcripts, but I had no idea it went to this extent."

"I didn't like attention. Still, don't."

"I understand that, but I'm looking at the grades you finished with while you were away and I'm truly astonished. Lily, if this is how you do this year, then the world can be at your fingertips. Colleges will be lining up for you."

"You think so?"

She nodded. "I know so. I like to believe all students can reach whatever goals they set. With some, unfortunately, it's not a reality. With you, I believe it truly is, and it's even more of a victory for you considering all the trials and hurdles you've had to overcome.

"My main goal is to make sure you stay on track. You've got an intense caseload here, and you're very likely to feel overwhelmed. I must do a quick evaluation, and then we're all good to go. I need you to be completely honest with me, no matter how uncomfortable the questions get. Can you do that?"

Lily crossed her legs. "I can."

Ms. Lanahan looked down at a sheet of paper on her desk. She picked up a pen and perched her glasses on the end of her nose.

"Are you in an environment now that you feel safe?"

Lily smiled fondly as she recalled what Chase had revealed to her the night before. "I am."

"Do you receive adequate doctor care?"

"I do," she said flashing a quick grin at Anastasia, who—in turn—winked back at her.

"Are you being provided the most basic of necessities—food, shelter, clothing, anything that is required to live?"

"Yes, ma'am."

"Do you feel like harming yourself or do you have suicidal tendencies?"

"No, ma'am. I can honestly say, I do not!" It felt like a weight had been lifted from her shoulders as she answered.

"Are you sexually active?"

Lily's eyes widened, and she felt a rush of color settle in her cheeks. She swallowed and then cleared her throat. "Um, n-no. I'm not sexually active."

"Do you plan on becoming sexually active?"

"Not anytime soon," she stated.

"Do you have any anxiety about rejoining your classmates?"

"A little bit, yes."

"Rate your anxiety on a scale of 1-10."

"About a 6."

Lanahan jotted down the last of her notes, and then removed her glasses. "Well, we're done here unless there is something more you can think of, either of you."

"Nothing that I can think of," Anastasia said.

"Nope!"

Lanahan closed the file on her desk and laced her fingers together on top. "Well then, let me be the first to say, welcome back Lilian. If you need anything or feel like you're being overwhelmed, please come see me immediately."

"I promise," she said and realized that she genuinely meant it.

"Excellent. Now, you still have about ten minutes before the first bell. Have a good day."

Lily laughed and left the office. Outside the door, she turned and looked at Anastasia. "I know you're aggravated with me, but I promise, everything is on track now. I'll call you after track today and fill you in on all the details."

"That works. Have a good day, Lily."

"Thanks."

Lily watched as Anastasia left the school. Then, with a deep breath, she hitched her backpack on her back and turned.

She began down the hall. Underclassmen milled around her, freshman looked scared and panicked facing a new building and new routine. She remembered what she'd felt her freshman year, and it was similar to what she was feeling now.

They went about their business, ignoring her and acting as if she didn't exist. Some looked at her in awe, like she was some superstar. It felt odd, but she knew it was only because she was a senior. At least that is what she hoped.

When she reached the senior hall, she paused. Once she walked around the corner, she would see some of the people that tormented her the most. The very same people that made her life a living hell.

"You can do this," she whispered to herself.

Squaring her shoulders and lifting her chin with confidence, she stepped forward and walked around the corner.

When no one seemed to notice her, she kept going. A few eyes turned in her direction, but most of them were out of curiosity. As she kept going, she began to gain confidence. Kiera and her cronies were nowhere in sight, and they were her biggest concern at this point.

She was getting closer to her locker. The second she spotted Chase and Tyler's heads above the crowd, as they leaned against the metal wall of doors, she felt relief flood through her. However, the closer she got, the more she realized that they weren't alone. They were encircled by a group of football players, cheerleaders, and other random people.

Lily realized that Chase and Tyler were the top dogs of the school. Somewhere along the way, they'd become the ones the girls wanted to date, and the guys wanted to chill with. They were popular. Lily tried not to let that intimidate her. She had just as much right to be there as everyone else did—possibly more so because none of the people flocking around knew them like she did.

She was just outside the circle when she suddenly stopped behind a girl with long, sleek black hair. For a split second, Lily considered bolting. Was she ready to deal with Kiera? *Could* she handle the girl? The girl was standing remarkably close to Tyler. She just prayed he wouldn't go down that road.

However, as her eyes wandered over to Chase, she stiffened. Molly Trent stood pressed against his side. The girl was beautiful with wide green eyes, thick and lustrous auburn hair, and pouty lips. A small bolt of jealousy shot through her at seeing how close the girl was standing to him. Lily frowned. She wasn't sure how to process what she was seeing. Her mind tried to go back to the night she'd almost kissed him in the kitchen, but she didn't let it go that far. She took comfort in the fact that Chase seemed to be ignoring Molly entirely as he continued to stare at his phone.

It struck her as weird when seeing Kiera pressing against Tyler didn't bother her as badly. As if sensing her distress, Chase lifted his gaze from his phone. His eyes bore into hers, and he straightened, moving away from Molly. He took a step in her direction, giving her a reassuring smile and a slight nod.

It was time to face it.

"Lils! What's shakin'," Chase said loudly.

This was it. Now or nothing!

Everyone stopped their conversations and slowly turned their attention in her direction. The last to turn around was Kiera.

Chapter 31

Your honor yourself by acting
with dignity and composure.

~Allan Lokos

The air seemed to crackle around them with tension. It seemed that everyone was holding their breath as the two girls stood facing one another for the first time in a year and a half. Kiera's looks had changed. She'd put on some weight. Something that Lily figured was due to giving birth. However, it didn't take away from the fact that the other girl was still beautiful. There was a small silver scar just beneath her dark eyebrow that Lily figured was a result of their fight.

Something clicked inside her, and she realized she was no longer intimidated by Kiera. She just smiled and stepped around the girl and reached for her locker. She twisted the combination lock while feeling everyone's gazes on her back. After placing her things inside and removing the books she needed for AP Biology, she turned and smiled sweetly.

"Okay, let's get things out in the open right now. Might as well get rid of the rumors right off the bat."

People shifted uncomfortably and looked at the ground. "First, yes, I was in a mental facility where I got the help and rehabilitation I needed. No, I did not join a cult. No, I did not try to kill myself. Yes, I was a cutter. I cut too deeply which is why people thought I attempted it. Yes, I did drugs. Yes, I had sex for said drugs. No, I did not sleep with the entire football team." She took a breath and continued.

"My mother is in jail for drugs and abuse, amongst other things. She was a whore. I. Am. Not. I was molested by one of her boyfriends, *not* my father. It was *violent*. This happened my freshman year, which is why I spiraled out of control. Do I believe any of this is any of y'all's

252

business? No, I do not. Am I going to talk about any of my experiences in depth with any of you? Definitely not! However, I do believe that if you're going to be talking about me, you need all the facts. Now, do any of you have any questions you need to ask? Because this is your only chance."

There was a cough, and it seemed like it was so quiet a pin dropping would sound like a shotgun blast. "No takers? Okay, good. Now, I'm here to have a fresh start and get through the day just like the rest of you. If you're interested in trying to start shit with me, move along. I don't have the time or the patience for it. I'm just like the rest of you. I want to have a good year, go to prom and then graduate."

She directed her last comment at Kiera. "And if *any* of you think bullying me, putting me down or otherwise trying to make my last days of school hell, then good luck. I've been through worse. You don't scare me. Not anymore."

Everyone was speechless. Some of them walked away, and others lingered. A few of them welcomed her back and gave her kind words about how "brave" she was or how they "admired" her. It was kind of surreal. When she turned, Chase and Tyler were looking at her as if she'd just sprouted a second head with horns.

"That was amazing," Chase finally said wrapping his arms around her and swinging her in circles.

Lily laughed. "Put me down, ya big ox."

When he placed her on her feet, she found Tyler smiling widely at her. "That was incredible." He gave her a quick hug. She was laughing and light headed with adrenaline when he stepped back. She realized that while everyone had wandered off, there were still two people that remained.

Kiera stepped forward, and Lily was having a hard time reading the other girl's face. It was blank except for a small crease in her forehead. Lily stopped laughing and stepped forward.

"It's good to see you back, Lily."

Lily's eyes widened, and a slight gust of wind could have knocked her over. She could see the actual sincerity in the other girl's eyes. Kiera was truly glad Lily was back. This didn't allow her to lower her defenses, though.

"Why don't we give them a minute," Tyler said to Chase and Molly.

Chase looked at Lily with worry, and she nodded. "I'll be fine."

Tyler grabbed Chase by the arm and pulled him away. They didn't go far, which was a secret relief.

"How are you?" Kiera asked.

"Um, fine?"

The other girl nodded and shifted nervously from one foot to the other. Finally, she let out a sigh. "I'm sorry. I'm sorry for all of it. I'm sorry for the way we—I—treated you; all the mean things I said and did to you. I was a horrible person. I didn't realize what you were going through. I know it's probably too late for an apology, but I needed to try."

A bevy of emotions welled up inside Lily's chest. "It's never too late for an apology, and you didn't know because you never took the time to find out. You were too busy being a bitch and making me look bad to take the attention off your life and drama. You were miserable with your life, and you used me as your whipping post. I won't say you're completely the reason I went away because you're not. But, you had a big hand in it. Even when I tried to apologize to you for the shitty things I said to you," she paused and took a breath. "Do you remember what you told me that day?"

Lily watched as Kiera's face crumpled. Tears rolled down the girl's cheeks as she nodded.

"You told me to kill myself. I nearly did kill myself, but not on purpose. You can't be like that to people, Kiera. Your words carry weight. *You* influence people. Everyone followed your lead. Half of those people wouldn't have even noticed me if you hadn't made it such a public show. You opened the door for people to attack me a long time ago. I can't tell you all the nasty names and dirty things people said to me because you made it okay for them to do so. It doesn't matter if you hate the person. Telling someone that they are better off dead is unacceptable. My blood would have been on your hands. Not only that, but because of how the others treated me, my blood would have been on their hands *because* of you. Is that something you were prepared to live with for the rest of your life? Your actions carry consequences.

Lily continued, "You can't use *I didn't know what you were going through or I wouldn't have done* it as an excuse. That doesn't give you a reason. You've been nasty to me since we were in kindergarten. What was your excuse then?"

She just shook her head, tears pouring down her cheeks. "I don't have one." Overhead the first bell rang. She had five minutes to get to class before the second bell rang, and she was nowhere near finished saying her peace.

"You never got the chance to know me." Lily was surprised at the intense amount of calm she felt. She wasn't mad as she spoke to Kierra because she was releasing the demons she'd clung to for so long.

"I-I know," Kiera sobbed. "I've wanted to come to you so many times and apologize, but I didn't know if you'd believe me."

"I wouldn't have. I'm still not sure if I do now. What gave you this change of heart?"

"A couple of things?"

"Such as?"

"Chase."

Her answer caught Lily off guard. "What about him?"

"After you were taken away, he showed up on my doorstep. He explained—yelled, actually—everything that happened and how it was my fault. At first, I didn't believe him. I figured because he was in love with you, he was just pissed. So, I asked Tyler. When he confirmed it—"

Lily did a double take and held up her hand. "Wait! Chase is in love with me? What?"

Kiera gave her a dumbfounded look and nodded. "Yes. He's been in love with you for years. Everyone in the school knows it. The guys in this school are scared of Chase, and know if they piss him off, they get Tyler pissed off too."

She opened her mouth to refute the statement. It wasn't true. "You know what, never mind. What was the second reason for this miraculous change of heart?"

"My daughter. When she was born, the things Chase said to me made me think about the kind of person I was. *I* didn't like me very much, which is why stuff happened. The second Rayna was placed in my arms, I realized that I wasn't going to be the mom my mother was. I wanted to be a better person, not for me, but for my daughter. I thought about how I would feel if the things I'd said and done to you had been done to my daughter. It made me sick. I decided that if I ever get to say I'm sorry, I would. So, Lily, from the bottom of my heart, I'm sorry for what I did. I'm sorry for the hell I put you through. Do you think you can ever forgive me? Maybe we can find a way around all of this and be friends," she asked in a hopeful voice.

Lily stared at her and truly believed her. However, Lily had to face her own truth. Kiera had fallen from grace and gotten a heaping dose of reality. She'd heard rumors about how she'd gotten pregnant and about how the father was some prominent businessperson from the city that dropped her like a bad habit. She didn't pay attention to the rumors because she knew what the receiving end was like.

She realized that Kiera was still waiting for her to answer. Lily let out a slow breath releasing the very last string of animosity she held for Kiera. "Yes, Kiera. I do accept your apology, and I forgive you. I think I forgave you a long time ago, but that's as far as it will ever go. Because we cannot be friends. Merely realizing what you've done and apologizing does not erase the years of hell you put me through."

"I do believe you, but I also think you're apologizing to make yourself feel better because you will never truly understand what it was like for me because you've never been there, and I can say this much with certainty. As much as I hated you, I would NEVER wish anything that

I've been through on you. I'm also not sure I believe this change of heart you're claiming to have, but only time will tell me if you're sincere.

"From here, we'll go our separate ways and live our separate lives. We live in a small town, and our paths will cross. I'm not saying I won't be polite because I will be, but that's as far as it will go."

And then, the last chains that had been shackling Lily down broke away. "I've got to get to class. Goodbye, Kiera."

Lily turned and walked away, tears of joy streaming down her cheeks. When she got to Chase and Tyler, looks of concern were etched deeply onto their face.

"Are you okay?" Chase asked immediately stepping close to her. She nodded and smiled.

"Never better." Her eyes locked with his and everything around them fell away. What Kiera had said about him still hummed through her brain. Was Chase really in love with her? How could he be in love with her?

He cleared his throat jerking her back to reality. "We need to get to class. The bell is about to ring."

"Oh, right."

She turned and found Tyler watching them with an amused smirk on his face. Heat climbed up the back of her neck when she realized that—for just a moment—she'd forgotten all about him standing there.

The three of them walked into their first class as the bell began to ring. She took a seat behind them and stared at the back of Chase's head.

He was dating Molly. There was no way he was in love with her. It just wasn't a possibility. Was it?

Molly was turned around in her seat talking to Chase as the teacher took roll call. Lily gritted her teeth when the girl giggled and touched Chase's arm. She then flipped her hair back over her shoulder and batted absurdly long lashes at him.

Seriously? Those had to be fake lashes. No way on earth could they be natural.

Chase leaned forward in his chair and whispered something in Molly's ear causing the other girl to giggle. Lily scowled.

Tyler was watching the exchange, but, at the same time, watching Lily watch Chase.

A knowing smile crossed his face when she met his gaze. Her scowl deepened. "What?" she mouthed.

He snickered, looked at the couple, and then tilted his head. "You're jealous," he mouthed.

Lily stubbornly shook her head. His only response was a silent laugh as he turned back to the front of the room.

She wasn't jealous. Was she?

Was she in love with her best friend?

Chapter 32

Love is the longing for the half of ourselves we have lost.

~Milan Kundera

Lily's life became about balancing work, school, and track. When she wasn't doing one or all three of those, she was concentrating on college applications and making decisions. When she was slow at the clinic, her nose was buried in homework.

After her conversation with Kiera, everything seemed to fall into place. People no longer tormented her. Sure, there were some that still didn't care for her, but she didn't care. She wasn't there to please people. She was there to do what she needed to do and get the hell out. Her grades were straight A's, and she couldn't help but feel proud of everything she'd accomplished.

She was still seeing Anastasia, but instead of once a week, they'd changed her appointments to every two weeks. They were beginning the process of weaning Lily off the anxiety meds. They'd already decided to take her entirely off the depression medication.

Tyler and Chase slipped back into the zone of football, so she didn't see as much of them as she would have liked. She realized it was okay. When they saw that she was doing well, their mothering died down a little bit.

When Chase wasn't on the football field or in the weight room, he was working on the ranch. With fall coming in quickly, they had to get things ready for winter. While things in Alabama were typically mild in the winter time, things could still get dangerous for cattle.

Sundays were reserved family time. This often included Tyler because things with his father continued to get worse. When she ventured to ask him about it, he usually shrugged it off, but she could tell the fights were beginning to take their toll on him. He started to stay at the house with Lily and Chase more often, primarily since his father was working from home more than ever.

If Diana and Trevor had a problem with it, they never mentioned it. They always welcomed him with open arms and a place to stay. On Sunday's, they all went to church. They then returned home to eat lunch as a family around the kitchen table. While Lily helped clean the dishes, the guys would either go outside and toss the football around in the backyard or pile on the couch and watch whatever game that was on.

Track had gone well for her, and she found herself ranked in the top three of the state. Ms. Lanahan said that because she placed so high, there could be chances for a scholarship for track. Lily didn't get her hopes up because, while she enjoyed running, it wasn't something she cared to pursue outside of high school. Nevertheless, it still made her feel accomplished.

It was the end of October, and the town was alive with activity. The Raven Bend Wildcats had made it to the championship for the first time in over a decade. All the shops boasted their support by painted windows the color of red and white. Streamers decorated the lamp posts. The air hummed with excitement, and while Lily didn't care much about the sport, she still found herself excited for the game.

She'd began talking and even hanging out with a few girls from her track team, Misty, Shawana, and Ginger. Misty was a cheerleader, and while Lily typically tried to avoid the peppy people, she couldn't help but gravitate toward Misty and her bubbly personality. She transferred from Montgomery three weeks into school. The perky little blond with eyes that were wide and almost too big for her face was always happy.

Shawana was from New York and had moved to Raven's Bend sometime during their junior year. The big city girl hadn't adjusted well to small town living, but she was adapting. During one of the track meets, Lily, Shawana, and Misty had been placed in a room with the very fiery redhead Ginger. Neither her name, nor the color of her hair was real, but no one questioned her.

She was the one that was as unpredictable as a tornado. One minute she could be sweet and kind then, in a flash, she could turn into the queen of the damned. However, Lily could see deep down how truly kind of a person she was.

Lily wasn't sure how or why, but the four of them all gravitated toward one another. While they didn't hang out all the time, they did every occasionally. Lily still wasn't comfortable around new people, and to her, these girls were very new. If they were going to be friends, she wanted it to be organic and not forced. So far, everything felt okay.

They'd made plans to go to the big game together. After picking Ginger up at her grandmother's house, they made their way to the game.

"Y'all, have you seen how fine Declan Shepard looked today in his jersey," Misty gushed as they pulled into the graveled parking lot of the football field.

"Girl, you've had eyes on that boy all year. Why don't you just ask him out and put us all out of our misery? At least we won't have to hear you mooning over him every chance you get," Ginger grumbled as she looked into the visor mirror and dabbed a finger beneath her perfectly winged eyes.

"Don't be nasty," Misty said poking her tongue out at her from the back seat.

Lily just smiled, but her mind was a million miles away. This would be the first time she would be going to the football field since everything started. She was nervous and worried at the same time.

"Hey," Ginger said once the other two girls had gotten out of the car and started toward the girl's locker room.

Lily blinked and looked at the other girl, giving her a shaky smile. Ginger frowned. "What's going on in that head of yours?"

Lily lifted her shoulders. "Mind's kinda busy tonight, I guess," she said trying to downplay what was going on.

Ginger didn't buy it. "Bullshit."

This caused Lily to laugh. Of the three girls, Ginger was the one she'd connected with the most. She'd come from a similar situation with her parents. They'd split when she was younger, and she'd been forced to live with her father. As it happened, he was an abusive drunk that liked to take his anger out on his young daughter.

While their experiences were vastly different, Ginger had experimented with almost every known drug to try to ease her pain. That was until she met her now boyfriend of three years. She'd lived a town over and transferred over to be closer. They were one of the cutest couples Lily had ever seen. Ginger may be rough around the edges, but where Allan was concerned, she was as soft as they came.

"I just haven't been back here since. . . ."

"Chase found you carved up like a turkey?"

The girl certainly had a way with words. "Well, yes."

She pursed her perfectly red painted lips. "Okay, you can do one of two things."

Lily arched a brow. "Dare I ask?"

"Don't matter if you ask or not. Imma gonna tell ya anyway," she said with a wink. "You can either stay out in the parking lot like a big ole chicken, or you can pull up them big girl panties and go root for your man."

"My man?"

"Don't even act like you don't know I'm talking about Chase."

Lily huffed out an annoyed sigh. "Why in the hell does everyone think we're together?"

"There are too many reasons to list."

"He's seeing Molly."

"You really are daft, aren't you?"

"I don't know what you're talking about."

"Girl, he is no more with Molly than I am."

"But nothing. Shut up and get out of this car. Then, after the game, we're going to go back to your house, you're going to change into a cute little dress, and we're going to Tyler's party."

"I don't even know why Tyler is having this stupid party. He never has before."

"Stop trying to change the subject and get out before I drag you out."

"Sheesh, you're bossy," Lily grumbled as she opened the door.

"And you love me for it," Ginger said as she looped her arm through Lily's. "And, don't worry," she whispered as they got closer to the crowd. "I'm right here with you." Ginger gave her arm a little squeeze.

"Thanks."

They paid their entry fee and made their way to the concession stand line. A cold sweat broke out on Lily's forehead as they got closer. The overly strong scent of popcorn mingled with the somewhat repugnant smell of processed cheese for nachos and pretzels. All around her people talked excitedly. Kids ran around with their faces painted red and white.

From where she stood, she could see inside the brick building. She could see the exact place where she'd done whatever it took to ease the demons she'd been fighting.

"I've got you," Ginger whispered. "Own it. Don't let it own you."

The only thing Lily could do was nod as they stepped closer. They were almost to the spot where Chase had found her. Of course, all traces of blood had been scrubbed away. *It's in the past. It's in the past. It's in the past. I'm better and stronger.* She chanted it repeatedly.

Ginger got her candy and popcorn, and the girls walked away. "You did it," Ginger said proudly. "You faced the one place you hadn't been back too. I'm so proud of you."

Lily wiped the sweat from her forehead and let out a shaky breath. A feeling of pride and accomplishment came over her. Ginger was right. Facing the place of her undoing was the last string to her past. It was, in large part, why she hadn't been able to attend any of the games. Tonight, she'd cut the final string away, and now she felt like a balloon drifting free into the air.

Once Lily had face down her fear, she relaxed and had a good time. She found herself getting lost in the enthusiastic atmosphere of the game. When the crowd cheered, she cheered. When they got upset and hissed at the referees for making a bad call, she was right there with them.

She watched the field excitedly. Chase and Tyler were both on offense. Chase had once been a quarterback, but somewhere along the years, he'd been moved to running back. Tyler had taken up the quarterback and was the star of the team.

The way the two played together was mesmerizing. They worked like a well-oiled machine in perfect sync with one another. Chase seemed to anticipate where Tyler was going to throw the ball before it ever left his hands. They were the stars, and she couldn't have been prouder.

She found herself watching Chase more than Tyler, though, Ginger's words lingering in the back of her mind. The way he moved was so fluid and graceful. It left her in awe. However, when he found himself on the receiving end of a dirty tackle, Lily jumped to her feet with everyone else.

"What kind of call was that ref?" she yelled.

Suddenly, the crowd went silent. Lily's eyes searched the ground as the guys that had tackled Chase slowing climbed off him one by one. However, once they were up, there was still one body still laying on the ground.

Panic engulfed her. Chase was laying on the ground, not moving. "Chase!" she cried. She started to bolt toward the aisle, but Ginger grabbed her by the arm.

"Stay here. They won't let you on the field," she said.

"I need to go to him," Lily argued frantically.

Ginger's grasp remained firm. "Let them do their jobs," she said pointing to the team of doctors and medics rushing out to the field.

Lily pressed her hands together in front of her lips. "Please get up. Please get up," she whispered. Still, he didn't move. There still wasn't a sound from the crowd as they all watched with anticipation. She could no longer see him due to the huddle around him.

All the players—from both teams—on the field and sidelines took a knee. Tyler was standing just outside the circle, helmet laying on the ground forgotten. He shifted nervously from one foot to the other. He looked over his shoulder and caught her worried expression. Even from where she sat, she could see the worry etched on his face. If Tyler was worried, then it was bad.

"He's not getting up," Lily said fearfully. Tears were filling her eyes and spilling over her lashes.

"He will," she assured.

Lily opened her mouth to reply when suddenly the huddle around Chase parted. He was being helped to his feet. The crowd let out a collective sigh of relief followed by a loud roar.

She dashed the tears away from her eyes and watched as he searched the stands. Immediately, his eyes sought her out. He nodded and gave her a wink. *I'm okay!* She nodded once and watched as he was helped from the field.

Relief, unlike anything she'd ever felt washed over her.

Ginger leaned in close and whispered. "Tell me again he's not in love with you. Better yet, tell me you're not in love with him."

Chapter 33

The truth is always near at hand, within your reach.

~Shunryu Suzuki

They pulled up the drive to Tyler's massive house. Cars were parked along the drive, down the street, and up the road beside the house. Even before they got out of the car, they could hear the deep throb of music. Through the windows, a strobe light pulse with the beat. The football game had ended with the Wildcats winning by one point and it looked like the entire school had gathered to celebrate.

"There are a ton of people here," Lily said as she climbed out of the car.

"Of course. Who would miss a chance to party at the house of one of the hottest guys in school?"

She didn't reply. Instead, they walked up the porch and through the front door. Lily was still in shock that Tyler wanted to throw a party in the first place. They typically never went to these kinds of things, let alone hosted them. Then again, Tyler had been acting out of character a lot lately. It was starting to bother her.

They were greeted at the front door with a wave of music and the smell of cheap keg beer. Bodies danced and bumped to the obnoxious music blaring from the massive sound system Tyler had installed. Immediately, Lily regretted deciding to show up, even more so than changing into the black dress she was wearing.

"I'm going to go find Allan. You good here?" Ginger yelled over the music.

Lily nodded and watched as her friend disappeared into the crowd. The walls felt like they were beginning to close in on her. This was not a place she needed to be.

Trying to shrink away from people dancing too closely to her, she wove her way through the throngs of sweaty bodies to the stairs. She cared nothing about the

266

party. As soon as she walked through the front doors, she knew it was a mistake. Big crowds made her anxious.

Upstairs, the music was quieter, and it was less crowded. There were people paired off, making out in darkened corners or doing other things behind closed doors. She hurried down the hall and stepped into the darkness of Tyler's room.

She reached for the switch, and when the light came on, she breathed a sigh of relief when she found it empty. The last thing she wanted to do was walk in on someone having sex. She shuddered at the thought. She kicked off her shoes and made her way over to the bed. Climbing in the center of it, she removed her cell phone from the pocket of her dress.

Me: *are you at the party.*

She drummed her fingers on her legs as she waited for a response. Five minutes passed before a message pinged through.

Chase: *yeah. Are you?*
Me: *yeah. Too many people*
Chase: *where are you?*
Me: *upstairs.*
Chase: *be there in a sec.*
Me: *you don't have to. I'm okay. Have fun.*

She stared at her phone, already knowing that he was on his way to her. A few minutes later, Tyler's bedroom door opened, and Chase slipped through.

"Hey," he said as he crossed the room quickly and sat on the bed in front of her. His brows were pulled together in worry. "Are you okay? Is something wrong?"

"Don't think parties are my thing anymore," she laughed softly.

"I'm surprised you're here at all," Chase said honestly.

"I'm surprised there's a party."

"Yeah, Tyler's been off since his dad's been around more. I think Elliot is finally trying to be a parent and is failing miserably."

"Understatement of the year."

"Do you want me to take you home?"

She shook her head. "No. You need to go down and celebrate. It was a big win for you tonight."

He scooted onto the bed beside her, crossing his legs at the ankle. "I'm not the only one that had a big win. I saw you in the stands. First time you've been to one of our games since you've been back. Big step, yeah?"

"Yeah."

"I'm proud of you," he said nudging her shoulder with his.

She looked down at her folded hands. "It wasn't easy. Ginger helped a lot with that."

He made a humming noise in his throat. "I like her. She seems like a good match for you. She's . . . abrupt."

Lily laughed. "Well, that's one way of putting it."

The silence stretched out between them. From somewhere downstairs came the sound of breaking glass followed by some angry shouts.

"You scared the hell out of me tonight," she grumbled. The sight of him lying motionless would be an image that would forever remain burned into her mind.

"Have you worried, did I?"

"Yes, butthole, you did."

"Had me scared too," he said honestly.

"How you feeling?"

"Eh, I've been hit harder."

"Seriously, Chase. How are you feeling?" she asked, turning a little so she could see him. There was a slight cut just under his hairline from where his helmet must have cut him.

"I've got a bit of a headache and a few bruised ribs. Nothing I haven't had before. Randy, my mom's first boyfriend after my stepdad left hit harder than those pansies on the field."

She didn't laugh.

He picked her hand up and laced his fingers through hers. She stared down at their locked hands. It was something that Tyler frequently did. Only this felt nothing like it had with Tyler. His palms were warm and calloused. The rough pad of his thumb rubbed the back of her thumb gently. Her body tingled with the contact. No, this was most definitely nothing like it was with Tyler.

She cleared her throat. "Are you sure you don't want to be down at the party? What about Molly?"

"What about her?"

"Didn't you come here with her?"

He shook his head. "Nah, she came with Winston."

Lily's eyes widened. "Really? Things aren't going well with you two?" she hedged.

"Why would you think that?"

"I don't know."

"Things are fine with us."

"Oh."

"Does that bother you?"

She tried to sound as casual as possible. Why would it bother her?

You already know the answer to that dummy.

"No."

"Liar."

Déjà vu struck, and they were back in his kitchen. They were having the same conversation.

"I'd much rather be in here with you," he said softly.

Her stomach fluttered as she recalled what Ginger had said about Chase being in love with her. Kiera had said the same thing. Lily just couldn't see it. Chase was just protecting her. He wanted to be there with her because she'd been anxious about being in such a crowded place. He was just protecting her, and that was it.

And what about that night in his kitchen? Her mind whispered. She'd thought about that night several times. She'd analyzed it until she'd gotten a headache. The only rational explanation was that it was a heat of the moment thing. There was no way Chase could love her.

"Hey," he said softly, pulling her out of her thoughts.

"Yeah?"

"Where were you just now?"

She turned her head and looked at him, and once again, she was lost to his crystal blue eyes. The intensity in which he looked at her stole her breath. She shifted on the bed, her thigh brushing against his. Suddenly she was hyper-aware of everything; the scent of the cologne he always wore; the warmth of his body sitting next to her; the thundering of her heart slamming against her ribs.

"I was just thinking."

"Yeah, I gathered that. What about?"

She tugged her bottom lip between her teeth and looked away. Should she ask him? What if he said no? But what if he said yes? She wasn't sure which was the scarier of the two answers.

The room felt warmer. Her throat was suddenly dry. Removing her hand from his, she scooted from the bed and walked over to the window. She couldn't think with him so close. Outside, the moon was just a sliver in the sky. Stars twinkled brightly from their black velvety bed.

Below, people were swimming in the heated pool. Someone was puking in the bushes below the window. She felt his presence without having to turn to see him. His reflection appeared next to hers in the glass. Their eyes locked.

The heat from his chest pressed into her back, giving her comfort. His breaths puffed out over the top of her head. Even with everything going on outside, his eyes never left hers.

"What were you thinking about, Lilian?" he whispered huskily.

She shook her head, knowing that once she asked the question, she could never take it back. There would be no going back. It could change the whole dynamic of their friendship. It could destroy everything.

She turned and looked up at him, and like the night in the kitchen, they were standing impossibly close. "Nothing." The single word came out barely in a whisper.

Reaching up, he gently combed his hand back through her hair, cupping the back of her head. He lowered his mouth, hovering it a breath away from hers.

"Liar."

"Chase," she pleaded quietly.

"Ask me. Ask me what you're wanting to." There was a pleading tone in his voice. His eyes begged her.

She swallowed the lump that had formed in her throat. One of her hands had fallen to his hip while the other rested against his chest.

This was it. There would be no going back, but she had to know.

"Are you in love with me?"

"Yes."

Then his mouth slanted down over hers. Her eyes fluttered closed, and everything melted away.

Chapter 34

Now is everything.
Whatever you do in this very moment is everything:
it's the past, it's the future, it's now.

~Chögyam Trungpa

Everything ceased to exist. The throb of the music downstairs faded. The sound of shouts and breaking glass disappeared. Chase gently moved his mouth over hers. She could tell he was taking his time and not pushing her, but the energy bubbling inside her demanded more. This kiss was nothing like her first kiss. Sure, Lucas's had been fun and exciting because it was her first, and in comparison, pretty awful.

Nothing in the world could have prepared her for the intense emotions that came with kissing Chase. Her lungs were beginning to ache, but she refused to back away. If she were going to suffocate, she would do it by giving her last breath to him.

The tip of his tongue teased her bottom lip but never went any further. Reaching up, she cupped the back of his neck. Her fingers glided through the silky-smooth hair. He seemed to shudder under her touch.

Finally, he broke the kiss, and she whimpered in protest. She didn't open her eyes because she was afraid if she did, that the last thirty seconds of her life would be a dream. If she opened her eyes, then the kiss hadn't happened. Maybe it hadn't happened. Maybe she'd fallen asleep in Tyler's bed and was dreaming about kissing Chase.

"Open your eyes, Lily," he whispered, pressing his forehead against hers.

"I'm scared too."

Reaching up, he brushed his thumb across her cheek. "Why?"

She swallowed and licked her lips. She was still able to taste him on her mouth. "I'm scared."

"Of what?"

"That what just happened didn't really just happen. That it was all a dream."

"Open your eyes, Lilian."

She chewed on her bottom lip and opened one eye and then the other. He was still standing there, right in front of her. His beautiful eyes sparkled down at her.

"Wow," she breathed. "That was. . . ."

"There are no words for what that was, baby," he said breathlessly.

Her heart skipped a beat. It wasn't the first time he'd called her baby, but for whatever reason, this time, it meant the most.

"Say it again."

"Say what?"

"Call me that again."

Reaching up, he cupped her cheek. She covered his hand with hers and turned into his touch.

"Baby," he breathed.

He pulled her into the circle of his arms, and she pressed her cheek against his chest. She listened as his heart raced through his chest, and as it slowed, it matched the rhythm of her own. It was as if their hearts were made to beat in rhythm with one another. She wrapped her arms around his waist, and they swayed back and forth, not to the rhythm of the music below, but to their own music.

His hands rubbed slow circles over her back. She felt everything in her body, mind, and soul clicking into place. It was as if they were two pieces of the same puzzle, but all this time, they'd been turned the wrong direction. Now, they were positioned just right, and they fit together seamlessly.

However, her thoughts began to race. Was this just something because he felt responsible for her? He felt the need to protect her, but accidentally got swept up in feelings that never existed. Her mind began to spin out of control, forcing her to take a step back.

He must have sensed where her thoughts were going because he shook his head. "Don't. I can see that busy head of yours working in overdrive. I'm just going to tell you to stop right now. This isn't a one-time thing. It's also not whatever crazy thing you're trying to come up with to rationalize it away. This," he said taking both of her hands in his, pulling her close, and pinning them between their chests, "this is where we are supposed to be. This is exactly where I want to be. *You* are exactly who I want to be with. It's always been you, Lily. Always."

"But what about Molly?"

"Molly and I are just friends and nothing more. We've been hanging out because—" He gave her a sheepish look.

"Because?"

"Because I wasn't sure how to do this. With you and me. We ran into each other not too long after you got out, and she asked about you."

Lily's eyebrows shot up. "She did?"

He nodded. "Yep, several times, actually. She admitted how badly she felt for the way Kiera treated you and for the way *she'd* acted. Apparently, not too long after everything happened, she tore Kiera a new one."

"You're joking."

"No, I'm not."

"So, you haven't *been* with her?"

"No. She's just been helping me. I needed a girl's perspective, and since she's a girl. . . ."

"Well, that makes sense."

"Lily, when I say it's always been you, I mean it. It's *always* been only you."

"But you've dated other girls."

"Dated, yes. A kiss here or there, sure. But that's it."

Her heart thumped so loudly, she was confident it was someone knocking on the door. "What are you saying, Chase?"

He lifted their hands and pressed a kiss to her fingers. "I've loved you since the first day I saw you. I've never seen you as a sister, like Tyler does. I've been waiting for *you*, Lily, and no one else."

"When you say waiting, you mean it as in *waiting, waiting?*"

Color tinted his cheeks and he nodded.

"You mean all the girls you dated, all the girls you've made out with, you never . . .?"

"Never. It's always been you."

Lily had no words. All this time, when she thought Chase was having sex, he wasn't. And it was because of her?

"You're waiting for me?"

He nodded. "And I'll wait as long as it takes."

A long-buried thought began to resurface. Why would he want me now? He knows what happened. There wasn't anything that happened in her life that he hadn't known about or been a part of. Still, she felt like she wasn't good enough.

Before her thoughts could ruin the moment, she looked up at him sheepishly. "You do know Tyler and I kissed, right?"

He laughed. "Yes, I know. He told me afterward, and I decked him."

"You did what?"

He gave her a guilty look. "It's not my proudest moment, but it was what forced me to realize how I felt. I'd tried to deny it. I didn't want to love you. You deserve someone like Tyler. I knew you'd never see me that way."

"What changed?"

"The way you looked at me."

"The way I looked at you? I don't understand."

"The night we were in my kitchen after our fight. I never went to Molly's. I sat at the end of the dock, *our* dock, for hours just thinking about you and everything else. Then when I turned around and saw you standing there staring at me in the kitchen, that's when I saw it. You were looking at me how I've always looked at you. I knew you felt something for me, but I couldn't—wouldn't—force it. If anything was going to happen, it had to be on your terms.

"Then, when you went out with that Dexter guy. I thought that maybe I'd been mistaken. I'd lost hope of us being together, but Molly told me to hang in there. I'd waited for you for over a decade, what's a few more days, weeks, or months."

Lily listened to everything he said, and tears rolled down her cheeks. But, for the first time in what felt like eons, they were tears of happiness. "And I'll keep waiting for you as long as you need me too."

"Chase, I—" Before Lily could finish her sentence, the bedroom door swung wide. Molly was standing on the other side, eyes wide with worry.

"Chase there's a problem downstairs."

He frowned. "What problem?"

"Some guys from Tucker showed up. They're downstairs stirring up a bunch of shit with Tyler, Winston, and some of the other guys."

"Damn it," he growled. He dropped a kiss to Lily's mouth. "Stay here. I'll be right back."

She nodded as he stormed across the room. "Stay with her," he said to Molly before leaving and slamming the door behind him.

Lily stared at the door with wide eyes and then looked at Molly. The other girl was nervous as she shifted from one foot to the other and avoided eye contact.

"I think it's time we talked," Lily said. When Molly's eyes widened with worry, Lily gave her a soft smile. The girl seemed to relax.

Lily sat on the bed and Molly took a few cautious steps forward. Her hands were folded in front of her. She looked terrified.

"Relax, Molly. I'm not going to hit you."

Molly visibly relaxed and laughed softly. "I wasn't sure. I mean you've got one hell of a left hook."

Lily flinched, remembering the fight she'd had with Kiera at the bonfire. Molly had been the one to take her friend to the hospital.

"Chase told me everything, about what you did for him and how you explained things. Thank you."

"Chase is a great guy, and he's loved you forever. It seemed like everyone knew it but the two of you."

"Kind of ironic how things like that happen," Lily snorted.

Molly sat on the edge of the bed and turned to face Lily. "When Chase first came to me to talk, I wasn't sure what I should do. I knew how you felt about Kiera and by extension, me. While I don't think I've ever given you a direct reason to hate me. But, I've never given you a reason not to. I should have stopped Kiera long before things escalated. That day she said those horrible things to you in the hall, about how you should—" She gulped back emotions as huge crocodile tears began to roll down her cheeks.

"About how I should kill myself."

Molly let out a hiccupping sob and nodded. "I couldn't believe what she'd said. I finally spoke up, but by the time I had caught up with her, the ambulances were already hauling you away. I lived in horror each day after that. I was so ashamed of everything. I had no idea how I was going to make things right, but I would when the time came.

"Then when I ran into Chase one day after he'd visited you, he broke down. Tyler was gone, and you were getting the help you needed. Things with his mom were starting to get better, but they were still pretty rocky."

Guilt plagued Lily. She hadn't thought about how alone Chase had been through all of this. He'd been the one taking care of her, and since Tyler had been gone, there was no one left to take care of Chase. She suddenly felt so selfish.

"I was so selfish. He needed me, and there was no one," she whispered.

Molly reached forward and grabbed her hand. "No! Never think that. You were getting the help you needed. I was helping Chase the only way I knew how. I was a friend, and I was hoping that by my helping him, at some point, I'd be able to have this very conversation with you."

"But you guys hid it from me and let me think you were dating."

She chewed on her bottom lip. "And that was my fault. He said he was going to tell you about us spending time together, but I wasn't ready. I was scared. Then, I saw the looks you gave me at school and knew we'd made the right decision. I know it was the same as lying to you, but I truly didn't know any other way."

"You could have come and talked to me."

"Would you have listened?"

"No. Probably not."

"I'm sorry, Lily. I truly am. I know you and Kiera will never be friends, and I don't expect *us* to either. I just need you to forgive me."

Lily listened to what Molly was saying. "Yes, you should have spoken up sooner, but it wouldn't have done any good. Things were already set into motion. They had to play out. I don't see any reason why we can't be friends," she finally said.

The girl's face split into a bright smile. "Really?!"

"Sure, why not?"

Molly clapped her hands excitedly and threw herself into a Lily with a hug. Lily laughed and then both girls erupted into giggles.

"So, judging from what I walked in on, and what I've pieced together, I take it, everything has finally come out into the open—feelings and whatnot? Tell me, was the kiss everything you've dreamed about? And don't tell me you haven't been thinking about it. He told me about the kitchen."

"He did?" Lily wasn't sure how she felt about their more intimate moments being shared.

"Well, he didn't tell me *everything*. The only thing he said was there was a moment. I asked for more, but he refused to tell me, the little punk."

"I can't believe I haven't seen what everyone else has been seeing."

"Sometimes, we're just not ready to see what we're meant to. I think deep down you knew, though. Almost like your soul was recognizing his, but was waiting until you were ready."

"That's pretty deep and very insightful actually. You're pretty good at this talking stuff. I can see why he came to you."

"It's what I plan on majoring in."

"What?"

"Psychology."

"Well, for what it's worth, I think you're going to be awesome at it."

"Thanks. There's something I want to ask; I'm just not sure how to do it?"

"Okay?" Lily said cautiously.

Molly fidgeted. "You see, I'm good with helping other people and advising on their love lives, but my own—not s'much."

She took a deep breath, and Lily realized the girl was genuinely nervous.

"Spit it out, woman!" Lily laughed.

"I like Tyler and I want to ask him out but I don't know how and I'm afraid he'll say no. I just thought that maybe you could help me or something. And now you and Chase might maybe be a thing, we could all go out on like a double date."

Lily gave her head a little shake as she listened to Molly's rapid—albeit rambling—admission. She held up a hand. "First of all, take a breath."

Flush colored Molly's cheeks as she nodded.

"And secondly, I'll see what I can do."

Part 3

Chapter 35

Embrace the glorious mess that is you are.

~Elizabeth Gilbert

"Have you guys rented your tuxes yet?" Molly asked Chase and Tyler as they walked down the sidewalk.

Both guys groaned, causing Molly and Lily to giggle.

"Chase got his," Lily said as she swung their linked hands back and forth.

"But it was under extreme protest," he grunted.

"Yeah, he complained the whole time, but he was a good boy and got a treat afterward."

"Okay, eww," Molly chuckled.

Lily flushed. "That's so not what I meant."

Chase laughed at the delicate blush that was staining Lily's cheeks. He let her sputter for a few moments longer because he found it adorable. He put his arm around her shoulder and then pulled her into his side. "It was a real treat. I got ice cream and cookies like a good boy."

Lily batted playfully at his chest.

"I got mine yesterday," Tyler said.

"And it matches my dress perfectly," Molly gushed. "He's lucky he got one at all," she said casting him a glance.

Lily looked at him. "Prom is tomorrow, and you *just* got your tux yesterday?"

Tyler only shrugged. Lily turned and backhanded Chase playfully in the chest.

"Owe, what was that for, woman?"

"Why didn't you get him to get a tux sooner?"

"He's a big boy!" Chase whined playfully.

"That's right, been wiping my own butt for a few weeks now!" Tyler joked.

Everyone laughed. "Honestly, I was so wrapped up with college stuff I just lost track of time. Besides, Molly said I didn't have too."

Lily chuckled and scoffed. "So, it's *your* fault?!"

"Hey, not everyone has their college already picked out, and bags packed. There are others of us that have loose ends to tie up before graduation."

"Well, *fine*," Lily laughed drawing out the word.

"Hey, come here. I want to talk to you."

Molly pulled Lily away from Chase and walked ahead of the guys a few steps. Chase watched the girls put their heads together as they walked and talked. His heart expanded. He and Lily had officially been together as a couple for six months. At first, he had to admit it was awkward and weird, especially when his mother decided it was time to have "a talk."

That had been all kinds of humiliating, but not nearly as embarrassing as telling her that he was still a virgin. She'd made such a huge deal out of it, but then their talk got serious. She said she wasn't going to get involved in his love life. She admitted to not deserving the respect of not having sex in the house, and she asked that he was at the very least careful. They both had such bright futures ahead of them and while having a baby at such a young age wasn't bad, it would provide several roadblocks that neither one of them were ready to handle.

Sex with Lily was something he thought about. Frequently. However, they'd had a discussion when they rang in the New Year and decided there was no need to hurry it. When she'd expressed that she wanted to wait until marriage, he'd agreed to it. Though, if he had to be one hundred percent honest with himself, at times, he questioned that decision. He'd never wanted someone as badly as he wanted her. Everything about her made him feel more alive than ever.

He loved the way she smiled—honestly smiled— and he thanked God every day for allowing him to see it. They'd started going to church together, and while he still had questions about a lot of things, there was a kind of peace he felt when he was there. He had to believe in some sort of Divine intervention because why else would he have found Lily just at the right moment that night. It was just after she'd been brutalized and before the monster came back for another round, possibly killing her in the process? Why else would he have found her in the nick of time at the school, or after her panic attack in her car?

To him, they all led to them finding their way to one another. He watched as the girls walked arm in arm down the sidewalk. The spring air was cool but not uncomfortably so. They'd just gone out with Tyler and Molly, something they did every other weekend. It was nice to have another couple around.

"How are y'all doing?" Tyler asked pulling him out of his thoughts.

"Doing good, great actually. Still taking things slow. She's doing remarkably though and never ceases to amaze me. I mean, she's been working so hard at the clinic and with her studies. If you didn't know all the hell she went through. You'd never know it by just looking at her."

"I know. Just goes to show you that outward appearances aren't everything. The stuff she went through would have destroyed some."

"I think Lily has always had more strength than she gave herself credit for."

"Or we gave her credit for. I'm just glad you two are finally together. It took you long enough!" he laughed.

Chase chuckled. "I know. The timing was just never right. Then everything happened and spiraled. What about you and Molly? How are things going there?"

"Not terrible," Tyler said with a sly smile. "She's pretty remarkable. She's been talking me through some issues with my dad. It's helped a lot."

"How's that going, with the old man and stuff?"

Tyler shrugged and frowned. "I gave up a long time ago on him. Right now, it's just about making it to graduation, and then I'm done. I won't have to deal with him anymore."

"Well you know you can move in with us at any time. Mom even made up the other guest room."

"Nah, he's gone until graduation anyway."

The original plan after Tyler turned eighteen was for him to move out and into the house with Chase and Lily. He would then have access to all the money his grandparents had left him, and his father couldn't touch him. Those plans changed when his father had some huge client to defend in Europe.

"When did he leave?"

"Day before yesterday."

"And he's going to be back for graduation next week?"

Tyler shrugged. "I seriously doubt it."

"Well, you've got us and my mom, Trevor, and Coraline. That's all that matters. We're your family. You do realize that, right?"

"Dude, what's with the touchy-feelies all of a sudden? Has Lily turned you into some sort of overly emotional drama queen?"

Chase rolled his eyes. "Don't be a douche. I'm just chatting."

"Well, ease up, dude. We're freaking Seniors. Prom is tomorrow, and we graduate next week! Woooooo!" he yelled excitedly. "*We're gonna get the hell outta here!*"

"*Woooooo!*" Chase whooped.

"Yeah!" Lily and Molly cheered. People on the sidewalks looked at them funny, but then somewhere ahead of them they heard more calls. It was Friday night in a small town. People were out on dates.

Again, down the street, someone yelled, "*Seniors!*" While another shouted something completely inappropriate, causing the four of them to erupt into a riot of giggles. Tyler clapped Chase on the back then ran ahead and grabbed Molly by the waist and slung her around.

Chase just watched in awe. This was his family. This was one of the moments in his life he would hold onto forever.

Lily turned and gave him a sweet smile, and his heart melted into a puddle in his shoes. It happened every time she looked at him with those amazing green eyes. She trotted to him and jumped into his arms.

"I love you," she whispered, kissing him softly.

"But not nearly as much as I love you," he whispered against her soft lips.

"Get a room or get a move on. We're gonna miss the movie," Tyler called.

Lily blushed and wiggled out of his arms. Locking her hand with his, they jogged to catch up with Tyler and Molly. Everything was perfect.

Lily stared at her reflection, unable to recognize the girl she saw in front of her. The woman staring back at her was not the skinned knees, scraped elbows, little girl. Her blond hair was pulled back into a sleek bun with a small crystal-studded comb as an accent piece.

She moved slightly to the left and the right. The glittering beads on her gown winked under the lighting in her room. The shimmering, almost iridescent silver material glistened. The bodice hugged her tightly with beautifully stitched embroidery weaving intricate patterns all the way down the front. The chiffon skirt fluttered lightly around her legs as she moved.

Turning to her right, she looked over her shoulder at the corset back of the silver gown. Questions buzzed around in her over hair sprayed head. Was it too much? Should she have gone with something not quite as revealing? As it was, the dress wasn't exposing that much. When picking out the V-neck, drop waist gown, Molly had assured her that it revealed just enough while being modest. The v dipped slightly between her breasts.

Molly had done her makeup in silvers and blacks, but not so much it was overpowering. She had to give the other girl credit; she really knew how to do all that contouring stuff. The makeup was so precisely done, it made her green eyes seem to glow. For the first time in her life, Lily felt beautiful. She felt like a woman.

As she studied her reflection, she caught a glimpse of the teeth marks that scarred her right shoulder. It was a scar that she had chosen to keep as a reminder of where

she came from, along with the scars on her forearms.
They were all a reminder of where she'd once been and a
place she never wanted to be again. She might get them
removed in the future, but for the time being, they served
a purpose. They reminded her that no matter what, never
again would she let someone overpower her. She would
never be a victim again.

A knock sounded on her door, jarring her from her
thoughts. "It's me. Can I come in?" Diana asked from the
other side of the door.

"Sure."

Diana stepped through the door closed it behind her.
Then she turned and stopped abruptly. "Oh Lily," she
whispered, pressing her hand to her chest. Tears filled the
woman's eyes. "You're so beautiful."

"You don't think it's too much?"

"Oh dear. Of course not."

"I don't know, Diana," she said looking at her
reflection once more. "Is this really me? I mean, I feel like
me, but her," she pointed to the mirror, "I don't know."

Diana moved to stand beside her. She placed a hand
on Lily's shoulder and looked at her in the mirror. "I still
see a little girl that was forced to grow up way before she
was ready. All of you've had to deal with all these adult
problems while you were children. You never truly got to
be kids. Now that you're practically adults, you don't
realize you've turned into adults. Does that make sense?"

"I think so."

"I'm proud I got to be here. I know I wasn't the best
person when y'all were kids, and I'll spend the rest of my
life making it up to Chase, but I'm here now. I'm always
here for you. My sweet darlin', you're the first daughter I
ever had." Tears rolled down the older woman's cheeks.

Lily's eyes misted over.

Diana laughed and fluttered her hands in front of her
face. "Okay, I can't make you cry. You'll ruin your
makeup. "I brought you these," she said holding a pair of
diamond, earrings with a dangling teardrop diamond in
the palm of one hand and a dainty, silver chain, with a
simple teardrop diamond.

"Diana," she gasped. "I can't wear those. They are stunning."

"I'm giving them to you like my momma gave them to me."

"But what about Coraline?"

She just shrugged and fastened the necklace around her neck. "I don't think she will appreciate them as much as you will."

After putting the earrings in, Lily inspected her reflection once more.

"Perfect. Now, it's time for you to go. Everyone is downstairs waiting for you."

Lily nodded and picked her silver clutch up from the bed. It was now or never.

Chapter 36

You come to love not by finding the perfect person,
but by seeing an imperfect person perfectly.

~Sam Keen

Lily held her breath as she walked down the stairs, partially because she was afraid she would trip and fall head first, and then the other reason was that she was nervous. She knew it was absurd to be nervous because this was Chase, and she was more comfortable around him than anyone. However, at the same time, that made it worse.

Diana cleared her throat, and everyone turned. Tyler's eyes widened as he let out a low whistle. Molly clapped and bounced up and down excitedly, her slinky dress bouncing with her. Lily smiled at them, but as she walked down the remaining steps, there was only one person she could see. There was only one person in the room, and he was looking at her like she was the most precious gem on earth.

While he stared at her, she also stared at him. His tux fit him impeccably, the silver vest and tie matching her dress perfectly. His blond hair had been trimmed and was styled with meticulous precision. In all her years of knowing him, she'd never seen him look so stunning. She could still see the ranch foreman, but she could also see a *GQ* cover model.

"Wow," he said his eyes widening as she got closer. Slowly, they raked over her starting at her head and moving to her toes.

"Why, Chase Kramer, are you speechless?"

The only thing he could do was nod, making her giggle. His eyes found hers, and he smiled in a way that she knew it was only meant for her. Her cheeks turned warm under his gaze.

"Lily, what this dope is having a hard time saying is that you look astonishing," Tyler said nudging Chase hard in the ribs.

Chase shook his head slightly as if coming out of a daze. "Y-yeah, w-what he said."

Lily blushed and shifted from one foot to the other.

"Okay, everyone, on the stairs. It is time for the picture portion of this evening," Diana said with a clap of her hand.

For the next thirty minutes every possible picture combination was taken; Lily and Tyler; Lily and Molly; Molly and Tyler; Lily and Molly; Molly and Chase; Tyler and Chase; Lily, Tyler, and Chase; then all four of them. The final pictures were of Lily and Chase. These were the ones that lasted the longest because halfway through, the batteries in the camera died, and Diana had to go hunt more down.

While Diana went hunting for batteries, Chase pulled Lily's back against her chest. "You look simply delectable." His voice was a low, husky whisper that made goosebumps scatter all over her skin. Her body tingled in reaction to his.

Leaning down, he pressed a kiss to her shoulder, over the scar. She tried to shift, but he wouldn't let her. "Don't," he said softly.

"You're not repulsed by me?"

"I'm repulsed at what he did to you. I'm repulsed that a grown man branded such beautiful skin," he said as he slowly drew his fingers down her arms. "But one thing I will never be repulsed by is you."

"I love you so much," she said. The amount of love she felt for him only seemed to grow more intense every single day. Then, when she thought it wasn't possible for her to love him anymore, she found a way.

"But I'll always love you more," he said as he nuzzled her neck and wrapped his arms around her waist.

"Huh-uh," she argued covering his hands with hers.

"Yick, you two with all your lovey-dovey mush," Tyler teased as he grabbed the remote from the table and began flipping through the channels.

Chase flipped him the bird, and everyone just laughed.

"I saw that Chase Michael," Diana said from the kitchen.

Chase whipped his head around, trying to figure out how on earth his mother could have possibly seen that. "That woman is like freaking Superman or something," he grunted. "I swear she can see through walls."

"I heard that."

"And apparently hear through them too," Tyler crowed. He jumped over the back of the couch and began to scuffle with Chase.

"I swear if you two break something, I'm gonna whoop ya both," Diana called from the other room.

Lily was laughing until her attention was pulled to the television. The air suddenly left her lungs in a *whoosh* as the walls in the living room closed in on her. The only thing she could see was the picture of the man on television.

Her skin began to twitch, and her fingers began to tingle. Her breathing began to accelerate. She walked into the living room on shaky legs. Her hands trembled as she fidgeted with the volume button on the remote, but her fingers felt like the tips were filled with lead. After a few tries, she finally managed to get the volume up. Behind her, Chase and Tyler continued to tussle, but she couldn't hear them.

"Lily?" Molly asked walking over to her. She placed a hand on Lily's arm. The sudden contact made Lily flinch. "Lily? What's wrong? Honey, you're white as a ghost."

She didn't answer. The only thing she could do was stare at the mugshot of the man on the giant screen television.

"Chase! Tyler! Something's wrong with Lily," Molly said frantically.

The raucous behind her ceased, and in a second, Chase was beside her but not touching her. "Lily, baby? Stay with me okay."

"I'm fine," she said weakly, gaining control of the panic attack trying to claw its way from the depths of her mind.

"Rewind it and turn it up," she said whispered, pointing to the television.

"I don't think that's a good idea," Tyler said.

"Please," she pleaded softly.

Chase took her by the hand, and she squeezed while Tyler pressed the back button on the remote. Lily held her breath as she looked at the mugshot of the man that ruined her life. The picture vanished and flashed to the anchor in the studio. They all listened as the report rolled on.

"Forty-five year old, Allan Watkins escaped police custody this evening when he became hostile from the back of the cruiser, resulting in officer Jason Clemmons to swerve from the road, hit a culvert and flip the car. Watkins was being extradited from Raven's Bend police department to Carter County on several charges of assault, five counts of sexual assault involving minors all under the age of thirteen, and three counts of public indecency.

"Watkins is believed to be armed and dangerous. If you know of his whereabouts or have seen a man fitting his description, please contact your local authorities. It is encouraged that you do not approach Watkins."

Tyler turned the television off. It seemed like everyone in the room was holding their breath. Lily's head throbbed. She could feel Chase's hand in hers and knew he was talking, but she couldn't hear what he was saying. He sounded so far away.

"He's . . . f-free?" she gasped anger burned brightly through her. "That bastard is free, and I'm living here in terror."

She began to breathe heavily as the panic and anger mingled inside her chest. Would he come for her? Was he going to finish the job he started? He'd told her if she told anyone, he'd kill her. Was that what he was doing now? Had he somehow found where she lived?

Sweat gathered on her forehead. "Lily, baby, listen to me," Chase said reaching for her.

"Don't. Touch. Me!" she shrieked turning away from him.

He jerked his hand back as if she'd burned him. "I'm s-s-sorry," she sobbed. Gathering her dress in her hands, she hurried through the front door down the steps. Halfway down the sidewalk, she stopped and sagged to her knees in a sobbing heap.

She didn't know how long she'd been out there, and she didn't care. Her panic attack never entirely came on, she figured it was due to the absolute rage. The front door opened and then closed softly. A few seconds later, she heard footsteps behind her.

"I'm fine."

"Well, I prefer to think *I'm* the fine one. I consider you to be more of a hottie, but hey, whatever floats your boat, baby," Chase said as he sat on the ground in front of her, crisscrossing his legs and propping his elbow on his legs. He rested his chin in his hands, giving her a dopey look.

Despite the emotions roiling inside her, she laughed. She sniffed and wiped her nose with the back of her hand. "Oh, that was so hot! Can you do it again?"

She laughed again. "You do realize I'm upset right?" She looked up at him, and his eyes twinkled mischievously as he gave her his infamous cheeky smile

He nodded. "And *you* realize that this is our prom night, and you're currently sitting out in my front yard in a rather expensive dress looking like a raccoon." He removed a handkerchief from his pocket and passed it to her.

She dabbed her eyes.

"I never knew his name," she said looking down at the handkerchief in his hands.

"Sometimes it's for the best."

She shook her head. "No. Not this time. Now, my demon has a name and not just a face."

"They're going to catch him."

Through watery eyes, she looked at him. "You don't know that."

"Oh, but I do because you see, I refuse to believe that a man like that gets a get out of jail free card."

"Five."

Chase frowned. "What?"

"Five kids were tormented by that man."

"Six," he corrected softly.

"How many more were there before me—after me? This is my fault."

"Whoa there," he said suddenly. The playfulness was gone from his voice. She could hear a soft edge to it. "Look at me."

She continued to look at the handkerchief she was twisting in her lap. "I said look at me," he barked, causing her to flinch.

Finally, she lifted her gaze. "Don't you dare, think that. You are not at fault for this. YOU are not the reason that sick bastard is the way he is. Do you understand me?"

"But if I—"

"*No!*"

She jumped at his sudden very sharp voice. He took her hands and together they climbed to their feet. "That is not your cross to carry. You were a child. You didn't know what to do. Your mother was a drugged-out junkie who didn't give two shits about you." Chase was getting mad now. His voice continued to rise. "Your mother was the one that was supposed to protect you from the monsters. Not two boys who didn't know shit. That man molested and tortured you for his own sick pleasure. You were innocent, and he took that from you. He stole years from your life. He stole from me. Don't you see, by stealing those years from you, he stole them from me?" He angrily jabbed his finger in the center of his chest. Tears rolled down his face.

"You're the love of my life."

"But why would you want me? He broke me. He damaged me in the worst possible way. I've been this way for so long that I don't know how to be anything else. No one wants something that is defective." Tears rolled unbidden down her cheeks, but she didn't care. She didn't have the strength to hold them back.

Chase took her hands and pulled them up between their bodies; the way he'd done the night they first kissed. "Look at me because I need you to hear me."

She lifted her gaze and met his eyes. "We're all broken in some shape or form, but it's how we put ourselves back together that matters. That's what I'm here for. I'm the one that is supposed to put you back together each time you break. I knew what I was getting into when we started this. I knew there were going to be tough days. I knew what I was doing."

"But how many times can you put something back together before there is nothing left."

Leaning forward he pressed his lips against hers. She could taste the saltiness of her tears on his lips. When he pulled away, he continued. "The girl in front of me right now, right here looking sexier than any person has a right too, may be broken, but she's beautifully so. *That's* all that matters to me. Because when I look at you, I don't see broken. I see the bravest girl I've ever met."

"I don't feel brave," she sniffed wiping her nose.

"You still don't get it do you?"

"Get what?"

"The path that that douchcanoe forced us to go down, *that* was the path to us. You're my soulmate. My soul called out to yours even before we truly knew one another. Why do you think we met all those years ago?"

"What if I never get better?"

"Then I will be there every step of the way. I'm all in, baby. Right here, right now. Even if something happens that forces us to go our separate ways, I'll be there in whatever way you need me."

"Promise?"

Chase held up his pinky and hooked it through hers, holding it tightly. "Always."

The front door opened, and Tyler stepped out. "Uh, guys. I think you need to get in here. *Now!*"

Chapter 37

We are alive in the present moment,
the only moment there is for us to be alive.

~Thich Khat Hanh

They walked back in the house and found everyone staring at the television. "What are we looking at?" Chase asked as he held a protective arm around Lily's waist.

Tyler pointed to the television and bumped the volume up as the same voice from earlier began the report.

"The short manhunt for Allan Watkins has come to an end. The Raven's Bend K-9 unit was called in, and within minutes, Watkins was tracked down to an abandoned trailer house at the edge of town. The standoff ended when Watkins opened fire on police officers, and the officers returned fire. Watkins was reported dead at the scene."

Again, silence filled the room. Lily couldn't believe what she was hearing. "He's gone? He's truly gone?"

"He really is, baby. That sonofa— "

"Ahem," Diana said.

"That *dirtbag* is gone."

Lily had no idea how to react. She was relieved, but there was something else inside her, but she couldn't place a finger on it.

Tyler walked over to where Chase and Lily stood. He placed his hand in the middle of her back and wiped away her tears. "You're free now, Lils. You'll still have to deal with what that beast did to you, but now, you're truly free to move on because you have closure. Watkins is dead and can't hurt anyone else ever again. There are some people out there that don't get that." He pulled her into his arms and held her tightly. "I'm so glad you're one of them that does," he whispered.

A car honked outside the house.

"Shoot. The limo's here," she said.

All eyes turned to her. "We don't have to go tonight if you don't want," Molly said. "We're all together, and that's all that matters. We can have our own prom right here if you want."

Lily shook her head and smiled. "I'm done hiding. It's time for me to live my life. Thank you all. I wouldn't be here if it weren't for you."

She took Tyler's hand and Chase's. They formed a triangle. "You two have been my everything for so long. I love you guys."

By the time she finished her short little speech, there wasn't a single dry eye. "Okay," Lily said. "Guys, go tell the limo driver we're gonna be a few minutes late. Molly and I have to put our faces back in place."

Lily took Molly by the hand and pulled her toward the stairs.

Tyler groaned. "So, what we thinking? Midnight?"

Lily and Molly both poked their tongues out at them and raced up the stairs as fast as their three-inch heels would allow them.

This was going to be the night they remembered, and they were all going to do it without a single care in the world.

Lily, Chase, Molly, and Tyler danced until their feet ached. They laughed and drank punch that someone had taken the liberty of spiking. Over their heads, white lights twinkled brightly. Couples danced and laughed, and for the first time in her entire life, Lily felt like a true teenager without a care in the world.

She'd gotten all her acceptance letters to all the colleges she applied too. The long hours of studying, all night cram sessions, and essays had paid off. While she had a chance to go to any one of them, her mind was already made up. She was going to bring it up earlier, but because of the circumstances the evening started under, she'd forgotten.

She and Chase had talked about what was going to happen after school. No matter where she decided to go to college, he would continue to work toward his ranch. He would do it where ever she chose to go. He claimed that it had taken him too long to catch her. He wasn't about to let her get away that easily.

Lily and Molly danced wildly together, and when it came time for a slow song, Tyler and Chase found them. "So, have I mentioned how beautiful you are this evening?"

Lily pursed her lips. "Not in the last five minutes."

"Well, I guess I need to rectify that." Slowly, he drew his fingers down her bare arm causing her to shiver. Excitement swelled in the pit of her stomach. The college acceptance letter wasn't the only thing she'd decided to give to Chase.

Leaning forward and lifting herself up on her toes, she pressed her lips close to his ear. "I'm ready if you are."

Chase stiffened and looked down at her. His eyes were full of passion and burning desire, but there was something else. Hesitation.

Taking her by the hand, he lead her from the dancefloor and out to the hall. She grabbed her clutch, and then they walked in silence until they were outside. He shrugged out of his jacket and draped it over her shoulders.

"What's going on?" she asked.

"You just told me you're ready. I assume you're not referring to going home, getting into our pjs and watching an all-night marathon of *Godfather* or *Halloween*."

She felt color rise to her cheeks. "I meant, if you want, we can reserve a room at the Hill Crest and spend the night there."

He raked his hands back through his hair and looked down at her. "I want to, sweet Lord do I want to more than anything on this earth."

Lily could feel his hesitation, and it made her nervous. "But?"

"I'm not."

"You're not what?"

"Ready."

"You're not ready to have sex with me?"

He groaned and nodded.

"Don't you want to?" She tried to keep the uncertainty out of her voice, but it didn't work.

"Did you not just hear me tell you that's exactly what I wanted to do?"

"I don't understand. I'm ready. I thought I wanted to wait until marriage, but I don't."

He shook his head. "What if I do?"

She blinked. "You want to wait until marriage before we . . .?"

He nodded. "Have sex? Yes. That is a big step in any relationship. Personally, I'm not ready for it yet. I certainly don't want to do it on a night where it's expected of us. I want it to be on our own terms when we're *both* ready. I'm not ready because I want to catch up on the time we lost. We have so much to catch up on, like spending time at the lake. Tyler is leaving next Saturday for California, and we don't know when he'll be back again. I don't want the heaviness of sex hanging over our heads, especially after everything you've been through."

"Are you saying you want to marry me?"

He scoffed. "Do you not remember me proposing to you when we were nine years old?"

She laughed because she remembered that day very clearly. He and Tyler had been picking on her relentlessly. She'd gotten tired of it and socked him in the nose. It was then that he said she was like Wonder Woman, and he wanted to marry her.

"We were just kids."

"We were, but I meant every word of it. I promise to ask you to marry me when the time is right in our life for it. I also promise, that for whatever reason, you decide that I am not your soulmate and need to move on, I will let you go."

The simple thought of being without him terrified her. "Don't say that Chase Michael." She took a step closer to him. "Don't you dare say that."

"You think you're going to keep me around?"

She shrugged and waved her hand in the air. "Oh, I don't know. Maybe, until I get bored."

He laughed, and she stood on her tiptoes and brushed a kiss against his lips. When she stepped away, she grabbed her clutch and snapped it open. Reaching inside, she removed a folded piece of paper.

"What's that?" he asked craning his neck to get a better look.

She unfolded the paper and handed it to him.

He scanned the contents. His eyes snapped up to his. "Are you serious?"

"Completely!"

Chase let out an excited whoop and grabbed her around the waist, swinging her in circles until they were both dizzy. She wobbled slightly once he put her back on the ground.

"I have to live on campus for the first year, but after that, we can figure things out, and it's only a thirty-minute drive to and from campus."

"Lily, that's amazing."

When Tyler and Molly came outside, they found the couple laughing hysterically.

"Did you tell him?" Molly asked.

Lily nodded.

"Tell him what?" Tyler asked.

"I've officially been accepted to the University of Alabama," she said excitedly.

Tyler engulfed her in a hug. "I'm so proud of you," he whispered. When he stepped back, she saw the pride in his eyes as they welled with tears. He sniffed and wiped them away.

"What do you say we celebrate?!"

"I think we're going to go home and do a movie marathon," Lily said. "I'm exhausted."

"Okay. We'll see you on Sunday," Tyler said pressing a kiss to Lily's cheek. "I'm so glad you're happy."

"I am."

Tyler took a step and watched the happy couple walk away. They'd been through so much, it was nice to see them get everything they deserved.

Turning, he smiled at Molly. "What do you say we get out of here?"

She gave him a beautiful smile. "I thought you'd never ask."

Chapter 38

Quiet people have the loudest minds.

~Stephen Hawking

"We did it!" Lily cried as the principal congratulated the graduating class of 2008. She removed her cap and threw it into the air with the rest of her classmates. She didn't have a chance to see where it landed because Chase grabbed her and spun her around.

Like two magnets, their mouths met in a kiss so steamy, several people around them began to cheer them on. When they finally pulled away, he was staring into her eyes.

"You did it."

She shook her head and looked at the two men and the girl that were her best friends. Tears rolled down Molly's cheeks as the four of them hugged.

"We've got the rest of our lives ahead of us!" Lily said excitedly as she hugged Molly and kissed Tyler on the cheek.

"Nothing is stopping you now!" Tyler said a wide smile spread completely across his face. "I'm so incredibly proud of you. Both of you," he said to Chase.

The two guys embraced each other in a manly hug. "I love you, brother," Tyler whispered.

"You too, Richie," Chase said.

"Aww," both girls said at the same time.

They guys made a big show of breaking apart by clearing their throats and making deep grunting sounds.

Trevor walked up to the group, Coraline was in his arms. Chase took the little girl into his arm and tossed her into the air.

"Lord, don't let your momma see you doing that," Trevor said looking around to make sure Diana wasn't lurking about.

Chase laughed and clapped Trevor on the back. "Don't worry. She's already gone back to the house to finish getting the party set up."

Trevor let out a sigh of relief. "She's been a basket case about you graduating, and Lily moving out to college."

"Well, she *is* pregnant, so. . . ."

Trevor grimaced. "I'm happy we're having another one, but the sweet Jesus best be keeping his hand on me because I'm gonna go nuts."

Everyone laughed as Trevor walked away.

"Molly, you coming to the house?" Lily asked.

She frowned. "I can't. I've got family in from all over the world, and I'm stuck at my house all night. I can't even go to the after party. Y'all going?"

Chase, Tyler, and Lily all shook their heads. After Tyler's house party was busted by the cops and his father came down on him, they all stayed away from those things.

"Nah, we're gonna movie night it tonight before Tyler leaves."

She nodded. Taking a step closer, she gave Tyler a huge hug. "Take care of yourself, okay? Don't forget to stay in touch."

He nodded. "See you later."

Molly said bye to Chase and Lily, and then turned and walked away. The day after prom, Molly had informed her that she and Tyler had decided to be friends. With him going to California and her staying local, they felt that it wasn't fair for either one to have a long-distance relationship.

Lily stood between the two guys, wrapping each arm around each of their waists. "Let's go celebrate."

As they had dozens of times before, each guy draped an arm around Lily, and they walked away.

"Goodnight kids. Don't forget to lock up before you go to bed," Trevor said as he made his way up the stairs.

"G'night," the three of them called up from the couch.

"I'm stuffed," Lily groaned, rubbing her full belly.

"Who knew you could eat that much?" Tyler joked.

"Hey, that's nothing. Wait until there's cheesecake involved," Chase teased.

Lily chuckled. "I'm not that bad."

"Like hell you're not. You stabbed me with a frigg'n fork."

She shrugged. "Hey, I told you not to touch it. You didn't believe me."

"I know, and I love you anyway." He pulled her into his side, and she stretched her legs out over Tyler's lap. She frowned when she noticed him unusually quiet.

"Hey," she said nudging him with her toes. "What's with the hum-drum, chum?"

He looked at his hands and shrugged. "You know, I get that my dad is busy and is a giant prick. You'd at least think that he'd bother to show up to his only son's graduation."

"I'm sorry, Ty," she said leaning forward and wrapping her arms around him, smooshing his face against hers. "I wuvs you though and Chase," she said playfully.

He rolled his eyes. "I know. You're all the family I've ever needed. You always have been. I don't know what would have happened to me if I had to spend all these years alone in that house."

"We were supposed to meet that night in the playground. You were part of our path," she said.

"Yup," Chase agreed.

Tyler looked at them. "Are you guys happy?"

Chase and Lily looked at each other and smiled. Then they looked back at him. "We couldn't be happier," she said. "Just wait until you get out to Cali, Ty. You're gonna go back to that one chick; your P.O.S. father can jump off a freaking bridge. He's worthless. We're your family. Always remember that. Three misfits that found each other by chance."

"Fate," he said. He climbed to his feet. "I need to get home."

"What? Why? We were just about to start the movies," Lily pouted.

"I have some last-minute stuff I need to handle."

"Oh, well. Okay." Lily and Chase stood. "Love you," she said wrapping her arms tightly around him.

He hugged her tightly. "Love you too, kiddo."

She stepped away, and he and Chase did a high five and a hug. "We did it, bro. We graduated."

Tyler laughed. "We did. Y'all stay outta trouble."

"Pfft, never."

"See you in the morning," Lily said.

"See ya," Tyler said as he walked out of the house.

Lily and Chase resumed their seats on the couch. "What you say, a date with Michael Myers to end a perfect evening?!"

"Sounds like a plan to me."

The dinging of her phone pulled Lily from her sleep. She looked around, trying to figure out where she was. She realized that at some point during the second movie, they passed out. Sitting up, she reached for her phone. A second later, Chase's phone pinged.

Lily rubbed the grit from her eyes and nudged Chase.

He lifted his head and looked at her with sleepy eyes. "Huh?"

"Your phone just went off."

He fumbled with his phone, and together they looked at their screens.

"That's weird," she said sitting up a bit straighter. "I just got an email from Tyler."

Chase looked at his screen. "I did too."

Lily tapped the email, and it opened. As she began to read, the world around her ceased to exist.

Chapter 39

Man is not what he thinks he is,
he is what he hides.

~Andrè Malraux

Lily. Chase.

I'm leaving you this letter because, honestly, there isn't any other way to do this. There are a few things I need to tell you before I say goodbye.

First, I am so happy that you're both finally happy. It makes writing this to you so much easier. I've watched you two over the years grow and blossom into two amazing people. The fact that you still found each other through the darkness is an inspiration. Hold onto that through these next several days. You're going to need it.

My mother was arrested for trafficking, as you know, but that's not all. I was six years old when she hired me out. You see, there are people in this world that pay high prices to have young boys for the night, or several. My mother saw this as an opportunity to make extra cash. This went on until she got arrested. I was her first experiment into the sex trade. When she discovered she could make more with other kids, that's when she moved on. When that happened, I thought she'd leave me alone. That never happened.

Lilly, all your medical bills have been paid. I knew I wouldn't be using my trust fund and I wanted to put it to good use. I've made arrangements, and the remainder of the money is to go to both of you guys. My father can't touch it. That's part of the reason I went to California this last year. I was making sure everything was in order. I'm leaving you the name and number of my lawyer. When you're ready, call him. My father is going to raise all kind of hell, but don't worry. My lawyer makes my father look like a kitten.

305

Go be a vet and, Chase, you can buy that little piece of land you've been looking at! This is my gift to you. A fresh start. A new place in life. I've watched you guys, and you're finally both so happy. You deserve it. I'm just sorry I can't be happy with you. I tried for so long. I went through the therapy. I went through the motions. When I went to California, I realized that I'll never be happy. No matter how hard I try. I'm not as strong as you, Lily.

I've been broken for too long. Focusing on you guys made the pain a little better. Seeing how you both needed me, made me have a purpose. Now, my purpose is finished, I can finally go. Knowing that you will be there to take care of each other.

I was in the park that night to kill myself. What you didn't see was the bottle of pills I had in my pocket. You two gave me life. You saved my life that night. Don't blame this on yourselves because it is not your fault. I'm telling you now, you could not have saved me.

The shit that she made me do. The way my dad turned the other way while it happened. That's how I got him to take care of things when you were in the hospital, Lily. I threatened to expose him.

Chase, you asked me why my father would do something like that for someone he didn't care about. I lied. He knew what was happening to me and did nothing to stop it.

I thought I was better, so I thought I'd come home and spend our senior year together. I was wrong. I saw the people she made me be with everywhere I went. Even if I didn't see them, I still saw them. I couldn't erase their faces.

Lily, I'm glad you found your peace and got your closure. But the people I was forced to be with . . . people would make a big deal if they were missing. They are powerful people.

Chase, I heard you talking to Lily that night in the kitchen about how people deal with trauma. I'm the kind that that buries it deep. I didn't spiral because if I did, things would have ended much differently. I wouldn't have ever known if you two were happy. I put my energy into you two because it took the focus off me.

I'm sorry I didn't tell you, but you would try to help, and there was no helping me. I was too far gone, and it just became too much. I promised myself I would go through graduation and have one final happy day with the two people that I love most in this world. I did that, and now I can go, knowing you were happy and I didn't ruin the day.

I love you guys. Cling to one another. Hold each other dear. I love you, brother. I love you, my sister. Think of me often because I'll be watching over you.

Forever in your hearts and never far away,
Tyler.

Lily's and Chase's hands shook as they read and re-read the letter.

"Please tell me this is a joke," she demanded, already crying.

Chase launched to his feet. "Get your shoes on. *Hurry!*"

Lily rushed to the door where she'd left her shoes and quickly pulled them on. They were just yanking the door open when Trevor came bounding down the stairs dressed in his first responder's gear. His face was white as a sheet. They didn't have to ask where he was going because they already knew.

8163 Claymore Avenue

"*No!*" Lily screamed.

Chase caught her around the waist and pulled her back. She kicked her legs and struggled against him. "Let me go! Damn it, Chase, let me go. We have to go to him. He needs us. Please, he *needs* us."

Trevor stopped in the entryway, eyes red and filled with tears. "I'll let you know as soon as I know something," he said, but Chase could see the look in his eyes. He already knew the answer. There would be no one at that house to rescue because it was too late. Tyler was already gone.

Trevor closed the door, and Lily wailed a soul-crushing cry into his shirt front. He clung to her for dear life as his heart shattered. They both crumpled to the floor in a sobbing heap and holding onto one another. They sat and let the pain engulf them completely. Diana sat on the bottom of the stairs and cried.

"I'll never forgive him," Lily keened. "I'll *never* forgive him."

Lily had won her battle, but Tyler had lost his.

Epilogue

Grief is like the ocean;
it comes on waves ebbing and flowing.
Sometimes the water is calm,
and sometimes it is overwhelming.
All we can do is learn to swim.

~Vicki Harrison

The cool spring breeze lifted tendrils of hair away from her face. She sat on the tone bench staring at the same thing she'd been staring at for the past two hours. It was the same thing she'd done every year for the past ten years.

She took a deep breath.

"I'm still pissed as hell at you, by the way. It's not as bad as it used to be, but at least I can tell you about it now. It's only taken me ten years. I have some stuff I need to say, so you're going to listen to me."

She angrily dashed the tears away from her face. "I hate you a little bit, but I understand why you did it. The biggest thing that hurts is that you didn't come to us. You made me promise to come to you when I hit my lowest point. I didn't and nearly lost my life, but you guys saved me. Why couldn't you just let us do that for you? And I know you're rolling your eyes at me from wherever the hell you are, but we could have helped you. We never had the chance. *You never gave us the chance!* You didn't even give us a chance to tell you goodbye. You stole that from us.

"I've read that damn goodbye letter a million times. I know what you said. Hell, I even get it, but it doesn't make me feel any better. I guess Chase made his peace with you a while back. You know I don't let go of things that easily."

Her shoulders were shaking with sobs. "I loved you so much. I still do. I'm so sorry, Tyler. I'm so, so sorry."

309

Lily slid from the bench, hitting her knees in front of the giant black tombstone with Tyler's name etched in white on the front. She pressed her head against the cold marble. "I miss you so much. I wonder every day what you would have been like today. I imagine you as a huge football star; People falling to the ground at your feet."

She sniffed and leaned back on her haunches.

"Okay, now that I've yelled at you, you want to know what's happened this past year?"

The cool breeze from earlier seemed to warm as it caressed her cheek. "First and foremost, you'll be glad to know that karma kicked your dad's ass all over the state of Alabama. He was just arrested for fraud. When his office was investigated, they found several letters from your mother about the things that happened to you. They also got him on perjury. He's going away for a very long time. I try not to be happy when bad things happen to other people, but the day I read that in the news was the day I felt like justice had been served for you. I'm just sorry it happened too late."

"Let's see, what else? OH! Chase expanded the ranch by a thousand acres. He's got the most successful cattle ranch in the entire state. We've also been selling horses to people all over the world. Someone from England even bought a mare for Her Majesty. Can you believe it?

"My practice is doing well. I opened another clinic in Tucker. I split my time between the clinic at the ranch and the one in Tucker. I won Veterinarian of the year. It was a pretty big ordeal."

She laughed. "Oh, and you'll get a kick out of this one. Abigail got sent to the principal yesterday. She punched a guy in the nose for saying she hit like a girl. When he started crying, she hit him again and said he cried like a girl. Chase found it hilarious, but there's a big thing on bullying nowadays. It wasn't like that when we were in school. If it had been, things might have gone a little differently. Both Abi and the little boy got in trouble. At least it was fair."

Behind her, she heard the door of a pickup slam closed.

"Tyler Matthew will be three in three days. He looks just like his daddy. Acts like him too, Lord help us all."

"Mommy. Mommy!"

Lily turned around and smiled as her daughter ran across the cemetery, her blonde ringlets bouncing and shining like spun gold. Behind her, Chase followed, their son sitting high on his shoulders. Her heart expanded and thumped wildly like it did the first night they kissed, and if it was possible, she loved him more today than she ever had.

Turning back around, she took a settling breath and then finished up. "I need to tell you two more things before I go. The first one is a secret." She flattened her hand over her stomach and smiled. "You're going to be an uncle again. I promised you when I first found out about Abigail that I would be the mother that neither of us had. I'm far from perfect, but I think you'd be proud. At least I hope you're proud of me from wherever you are."

Fresh tears slipped down her cheeks as she traced Tyler's name with her finger. "And the second thing is . . ." She took a deep breath. "I forgive you."

She climbed to her feet and brushed the dirt and leaves from her knees just as Abigail flung herself into her arms. "Hey, punkin," she said nuzzling her daughter's cheek.

"Daddy gave us ice cream for breakfast and cake for lunch."

"He did, did he?" She shot a questioning brow at her husband.

He gave her an impish look, those darn baby blues her undoing every time. "Hey, she begged me."

"Uh-huh. Just like she begged you for an extra bedtime story and an extra scoop of ice cream on her sundae at your momma's?"

"*That* was all Nana and Popa's doing!"

"Sure it was."

She wrapped her arm around her husband's waist. "You know, you're going to have to learn that little two letter word eventually. What about when she starts dating?"

"No! Hallelujah, I'm cured!"

She heaved a dramatic sigh. "You're hopeless, Chase Michael Kramer."

"And you love me for it, Lilian Victoria Kramer."

"If I halfta."

He brushed a feather light kiss across her lips, and it caused her toes to curl. When he pulled away, she smiled. "Well, I can already tell you're a lost cause with these two. Maybe number three with be different."

His eyes widened. "Really?"

"Yeah. Just saw the doctor this morning."

"WooWeee! You hear that, guys? We're gonna have another baby!"

Abigail frowned. "Ah, man. Another one?"

Chase and Lily exploded into laughter.

"Are you ready to go home, baby?" Chase asked Lilly.

"I'm ready to go anywhere you are."

He placed a kiss on her forehead and she smiled. Before she left, she put her hand on the cool stone one more time.

"Oh, before I forget, Chase added. "Earl called and said they are redoing the dock at the lake. He brought something by the ranch this morning."

"Oh?"

He reached into the back pocket of his jeans and removed a piece of faded wood. Tears sprang to her eyes. She'd forgotten all about it.

Gently, she traced her fingers over the weathered marks. The first ones they'd carved were worn completely away, but the last set was still there.

Kneeling, she placed the piece of wood at the base of the stone. She kissed the tips of her fingers and pressed them onto his name."

"Bye Tyler. I love you. Promise you'll check in on us from time to time?"

She pushed to her feet and began to walk off, but stopped when they reached a bright, sunny spot. She took a deep breath and closed her eyes. Then, tilting her head back and spreading her arms wide, she let the warm rays of the sun touch her face, just like they all did the first day of senior year down on the dock. The gentle breeze was back, and this time she could have sworn she heard two words.

Pinky Promise.

The End

I want to say thank you to everyone who picked up a copy of The Path to Us. This was not an easy book to write. There are many topics in it that affect our young people— and even adults—every day.

Today it is estimated that on average 3,400+ teens in grades 9–12 attempt suicide. Suicide is one of the deadliest epidemics affecting teens and young adults. It ranks higher than cancer, heart disease, AIDS, stroke, and many more *combined*.

If you, or someone you love, may be thinking about suicide, please find help by calling the National Suicide Prevention Lifeline. 1-800-273-8255. Someone is always there willing to lend an ear and listen.

Another subject that was hard to approach was rape. Every 98 seconds someone is sexually assaulted. It's an ugly act that can leave many physical and emotional scars. It tears away the victim's identity and leaves them feeling hopeless and ashamed. There is help out there. YOU ARE NOT ALONE. For more information, you can visit www.rainn.org or call toll free 1-800-656-HOPE (4673)

THANK YOU.

GOD BLESS!

A lot of music played while creating this book. Below are some of my favorites that fit perfectly with the story. You can also follow the playlist on Spotify.

https://spoti.fi/2Harjml

*** Last Night Alone . . . Skillet (Main theme song)

*** Never too late . . . Three Days Grace

*** Disappear . . . Hoobastank

***Everything I do . . . Bryan Adams

***Nobody Knows . . . Tony Rich

*** Just the way you are . . . Bruno Mars

*** Little do you know . . . Alex & Sierra

*** Seasons of Love . . . Rent

*** This is Me . . . Keala Settle

*** Here without you . . . 3 Doors Down

*** Bruises . . . Train

***Sound of silence . . . Disturbed

*** Say Something . . . A Great Big World

*** Rise Up . . . Imagine Dragons

*** Thinking Out Loud . . . Ed Sheeran

***Demons . . . Imagine Dragons

***Far Away. . . Nickleback

***Lost Boy . . . Ruth B

*** These are the moments . . . Edwin McCain

***Photograph . . . Ed Sheeran

***Say You won't let go . . . James Author

***Purpose . . . Justin Bieber

***Count on me . . . Bruno Mars

***Endlessly . . . Green River Ordinance

***Hold my hand . . . Hootie and the Blowfish

***You and Me . . . Lifehouse

Check out other books
from Christine James:

The Chosen Chronicles:

Risen

Bloodlines

Final Redemption

Abroad
(co-written with author Amelia Cole)

The Guardians: UnderCity

Swelter

www.ingramcontent.com/pod-product-compliance
Lightning Source LLC
Chambersburg PA
CBHW060517180626
46817CB00002B/385